Fortune's Rocks

ANITA SHREVE

Fortune's Rocks

A NOVEL

Little, Brown and Company

BOSTON | NEW YORK | LONDON

First Edition

The characters and events in this book are fictitious. Any similarity to real persons, living or dead, is coincidental and not intended by the author.

Library of Congress Cataloging-in-Publication Data

Shreve, Anita.
   Fortune's rocks / by Anita Shreve. — 1st ed.
     p.   cm.
   ISBN 0-316-78101-0
   I. Title.
PS3569.H7385F67 2000
813'.54 — dc21   99-42665

10 9 8 7 6 5 4 3 2

MV-NY

Printed in the United States of America

for

John Osborn

gifted reader, great cook

· I ·
Fortune's Rocks

*I*N THE TIME it takes for her to walk from the bathhouse at the seawall of Fortune's Rocks, where she has left her boots and has discreetly pulled off her stockings, to the waterline along which the sea continually licks the pink and silver sand, she learns about desire. Desire that slows the breath, that causes a preoccupied pause in the midst of uttering a sentence, that focuses the gaze absolutely on the progress of naked feet walking toward the water. This first brief awareness of desire — and of being the object of desire, a state of which she has had no previous hint — comes to her as a kind of slow seizure, as of air compressing itself all around her, and causes what seems to be the first faint shudder of her adult life.

She touches the linen brim of her hat, as she would not have done a summer earlier, nor even a day earlier. Perhaps she fingers the hat's long tulle sash as well. Around her and behind her, there are men in bathing costumes or in white shirts and waistcoats; and if she lifts her eyes, she can see their faces: pale, wintry visages that seem to breathe in the ocean air as if it were smelling salts, relieving the pinched torpor of long months shut indoors. The men are older or younger, some quite tall, a few boys, and though they speak to one another, they watch her.

Her gait along the shallow shell of a beach alters. Her feet, as she makes slow progress, create slight and scandalous indentations in the sand. Her dress, which is a peach silk, turns, when she steps into the water, a translucent sepia. The air is hot, but the water on her skin is frigid; and the contrast makes her shiver.

She takes off her hat and kicks up small splashes amongst the waves. She inhales long breaths of the sea air, which clear her head. Possibly the men observing her speculate then about the manner in which delight seems suddenly to overtake her and to fill her with the joy of anticipation. And are as surprised as she is by her acceptance of her fate. For in the space of time it has taken to walk from the sea-wall to the sea, perhaps a distance of a hundred yards, she has passed from being a girl, with a child's pent-up and nearly frenzied need to sweep away the rooms and cobwebs of her winter, to being a woman.

It is the twentieth day of June in the last year of the century, and she is fifteen years old.

Olympia's father, in his white suit, his hair a fading ginger and blowing upward from his brow, is calling to her from the rocks at the northern end of the beach. The rocks upon which it has been the fate of many sailors to founder, thus lending the beach and the adjacent land the name of Fortune. He cups his mouth with his hands, but she is deaf from the surf. A white shape amidst the gray, her father is a gentle and loving man, unblemished in his actions toward her, although he believes himself in possession of both her body and her soul, as if they were his and not hers to squander or bestow.

Earlier this day, Olympia and her father and her mother journeyed north from Boston by train to a cottage that, when they entered, was white with sheets and oddly without dust. Olympia wished when she saw the sheets that her mother would not ask

Josiah, who is her father's manservant, to take them off the furniture, because they made fantastical abstract shapes against the six pairs of floor-to-ceiling windows of the long front room. Beyond the glass and the thin glaze of salt spray lay the Atlantic with its cap of brilliant haze. In the distance there were small islands that seemed to hover above the horizon.

The cottage is a modest one by some standards, although Olympia's father is a wealthy man. But it is unique in its proportions, and she thinks it lovely beyond words. White with dark blue shutters, the house stands two stories high and is surrounded by several graceful porches. It is constructed in the style of the grand hotels along Fortune's Rocks, and in Rye and Hampton to the south: that is to say, its roof curves shallowly and is inset with evenly spaced dormer windows. The house has never been a hotel, but rather was once a convent, the home of the Order of Saint Jean Baptiste de Bienfaisance, twenty sisters who took vows of poverty and married themselves to Jesus. Indeed, an oddity of the structure is its many cell-like bedrooms, two of which Olympia and her father occupy and three of which have been connected for her mother's use. Attached to the ground floor of the house is a small chapel; and although it has been deconsecrated, Olympia's family still cannot bring themselves to place their own secular belongings within its wooden walls. Except for a dozen neat wooden benches and a wide marble stone that once served as an altar, the chapel remains empty.

Outside the house and below the porches are massive tangles of hydrangea bushes. A front lawn spills down to the seawall, which is little more than a rocky barricade against the ocean and which is covered at this time of year with masses of beach roses. Thus, the view from the porch is one of emerald leaves with blots of pink against a blue so sparkling that it is not so much a color as the experience of light. To the west of the lawn are orchards of Sheepnose and Black Gilliflower apples, and to the north is the beach, which stretches two miles along the coast. Fortune's Rocks is the name not only for the crescent of land that cradles this beach but also for the gathering of summer houses, of which the Biddefords' is but one, on its dunes and rocks.

From the rocks, her father waves to her yet again. "Olympia, I called to you," he says when she, with her wet hem, climbs up to the rock on which he is standing. She expects him to be cross with her. In her impatience to feel the sea on her feet, she inadvertently went to the beach during the men's bathing hours, an activity that might be acceptable in a girl but is not in a young woman. Olympia explains as best she can that she is sorry; she simply forgot about the men's bathing hours, and she was not able to hear him call to her because of the wind. But as she draws nearer to her father and looks up at his face and observes the manner in which he glances quickly away from her — this is not like him — she realizes that he must have witnessed her bare-legged walk from the seawall to the ocean's edge. His eyes are watering some in the wind, and he seems momentarily puzzled, even bewildered, by her physical presence.

"Josiah has prepared a tray of bread and pastes," her father says, turning back to her and recovering from the slight loss of his composure. "He has taken it to your mother's room so that you both might have something to eat after the long journey." He blinks once and bends to his watch. "My God, Olympia, what a shambles," he adds.

He means, of course, the house.

"Josiah seems to be handling the crisis well enough," she offers.

"Everything should have been prepared for our arrival. We should have had the cook by now."

Her father wears his frock coat still. His boots are heavy and black and covered with dust, and she thinks he must be extraordinarily hot and uncomfortable. Clearly, he dressed this day with some indecision — trailing Boston behind him even as he was anticipating the sea.

In the bright sunlight, Olympia can see her father's face more clearly than she has all winter. It is a strong face, full of character, a face he inherited from his father before him and then later, through his own behavior, has come to deserve. His most striking feature is the navy of his eyes, a blue so vivid that his eyes alone, even with the flecks of rust in the irises, suggest moral rectitude. A fan of wrinkles, however, as well as folds of skin at the lids, soften the suggested righteousness. His hair is graying at the sides and thinning at the front, but he has high color and has not yet begun to grow pale, as is so often the fate of ginger-haired men in their middle age. Olympia is not sure if she has ever thought about her father's height, nor can she accurately say how tall he is — only that he is taller than her mother and her, which seems in keeping with the proper order of the universe. His face is elongated, as Olympia's will one day be, although neither of them is precisely thin.

"When you have finished your tea, I should like to see you in my study," her father says in the ordinary manner in which he is accustomed to speak to her, though even she can see that something between them has changed. The sun etches imperfections in his skin, and there are, in that unforgiving light, tiny glints of silver and ginger spread along his jawline. He squints in the glare.

"I have some matters I need to discuss with you. Matters relating to your summer study and so forth," he adds.

Her heart falls at the mention of summer study, since she is eager to have a respite from her singular, yet intense, schooling. Her father, having lost faith in the academies, has taken her education upon himself. Thus she is his sole pupil and he her sole teacher. He remains convinced that this education is progressing at a pace not dreamt of in the academies and seminaries, and that its breadth is unsurpassed anywhere in New England, which is to say, the United States. Possibly this is true, Olympia thinks, but she cannot say: It has been four years since she last attended classes with other girls.

"Of course," she answers.

He looks at her once and then lets his eyes drift over her right shoulder and out to sea. He turns and begins to walk back to the cottage. As she gazes at his slightly hunched posture, a physical characteristic she has not ever noticed before, she feels suddenly sad for her father, for the thing that he is losing, which is the guardianship of her childhood.

She floats through the house, appreciating the sculptures made by the white sheets strewn over the furnishings. A coatrack becomes a maiden ghost; a long dining room table, an operating theater; a set of chairs piled one on top of the other and shrouded in white becomes a throne. She climbs the stairs in the front hall to her mother's rooms.

Her mother is resting unperturbed on a peacock chaise that has been uncovered and looks directly out to sea. She seems not to notice the man perched on a ladder just outside her window. He has in one hand a bottle of vinegar and in the other a crumpled wad of newsprint. Josiah wears an overall for this task, although he also has on a waistcoat and a formal collar underneath. Later, when the windows have been cleaned, he will take off the overall, put his suit coat back on, adjust his cuffs under the sleeves, and walk into the study, where he will ask Olympia's father if he wishes his customary glass of London porter. And then Josiah, a man who has been with her father for seventeen years, before her father's marriage and her birth, and who has without complaint taken upon himself the washing of the windows in her mother's rooms because he does not want her view of the ocean to be obscured on this, the first day of her summer visit (even though such a task is thoroughly beneath him), will walk down the long pebbled drive and onto Hampton Street to lay into the new man who was to have had the house prepared before Olympia's family arrived.

Since Olympia's mother is partial to hues of blue, even in the summer months, she has on this day a wisteria crepe blouse with mother-of-pearl buttons and long deep cuffs that hide her wrist-bones and flatter her hands. At her waist is a sash of Persian silk. This preference for blue is to be seen as well in the fabrics of her room — the pale beryl sateen puff on the bed, the peacock silk brocade of the chaise, the powder velvet drapes at the windows. Her mother's rooms, Olympia thinks, suggest excessive femininity: They form a boudoir, separate, cut off from the rest of the house, the excess not to be condoned, not to be seen by others, not echoed anywhere else in the austere furnishings of the cottage.

Her mother lifts a cup to her lips.

"Your skin is pink," she says to Olympia lightly, but not without a suggestion of parental admonition. Olympia has been told often to wear a hat to protect her face from the sun. But she was unable to forgo for those few happy moments at the water's edge the sensation of heat at the top of her head. She knows that her mother does not seriously begrudge her this small pleasure, despite her inordinate re-gard for beauty.

Beauty, Olympia has come to understand, has incapacitated her mother and ruined her life, for it has made her dependent upon people who are desirous of seeing her and of serving her: her own father, her husband, her physician, and her servants. Indeed, the preservation of beauty seems to be all that remains of her mother's life, as though the other limbs of the spirit — industriousness, cu-riosity, and philanthropy — have atrophied, and only this one ap-pendage has survived. Her mother's hair, which has been hennaed so that it has taken on the color of a roan, is caught with combs at the sides and rolled into a complex series of knots that Olympia herself has yet to master. Her mother has pale, pearl-gray eyes. Her face, which is both handsome and strong, belies her spirit, which is uniquely fragile — so fragile that Olympia herself has often seen it splinter into glittering bits.

"Josiah has prepared a tray," her mother says, gesturing to the display of paste sandwiches.

Olympia sits at the edge of the chaise. Her mother's knees make small hillocks in the indigo landscape of her skirt. "I am not hungry," Olympia says, which is true.

"You must eat something. Dinner will not be for hours yet."

To please her mother, Olympia takes a sandwich from the tray. For the moment, she avoids her mother's acute gaze and studies her room. They do not have their best furnishings at Fortune's Rocks, because the sea air and the damp are ruinous to their shape and surface. But Olympia does like particularly her mother's skirted dressing table with its many glass and silver boxes, which contain her combs and her perfumes and the fine white powder she uses in the evenings. Also on the dresser are her mother's many medicines and tonics. Olympia can see, from where she sits, the pigeon milk, the pennyroyal pills, and the ginger tonic.

For as long as Olympia can remember, her mother has been referred to, within her hearing and without, as an invalid — an appellation that does not seem to distress her mother and indeed appears to be one she herself cultivates. Her ailments are vague and unspecific, and Olympia is not certain she has ever been properly diagnosed. She is said to have sustained an injury to her hip as a girl, and Olympia has heard the phrase *heart ailment* tossed about from time to time. There is, in Boston, a physician who visits her frequently, and perhaps he is not the charlatan Olympia's father thinks him. Although even as a girl, Olympia was certain that Dr. Ulysses Branch visited her mother for her company rather than for her rehabilitation. Her mother never seems actually to be unwell, and Olympia sometimes thinks about the term *invalid* as it is applied to her mother: invalid, *in valid,* not valid, as though, in addition to physical strength, her mother lacked a certain authenticity.

As a result of these vague disabilities, Olympia's mother is not the caretaker in the family, but rather the one cared for. Olympia has decided that this must suit both of her parents well enough, for neither of them has ever taken great pains to amend the situation. And as time has gone on, perhaps as a result of actual atrophy, her mother has become something of a valid invalid. She seldom leaves the house, except to have her husband walk her at dusk to the seawall, where she will sit and sing to him. For years, her mother has maintained that the sea air has a salubrious effect on both her spirits and her vocal cords. Despite the humidity, she keeps a piano at Fortune's Rocks as well and will occasionally leave her rooms and play with some accomplishment. Olympia's mother has wonderful bones, but Olympia will not inherit her face or the shape of her body or, thankfully, the brittleness of her spirit.

Olympia's mother, who met her father in Boston at a dinner arranged by her own father when she was twenty-three, did not marry until she was twenty-eight. Although she was considered a handsome woman, it was said that her nerves, which were self-effacing to a degree of near annihilation, rendered her too delicate for marriage. Olympia's father, ever one for a challenge and captivated by those very characteristics that frightened other men away — that is to say, her mother's alternating fuguelike states of intense quiet and imaginative flights of fancy — pursued her with an ardor that he himself seldom admits to. Olympia does not know what to make of her parents' married life, for her mother appears to be, though sensitive to a fault, the least physical of all women and oftentimes, if surprised, can be seen to flinch at her husband's touch. Olympia's thoughts balk, however, at crossing the veil to that forbidden place where she might be able to imagine in detail her parents' marriage.

For it is a marriage that has seemed to thin as it has endured, until it appears to Olympia, by the summer of her fifteenth year, that there is only the one child and the vaguest and most formal of connections between them.

"You are quiet, Olympia," her mother says, eyeing her carefully. Though fragile, her mother can be astute, and it is always difficult to hide from her one's true thoughts. Olympia has been, indeed, thinking about her walk along the beach, viewing it as if from beside herself, seeing the somewhat blurry and vague figure of a young woman in peach silk conveying herself to the water's edge under the scrutiny of several dozen men and boys. And in her mother's room she blushes suddenly, as if she has been caught out.

Her mother shifts slightly on the chaise. "I fear I may already be too . . . too tardy in this discussion," she begins diffidently, "but I cannot help but notice — indeed, I think I am quite struck by this — that is to say, I am very mindful today of certain physical characteristics of your person, and I think we must soon have a talk about possible future occurrences, about necessary and delicate dilemmas all women have to bear."

Though the sentence cannot be parsed, her meaning can be; and Olympia shakes her head quickly or waves her hand, as though to tell her she need not go on. For she has relied heavily upon Lisette, her mother's maid, for information on matters of the body. Her mother looks startled for a moment, in the manner of someone who has hastily prepared a lengthy speech and has been stopped midsentence. But then, as she sits there, Olympia observes that relief overtakes her mother and flatters her features.

"Someone has discussed this with you?" her mother asks.

"Lisette," Olympia says, wishing the conversation over.

"When was this?"

"Some time ago."

"Oh. I have wondered."

And Olympia wonders, too, at the silence of Lisette regarding the daughter of her mistress. She hopes the woman will not receive a scolding for this confidence.

"You are settled?" her mother asks quickly, eager now as well to change the subject. "You are happy here?"

"Quite happy," Olympia answers, which is true and is what her mother wants to hear. It is essential that her mother's placidity not be disturbed.

At the window, Josiah moves on the ladder, causing both of them to look up in his direction.

"I wonder . . . ," her mother says, musing to herself. "Do you think Josiah a handsome man?"

Olympia looks at the figure framed seemingly in midair. He has light-brown hair that waves back from a high forehead and a narrow face that seems in keeping with the length of his slim build. Mildly astonished as Olympia always is by any sudden and surprising crack in her mother's long-practiced poise, she cannot think of how to answer her.

"Do you imagine that he keeps a mistress in Ely Falls?" her mother asks, pretending to wickedness. But then, after a brief heartbeat of silence, during which Olympia imagines she hears her mother's longing for (and immediate dismissal of) another life, she answers herself: "No, I suppose not," she says.

Altogether, it is a day on which everyone around Olympia seems to be behaving oddly. She does not know whether this is a consequence of truly altered behavior on their part, or of her perception of herself, which she thinks she must be giving off like a scent. How else to explain the uncharacteristic inarticulateness of her father, or the forays of her mother into subjects she normally avoids?

"I should like you to take the tray with you when you go. To help Josiah, who is quite overwhelmed, I fear."

Olympia is not as surprised by this non sequitur as she might be, since her mother has a gift for abandoning subjects she has suddenly decided she does not wish to discuss further. Olympia stands up from the chaise and bends to lift the silver tray, happy to help Josiah, whom she likes. She is relieved to be dismissed.

"You must be more protective of yourself," her mother says as Olympia leaves the room.

After Olympia has returned the tray to the kitchen, she walks into her father's study, where he sits, in an oversize mahogany captain's chair, reading, she can see, *The Shores of Saco Bay* by John Staples Locke, the first of the many volumes he will devour during the summer. Her father is, both by profession and by inclination, a disciplined and learned man, discipline being, in his belief, a necessary hedge against dissolution; therefore, he does not like to change his routine even on this first day of vacation, despite the lack of preparation for their arrival and the resulting chaos.

During this summer, as in past summers, her father will invite to their cottage a succession of guests whom he has met largely through his position as president of the Atlantic Literary Club or as editor of *The Bay Quarterly,* a periodical of no small literary reputation. He will hold lengthy discussions with these people, who are most often poets or essayists or artists, in a kind of continuous salon. During the day, he will oversee the recreation of the visitors, which will be bathing at the beach or tennis at the Ely Tennis Club or boating through the pink-tinged marshes of the bay at sunset. Evening meals will be long and will last well into the night, even though his wife will excuse herself early. The women who will come to these dinners will wear white linen dresses and shawls of woven silk. Olympia has always been fascinated by the clothing and accessories of their female guests.

Her father glances down at the hem of her dress, which is still damp. She asks him what he recommends that she read first this summer. He removes his spectacles and sets them on the green marble table beside his chair, which is a replica of the table he has in his library in Boston. Around them, the windows are thrown open, and the room is flooded with the peculiar salt musk of the outgoing tide.

"I should like you to read the essays of John Warren Haskell," he says, reaching for a volume and handing it to her. "And then you and I will discuss its contents, for the author is here at Fortune's Rocks and is coming to stay with us for the weekend."

And this is the first time she hears John Haskell's name.

"Haskell is bringing his wife and children with him," her father adds, "and I hope you will help to entertain them."

"Of course," she says, smoothing her palm across the book's brown silk cover and fingering its gilt-embossed title, "but as to these essays, I do not know the author."

"Haskell is a man of medicine, and lectures occasionally at the college, which is where I originally met him; but his true calling, in my estimation, is as an essayist, and I have published several of his best. Haskell's interests lie with labor, and he seems most particularly keen on improving living and working conditions for mill girls. Hence his further interest in Ely Falls."

"I see," she says to her father as she riffles through the pages of the modest book. And though she is already slightly bored with this topic, later she will sift and resift through the memory of this conversation for any tiny morsel she might have missed and thus might savor.

"Haskell keeps a clinic in east Cambridge," her father says. "He is offering his services at Ely Falls for the season, as he is replacing one of the staff physicians who is taking a leave." Her father clears his throat. "Haskell regards this as the most fortunate of circumstances, for not only will it allow him to remain close by while his own cottage is being constructed farther down the beach, but he should be able to study firsthand the conditions that interest him so. And as for me, I also regard his visit as a fortunate circumstance, for I do enjoy the man's wit and company. I think you will be charmed by Catherine, who is Haskell's wife, as well as by the children."

"Am I to be a governess then?" Olympia asks, mostly in jest, but her father takes the question seriously and looks appalled.

"My dear, certainly not," he says. "The Haskells are our guests for the weekend only, after which Haskell shall stay on, as he has been doing, at the Highland Hotel until their cottage is finished, which should be by the end of July. Catherine and the children will stay in York with her family until then. Heavens, Olympia, how could you have imagined I would exploit you in such a manner?"

Her father's study is dark, though the windows are open; and his books, which have been partially unpacked by Josiah, are already beginning to warp in the damp air. Each Monday throughout the summer, Josiah will place the books in tall stacks and weight these stacks with heavy irons to help return them, for a few hours, to their original shape and thickness.

Olympia moves about the room, touching various familiar objects that her father has collected through the years and keeps at Fortune's Rocks: a malachite paperweight from East Africa; a bejeweled cross her father purchased in Prague when he was nineteen; a stained ivory letter opener from Madagascar; the silver box that contains all of her mother's letters written when her father was in London for a year before they were married; and a stained-glass desk lamp fringed with amber crystals at the edges that once belonged to Olympia's grandmother. Her father also collects shells, as a small boy might, and when they walk together at the beach, he is never without a container in which to put them. On his shelves are delicately edged scallop shells, the darkly iridescent casings of lowly mussels, and encrusted white oyster shells. When her father smokes, he uses the shells for ashtrays.

He watches her move about his study.

"You enjoyed your first visit to the beach?" he asks her carefully.

She picks up the malachite paperweight. She is not certain she could describe her walk along the beach even if she wanted to.

"It was excellent, after so long a winter, to feel the sea and the sea air," she answers. But when she looks up at him, she sees that he has put on his spectacles in a mild gesture of dismissal.

From her father's study, she walks out onto the porch. She has the book her father gave her, but she is too distracted to open it. During the winter, she attained her full height, so that when she sits on a chair on the porch, she can now see over the railing and down the lawn, which needs cutting. A blossom she cannot identify is sending a luscious scent into the air, and that scent, combined with the sea, is creating an intoxicating and soporific cloud all about her.

She unfastens the top two buttons of her dress and fans her neck with the cloth. She takes off her hat and lays it down, whereupon it immediately skitters along the porch floor until it wedges itself on the bottom rung of the railing. She slips her hands under her dress and removes her stockings from her garters as she did earlier at the bathhouse before walking down to the sea. She rolls the stockings into a ball and sits on them, and then lifts the hem of her dress, which has now grown stiff from the seawater, to her knees. She stretches out her legs, startled by the whiteness of her skin, which she has hardly ever in her life given any thought to. The coolish moist breeze tickles the back of her knees and the calves of her legs. She imagines the shocked face of Josiah or her father or her mother were any of them to come around the corner and catch her in her dishabille; but she decides the exquisite pleasure of the air against

17

her limbs worth the later mortgage of the consequences. Her eyes relax at the horizon, the place where the sea meets the sky, where it appears that all movement has been suspended. And indeed, it seems this day that she herself hovers in a state of suspension — that she is waiting for something she can hardly imagine and is only beginning to be prepared for.

OLYMPIA LIKES TO THINK about the original inhabitants of the house, the sisters of Saint Jean Baptiste de Bienfaisance, twenty French Canadian girls and women from the province of Quebec. Though the sisters had taken vows of poverty and were attached to the parish of Saint Andre in Ely Falls, they lived in the cottage at Fortune's Rocks with all the beauty that such a prospect had to offer. Sometimes Olympia imagines the nuns sitting contemplatively on the porch, looking out to sea; or lying on their narrow horsehair beds in cells adorned with only a single cross above a rustic table; or praying together in the small wooden chapel with French thoughts and Latin words; and then traveling across the large expanse of salt marsh between Fortune's Rocks and Saint Andre's so that they could attend services with the French Canadian priests and immigrants. Olympia is sometimes puzzled by the contrast between the lush grounds of the cottage and the austere habits of the women who dwelt in it; but since she is not a Catholic, she cannot think too long about the theology behind this paradox. In fact, she does not, early in the summer of 1899, when she is lost in speculation about the women who must have glided in slippers along the polished floors of the house, know a single person of the

Catholic faith — a deficit that troubles her, since it seems to be yet another manifestation of her overly sheltered existence.

She has been to Ely Falls only once, and that was the previous summer, when her father took her into the city to see that natural phenomenon that empties into the Ely River and makes the location such a desirable one on which to build a textile mill. They journeyed by carriage from Fortune's Rocks into the heart of the city, with its massive dark-brick mills and its narrow tiers of worker housing, and it was, as they made their way, she thought, as though they moved through layers of names: from the Whittiers and Howells of Fortune's Rocks, a class of wealth and some leisure who come north from Boston each year for the summer months; to the Hulls and Butlers of Ely proper, old Yankee families who live in sturdy clapboard houses and who own and run the mills and the surrounding shops; to the Cadorettes and Beaudoins of Ely Falls, first- and second-generation French Canadians from Quebec who emigrated to southern Maine and to the coast of New Hampshire looking for work. Residents of Fortune's Rocks, which is largely uninhabitable in the winter because of the severity of the storms out of the northeast, are continually trying to secede from the government of Ely; but that government, which encompasses Fortune's Rocks and Ely Falls, remains loath to let the wealthy inhabitants of Fortune's Rocks escape, because the tax revenues from the summer cottages are considerable. Her father, who is moderately progressive in his views, is not supportive of secession. He has told his daughter repeatedly that he believes it is his moral duty to contribute to the welfare of the inhabitants of the mill town, even though that town government is inexpressibly corrupt.

Though that day with her father Olympia was indeed rapt by the majestic sight of five million gallons of water a minute falling a height of sixty feet into a diamond-strewn spray that fueled the spinners and the looms of the mills at Ely Falls, it was the nearby utilitarian, and indeed often shabby, town houses, where the mill girls boarded, that intrigued her more. As they rode through the city in their carriage, her father delivering, since he was a man of letters and two generations removed from the shoe manufacturing in Brockton, Massachusetts, that had produced his own family's wealth, a lucid commentary on the exploitative economics of textile manufacturing — a commentary that was understood to be as integral to her education as the works of Ovid and Homer she had been reading in the spring — it was all Olympia could do not to cry out to her father to stop the horse. For she wanted so to gaze upon the facades of those buildings, with the odd book or feathered hat or milk glass pitcher in a window, and imagine, with only the angle of the hat or the simplicity of the pitcher to guide her, the lives of the women behind those enigmatic windows. In those rooms, Olympia believed, were girls not much older than her, living lives she desperately wanted a glimpse of, if not actually to try on. Lives so much more independent and adventurous than her own, however appreciative she was of her comfort. And she still does not know if her own restlessness, which has always seemed to be part of her spirit, is a result of her orderly and comfortable upbringing, or whether she is simply destined, by the same biological inheritance that causes her mother to be intolerant of even modest episodes of reality, to have a less complacent, and perhaps more curious, temperament than her peers. But she did not cry out to her father that day; for if she had, he would have regarded her with astonishment and dismay and would have assumed it necessary to readjust his assessment of her maturity and judgment.

In 1892 Bishop Pierre Bellefeuille of Saint Andre's Church, having decided that the parish would be better served if the sisters moved into the city so that they could take over the management of the hospice and the orphanage, sold the convent to Olympia's father, who happened to be in the smoking room of the Highland Hotel on the evening that Father Pierre came for a drink and mentioned the upcoming sale. Her father graciously (and rather prudently, as it happened) offered to buy the convent sight unseen and gave Father Pierre a check for the entire amount right there in the smoking room. The conversion took a month — primarily the turning of twenty tiny bedrooms into eight modest ones and one larger set of rooms for her mother, as well as the installation of indoor plumbing, a luxury the sisters had not permitted themselves.

Olympia is sitting, as she idly contemplates the nuns and their convent and the town of Ely Falls, on a wooden bench inside the deconsecrated chapel, which is attached to the northern side of the house. It is a small building with a peaked roof and clear-glass windows through which one can gaze at the many charms of nature, if not actually of God, although Olympia is sure the sisters would have had it otherwise. Apart from the shape of the chapel and its pews, the only religious artifact is its altar — a squat, heavy slab of delicately veined white marble that looks naked without its cross and candelabra and other accessories to the Catholic Mass.

It is the late morning of the day of the summer solstice, and through an open window Olympia is trying to capture on her sketch pad the look of a wooden boat, unpainted, its sails old, a dirty ivory. But she is not, she knows, terribly gifted as an artist, and her attempts to render this boat are more impressionistic than accurate, the main purpose of her sketching being not so much to improve her drawing skills as to provide herself with an opportunity for idle thought. For at this time in her life, Olympia is much occupied with the process of thinking: not constructive thinking necessarily, and nothing that will produce brilliant solutions to problems, but rather drift thinking, like dreaming, the thoughts moving randomly from one place to another, picking something up, looking at it, putting it down again, the way people move through shops. As she takes her daily walks along the seawall (or through the Public Garden at home), or sits on the porch gazing out to sea, or joins her father's guests at the dinner table, observing the way the flattering yellow candlelight plays amongst the faces of the visitors, her thoughts wander and the scenery shifts. Although at the dinner table she will sometimes play a game with herself in which she tries to reconcile what an individual might be saying at any given moment with the unrelated and truer thoughts she imagines the person to be having, a game that has caused her to be unusually attentive to character.

So her sketching is a ruse for a larger scheme. But though it is, and she is more than a little content simply to be left alone on a bench in the chapel, she is mildly disturbed by her inability to capture, even approximately, the relative size of the boat when compared with the islands behind it. Thus she is slightly distracted by her task when she hears, faintly at first and then with more clarity, the urgent and excited voices of children. When she stands up to peer through the window at the house, she sees that there are indeed children on the front porch; and although it seems as though an entire schoolroom has descended upon them, she can count only four slender bodies. Of course, she knows at once that this means that John Warren Haskell and his family have arrived and that she should go in to greet them.

Olympia sees immediately, as she walks across the lawn, that the children are all related: There are three dark-haired girls, ranging in age from about twelve years to three, and one boy, slightly older than the youngest girl, whose hair is thick and smooth and so yellow as to startle the eye. As Olympia reaches the porch steps, her sketchbook under her arm, and the children, curious, peer over the edge of the railing at the stranger in the white linen dress drawing nearer to them, she sees that they all have dark eyebrows (even the boy) and the same strong, wide mouth. The two older girls have shed their baby fat and are quite slender; the eldest girl, Olympia notes, will one day have considerable height since her shoulders are already broad and her legs long. The girl stands with her feet spread slightly apart and with her hands on her hips. Her pale blue dress, with its white collar and delicate embroidery, seems at odds with her athletic stance; and she is, as Olympia watches her, slightly challenging in her posture.

The other girl is shy and has a hand to her mouth. The youngest girl and the boy are continuously in motion, unable to stop at any one place upon the porch for fear of missing another vista that might prove to be almost unbearably exciting. As the children take in the lawn and the rocks and the sea and then the young woman who is approaching them, they have about them an expression Olympia recognizes from herself the previous day: a nearly frenzied inhaling of the first stingingly heady breaths of summer.

Once on the porch, she stops first to say hello to the two smaller children, who bend their heads in embarrassment, and then to the middle girl, who shyly takes Olympia's hand but does not utter a word, and then to the oldest girl, who tells Olympia her name is Martha.

"I am Olympia Biddeford," she says. The girl takes her hand but looks over her right shoulder.

"And I am John Haskell," she hears a voice announce behind her.

Olympia makes a half turn. She sees walnut hair, hazel eyes. The man nods almost imperceptibly. His shirt is wilted in the humidity, and the hems of his trousers are frosted with a fine layer of wet sand. He stands with his hands in his pockets, his braces making indentations in his shoulders. The cuffs of his shirt are undone, though he has not gone so far as to roll them. She guesses, in the brief period of time it takes him to cross the porch and extend his hand, that he is about the age of her father, perhaps a year or two younger, which would put him at about forty. He is not stocky exactly, because he has height, but he is broad-shouldered. She has the sense that his clothes confine him.

As he takes her hand, he steps from the shade of the porch into a rectangle of sunlight. Perhaps there is the barest trembling of her fingers in his palm, for he quickly tilts his head so that the sun is not in his eyes. He glances down at their clasped hands and then again at her face. He does not speak for some seconds after that, nor does she. Not a word, not a greeting, not a pleasantry. And Olympia thinks that her mother, who is just coming out onto the porch at this time, must see this silence between them.

"I am pleased to make your acquaintance," Olympia says finally.

"And I yours," he says, releasing her hand. "You have met Martha."

Olympia nods.

"And this is Clementine," he says, gesturing to the shy middle girl. He turns around to find the smaller children. "And those in motion are Randall and May."

Olympia feels, through the body, a sensation that is a combination of both shame and confusion.

"Do you swim?" Martha asks beside her, her voice breaking through the warm bath of John Haskell's greeting like a spill of ice water upon the skin.

"Yes, I do," Olympia says.

"Are there shells upon the beach?"

"Many," she answers.

Olympia wants suddenly to leave the porch and the watchfulness of her mother, who has not moved over the threshold of the doorway nor spoken a word.

"What kind?"

"What kind of what?" Olympia asks distractedly.

"Shells," Martha says with some impatience.

"Well, there are oysters and mussels, of course. And clams."

"Do you have a basket?"

"I think one can be found," she says.

John Haskell walks away from them. He leans against the railing of the porch and studies the view.

"Where?" Martha asks.

"There are several in the kitchen," she says.

"What are you working on?"

Olympia does not at first understand the question. Martha points to the sketchbook under her arm.

"A picture," she says. "It is not very good."

"Let me see it."

Although she does not want to, Olympia can find no reason to refuse Martha this request.

"No, it is not," Martha says in a disarmingly forthright manner when she has looked at the drawing.

"Martha," John Haskell says in mild admonition. "We should not detain Miss Biddeford any longer. Walk with me, please."

Olympia watches as John Haskell and his daughter descend the wide front steps of the porch and make their way across the lawn, Martha not reaching his shoulders. Olympia turns and looks at her mother, who regards her thoughtfully. Olympia moves toward her and makes as if to brush past her, and asks (and she can hear the new false note in her voice) if she should take the smaller children out for a walk along the seawall. And then immediately, before her mother has a chance to speak, Olympia answers herself: "Let me just change my boots and fetch a shawl," she says, slipping past her mother. And if her mother speaks a word to her, Olympia does not hear it.

Olympia's room is soothing to the eye, and she is not unlike her mother in that within its four walls she often seeks refuge. It has been papered in a pale azure that echoes the sky; against this background are tiny bouquets of miniature cream roses. The room is large enough for only her single bed, a small bedside table, a dresser, a ladies' writing desk, and a chair. Olympia has put the writing desk up against the window so that she might see out across the lawn and to the ocean, a view she never tires of, not even on the worst of days the New Hampshire coast has to offer. Framing the window are white muslin curtains with their panels tied back so that the soft cloth provides a diamond opening to the sea. She thinks it may be the diffused light through the white gauze that almost always causes a sensation of tranquillity to descend upon her whenever she shuts the door and realizes that at last she is alone.

But this day, there is no peace to be had in that room or in any other. She walks to the window and away again. She lies on the bed and then is immediately up and pacing. She walks to the glass over the dresser and peers at her face, turning her face from side to side to observe it, trying to imagine how it might be seen in the first few seconds of a greeting, what judgments might be made about her physical beauty or lack thereof. She turns sideways and studies the length of her figure and the manner in which her dress falls from her bosom. She leans forward almost into the glass itself to peer at the skin above the scalloped collar of her dress, and in doing so, she sees that her face is mottled at the cheekbones. She is suddenly certain her mother must have noticed this staining as well. She wonders then about her mother, who surely is waiting to see if Olympia will descend soon with shawl and boots to take the children for a walk on the beach, as she has promised. And at that moment, as if in answer, there is a knock.

Composing herself as best she can, Olympia moves to the door and opens it. Her mother stands across the threshold, her arms folded, her mouth open in a question that does not entirely emerge. It is purely serendipitous, and more fortunate than Olympia deserves, that she looks as ill as she professes to be. She lies to her mother, shamelessly and extravagantly, and tells her she is uneasy in her bowels, possibly from something she has eaten. She does not feel feverish, she adds, but she has been resting for a moment. And then before her mother can speak, Olympia asks if her mother has told the children yet about the walk, for she doubts she will be able to take them to the beach as she planned.

"I see," her mother says, though Olympia notes the doubt in the cast of her mother's mouth. Olympia has lied before, white lies to protect her mother from discovering some small truth that might worry her needlessly, but Olympia is not aware of ever having lied to protect or excuse herself. And she thinks then that though her mother often chooses to dwell in a world in which few decisions need to be made, she is making one then. And that her mother is, in her way, nearly as discomfited by Olympia's obviously agitated state as she is.

"You will not come down then for supper," her mother says, and Olympia hears in her voice that this is not a question, but a statement.

When she is gone, Olympia lies on her bed. She stares at nothing at all and tries to calm herself with the sound of the waves breaking against the sand. And after a time, this effort begins to bring the reward of regular breath. So much so, in fact, that she sits up, searching the room for occupation. Her knitting is in a carpetbag by the dresser, her sketchbook abandoned on her desk. On her bedside table, she sees the book her father gave her the day before. She picks it up and fingers the slightly raised lettering of the gilt title. She takes the book with her to the room's single chair and begins to read.

That afternoon, Olympia reads John Haskell's entire book, not to educate herself or to understand its contents, which only yesterday seemed a tedious challenge, but to search for clues as to another's mind in the specific combination of words, as if the structure of the sentences and the words therein were formulas that once deciphered might reveal small secrets. But she is, as she reads, despite her true intentions, absorbed in the matter of the book itself. The premise is deceptively simple and unusual, at least in Olympia's limited experience. In *On the Banks of the Rivers,* John Warren Haskell presents to the reader seven stories, or rather, Olympia thinks, portraits — portraits that are extraordinarily detailed and drawn with seeming objectivity — of seven persons associated with the mills at Lowell, Holyoke, and Manchester: four female workers and three male. In the rendering of these portraits, there is little rhetoric and no observable attempt on the part of the author to praise or to injure any of the men or women. Instead, the reader is given a depiction of a way of life that speaks, through the images of the daily struggles alone, more eloquently, Olympia decides, than rhetoric ever could of the nearly intolerable lot of the millworker. The portraits are raw and have passages that are to her both illuminating and difficult to read — not in their language but in the pictures they call forth; for the knowledge of the author in domestic and medical matters is exceedingly detailed. She wonders briefly about her father's motivation in exposing her to this material, although this is not the first time he has given her difficult or questionable subject matter that other teachers might suppress. He has always encouraged Olympia, in their dialogues, not to turn away from the painful or the ugly, at least not in print.

That afternoon, in her room, without moving from her chair, she lingers over words: *male-spinner* and *scabs* and *colomel.* She flinches at the description of a surgical intervention for an early cancer. She is fascinated by the plumbing of the boardinghouse. And she wonders, more than a little idly, how John Haskell can know of machine knitting as well as the pain of childbirth. As she reads and wonders these things, she is admitted, page by page, into the breadth of the man's knowledge of the human body and of human nature, so that she feels as though she has spoken with John Haskell at length, when, of course, she has not.

When she looks up, she sees that the light has reached that excellent period in the day when all objects are given more clarity than they have had before. And she is able to convince herself that she has somehow deftly managed to trade an unacceptable set of feelings for an acceptable set, namely, to have spun respect from confusion, admiration from agitation, and that this alchemy permits her to contemplate descending for the evening meal in an almost normal state.

IN TIME Olympia will learn of the obsession with the "other," that person from whom the theft is made — the wife, the former mistress, the fiancée. Of the relentless prurience that causes another woman to become an object of nearly intolerable curiosity. Of tormenting fascination that doesn't abate. She will discover that summer that she wants to know the most intimate of details about Catherine Haskell's life: if she sleeps alone in her bed or entwined with her husband; what words of tenderness she whispers and thus receives; if she hears, as Olympia does, the momentary pause and then the low, hushed cry, secretive and thrilling, that only a lover should be privy to. Do they share, she will wonder, Catherine Haskell and her, certain memories, events replayed at different points in the continuum of time, so that her memories are not her own at all, but merely repetitions of Catherine's? So that, in the continuum of time, each woman is similarly betrayed?

And in years to come, Olympia will ask herself if she did not, in fact, enter into a kind of love affair with Catherine Haskell, if her curiosity about the woman and about the years she had with John Haskell that Olympia did not, years in which marriage vows were made and celebrated, children were born and treasured, a marriage bed was entered and left a thousand times, did not constitute a twisted form of love itself, a love that could never, by its very nature, be returned or sated.

Olympia makes the decision to go down to supper and confronts the reality of her unkempt appearance in the mirror over the dresser. Although they have a laundress at Fortune's Rocks, Olympia does not have a personal maid (nor does she in Boston), since her father believes self-sufficiency in matters of dress and personal hygiene to be an essential part of the education of a young woman. Nor does he approve of vanity in a girl, and to that end he has urged Olympia to keep her toilet and her wardrobe as uncomplicated as possible, without straying into the realm of the eccentric. It would appear that this schooling in simple taste applies only to his daughter, however, and not to his wife: Her father seems pleased with her mother's lavender-blue silks and navy voiles and also with the elaborate and time-consuming coils and combs of her hair. Olympia's mother, of course, does have a personal maid, who is Lisette.

Olympia has never minded her father's admonitions to her on the subject of dress and appearance, for she has grown accustomed to caring for herself. Indeed, she thinks she would find it distasteful to share, for the purposes of maintenance only, the intimacies of her body. That being true, however, she does have an unpleasant half hour in her room, discarding one dress for another, bewildered by a modest assortment of jewelry, and unsure of whether to let her hair down or keep it pinned up, both choices seemingly fraught with underlying resonance: Is she a girl or is she a woman? Is this supper a casual event or is it more formal? Would her father like to see her with her hair down but her mother with it up? Olympia settles for loose hair with a ribbon and a navy blue and white linen dress that has about the bodice rows of white piping that suggest a sailor's collar. But just as she is about to leave the room, she catches a glimpse of herself in the mirror, and she is somewhat horrified to see that she resembles more an overgrown schoolgirl than a young woman about to attend a supper party on the evening of the summer solstice. Frantically unfastening the buttons of the bodice and pulling the offending dress over her head, she selects from the clothes on the bed a white handkerchief linen blouse and a long black wool challis skirt with a high-fitted waist. She tears the equally offensive ribbon from her head and begins to pin her hair into a high knot. Her hair at this time of year, before it has collected its summer highlights, is oak-colored and heavy and requires an extraordinary number of hairpins to secure it in place. Even so, she finds she has to allow loose strands to wander to her shoulders, or she will miss supper altogether. Prudently, she decides not to glance at her appearance in the mirror as she leaves the room.

She hears muffled voices in the direction of the porch and so takes a detour to the dining room, unwilling yet to enter into conversation. Since it is the first supper party of the season, the table has been more elaborately set than usual, with cloisonné china, her mother's cut-crystal goblets, and masses of miniature cream roses strewn seemingly haphazardly, but with her mother's artful eye, upon the white damask of the tablecloth. Dozens of candles, in sconces and in candelabra, have been lit and are reflected in double mirrors over two opposing mahogany buffets, so that everywhere there seems to be an infinite number of yellow-warm flickering lights. As it is still only dusk, she can see, through the large screens at the windows, hedges of beach roses that border the south side of the lawn, and beyond them the orchards. The air through the screens is soft and swims over the body like a spirit making its way through the room. Olympia follows this spirit's trail by watching the flickering flames of the candles. Beyond the door to the butler's pantry, she can hear raised voices and the sound of metal clanging upon metal. And then she hears another sound, the sibilant rustling of skirts in the doorway.

"You must be Olympia."

Olympia notices first, as doubtless everyone must, the wide green eyes, a green as transparent as sea glass. Catherine Haskell advances, and Olympia is surprised to discover that the woman is not as tall as her and that she has an almost imperceptible limp.

"What a lovely room," Catherine says, removing her hat and taking in the table in a glance. Her hair, Olympia sees, is a most unusual color: a dark blond woven with a fair percentage of silver threads, so that it has taken on the appearance of gossamer.

"You must be Mrs. Haskell," Olympia responds, finding her tongue.

"I can never get used to the gloriousness of Fortune's Rocks, no matter how often we come here," Catherine says, trying to twist a stray strand of hair into a knot at the nape of her neck. Olympia is struck by her smile, which is not exactly a smile of self-satisfaction, but seems rather to be one of genuine contentment.

"I have been walking," Mrs. Haskell says, explaining the hat and lifting it in her hand. She has on a green taffeta dress with many underskirts — an odd choice, Olympia thinks, for a walk. Perhaps Catherine Haskell was simply too impatient to change her clothes, as Olympia was the day before. Olympia notices that her boots and the hems of her skirts have dust on them.

"I was afraid I would delay supper," she says.

Olympia shakes her head.

"I hope the children have not been pestering you," Catherine says. "Have you met them? I know that Martha will have been charmed by you and will want to question you about all manner of things, and you must send her away whenever you want."

"Oh, not at all," Olympia says, thinking that Martha was not in the slightest charmed by her. "I have hardly seen them, except to meet them, as I have been in my room all afternoon."

"Really? On such a fine day? Whatever for?"

Instantly Olympia regrets having confessed confinement in her room, and she sees as well that she cannot tell this woman that she has spent the entire afternoon reading her husband's essays. Although Olympia cannot articulate precisely why at that moment, the idea feels ill-mannered and intrusive, as if she had been studying an album of private photographs.

"I have been resting," she says.

"Oh, I hope you are not unwell."

"No, I am very well," Olympia answers in confusion, looking at her feet.

"Catherine," the woman says slowly, pronouncing her name in three syllables. "Please call me Catherine. Otherwise, you will make me feel too old."

Olympia looks up and tries to smile, but she can see that Mrs. Haskell is examining her, the eyes straying to her waist, to her hair. And then returning to her face, which she holds for a moment before glancing away toward the porch.

"Do you suppose," Mrs. Haskell asks, "that I might have time to slip up to my room and change into another dress, one that has not been dragged along the sand and the sea moss?"

It is not really a question, for surely Olympia is not the arbiter of the supper hour. Mrs. Haskell leaves the room with the same sibilant swishing of her skirts with which she entered.

Olympia leans for a moment against the frame of the door, and as she does, she happens to see, through the screen of a window, a small seal beach itself upon a rock.

That night they are seven at dinner, with the addition of Rufus Philbrick from Rye, who owns hotels and boardinghouses in that town, as well as Zachariah Cote, a poet from Quincy who is having a holiday at the Highland Hotel. (A seventh place is hastily set for Olympia, who was not expected.) The children, having eaten earlier, have been removed temporarily from the house by the Haskells' governess, who has obligingly taken them for an evening walk along the beach. Mr. Philbrick, a large man with pure white whiskers and beard, has on a striped jacket with cream trousers. Olympia takes him for a dandy as well as a man of property. Cote, whose poetry she has sampled and set aside, his saccharine and sorrowful images not to her liking, is a remarkably handsome man with dark blond hair and astonishingly white teeth, an asset he must be vain about, Olympia thinks, for he seems to smile a great deal. (And are those really lavender eyes?) Her mother, in hyacinth chiffon, with pearl combs in her hair, seems to be in an animated mood, which sets off but the faintest of alarms in Olympia's mind, and she imagines in the mind of her father as well; for they have both known such episodes of brilliance and gaiety before and have reason to fear the collapse that sometimes follows. But such is the flickering beauty of the room with its seven diners, and with the candles reflected again and again in the double mirrors over the buffets, and with the moist air moving through the screen, air that hints of such a wealth of nights to follow that Olympia feels rich with their luxury, that she cannot be anything but exhilarated.

Olympia is greeted and spoken to and queried early in the meal, a mild flurry of attention that she has learned to expect and respond to. When the guests have asked all the obligatory questions, and the fish chowder has been exchanged for escalloped oysters, she will be left to listen to the others, which is the part of the meal she enjoys best.

She forms quick judgments about the guests. She sees that Zachariah Cote, in his conversation and in his gestures, is too eager to please her father, who has not yet decided whether to publish the poet's verse. And she finds that this particular display of eagerness, as it inevitably will be under such circumstances, is more pathetic than charming. She prefers the rather gruff demeanor of Rufus Philbrick, in his odd striped suit, with his sharp-tongued replies to her father's queries. For these in turn produce joviality in her father, since he knows his evening will contain at least a modicum of wit. Olympia's mother seems to drink a great deal of champagne and not to touch her meal, and periodically Olympia's father glances over at his wife or lays his fingers briefly on her hand. Olympia knows that he hopes his wife will excuse herself early in the evening before she begins to disintegrate. Catherine Haskell, in a dress of heliotrope crepe de chine, which dramatically sets off her blond and silver hair, responds politely to queries from the men and gravitates protectively toward Olympia's mother, complimenting her with apparent sincerity on the masses of miniature roses on the table and asking her opinion about the advisability of the girls' boating in the marshes in the morning.

John Haskell is seated at the far end of the table, and from time to time Olympia can hear his voice. It seems that the men, including Haskell, are relating to Cote, who is not familiar with the area, a story involving the poetess Celia Thaxter, whom her father has published often and admires. Thaxter, Olympia knows, had a peripheral, though critical, role in a local murder some twenty-five years earlier. But since this is an oft-told tale for Olympia, and a rather gruesome one at that, she lets her thoughts drift for a period of minutes until such time as the lamb medallions and the rice croquettes will be served and good manners will once again compel the guests to include her. She is informed enough this summer on some subjects to enter into conversation if invited to do so, a fact that her father knows; and it is possible that at any moment he might demonstrate the education of his daughter by drawing her into a debate about American liberalism or Christian social reform. But that night she observes that her father, too, seems to be more than usually animated, almost flushed, and she thinks this must somehow be attributable to the double beauty of Mrs. Haskell and her mother, and the further doubling — no, quadrupling — of their handsomeness in the double mirrors over the buffets. Indeed, Olympia discovers, as she looks around the table, that all of the men are well positioned in regard to the double mirrors and thus are recipients of an infinite multiplication of the charms inherent in a certain tilt of a head, a long throat leading to a cloud of silver and gold gossamer, a smile quickly bestowed, a slight furrowing of the brow, the drape of pearls upon a white bosom, the fall of a strand of hair that has come loose from a jet and diamond-studded comb. And she, too, is deeply attentive to these charms, as an apprentice will be to a carpenter or a smith. But when, in the course of her drifting thoughts, she glances over at the opposite end of the table, she sees that John Haskell is gazing not at the charms of his wife or of Rosamund Biddeford, either in the flesh or in the double mirrors, but at her.

There is no mistaking this gaze. It is not a look that turns itself into a polite moment of recognition or a nod of encouragement to speak. Nor is it the result of an absentminded concentration of thought. It is rather an entirely penetrating gaze with no barriers or boundaries. It is scrutiny such as Olympia has never encountered in her young life. And she thinks that the entire table must be stopped in that moment, as she is, feeling its nearly intolerable intensity.

She bends her head, but perceives nothing, not the fork in her hand, the lace at the sleeve of her blouse, nor the lamb medallions on her plate. When she raises her eyes, she sees that his gaze is still unbroken. She cannot, finally, keep the bewilderment from her face. Perhaps because of her confusion, which must suddenly be apparent, he turns his head away quickly toward her father, as if he would speak to him. And it is then that her father, doubtless startled by Haskell's abrupt attention (or possibly unconsciously aware of the man's gaze in his daughter's direction), says to the assembled group, "I have given Olympia John's new book to read."

The silence that follows is more dreadful than any untutored comment she might have uttered in its place, a silence in which her father and his guests wait for her to speak, a silence during which she risks turning her father's pleasure into disappointment. So that after a time, he is compelled to say, with the faint echo of the schoolmaster in his voice, "Is not that so, Olympia? Or perhaps you have not yet had time to glance at Haskell's essays."

She raises her chin with a bravado she does not feel and says to John Haskell rather than to her father, "I have read nearly all of the essays, Mr. Haskell, and I like them very much."

She breathes so shallowly that she cannot get air into her lungs. Another silence ensues, one that, as it unfolds, begins to annoy her father.

"Surely, Olympia, you can be more specific," he says finally.

She takes a breath and lays down her fork.

"The form of your essays is deceptively simple, Mr. Haskell," she says. "You appear to have written seven stories without judgment or commentary, yet the portraits, in the accretion of detail, are more persuasive, I believe, than any rhetoric could possibly be."

"Persuasive of what?" asks Philbrick, who has not read the essays.

"Persuasive of the need to improve the living conditions of millworkers," she answers.

39

John Haskell looks quickly at Philbrick, who does, after all, own a number of boardinghouses in Rye, as if to ascertain whether the man will be offended by further discussion of the topic. But Haskell doubtless also sees, as she does, the small smile on her father's face, a smile that indicates to her that perhaps his insistence that she speak about the book is, in fact, part of his plan to engage in lively debate. Haskell then turns from Philbrick to Olympia. She prays that he will not say that she is too kind in her comments, for she knows that to do so will be to dismiss her entirely.

"Your portraits are raw and have passages that are to me both il-luminating and difficult to read," she continues before he can speak, "not in their language but in the images they create, particularly as regards accidents and medical matters."

"This is quite true, Olympia," her father says, beginning slightly to recover his pride in his daughter.

"I think it would be the rare reader indeed who could come away from those portraits unmoved," she adds.

"Your perceptions would seem to belie your age," Rufus Philbrick interjects suddenly, appraising her with keen eyes. She finds she does not mind the frankness of his gaze.

"Not at all," her father says. "My daughter is exceptionally well schooled."

"And what school might that be?" Zachariah Cote asks, address-ing her politely. Olympia does not like the man's sudden smile, nor the exceptional length of his side-whiskers, nor, more important, the way in which the conversation has turned to her rather than to the work of John Haskell.

"The school of my father," she says.

"Is that so?" asks Rufus Philbrick with some surprise. "You do not attend classes?"

Her father answers for her. "My daughter went to the Commonwealth Seminary for Females in Boston for six years, at which time it became painfully apparent that Olympia's learning was far superior to that of her instructors. I removed her and have been schooling her at home instead; although a year from now, I hope to enroll her at Wellesley College."

"Have you minded?" Catherine Haskell asks quietly, turning in her direction. "Being separated from other girls your age?"

"My father is a gifted and kind teacher," Olympia says diplomatically.

"So you know a great deal about the mills?" Rufus Philbrick asks John Haskell.

"Not as much as I would like," he answers. "One of the disadvantages of creating portraits to tell one's story is that they seldom allow the writer to reveal a full historical perspective, and I fear this is a major flaw of the book. I think that understanding the history of any given situation is critical to comprehending it in the present. Do you not agree?"

"Oh, I think so," Olympia's father says.

"In the early days of the mills," Haskell continues, "when the workers were mostly girls from Yankee farms, the mill owners took a benevolent attitude toward their employees and felt obliged to provide decent housing and clean infirmaries. The girls were housed two to a room and were fed communally three times a day in the dining room. In many ways, the boardinghouse was a home away from home, something like a college dormitory. There were libraries and literary societies for the girls, for example, and concerts and plays and so on. A young woman could be said to have had her horizons broadened if she went into the mills."

"Even so, I have heard," says Rufus Philbrick, "that the girls worked ten or twelve hours a day, six days a week, and to ruin one's eyesight or to become diseased was not uncommon."

"This is absolutely true, Philbrick. But my point is that when the Yankee girls began to go home and were replaced by the Irish and French Canadians, conditions deteriorated rapidly. These immigrants have come in families, large families that are forced to crowd into rooms previously meant only for two. The original housing cannot sustain such a large population, and the sanitary and health conditions have broken down. It is only in the past several years that progressive groups have begun to take on the cause of better housing and clinics and care for children."

"I have heard something of these progressive groups," Zachariah Cote says, looking around at the assembled group.

"Last April," says Haskell, "I and several other physicians from Cambridge journeyed up to Ely Falls and conducted a survey of as many men, women, and children as we could cajole into participating. The inducement, seven dollars per family, was sufficiently appealing that we were able to examine five hundred and thirty-five persons. Of these, only sixty could be considered to be entirely healthy."

"That is an astoundingly poor ratio," Olympia's mother says.

"Yes, it is. The boardinghouses, we discovered, were riddled with disease — tuberculosis, measles, white lung, cholera, consumption, scarlet fever, pleurisy — I could go on and on. I have already gone on and on."

"One of the difficulties, John, as I understand it," says Olympia's father, "is that some of the immigrants do not have strong cultural opposition to child labor. The Francos, for example, see whole families as *working* families, and thus they try to evade the child-labor laws by having the children do piecework at home, sometimes, depending upon how desperate the family is, for fourteen hours a day in a room with little or no ventilation."

"What sort of piecework?" Catherine Haskell asks.

"The children sew or baste or rip out stitches," her husband explains. "Simple, repetitive tasks." He shakes his head. "You would not believe these children if you saw them, Philbrick. Many are diseased. Some are stunted in their growth and have ruined their eyesight. And these children are not twelve years old."

The conversation pauses for the contemplation of this startling fact that must be properly digested before the talk can continue. Olympia pokes at her rice croquettes. With the fleeting bravery that comes of being encouraged in conversation, she once again addresses John Haskell.

"And something else, Mr. Haskell," she says. "There is a fondness in your portraits. I think you must bear these workers no small amount of affection."

John Haskell responds with a small but distinct smile in her direction. "I had quite hoped that such affection would be apparent to the reader," he says, "but it seems to have escaped the notice of my reviewers entirely."

"I believe the critic Benjamin Harrow is better known for his gravity than for his good humor," says her father, smiling.

"I wonder if these are not, strictly speaking, something other than essays, John," says Zachariah Cote, still trying to find a way into the conversation, which has been moving along well enough without him.

"They are not essays in the strictest sense, to be sure," says John Haskell. "They are profiles only. But I like to think the details of a life form a mosaic that in turn informs the reader about something larger than the life. I have drawings as well of these workers, which I commissioned and which I should have liked to have included in my book, but my publisher persuaded me that pictures would detract from the seriousness of my work, and so I did not — a decision I regret, by the way."

"I regret it as well," Olympia says. "I, for one, would very much like to see drawings of the people you have written of."

"Then I shall oblige you, Miss Biddeford," he says.

And Olympia can see, in the quick turn of her mother's head, that she has perhaps been too bold with her request.

"But does that not destroy the very purpose of the written portrait?" Philbrick asks. "How can one's words ever equal the accuracy of a picture?"

"Surely there remains a great deal that cannot be caught in a likeness," John Haskell says. "Historical facts, for example, or the joy of a marriage. The anguish resulting from the death of a child. Or simply a broken spirit."

"But I for one have always thought that a life can be read on a face," says Philbrick. "It is how I do my business, by what I see in a face. Loyalty. Honesty. Cunning. Weakness."

"Well, then, we are in luck," says Catherine Haskell brightly. "For my husband has brought his camera with him. Perhaps we may persuade him to make photographs of each of us tomorrow. After which we can decide for ourselves whether character may be read in the face."

"Oh, surely not!" exclaims Olympia's mother, mistaking the gentle teasing of her guest for a summons. "I shall never have a photograph made of myself. Never!"

This note of alarm, as inappropriate to the evening as any note sounded, yet as significant to the summer as if a pianist had inadvertently fingered the wrong keys and had produced a measure of heartbreakingly beautiful music, vibrates through the room and then slowly dies away.

"My dear," says her husband, reaching across to touch, and then to still, his wife's trembling hand in a gesture Olympia will always think of as one of infinite grace, "I should never permit anyone to photograph your beauty, for I should be insanely jealous both of the photographer and of anyone who dared to look at the finished product."

And whether it is the faint reminder of danger or the humbling recognition of the generosity of married love, each of the guests is rendered silent as Lisette brings to the table the Sunderland pudding, which she begins to spoon and serve.

The notes of Chopin's "Fantaisie-Impromptu" float through the tiny squares of the wire screens and onto the porch, where the men sit with cigars and large delicate bubbles of brandy. Olympia's mother has, as expected, excused herself, and her father has returned from seeing her to her bedroom. Catherine Haskell plays with an accomplished, even plaintive, touch that is, Olympia thinks, to be much admired. Moths flutter about the lanterns, and she sits away from their light as well as from the men. Since there are no women on the porch, she cannot join the men, but neither can she bear to be kept inside on such a fine evening.

The moon makes long cones upon the sea, which has settled with the darkness and resembles, as it approaches high tide, a magnificent lake. The continuous susurrus of the surf is soothing in and about the conversation and the piano's notes. Olympia cannot hear what the men are saying, but the sound of their voices is instantly recognizable: the assured and gracious, if sometimes pedantic, pronouncements of her father; the short staccato bursts of enthusiasm and advice from Rufus Philbrick; the somewhat breathy and all too deferential note of Zachariah Cote; and, finally, the low, steady sentences of John Haskell, his voice seldom rising or falling. She strains to pick out words from the talk: *merchandise . . . Manchester . . . carriage-maker . . . travesty . . . benefits . . .* Masculine words drenched in smoke and slightly slurred on the tongue. From time to time, the men lower their voices conspiratorially, with heads bent toward one another, and then suddenly, with harsh bursts of laughter, they move apart. At these moments, Olympia thinks perhaps she should leave

45

the porch. But so deep are her lassitude and physical contentment that she cannot rouse herself to action. It strikes her as possible that she might simply fall asleep in the chair and remain in it the entire night, this entire short night of the summer solstice. That she might watch the sun rise over the sea at dawn. And so it is that she does not notice that Catherine Haskell has stopped her playing until she hears the woman's voice behind her.

"Did you know that nearly all civilizations have regarded the night of the summer solstice as possessing mystical powers?" she asks.

Olympia sits up straighter, but Catherine puts a restraining hand on her shoulder. She takes a seat near to Olympia and looks out over the railing.

"Your playing is very beautiful," Olympia says.

Catherine Haskell smiles vaguely and waves her hand, as if to dismiss such an unearned compliment.

"Not as beautiful as your mother's, or so I have heard," she says. The heliotrope crepe de chine of her dress has the effect, in the darkness, of disappearing altogether, so that she seems, in the dim light of the lanterns, to be merely two slender arms, a throat, a face, and all that hair.

"And that the earliest setting of the blue stones at Stonehenge is aligned with the moment of sunrise on the summer solstice? On that day, sacrifices were made. Some think human sacrifices."

"On this night I could believe anything possible," Olympia says.

"Yes. Quite."

Olympia can hear the creak of wicker as Mrs. Haskell leans back and begins to rock in the chair. Her white slippers glow faintly in the moonlight.

"Your mother is not unwell, I hope," Catherine says.

"She tires easily," Olympia explains.

"Yes, of course."

46

Olympia hesitates. "She is delicate in her constitution," she says.

"I see," Catherine Haskell says quickly, as though this is something she has already divined. She turns her head toward Olympia, but Olympia can see only a quarter moon of face.

"I think you must be like your father," Catherine says.

"How is that?" Olympia asks.

"Protective. Strong, I think."

Beyond them there is another short burst of laughter, causing them both to glance in the direction of the men. The two women examine the tableau in the lantern light.

"Of course, you have your mother's beauty," Catherine adds. She smooths out an invisible skirt with her alabaster arms. "I have always thought there is a moment in the life of a girl," she begins, and then pauses. They hear John Haskell's voice rise briefly above the others with a fragment of a sentence: *have deteriorated with the coming of the* . . . "By 'moment,'" Catherine continues, "I mean a period of time, a week, or months perhaps. But finite. A moment for which the bones have been forming themselves. . . ." She stops, as if searching for the appropriate words with which to continue. "And in that moment, a girl becomes a woman. The bud of a woman perhaps. And she is never so beautiful as in this period of time, however brief."

Olympia is glad that it is dark and that her face cannot be seen, for she can feel it becoming suffused with color.

"What I mean to say, my dear," Catherine adds, "is that I believe you are just on the cusp of your moment."

Olympia looks down at her lap.

"Your beauty is in your mouth," Catherine says further, and Olympia is jolted by this frank pronouncement.

"Of course, it is in your face," the older woman adds hastily, "but primarily your mouth, in its unconventional shape, its fullness. Your mouth is worthy of its own portrait."

Olympia hears the deliberate repetition of the word *portrait*. In the darkness, the kitchen's screen door squeaks as it is opened and then slapped to. The cook must be on her way home. Olympia is too unsettled to form a reply that is not fatuous, and she is as well a bit alarmed by the intimacy in Catherine Haskell's comment, for she hardly knows the woman at all. Although later, from the perspective of years, Olympia will think that Catherine's pronouncement was delivered more to herself than to Olympia, as if by defining a thing, one could successfully defuse its power.

"Well, you are lovely altogether," Catherine Haskell says, employing a different tone, the casual voice of a favorite aunt or a cousin, as if she has sensed Olympia's misgivings. "And I have no doubt that this will be your summer."

"You flatter me too much, Mrs. Haskell."

"Catherine."

"Catherine."

"And I do not flatter you half enough. As you shall see. If I may ask a favor?"

Olympia nods.

"I wonder if you would take the older girls boating while we are here. I know that Martha would adore it."

"I would be happy to," Olympia says.

"Martha and Clementine only, I think. The others are too young."

"We have the lifesaving dresses," Olympia says.

"Even so, I would rather you take them, if you would. I do not trust Millicent's judgment. You have met the children's governess? On other matters, yes. But not boating. She has little experience with the water."

A masculine voice, wheedling and insistent, rises a note above the others. Instinctively, Catherine Haskell and Olympia glance together toward the men by the porch door, at the flurry of moths over their heads.

"Cote seems such an ass," Catherine whispers. And Olympia laughs, at least as much in relief as in recognition of her own thoughts.

But as she laughs, and perhaps this is only a trick in the moonlight, the white skin of Catherine Haskell's face seems fleetingly to become thin and drawn.

"Do not be up late," the older woman says, putting a hand on Olympia's wrist for support as she stands, and Olympia is again reminded of her limp. Catherine's fingers are shockingly cold.

"How warm you are," she says, looking down.

Her face hovers only inches from Olympia's, so close that she can smell Catherine's breath, which is sweet with the mint from the lamb. For a moment, Olympia thinks that Catherine will kiss her.

Olympia knows other facts about the solstice. That it rests in Gemini, and that on this day at Aswan, which lies five hundred miles southeast of Alexandria, the sun's rays fall precisely vertically at noon. That visionary cults paint their bodies in symbols on the solstice and salute the sun with lamentations until they either fall unconscious or have their expected visions. That the solstice produces the highest tides of the year, particularly so if it happens in concert with a full moon. The moon is not entirely full this night, but nearly so, and will be a source of worry, Olympia knows, for those few who inhabit houses too near to the beach at Fortune's Rocks.

She slips off the porch and walks along the edge of the lawn in shadow, so as not to attract the attention of the men. She makes her way to the seawall and finds a dry rock on which to sit. She perches herself on a natural ledge over a glistening calligraphy of seaweed that is remoistened each time the waves enter the rock crevice nearest to her and send up a spray. The tide is indeed high and teases even the uppermost of the stones. As one draws closer to the water, the temperature drops accordingly, and she is somewhat chilled as she sits with her legs bent under her. The porch of the house, some hundred feet away, is bathed in pools of yellow light that flicker in the light breeze. Though she can see the cluster of men by the door, she cannot hear their voices for the surf.

She removes her slippers and stockings and sets them near to her. She presses the soles of her feet into the slippery sea moss of the rock below. The sensation is a queasy one, immediately giving rise to thoughts of the thousands of forms of sea life just beneath the deceptively calm surface of the water. The summer previous to this one, her father insisted that Olympia have bathing lessons, since he does not allow anyone who cannot swim to use the boat alone. They went to the bay for these lessons, and she was at first so frightened by the feel of the muck between her naked toes, and by possible contact with any number of slippery sea creatures, that she learned to swim in near record time. At least well enough to permit her to have some chance of saving herself should she fall overboard reasonably close to shore. And all this despite the extraordinary, if not altogether comical, appearance her father made in his bathing costume, and his extreme embarrassment to be so unarmored. (And it occurs to her now that the speed with which she learned to swim may, in addition to her fear of touching the slimy unknown, have been a result of his haste to change into more suitable attire.)

She does not know how long she sits upon the rocks, watching the tide rise to its highest point. She is having thoughts of returning to the house when an errant wave washes up over the rock on which she is sitting and steals a slipper like a thief vanishing instantly into the night. She stands up at once, physically shocked by the icy water, which has soaked the back of her skirt. She bends to snatch the slipper, which she sees bobbing just out of reach, and in doing so receives another frigid soaking as a result of a wave that claims not only the other slipper but also her stockings. She scuttles backward and then stands up again. It is clear that she will never retrieve the slippers and stockings. She watches them make slow progress outward from the rocks, one of the shoes disappearing altogether. Shivering slightly, and wet all along the back of her petticoat, she turns to make her way to the house. She crosses the lawn, which is glistening with dew and blackened in the dark. She is fervently hoping that no one will hear the screen door open and close when she enters the house.

She is halfway across the lawn when she begins to discern, in the shadows of the porch, a lone figure. Her heart plummets to a cold place within her chest. Her father, vexed, has been waiting for her, and he will be furious to have been kept up for so long. But when she takes a few steps farther, she can tell, by the posture and size of the person, that it is not her father. Anxiety is replaced by relief, but that relief quickly gives way to apprehension.

She stops mid-stride and pauses for a moment. She has been seen and now cannot turn around without seeming either rude or frightened, neither of which she wishes to appear to be. With forced ease, she continues on her walk. John Haskell stands and walks over to the steps. He gives her his hand, which she briefly takes.

"You have forgotten your shoes," he says.

"I have lost them to the sea," she answers.

"And the sea will not give them back, I fear."

She allows him to lead her onto the porch.

"I told your father I thought you had gone to bed," he says, "but I can see that I was mistaken. It is very late. You should go up."

"Yes," she says.

"You look pale," he says. "Let me fetch you some hot tea."

"No," she says, waving him off. "I will just sit a second and catch my breath."

She feels a hand at her elbow, guiding her to a chair.

"You are soaked," he says.

She knows he has seen the back of her skirt.

He hands her a cup. "This is mine," he says. "Please, humor me and take a sip."

She takes the cup in her palms and brings it to her lips. The hot tea burns its way through her body and causes a warming tingle to spread to her limbs. She takes another sip and gives the cup back to him.

Since dinner, Haskell has loosened his collar. His jacket lies over the back of the wicker rocker on which he is sitting. She is painfully aware of her bare ankles and feet, which she tries to hide by sitting up straighter and tucking the offending appendages out of sight.

Setting the cup aside, John Haskell leans back in his chair, which is so close to hers that if she extended her hand, she could touch his knee. The shivering begins in earnest in her upper arms.

"You lingered at the seawall too long a time," he says.

"It is the night of the summer solstice," she answers, as if that were explanation enough.

"So it is. You were too kind to me in your earlier comments on my book."

And there it is, she thinks, the dismissal. But she is mistaken.

"You would seem to be my perfect reader," he adds.

"Of course not," she says quickly. "Your intent will be apparent to any reader."

"If I can but reach them," he says. "I fear I have erred in producing a book that will have only a handful of readers. I should have published a pamphlet, as my instincts originally urged me to. But pride, I fear, got the better of me."

"You feel some urgency to reach a wide audience?" she asks.

"I must," he says. "The conditions are appalling. Enlightenment, I fear, has been replaced by successive layers of contempt and neglect."

"I see," she says. She knows that she should go up and change into dry clothes, but she is unwilling to leave the porch just at that moment. "And you wish to regain some of that lost ground?" she asks.

He shakes his head. "Nothing so grand," he says. "It is the health of the millworkers with which I must first concern myself. Their personal health, their sanitary conditions, their medical care, all of which are quite wretched, I can assure you."

"And so you will work at the clinic."

"Yes, I have already begun."

A small silence fills the space between them.

"It is more than kind of you to ask to see the pictures," he says.

"I *should* like to see them," she repeats.

"Well, then I shall send for them."

"I would not want you to go to any trouble," she says.

"No, none at all."

"I must go," she says, standing abruptly. And in doing so, her hair, which has been jostled in her walk across the lawn (or perhaps in the startled movement of her head when the sea soaked her skirt), lists slightly to one side and releases a comb, which clatters to the porch floor. John Haskell, who has stood with her, bends to retrieve it.

"Thank you," she says, holding the comb in her palm.

"How poised you are," he says suddenly. He tilts his head, as if to examine her from another angle. "How self-possessed. Quite extraordinary in a young woman of your age. I think it must be a result of your singular education."

She opens her mouth, but she cannot think how to reply.

"I was there yesterday," he says. "On the beach. I saw you at the beach."

She shakes her head wordlessly, then turns on her heel, belying in an instant the truth of Haskell's compliment.

AFTER HER ENCOUNTER with John Haskell on the porch, Olympia climbs up to her bedroom in an agitated state. She opens the window, puts her hands on the sill, and bends her head. A fine dampness covers her face and hair and throat.

She dresses in a white linen nightdress, a garment she has not worn since the previous summer. The thinness of the fabric is a pleasure to her, although she notes that she has grown so much during the winter months that the sleeves are at least an inch too short. At the cuffs is a delicate tatting her mother has knotted, tatting being a skill that suits her invalid status and one she has tried to pass on to her daughter without success. Olympia sits on her bed and, as usual, plaits her hair, her feet bare against the slightly damp wooden floorboards. She has long grown accustomed to the ever present humidity; indeed, it is not uncommon to slip between slightly dampened sheets at night or to retrieve from the armoire dresses that have quite lost their stiffness in the sea air.

Sometime after she has finished tying up her hair, she crawls into her bed and falls into a troubled sleep. Her dreams are different from any she has ever had before, different in their texture and in their substance. They are somewhat shocking, but not terrifying, since they contain the most private and pleasurable of physical sensations she has ever experienced in her short life. She wakes in a state of much confusion, lying in a tangle of twisted linen, believing she has spoken to John Haskell just moments before, when, of course, she has not. And she wonders fleetingly if there might be something wrong with her, if she has been, in fact, hallucinating, if she is in danger of becoming her mother's daughter after all. But then she dismisses this speculation, for the dreams that she has had, and the sensations that have been visited upon her, feel, in spite of their extraordinary novelty, welcoming, as is a warm bath. And if these sensations do not seem entirely *good,* they feel deep and authentic. And she is, in truth, loath to watch them thin and dissipate with the morning sun.

That morning, with Philbrick and Cote and, of course, the Haskells still in residence, they are all occupied with photography, an undertaking Olympia finds as intriguing to observe as to participate in. The sittings begin shortly after breakfast, Haskell wisely deciding to start with the children so that they might be released to other pursuits early in the day. The camera is an English one and quite a handsome instrument with its mahogany case and brass fittings. Inside the camera, Haskell explains, is a metal cone lined with black velvet into which one puts the film. Once exposed, it is withdrawn from the other side. The camera holds film for forty exposures, he adds, so there will be enough for several photographs of each of them. Olympia is relieved to see that the camera is one that can be held in the hands and that the enterprise will not be the agonizing one she has heard about — an enterprise in which the unfortunate subject is made to remain still on a chair while the camera, anchored upon a stand, records in a painstakingly long process the rigid expression of the participant, any smile or movement on the part of the subject ruinous to the result.

To capture the best light, which there is in abundance this day, Haskell uses the front steps for his venue. While one of them is being photographed, the others come and go upon the porch and busy themselves with reading or with conversation or simply with gazing out to sea, a seductive activity that can consume many hours in a day. Olympia takes a chair near to the proceedings and watches Haskell work. And as she watches, she discovers that a dream creates a nonexistent intimacy, that one feels, all the next day after the dream, as though certain words have been said or actions taken *which have not*. So that the object of the dream feels familiar, when, in fact, no familiarity exists at all.

Haskell, in a white linen suit and cravat, with a straw hat which he removes when he begins to work in earnest, suggests from time to time a tilt of the head, a placement of an arm. Occasionally he reaches across the photographic space and moves the shoulder just so. As might be expected, the children are impatient, and it is an effort for them just to sit still. Olympia is impressed, however, by Haskell's lack of sentiment in posing his youngest children, Randall and May, waiting for a moment when both have spotted a fishing boat not far off shore and are gazing with rapt but keen attention, their eyes wide and their mouths slightly parted, at the novel sight. Later Olympia will see the photographs after they and the camera have been sent back to Haskell from Rochester, and she will be impressed with their clarity, a sharp precision of line and facial feature one tends not to observe in reality, since the face may be in shadow or the glance, of polite necessity, too short.

On the porch steps, Martha looks like a young girl aching to be taken seriously; Clementine, someone for whom it is an effort to lift her eyes to the camera. Both wear white dotted Swiss pinafores with pale blue underdresses, and each has a ribbon in her hair. Haskell poses his wife sitting sideways, the slightest suggestion of a pearl-buttoned opera boot peeking out below her skirts, her body and her face in profile. Catherine, Olympia notes, has a lovely profile, not flat or sharp-chinned, but rather one with high cheekbones and a long neck. Mrs. Haskell's bearing, though seemingly relaxed, is flawless. She has on this day a straw hat with a wide ribbon and many flowers on its brim. It sits atop her head with her abundant hair caught in rolls beneath. Most striking, however, is her costume, a white suit of the finest linen, nipped tightly at the waist, the peplum of the jacket draping itself becomingly over her hips, a suit that suggests both casual elegance and a disdain for frills. As Haskell photographs his wife, he communicates with her in a language of easy gestures and single syllables, a code that signals comfort, if not actually a fair degree of intimacy.

Philbrick, who is much interested in the make and mechanics of the camera, which, Haskell tells him, is called a Luzo, has on his striped jacket of the night before. He refuses to sit still, continually getting up to peer into the viewfinder and to ask why the image is up-side down and to marvel how it is that Haskell can accurately make out facial features. Cote has worn a navy frock coat that accentuates the planes of his face, and with it a silky white shirt. Her father, not surprisingly, has Haskell photograph him standing, complete with hat and waistcoat and pocket watch, since he is of the mind that one ought not to promote too much informality at the beach. Even Olympia's mother, in the end, relents and allows herself to be photographed, albeit behind a veil with her eyes lowered, flinching each time she hears the shutter click, as though she might be shot.

Toward the end of these proceedings, Haskell glances over at Olympia.

"You have been so observant," he says to her, "I think you could do this yourself."

"It is fascinating, surely," she answers, deciding not to add that she thinks one can learn at least as much from watching the subject pose himself as from the finished photograph.

"Well, then, let us see what we can do with you," he says, and she notes that he, like his wife on the previous night, speaks with the fond tone of a relative. "Please. Sit here on the steps," he says, gesturing with his hand.

She does as he has asked, smoothing her skirts under her and tilting her knees to the side when the folds of the material rise above her lap. She is determined not to be a difficult subject, but something about her pose feels ungainly. It must strike Haskell as awkward as well, for she is aware of the keenest interest on his part. For a few moments, she feels that every flaw of her face or of her figure must now be apparent to the man; and she thinks that in this it is perhaps not so unusual for Haskell to have been drawn to both photography and medicine. For do not both require severe attention to the body?

She has dressed this day in a white handkerchief linen chemise that billows out over a broad navy sash she has tightened to within an inch of her life. She has a navy shawl about her shoulders, and on her head a white broad-brimmed hat that she thinks would have benefited from a sprig of beach rose or even a single hydrangea blossom had she thought of it earlier. Somewhat restlessly, Haskell moves toward her and then away, to her left and to her right, occasionally looking up from the viewfinder and studying her face.

"Olympia, lift your shoulder . . . ," he says. "There. Now turn your head toward me. Slowly. Yes. Now stop. Good. Hold that."

She does as she is told.

He squeezes the shutter, simultaneously looking up and moving the film through the camera.

"No," he says in a disappointed tone, as much to himself as to anyone else.

"She looks fine to me," says Philbrick, who, having already had his sitting and having examined every aspect of the camera, is now impatient to reach the beach during the family bathing hours of noon to one and, perhaps more important, to eat the picnic that will be brought there.

"Lovely pose," says Catherine, who is knitting.

"I think she should sit up straighter," her mother says. "Olympia often slouches."

"Relax your arm," Haskell says, "and tilt your head like this."

He demonstrates.

Slightly annoyed at all the instruction, Olympia lifts her arms and removes the pin that secures her hat to her hair. She pulls the hat off quickly and tosses it to the steps. She folds her hands in her lap. She thinks her mother, sitting near the railing, actually says, "Oh no," for no female has been photographed this morning without a hat, not even the girls.

Haskell stands unmoving for a moment. And then he steps forward. She thinks he might speak to her. Instead, he lifts her chin with his fingertips. He raises her chin high and then higher, so that she is forced to look into his eyes. He holds this pose at its apex, studying her face, and then he allows his hand, which she is quite certain is hidden from the others' view, to trail under her chin, to her throat. The touch is so brief and soft, it might be a hair floating across the skin.

This fleeting brush of his fingers, the first intimate touch she has ever had from a man, triggers a sudden image from the previous night's dreams. Her gaze loosens and swims, and color comes into her face. There must be on her cheeks the hectic flush of confusion, she thinks. And she is afraid that she will, in the several seconds she is required to remain still, betray the content of the scenes and pictures that float before her eyes.

She waits for some confirmation that the others have observed Haskell's touch. But she realizes, from the impatient and bored tones of the onlookers, that no one has noticed the moment at all. And she wonders then: Did it really happen, or did she imagine it?

Later, when she sees the photographs for the first time, she will be surprised at how calm her face looks — how steady her gaze, how erect her posture. In the picture, her eyes will be slightly closed, and there will be a shadow on her neck. The shawl will be draped around her shoulders, and her hands will rest in her lap. In this deceptive photograph, she will look a young woman who is not at all disturbed or embarrassed, but instead appears to be rather serious. And she will wonder if, in its ability to deceive, photography is not unlike the sea, which may offer a benign surface to the observer even as it conceals depths and currents below.

"Very good," says Philbrick, standing. "I, at least, am off to the beach."

As promised, they make their expedition at noon, all of them, that is, except for her mother, and then Catherine, who remains behind to keep her mother company. Josiah has packed an elaborate picnic in a wicker basket, so large it requires two boys to haul it. The day continues to be bright and breezy, and although the surf is decidedly energetic, everyone except Olympia and Haskell ventures into the water. Olympia has deliberately chosen not to wear a bathing costume, being uncomfortable in that company to be in such a state of undress. Haskell has not had time to change, since he has been working with the camera until the last minute. Indeed, he still has it with him in its mahogany box.

The day and the hour seem to have brought out nearly all of the population of Fortune's Rocks. Olympia observes many children under the watchful eye of governesses. One woman, taking care of eight babies, has placed her charges in laundry baskets. From where Haskell and Olympia sit, they can see only tiny heads and faces bobbing and peering out over the baskets' rims, altogether a most comical sight. In other groupings, there are women overdressed in black taffeta dresses with elaborate hats and gloves and boots and ruffled parasols, as though desperate not to let a single grain of sand or ray of sunshine touch their bodies. Olympia wonders how it is they do not melt from being swathed as they are in so many garments. In other gatherings, men stand in bathing costumes that quite cost them their dignity: The apparel has the impoverished look of union suits, and the cloth sags in an unfortunate manner when wet. But at the beach, she thinks, is there not a certain license in dress, a latitude in custom?

After they have set up their picnic on the rug, Philbrick and Cote and (reluctantly) her father accompany Martha and the other children, in sailors' costumes and dark stockings, to the water's edge, some fifty feet away. Haskell and Olympia are left behind. This is not contrivance on their part, Olympia knows, although she is certain they are both aware of the somewhat awkward circumstances as the others leave them. Haskell sheds his jacket and his shoes, removes his tie and his socks, and rolls the white flannel of his trousers to just below the knees. He leans back on the rug, propped up on one elbow, and watches the bathing party proceed to the ocean.

To busy herself, Olympia prepares a plate of boiled eggs and rolled tongue and bread and butter, and hands it to Haskell, who takes it from her. She makes a plate of food for herself. They eat side by side, Olympia on a small stool that has been brought for the occasion. They do not speak for some time. Occasionally, a gust of wind makes one or the other of them reach forward to anchor a corner of the rug or to lay a hand on a hat that threatens to stray. She pours lemonade into glasses and gives him one.

"What do you do when you are at the clinic?" she asks, her voice sounding strained, at least to her.

"A bit of everything," he says. "Set broken bones, amputate mangled fingers, treat diphtheria and pneumonia and typhoid and dysentery and influenza and syphilis . . ." He pauses. "But this is not a fit discussion for a young woman," he says, wiping his mouth with his napkin. His eyes are shaded by the brim of his straw hat.

"Why not?"

"Have you ever been to Ely Falls?"

"Only once," she confesses. "With my father last summer. But I did not see much. My father made me remain in the carriage while he went about his business."

"My point exactly. It is a fearful place, Olympia. Overcrowded and filthy and disease-ridden."

The wind lifts her skirts, which she smooths over her knees. So bright is the glare of the sun on the water that even with her broad-brimmed hat she finds it necessary to squint.

"Do you think," she asks, "that one day I could accompany you to the clinic? You speak of appalling conditions, and I should like to see them for myself. Perhaps I could help in some way. . . ."

"Poverty is raw, Olympia. And ugly. The people are good enough — I do not mean to suggest that they are not — it is simply that the clinic is not a suitable place for a young woman."

"Tell me this then," she says, feeling slightly challenged and unwilling to forfeit the debate so quickly. "Are there fifteen-year-old female workers in the mills?"

She knows perfectly well that there are.

"Yes," he says reluctantly. "But that does not mean they should be there."

"And are fifteen-year-old females permitted into the clinic?"

He hesitates. "Sometimes," he says. "As patients certainly. Or to tend to their mothers."

"Well, then . . ."

"It is not a good idea," he insists. "In any event, I should have to ask your father for permission, and I sincerely doubt he would give it."

"Perhaps not," she says. "But he may surprise you. He holds unusual views as regards my education."

Haskell lifts up a handful of sand and watches it fall through his fingers. He takes off his hat, lies back on the rug, and closes his eyes.

Does he know she watches him then? He seems peaceful, as if he were dozing or sleeping. The lines of his face and his body are elongated, so that there is a hollow at his throat that echoes a hollow at the base of his shirt. Below his knees, his legs are bare; and she is struck by how smooth his skin is, how silky with dark hairs.

She looks quickly to the water and back at Haskell. She knows it will be only moments before the others return, wet and chilled and wrapped in rugs, their feet encrusted with fine wet sand, wanting food and drink and feeling both virtuous and vigorous for their exercise in the sea. She saw Haskell with the camera often enough earlier this morning to know how it is done. Quietly, so as not to disturb him, she lifts the camera from its case and peers through the viewfinder.

Beyond Haskell, in the background, is a fish house and a large family of bathers, some of whom, Olympia realizes, are watching her with the camera. They must be a family from Ely Falls, she decides, for they do not have much in the way of a picnic. They are crowded, all eleven or twelve of them, onto only one rug, so that those at the periphery are half sitting on the sand and have to lean into the center of the group. They have all been swimming, she determines, even the women, for their hair is unkempt and slicked back against their heads. They stare in a curiously impolite manner. She thinks that at least one or two of the children must be undernourished, as they have a sunken appearance about the cheeks.

She squeezes the shutter.

Startled, Haskell opens his eyes. She sets the camera back into its case.

"Olympia," he says, sitting up.

She closes the top and fastens the latch.

Simultaneously, they see Olympia's father emerging from the sea and draping himself in a robe he has left by the water's edge so as not to have to appear too long in public in his wet bathing costume. She watches her father walk from the sea to where they sit, wondering if he has seen her take Haskell's picture. When he reaches them, she thinks he cannot fail to note the strain which lies between Haskell and her and which they both immediately seek to defuse with over-attention to her father's needs, Haskell standing with a wrap, Olympia preparing a plate of food. But her father does not ask her about the time she has spent with Haskell, either then or later.

The others soon follow her father, Zachariah Cote a somewhat comical spectacle in his union suit, which reveals rather large hips and suggests that the man is better suited to a frock coat. (But which man is not? Olympia wonders.) Philbrick, with little modesty or self-consciousness, walks briskly to the rug, sits down to lunch, and begins to consume his meal with enthusiasm. Unable to remain calm in their company, Olympia stands and walks to the water's edge with wraps for the girls, who twirl themselves into the dry cloths as if forming cocoons. Even Martha seems happy to see her, although somehow the girl has gotten sand into her stockings and they bag with the weight and make odd lumps against her legs.

They walk back to the rug as if Olympia were a governess and they her waterlogged charges. Along the way, when she chances to look up, she sees that Haskell has gone.

He does not reappear for dinner in the evening. When Olympia inquires as to his whereabouts, Catherine says that he has been called away to the clinic. Olympia struggles through the meal with little appetite. She minds Haskell's absence more than she ever could have anticipated. It is the first of many nights she will now spend when her life, which seemed complete enough only the night before, appears to be missing an essential piece.

Wishing to be alone, she pushes her chair back. Thunder shakes the house, and Olympia can feel the vibrations through the floorboards. A streak of lightning needles the sky outside the windows of the dining room.

"A storm," Catherine says.

"The man who brings the lobsters said there would be," her mother answers.

"I must go upstairs to close my window," Olympia says, relieved to have an excuse to leave the table.

"Did you know," her father asks the gathering, "that such a heavy clap of thunder will cause many of the lobsters in the waters hereabouts to lose at least one of their claws?"

"Fascinating," Catherine says.

The rain starts then, a heavy rain that slants under the eaves and beats against the panes of glass in the windows, as if it would be let in.

Olympia walks upstairs to her room and lies down on the bed in a state for which she has had no preparation and of which she cannot speak — not even to Lisette, who might have some practical advice. For how can Olympia admit to any person that she harbors such extraordinary and inappropriate feelings for a man she hardly knows? A man nearly three times her age? A man who seems to be happily married to a woman Olympia much admires?

After a time, she sits up in the bed and reaches for the volume that is still on her night table. She begins to read Haskell's book anew. She reads until her eyes blur and her senses dull and she can contemplate with equanimity her preparations for bed.

Later she will learn that Haskell did not go to the clinic that night, but rather walked with troubled thoughts along the beach until he was surprised by the sudden storm, which almost immediately drenched him and caused him to have to run back to the house for shelter.

Just before daybreak, Olympia is awakened by a hoarse cry. For a few moments, she thinks it part of another dream she cannot quite escape, until she realizes that the shouting comes from below her bedroom window. As she climbs out of bed, the hollering grows louder, and she can hear now that it involves several men.

Because the air has become chillier, she reaches for the shawl on the chair. When she looks out her window, she sees that all along the beach of Fortune's Rocks, bonfires have been lit and are now blazing. She does not at first understand the meaning of these fires until she notices the men in lifesaving dress and cork belts standing by the fire nearest to the cottage. Other men, among them Rufus Philbrick and her father and John Haskell, hover in their dressing gowns at the perimeter of this group. Since everyone is gesturing toward the sea, Olympia looks out to discover what it is that so excites them; and she is startled to see a large dismasted barque foundering in the white foam of the breakers not three hundred feet from shore. The bow of the vessel has shattered and has a ragged and splintered appearance. As she watches, the rudderless ship rises and rolls and hits the rocks that have been the site of not a few shipwrecks.

The doors of the Ely station, built only the year before, are flung open. A half dozen men in oilskins and crotch-high waders begin to maneuver to the water's boisterous edge the long, slim lifesaving boat that is kept always ready for such occasions. By now, the operation has drawn a crowd, and Olympia is compelled to throw her shawl over her shoulders and make her own way down to the beach.

She stands in the cold and darkness, just beyond the revealing light of the bonfires, the gale already unraveling her patient plaiting of the night before. The wind blows sparks from the fires and threatens to extinguish the signal lights from the red-globed lanterns. In the foaming currents, Olympia can see that the disabled vessel has pitched to an unnatural angle and that men and also women are abandoning her decks for the rigging.

She feels a hand on her arm and, startled, turns. "Olympia," Catherine Haskell says, unfolding a cloak and laying it across Olympia's shoulders. "I saw you from the porch. You should not be out here."

Olympia accepts the gift of the cloak by drawing it more tightly around her. "What has happened?" she asks Catherine.

"Oh my dear, it is so dreadful. Such a horror. I only hope the lifesavers can get to them."

"Who are they?" Olympia asks.

"According to Rufus, it is an English ship out of Liverpool. They were meant to put in at Gloucester, but the storm has blown them off course."

The gale makes conversation difficult. Catherine's hair blows all about her face, and the skirts of Olympia's nightdress snap at her shins. Together they watch as a gun is brought out of the station on a wagon and aimed at the ship.

"What are they doing?" Olympia asks.

"It is for the breeches buoy," Catherine answers.

A signal flare lights up the wounded vessel. A woman falls soundlessly from the rigging, and someone on the beach screams. Catherine turns to Olympia and pulls her toward her, as if to shield her face. But Olympia is taller than Catherine, and the embrace is cumbersome and mildly awkward; so they separate and watch as a man is swamped by a cresting wave.

"My God," Catherine says.

So sheltered has Olympia's life been up to this point that she has never seen death, nor anything resembling it. She flinches at the sudden boom of the gun. She watches as a ball with a rope attached spools out across the waves and lands behind the ship. A taut line is immediately established from the shipwreck to the shore. One of the men in lifesaving dress steps into the breeches buoy, a device that resembles nothing so much, Olympia thinks, as a large pair of men's pants attached to a wash line. As the men on shore haul the line through a pulley, the officer makes slow progress toward the vessel, his legs dangling unceremoniously just inches above the surf.

At the water's edge, John Haskell and Olympia's father take hold of the stern of the lifesaving boat and run it into the water. Her father's face is grave, his features wholly concentrated. The sash of his dressing gown has come undone, and Olympia is surprised to see, as she seldom does, his thin white legs. Although Olympia is embarrassed for his body, she is nevertheless proud of her father's strength in this matter: Haskell and her father seem oblivious to any possible discomfort from the wind or the sea or their endeavors as they both join in the effort to pull the line. Later Olympia and Catherine will learn that the ship, which was called the *Mary Dexter* and carried

Norwegian immigrants, sustained damage at the docks in Quebec; but the captain, too eager to finish the journey, unwisely left before repairs could be made.

Catherine and Olympia watch as the breeches buoy returns along the line, not with the man who only moments ago traversed it, but rather with the slumped form of a woman who is in turn carrying a child.

"She will drop the child," Catherine exclaims.

Those at the shoreline must have the same fear, for Haskell sheds his dressing gown and wades into the surf in his nightshirt to snatch the feet of the cargo. When he has the woman in his grasp, he brings her onto dry ground and, with the aid of Rufus Philbrick, disentangles her from the contraption. Another officer steps into the buoy and sets off for the wounded ship.

"I must go to him," Catherine says. "Will you be all right here?"

"Yes, yes, of course," Olympia says. "I am fine."

Olympia watches as Catherine Haskell runs against the wind toward her husband. While Olympia's father attends to the female passenger, wrapping her in a blanket Josiah has brought to the scene, John Haskell lays the child immediately upon a rug and begins to administer lifesaving breaths. Olympia watches as Catherine puts a hand to her husband's back, and he looks up at her. He tells her something, perhaps gives her instructions, for she immediately takes charge of the woman Olympia's father has been attending to. Haskell, apparently having restored the child's breathing, scoops the girl into his arms and begins to walk briskly with her toward the house. Olympia inhales sharply. For she can see that in order to get to the house, he will have to pass by the place where she is standing at the perimeter of the rescue effort.

Her hair blows all about her face, and she has to hold it back to see him. He carries the child close to him, but flat, level with the ground, his arms cradling her underneath. He does not pause, he cannot stop now, but he nevertheless looks directly at Olympia as he passes her. It is only a moment, because he is moving fast. Perhaps she speaks his name, not *John* but rather *Haskell,* which is how she has come to think of him. And in an instant, he is gone.

She stands as if she had been hollowed out.

She hears her father calling to her. She waves to him. She wants to help; of course she does. She tries to run, but there is something wrong with her legs, as if her body were momentarily paralyzed. Her father beckons her impatiently on, and she can see his need is urgent. The sand is a drag against her feet, and her movements are sluggish, as they sometimes are in dreams. She tries to run, but she steps on her nightdress or her legs buckle, and she stumbles.

When she looks up, she can see that her father is walking toward her and saying her name. She shakes her head; she does not want him to see her like this. He bends over and puts his hand on her shoulder. His touch is foreign and strange, for they do not ever embrace, but the unfamiliar touch brings her to her senses. She rubs her eyes with the sleeve of her nightdress.

"Olympia?" he asks tentatively.

Awkwardly, she stands. It is almost daybreak now, and she can see the sinking vessel and the drama unfolding there more clearly than before.

"I am fine, Father," she says. "I tripped on my nightdress."

She slips her arms into the sleeves of the cloak Catherine has brought her.

"Tell me what you want me to do," she says. "I want to help."

In the early morning hours of June 23, 1899, seventy-four passengers and one ship's officer from the *Mary Dexter* drown, while fifty-eight passengers and seven marine officers are brought across in the breeches buoy. Another man, a lifesaving officer from Ely, is lost in the rescue effort. The lifesaving boat itself, with nearly a dozen volunteers, pulls away from the unfortunate barque just before the vessel pitchpoles into the sea and splinters into wooden lathes against the rocks.

Despite the gravity of the wreck, the citizens of Fortune's Rocks cannot help but be somewhat prideful about the success of the breeches buoy, which has not ever been tried before at the Ely station.

Because the house is an unusual one in that it was once a convent, there are still a great many cell-like rooms with beds and dressers on the second floor, several of which are occupied by help, but many of which are vacant. With the Haskells in residence, a kind of field hospital is established, and they become, her small family and their guests and servants, its officers: her father the retired general recommissioned for the event; John Haskell the medical officer with all the responsibilities and intimacies that such a position demands; Catherine Haskell the nursing sister in her simple gray dressing gown with the white apron she found in the kitchen; Josiah the veteran sergeant, excellent in a crisis, his organizational skills beyond compare; Philbrick the quartermaster, who takes upon himself the task of securing foodstuffs for the bursting household; Zachariah Cote a kind of AWOL soldier, who feigns sleep during the entire lifesaving effort and who seems to think his only contribution lies in sitting with Olympia's distraught mother in her rooms; and Olympia the fledgling private initiated into the ranks of adulthood by default, there being few other able women present.

Olympia does not get any more sleep that night, since she and the others are employed in numerous tasks. Because no one amongst the

Norwegian immigrants speaks even the most rudimentary English, nor any of the Americans Norwegian, Olympia is called upon to decipher requests and pleas by facial expressions alone and is often reduced to hand gestures for replies. As a large number of the Norwegian menfolk have been lost to the sea, many of the women are deranged by grief. One such woman, with chestnut hair and light gray eyes, has with her five children under the age of eleven. Her face, when she enters the house, is wild, as if she were still in mortal terror for her life, and she is at first unable to care for her children, who are bathed and dressed by Olympia and Catherine. It is frustrating to Olympia not to be able to speak even the crudest expressions of sympathy to the Norwegian woman, although she hopes that her gestures and the tone of her voice are reassuring enough. Olympia notes that she, like most of the refugees who have come into the house, is in a physically deplorable state, even considering her ordeal; and this causes Olympia to wonder at the conditions aboard the immigrant vessel even before it foundered.

All along the hallways of the cottage is a cacophony of sound — children crying, women speaking excitedly in a foreign tongue, Josiah and the other servants moving briskly from room to room. A copper tub is set up in the kitchen, a cloth hastily erected. Olympia's job is to bathe the children, female and male alike; and thus she observes that even the most stringent of mores, kept highly polished in normal times, may be quickly abandoned in times of crisis.

By mid-morning, some order has been established. Olympia is bathing a small girl with silver curls whose name may or may not be Anna. Though Olympia has little verbal communication with the child, they manage to convey a great deal by way of an inventive soap sculpture of a sailing vessel that floats for a time and then disappears into the cloudy water. As small children will, the girl seems recovered from her near fatal mishap, and she appears to be, for the moment, simply enjoying her bath. As Olympia kneels before the tub, enduring the child's brief annoyance when she washes her hair, she hears a sound behind her. When she turns, she sees that John Haskell has entered the room.

"Do not let me disturb you," he says, pinching the bridge of his nose with his thumb and forefinger. He leans against a pine table and crosses his arms. He seems tired, which she knows he must be. He has hours ago changed into dry clothes, although his hair is somewhat unkempt.

Shielding the child's face with her hand, Olympia pours another pitcher of water over the silvery head. The girl squeals and fidgets, encouraging her to finish the task with dispatch. Through an open window, Olympia notes the ribs of the unfortunate barque, a sight that calls to mind the skeleton of a beached and stripped whale. And how strange it is to see the lifesaving station, which was the locus of such frenetic activity just hours earlier, rendered tame and even charming in the sunlight. The building is a handsome structure with many wide windows and a large tower with a widow's walk. Intricate carvings decorate the eaves of the red roof, which rises to a sharp peak. How tidy and neat the scene appears, she thinks. And how un-apologetic Nature seems to be in her calm indifference.

"It was a brave effort," Haskell says.

"Yes."

"Sixty-five souls saved, and only one lifesaving officer lost. That is" — he calculates a moment — "slightly less than fifty percent of the ship's passengers and crew saved and only eight percent of the lifesavers lost."

She ponders his calculations.

"Were I the wife of the man who was lost," she says, "I might consider that poor return for the risk, for to me and my children the loss would be one hundred percent."

He studies her for a moment. "I think you quite beyond your years in understanding," he says. She flushes with pleasure, though later she will wonder if the remark did not contain more hope than accuracy.

"What of the others?" she asks quickly.

"We have several with broken bones, one with a serious injury to the neck that may leave the man paralyzed. Philbrick is even now trying to arrange to have the injured and sick transferred to the hospital at Rye, but Mason has declared the house quarantined and has said that no one may leave."

Haskell refers to the health inspector from Ely Falls, who arrived in the early hours. He comes to the tub and lifts the Norwegian girl from the water, the suds falling on his shirt. Olympia hands him a flannel, and he swaddles the girl in the cloth. He lays her on the kitchen table and examines her in a way Olympia finds thoughtful and gentle, despite the demands on his time and the sense of urgency all around them. She stands to one side, not certain whether to stay or to go, and in the end, indecision keeps her still.

She watches as Haskell retrieves a dry cloth from a basket Josiah has brought. He wraps the child again. He holds the girl in the crook of his arm — such a tiny thing in his confident grasp — and speaks to her constantly of this small thing and that, his words incomprehensible to her but their soothing quality apparent in the drowsy look in her eyes.

"Did Mr. Mason say how long he expects the quarantine to last?" Olympia asks, thinking of the mild unpleasantness of being unable to leave the house.

"No, he is like all petty officials in the arbitrary wielding of very little power. No, he will not say, and this is of some annoyance to me, as Catherine and the children are to leave for York later today."

Olympia busies herself with the wet cloths on the floor of the kitchen.

"Where will Mrs. Haskell and your children stay in York?" she asks.

"Catherine's mother has a cottage. My wife will return here on weekends, of course, and then will come to stay for good in August if the new cottage is finished, which I hope it shall be."

Olympia drops the cloths into another basket in the corner of the room and walks toward John Haskell.

"Let me," she says, lifting the girl out of his arms.

And it seems a most elemental gesture — to take a child from a man.

*O*N THE THIRD DAY after the wreck of the *Mary Dexter*, the visitors to the house are released from quarantine. Olympia wonders what will happen to the refugees. Since they now have no assets with which to negotiate their way in America, many of them are incorporated into the mills at Ely Falls, and what happens to the very young children, such as Anna, she never learns.

Catherine and the children travel on to York. Haskell again takes up residence at the Highland Hotel. For some time, Olympia does not see him, since he works at the clinic in Ely Falls most of the hours of the day, and there is no natural opportunity for them to meet.

Outwardly, Olympia passes her time in the usual manner. She reads books from a list her father has made up for her. Later she will remember *The Valley of Decision*, *A Tale of Two Cities*, and *The Scarlet Letter* in particular, since they are all works written in one century about another, the purpose of which is an issue her father and she debate at some length (her father taking the position that the social mores of a previous era might better highlight certain moral dilemmas of one's own time, and Olympia holding to the notion that Edith Wharton or Charles Dickens or Nathaniel Hawthorne might simply have been drawn to the baroque language and richer color of an earlier era). As Olympia's drawing skills have been seen to be inferior, she is given instruction by the French painter Claude Legny, who is residing at the Isles of Shoals for the season and who consents to ferry over to the mainland on Friday mornings to give her lessons. Though Olympia has a few talents, illustration is not among them, and she knows that she disappoints the man. She can see a thing well enough, can even describe it quite passably in words, but she cannot translate the subsequent vision to the fingers of her right hand. It is not unlike an adult giving instructions to a child, and the child rendering a result that, unfortunately, does not possess even a childlike charm.

She has more success, however, with riding and tennis. As for the riding, which she takes up at the Hull farm in Ely, it is a skill she has already mastered and therefore cannot lay claim to as an accomplishment this summer. The tennis, however, is new to her and is one of the few organized activities that require all of her concentration and provide brief respites from her thoughts and daydreams.

For more than anything else, the days that pass are ones that hold her in a state of suspension, somewhat in the way of an elongated pause in a beautiful piece of music — an interrupted prelude. Sometimes, it is all she can do to focus on any activity or task at all. She frequently feels dazed and preoccupied, unable to shake herself free of troubling thoughts. Indeed, she wonders from time to time if she is not possessed: Every moment that has passed between Haskell and her is examined and reexamined; every word that they have exchanged is heard and reheard; every look, gesture, and nuance interpreted and reinterpreted. While she sits at the dining table, or writes letters on the porch, or reads to her mother in her room, Olympia invents dialogue and debate with Haskell and weaves amusing anecdotes for him around the most seemingly banal events

77

of her daily life. In truth, her normal routines appear now to exist solely for the purpose of self-revelation, of revealing herself to a man she hardly knows. But though she repeats the same conversations and scenes over and over in her mind, she cannot exhaust them. It is as if she drinks from a glass that continuously refills itself, the last long, cool swallow as necessary as the first, her thirst unquenchable. Occasionally, her relentless scrutiny of the brief time she has spent in Haskell's presence is an agony to her, for she can see no satisfactory conclusion to what has begun, nor any possible way at all to go forward. She is only fifteen, and Haskell is nearly her father's age. He is married and has children. She is still in her father's care. She is but a child herself, perhaps even a deranged and obstinate child, fixed upon a fantasy that has for its roots only a few brief episodes that, for all she knows, she may have misinterpreted. Even so, she tortures herself with her endless imaginings, and there is no hour in which Haskell does not dominate her thoughts. Which causes her to wonder if there is not, existing simultaneously with the torment, an intensely pleasurable element to her self-created distress. Despite the fact that she seems barely present in the universe her physical body inhabits, the days seem more alive and arresting than any she has ever experienced before. Colors enhance themselves; music, which has before been only pleasant or difficult, now has the ability to transfix; the sea, to which she has always been drawn, takes on an epic grandeur and seems endlessly seductive — so much so that she is often sharply impatient of any demand upon her time that takes her away from simply gazing at the water and letting her thoughts float upon its surface.

The beach at Fortune's Rocks has always been a democratic one, and at no time more so than on the Fourth of July, when all of the population of the summer community, as well as that of Ely and Ely

Falls, gathers for the traditional clambake. The stretch of sand from the seawall to the water's edge is crowded with summerfolk, tradesmen and their families, and many Franco-Americans and Irish from the mills. An enormous fire is built and covered with wet seaweed, so that the steam that arises appears to be rising from the sand itself. And all around this fire stand men of every class and economic means, some in formal dress, others in more casual and festive attire, nearly all of them enjoying the potent liquid refreshment in the stoneware jugs that have been dug into the sand. Periodically, large slatted baskets of clams are carried down to the fire and heaped, along with potatoes, upon the seaweed. When a particular batch is considered properly steamed, tin dishes are brought out and filled with the food. The women, some with parasols, rest on wooden stools, while the children sit cross-legged on the rugs. Since there is a kind of lawlessness associated with this event, both men and women have on bathing costumes and are frolicking in the breakers. Occasionally a bather is carried to the surf by a servant and lowered into the water to lessen the shock of the cold. The water seldom rises above sixty-five degrees Fahrenheit, a temperature that is announced each noon hour by blasts from the Highland Hotel (six long blasts, five short). Near the bathers, Olympia can see that the Ely Club is conducting footraces along the low-tide flats on sand so hard, one could play tennis on it. Parked along one portion of the seawall are carriages and horses and one or two motorcars as well, novelties that quite intrigue the children, who crowd about the vehicles, not daring to touch them for fear of making them start up and run away. (An odd foreshadowing of calamity, as the following summer one of the motorcars is inadvertently turned on by a young boy; and the automobile does overshoot the seawall, burying itself but fortunately not the child in the soft sand at the high end of the beach, where it remains for a year, until a team of horses is able to drag it out.)

Olympia has worn this day a costume she particularly likes: a thin, light-gray chemise, belted at the waist, over a simple navy linen skirt. For some reason she cannot articulate, possibly having to do with the general air of license that infects the day, she has not worn a hat. She also has on a navy shawl in anticipation of sea breezes that do not come; indeed, so warm is it this day that she soon abandons the shawl altogether and unbuttons the cuffs of her blouse and rolls the cloth along her forearms. And she supposes the reason she likes these clothes so well is that they are easy and free and do not call attention to themselves. For what she most covets is the freedom to observe the people around her while remaining if not invisible, then not obvious in her scrutiny. As to the infection of liberty, she has heard that there are more love affairs begun, proposals offered, and dormant marriages rekindled on this day than on any other of the year, a supposition borne out annually by the abnormally large number of births during the first week in April.

Her tolerance for public occasions being unnaturally thin, Rosamund Biddeford sits with Olympia for a short time, eats precisely one clam that somehow the communal cooking seems to have tainted for her, complains mildly of a headache from the sun, and summons Josiah to see her back to the house. As none of this is unexpected, Olympia is quite content to sit upon her canvas chair by herself, sated with a dish of steamed clams and oyster crackers, and observe the comings and goings of all the celebrants in their various attire. And as she does so, she keeps a weather eye on her father, who hovers near to the fire with several other men and who appears to be drinking an immoderate amount of whiskey. Occasionally neighbors speak to Olympia, and some invite her to join them; but she declines, saying untruthfully that she is awaiting her mother's return.

After a time, however, Olympia finds herself restless, unwilling to sit still for so long on such a fine day. And so she begins to stroll along the beach, weaving in and out of families and social groupings, some of them rather elaborate with canvas gazebos, ice chests, and fine linen and silver. Others are more humble with only the tin plates and the cups of lemonade that have been provided for the occasion. She sees one family, even the children, dressed as if for church, sitting as formally as their posture will allow. And near to them is a Franco-American family from the mills, likewise dressed in their best finery, but not as stiff, for clearly they have put the several bottles of wine they have brought with them to excellent use. Their gathering seems joyous, if not actually raucous.

All along the beach, on the cottage porches, informal parties are being held, as is traditional on the Fourth. Olympia and her family have been invited to some of these parties. Because this is the first year Olympia is allowed to call upon someone of her own acquaintance alone, without the assistance or protection of her parents, she earlier thought of making a point of stopping by the Farragut cottage; Victoria Farragut is a young woman whose company she has sometimes enjoyed. But Olympia finds that she is reluctant, as she digs the toes of her boots into the sand, to enter into conversation with others, and so she passes by the Farragut cottage, noting the conviviality of all the people on the porch, but keeping her face averted. She does not want to be seen and called to.

After a time, she sheds her boots and begins to walk barefoot, which she has been encouraged to do by not a few good-natured strangers she has passed. Since she fully intends to slip her boots back on when she returns to the clambake fire, she is not concerned about being seen by her father, who would, of course, disapprove. For some time, she feels bold and flirts with the sea, lifting her skirts just enough for her feet to skim the spills of water upon the shallow sand and jumping quickly out of the way when a more substantial wave threatens.

As she draws nearer to the Highland Hotel, however, her progress grows more tentative. The hotel is grand in the way of many of the hotels scattered along that part of the coast; but none of them, she thinks, is as appealing as the Highland, with its excessively deep porches, its pristine white railings, and its black wicker rockers lined up against the railings like sentries on their watch. Men and women, on their way to and from the hotel, pass by her, carrying with them a distinct air of festivity. She watches as a cluster of employees poses on the steps of the hotel porch for a photograph; they seem unable to contain their merriment at the enterprise, much to the consternation of the hapless photographer. Behind them, plates of oysters are being passed among the many hotel guests, some of whom are splendidly dressed, the women with hats so large and ornate that they seem like lush peonies that might bend the slender stems beneath them. Other men and women, with racquets in hand, lounge less formally at the far end of the porch and appear to be waiting for a game of tennis to begin.

Her eye scans the porch and pauses at a figure seated in a rocker. Collarless and hatless, he is reading a pamphlet. She stops abruptly in the sand. Her sudden stillness must stand out in the scene, for he glances in her direction.

She turns around and begins to walk briskly along the beach, her boots in her hand. She can hear nothing but the surf of foolishness in her head: Whatever was she thinking to be so bold as to present herself at the hotel? *Knowing* that she might encounter Haskell? *Knowing* how inappropriate such a presentation would be? With her body bent forward, she is determined to retreat to the other end of the beach as soon as possible. And so it is that she does not at first hear her name called, and it is only when she feels a restraining hand upon her arm that she stops and turns.

"Olympia," Haskell says, breathless from trying to overtake her. "I spotted you from the porch."

She drops her skirts.

He bends to catch his breath. "I have regretted not having had the chance to visit with you and your father," he says, "as I very much enjoyed my stay with your family."

"And we as well," she says politely.

He rights himself and puts his hands on his hips. "And how are your father and mother?" he asks. "Well, I trust?"

"Oh, yes, very well," she answers. "And Mrs. Haskell and the children? Are they with you on this holiday?"

"No," he says. "I must be at the clinic in an hour, and I have given most of the others the afternoon off. It seemed pointless to send for Catherine when I could not join her in the festivities. In any event, I shall be with her in York tomorrow."

Olympia crooks an arm over her forehead to shade her eyes from the light. She is forced to look up at Haskell in order to speak to him.

"And how is your work at the clinic?" she asks.

"Difficult," he says without hesitation. "There has not been sufficient time for me to reorganize the staff in the way it must be done, and I am still awaiting supplies and medicines from Boston, which have been unpardonably late in arriving."

"I am sorry to hear that," she says.

"Oh, I think we shall manage all right. Although I shall be dreadfully short-staffed this afternoon," he adds, putting his hands into his trouser pockets. He seems to have recovered his breath. "May I accompany you back to wherever you are going?" he asks. "I should welcome an opportunity to greet your father if he is here with you."

His eyes scan her face.

She turns, and they begin to walk toward the bonfire. The beach slopes precipitously, and she is nearly as tall as he is. She imagines that her gait is self-conscious, her movements stiff and unnatural, for she feels unnerved in his presence. Haskell, however, seems considerably more relaxed and occasionally bends to pick up a shell or to send a flat stone skipping across the waves. After a time, he asks if he can stop for a moment since his boots are filling with sand. He puts the boots down where they stand, out of reach of the incoming tide, and says he will collect them later, which she thinks reflects rather more trust in human nature than perhaps is prudent. They walk together again, and though there are a thousand questions she wants to ask the man, she finds she is rendered silent. Voluble in her imaginings, she is inarticulate in his presence.

The sea that day is a brilliant aquamarine, a color seldom observed off the coast of New Hampshire, where the ocean most often presents either a deep navy or a gunmetal gray appearance. Indeed, so rich and lovely are the water and sky and light together that Olympia thinks that Nature, in her generosity, must be in a celebratory mood herself on this, the one hundred and twenty-third anniversary of the country's independence.

"Have you eaten?" she asks.

"The food at the Highland, I am sorry to say, is remarkably poor, despite the high standard of the service. I think they need another cook."

"You are in luck today, then, for the clambake is providing a savory meal for everyone. Do you know about this tradition?"

"I heard about it at breakfast and have watched the staff slink away in their finery all morning. I'm quite glad to be offered a meal, as I'm sure the dining room is like a ship deserted. Your face is growing pink," he says. "I think you should have worn your hat."

They walk side by side, the walking irregular and slow-going in the sand. Occasionally one or the other of them stumbles, and a sleeve brushes a sleeve or a shoulder a shoulder. The heat causes a prism of air above the sandy beach that distorts the view. Waves surprise them, and Haskell yelps once from the cold, which is always a shock upon the tender skin of the ankles, no matter how often one visits this part of the coast of New England.

In the distance, Olympia can see that the festivities have gathered some momentum in her absence. Men and boys are playing with balls and nets and racquets. Nearer to the water, where the sand is harder, several couples have set up wickets and are engaged in croquet, although it seems a fruitless enterprise since all the balls naturally roll toward the sea. Beyond the seawall and the fish shanties, hucksters hawk their wares from carts: ice-cold tonics, Indian baskets, ice-cream cones, and confections of all sorts.

She stops suddenly, unwilling to reenter the crowd so soon. Haskell strolls on for a few paces before realizing that she is behind him. He walks back to where she is standing.

"What is it?" he asks her. "What is wrong?"

Her eyes skim the tops of his shoulders, his braces making indentations in his shirt. She is perspiring all about her collar and wishes she could unbutton it. She sees a blue-and-orange-striped balloon rise above his right shoulder.

The balloon ascends slowly into the thickish air — a massive thing, both gaudy and majestic. The balloon gains height and floats in their direction. Two men are standing on the parallel bars suspended from the balloon. They wave to the throng below. Olympia wonders at the view of Fortune's Rocks the men must be having, and for a moment, she feels envious and wishes to be aloft with them.

"Olympia, are you not well?" Haskell asks again.

He stands so close to her that she can see the pores of his skin, smell the scent of him mixed with the starch of his shirt. There are perspiration rings under his arms. She wants to lie down. She watches as the balloon begins to ascend more rapidly and to pass overhead. And then she is startled by the sight of the aeronauts cutting loose from the balloon and falling to earth with parachutes. They scarcely seem to drift. In the distance, she can hear the muffled elation of the crowd.

Slowly and without preamble, Olympia takes hold of Haskell's hand and lifts it to her throat. She opens his fingers and presses them against her skin.

There is a long moment of silence between them.

"Olympia," Haskell says quietly, withdrawing his hand. "I must say something to you now. In a moment, we shall be at the fire and with your father, and there will be no more opportunity."

Her breath catches in her chest.

"I have reproached myself a thousand times since that day at your house when I took liberties with you," he says. "When I was photographing you. I felt then that I could not help myself, though it is pure cowardice to hide behind the excuse of helplessness now."

She shakes her head slightly.

"It is unpardonable, unpardonable," he says heatedly. "And I do sincerely ask your forgiveness, and you must give it, as I cannot work properly for thinking of it and of the harm I have done to you."

All about them, children squeal and run, oblivious to the drama that is taking place so near to them. Gulls, ever hopeful of a discarded morsel, swoop dangerously low to their heads. Haskell opens his mouth and closes it. He shakes his head. He turns once quickly toward the sea and then back again.

The aeronauts land on the sand. The balloon continues to fly overhead.

"I am going now," Haskell says. "If your father has seen us together already, please tell him that I have been urgently called away. And it is true. I am going now to the clinic. I will not visit you again. You understand that. I will not call on your family, however awkward that may prove."

And because she thinks he truly means to leave her then, she reaches for his arm; and though she catches only a small bit of his shirt cuff, it is enough.

"I shall go with you," she says calmly. She does not feel reckless. She is sure of her words and clear about their implications. "You yourself have said you would be dreadfully shorthanded this afternoon."

"The clinic is no place for . . . ," he begins, but then he stops. They have already had this conversation.

"I trust I can fetch and carry as well as the next person. Did I not prove myself the night of the shipwreck?"

"Olympia, you will regret this," he says gravely.

She looks out toward the horizon, where the balloon is only a speck. She wonders where it will finally land.

"Then allow me at least to have it before I regret it," she says calmly.

He opens his mouth as if to speak, but then hesitates. "No, I cannot allow this," he says finally, and leaves her.

She watches him walk away until he is only a blurry dot on the sand. When he is almost out of sight, she begins to follow him. For a time, she walks at a normal pace, and then she breaks into a run.

SHE WAITS, as they have agreed, at the back of the Highland while he fetches a carriage from the stables. She stands, with sand in her boots, praying that she will not encounter anyone known to her or to her father, for she will not easily be able to explain her presence by the road nor, if Haskell were then to appear, her intention to accompany him in the carriage. She hopes her father has had enough to drink that he will take his customary Fourth of July nap on the sand by the seaweed fire, as do many of the men on this day, a democratic falling-out if ever there was one.

Haskell comes around the corner in a small buggy with a canopy that bobbles wildly on the rutted dirt road. The coach is painted bottle green and has yellow wheels. On its side is written, in chaste script, *The Highland Hotel.* He has gathered from his room his physician's satchel and his jacket and hat, and he presents such a pleasing aspect to her eye that despite her nerves, despite the fact that she has begun to tremble at the audaciousness of her actions, she cannot help but feel a gladness in her heart at the anticipation of riding beside him. He steps down from the carriage to help her up.

They drive the length of the winding road between the bay and the ocean, passing many cottages and stone walls and carriages that jostle along the hard-packed dirt surface, much as they are doing. Men on bicycles ring their bells at them and tip their hats, and a family of Gypsies with begging tins tries to stop the buggy. This part of the world is flat, demarcated only by stone walls, clapboard cottages, a few trees, and low scrub pine. They pass a large party of revelers in a hay wagon, and as they make the turn at the end of the coast road, she sees again the lifesaving station. She wonders if the crew inside are allowed to partake of the festivities, and then thinks not, since Nature in her whims and frenzies knows not a holiday. At the very least, she imagines that the officers will have to be on the lookout for errant bathers who might be swallowed up by the breakers.

Behind the lifesaving station, the sun glints off the ocean with such ferocity that she cannot see her father's house on the rocks at the end of the beach — which is fine with her since she does not much want to be reminded of it just now. She turns her head toward the bay, which presents a calmer prospect with its flotilla of sloops and yawls at anchor. She can see the brown and ochre Congregational church tower, the weathered fish cooperative, and the long pier that attracts commercial and pleasure vessels alike. Farther inside the bay are many skiffs and tenders with gentlemen at the oars and ladies sitting stiff-backed in the stern, enjoying their gentle outings under frilled parasols.

In a short time, they leave Fortune's Rocks and enter the marshes, a watery labyrinth of long reeds, rare birds, and pink and white lilies. She likes best to travel through the marshes in a skiff at sunset, or rather in that half hour before sunset when the rusty light of the lowering sun sets the grasses ablaze and turns the water a metallic pink. Sometimes, on these solitary excursions, she will deliberately lose herself amongst all the shallow passageways, finding a kind of quiet thrill in the ginger-colored reeds. The challenge is then to make her way back through the watery maze, and she remembers only one time when she discovered herself at an unproductive dead end and had to summon help from a boy who was fishing along the harder ground of the shore.

Silently, they travel through the village of Ely with its stolid wooden houses built a century earlier by men who shunned adornment. In the center of the village is a butcher's shop with a meat wagon parked to the side, a blacksmith's shop, an apothecary, the town pump. Because of the holiday, there are no people about. Indeed, the stillness is almost eerie, as if a contagion has decimated the population, although Olympia knows it to be a fever of high spirits that has infected the people here and has caused them to flee their village.

They follow the trolley route into Ely Falls, where the buildings are darkened by soot from the mills. They do not speak much, some pleasantries, which sound strange on her tongue. She tries to attend to the world around her, but her mind remains preoccupied. Both the beauty of the marshes and the bustle of the city seem, as they ride to the clinic, mere scenery or chorus to the real drama at hand: the silent, unspoken one played out by Haskell and her.

The main street of the city is thronged with shops, all decorated with yards and yards of festive bunting: druggists, confectioners, saloons, milliners, watchmakers. They pass a chowder house, a shoe factory: Coté and Reny. Over the shops are more French names and some Irish: Lettre, Dudley, Croteau, Harrigan, LaBrecque. Turning a corner, they come abreast of a parade in honor of the holiday. Olympia notes the men in Napoleonic costumes and the marching bands, the fire brigades on safety bicycles. The parade ends, they discover when they are forced to make a detour, at a two-pole big top that seems to have attracted at least half the city.

The mill buildings themselves are massive and dominate the town.

Most are brick structures with large windows, stretching all along the banks of the Ely River. Beyond these factories is the worker housing, row upon row of boardinghouses with a drab, utilitarian appearance. Perhaps the blocks of houses once looked fresh and appealing, but it is clear that the buildings, which have neither shutters nor paint, have been left to ruin with few attempts at repair.

They stop before an unprepossessing brick edifice, one of many in a row. Haskell helps her down, and he swings his satchel from the floorboards. She walks behind him to the front door, where he puts his hand upon the latch. He hesitates and looks about to speak.

She shakes her head quickly to forestall his words. "Do not trouble yourself about me," she says. "It is all right what we have done."

Although they both know — as how could they not? — that it is not all right. It is not all right at all.

It is the noise Olympia notices first. In a large room, which she takes to be a waiting room, she can hear a group of small children squealing and shouting as they chase one another through the aisles. Near to them, a woman who seems to huddle into herself is alternately crying and cursing. Men in varying states of dress and undress roughly cough up phlegm, and a mother, in a harsh voice, scolds a group of boys who are trying to crowd all together onto a scale. Olympia hears as well the irritated mutterings of patients who have been kept waiting on the holiday, and the moans of other patients who are clearly in pain: an old woman weeping, and a younger woman, in labor, grunting in a terrible manner. These people sit or lie upon a series of wooden benches that resemble church pews in their arrangement; and the entire gathering seems to her like nothing so much as a bizarre and noisy congregation waiting rudely for its minister. As Haskell strides purposefully through the room, a kind of order begins to descend, as though the patients can already perceive their relief. Haskell speaks immediately with a nurse who has on a starched white muslin cap and a blue serge dress with sleeves Olympia assumes once were white but now are dotted or smeared with blood and other substances she does not want to think about. The nurse holds a sheaf of papers in one hand and a watch chained to her belt in the other. It is an unfortunate posture, as the implication seems to be that she is scolding Haskell for being tardy.

"The holiday is worse than a Saturday night for the drunkenness and injuries resulting from inebriation," the nurse says to Haskell in an accent of broad vowels that Olympia recognizes as native. "There are seven patients who have come in with food poisoning from a tin of tainted meat, and there are three boys who fell into the runoff from the Falls, and what they were doing trying to cross the river there, I cannot tell you, but they are, as you might say, all battered to pieces. And as we are short-staffed today — well, there is no wonder we are in such a state. Oh, and there is a child, the Verdennes boy, who came into the clinic not an hour ago with the diphtheria croup, and I am sorry to say that he has passed on, sir."

(The half hour she detained Haskell on the beach, Olympia thinks, with the first of many small shocks of that afternoon.)

Haskell looks disturbed, but not overly so. Perhaps he knows that the child would have died even had he been there.

"This is Miss Olympia Biddeford," he says, turning to her. "Olympia, this is Nurse Graham," he adds by way of introduction.

Nurse Graham, who looks to be in her mid-twenties, narrows her eyes at Olympia, but her scrutiny is fleeting. She has other, more pressing matters on her mind.

"I promised my family, sir, that I would be finished at two o'clock," she says.

"Yes, of course," Haskell answers. "Is there anyone in the back?"

"Yvonne Paquet is here, sir. And Malcolm."

"Enjoy yourself then," he says, turning then to survey his flock, who now have fallen mostly silent and are watching him with great interest. Haskell takes in air and holds it, and then lets his breath out in a long, slow sigh.

"Let us begin," he says to Olympia.

The clinic occupies the ground floor of what was recently a textile warehouse. It has several rooms, one of which Olympia has ample opportunity to examine, since it is the chamber in which Haskell has set up his temporary office. In it are a desk and a cot and many cabinets filled with medicines, which Haskell frequently asks her, as the afternoon progresses, to fetch for him: quinine, aconite, alcohol, mercury, strychnine, colonel, and arsenic. There is an eye chart and a scale with many weights, an atomizer, a graduated medicine glass, and long metal trays of instruments — knives and needles and scissors. She notes a large glass bell jar, a microscope, and several flannel-covered bags, the purpose of which she never discerns. On a stove nearby are pots of water boiling continuously.

Nurse Paquet, a sallow and sullen girl not much older than Olympia, interviews the patients while Olympia functions as a nurse attendant, fetching bandages and medicines and tonics, cleaning instruments and returning them to the boiling water, and, once or twice, holding a limb or a child's hand while Haskell goes about his business. The first patient he sees that day is a man who has lost his arm to a spinner, which mangled it up to the elbow some weeks before. Haskell begins to unwind the man's dressing with the most careful of motions. He speaks in a soothing voice, trying to distract the mechanician with queries and jokes, and Olympia deduces that securing a patient's trust and cooperation is the first order of business in any treatment. Haskell is, she observes that afternoon, a gentle, not to say tender, physician.

"Olympia, fetch me some clean dressings," he instructs. "There, in that metal cabinet."

She finds the gauze and torn strips of cloth where he has said she would and hands them to Haskell.

"Contrary to established medical opinion, there is no intrinsic value to pus," he says, unwinding the filthy bandages and gesturing to the exudation of a purple stump that emits such a powerfully noxious odor that she involuntarily puts the back of her hand to her nose and steps away. "It does but tell us that the patient is suffering and that the wound is infected," he continues. "I have given orders that any person who walks into the clinic with a malodorous dressing should be seen to at once, but it is sometimes difficult to convince a provincial nursing staff who have been taught otherwise."

Olympia looks over at Nurse Paquet, whose sullen expression does not change. Olympia watches as Haskell removes instruments from the pots of boiling water. After he has thoroughly cleaned the wound with carbolic acid, he begins to scrape away at the infection. The patient, despite Haskell's soothing words and deft curettage, cannot keep himself from crying out at the pain. Olympia does observe, however, that Haskell is quick and precise in his gestures and that when the pain seems to be intolerable, he stops and administers laudanum by a teaspoon to ease his patient's distress — which, miraculously, it does. The man, who ceases his shouting and trembling, lies still as Haskell finishes the job and bandages up the wound again.

That afternoon Haskell sets a broken leg, gives numerous injections, uses a pulmotor on a young man in the last stages of white lung, and treats another man who complains of a parched tongue, fevers in the night, and pain near his nipples. He diagnoses a case of scarlet fever on the basis of a telltale, ash gray patch on the palate, he cleans an abcess, he thumps a child's back for pleurisy, and he dispenses tonics. One of the boys who fell into the river dies that afternoon as a result of his injuries, and the woman who was grunting in the waiting room is delivered of a healthy girl (though not by Haskell himself).

Through all of this, Olympia is watchful, as though she were being introduced to a second language and must pay close attention. Several times she feels her stomach rise toward her throat, but she is determined to betray no weakness. Occasionally Haskell bids her don a mask in the presence of highly infectious disease, and he constantly reminds her to wash her hands, which she makes nearly raw by the time the afternoon is over. And though she seeks to keep her composure, it is impossible to remain unmoved by the persons who are treated by Haskell, and sometimes she finds herself close to tears. Toward the end of her visit to the clinic, a boy and a woman come in with itching between their fingers, which have begun to bleed rather badly. Haskell diagnoses scabies. But the true malady, Olympia can see at once, is poverty, the likes of which she has never come across before. The woman is inebriated, and Olympia thinks the boy may be, too, although he cannot be more than ten. The woman has on a blouse of faded green silk with a narrow scarf of black wool tied round her neck. Her hair hangs down from a soiled boater in hacked clumps. The boy's clothes — an old cotton shirt, trousers, and a waistcoat — are so big for him, they have to be rolled and braced. The mother's black boots are broken, and the boy is barefoot.

When Olympia looks at those narrow feet, encrusted not with sand but with filth, she feels a rush of shame. To have reveled in being barefoot just hours earlier now seems almost unnecessarily insensitive. How can she disdain what so few have? Haskell looks over at her then, and she thinks she must be pale.

And he does look at her this day. He does. Many times. A dozen times, perhaps. He catches her eye, and though no words pass between them — and he does not change his expression nor interrupt his conversation with a patient — each glance to Olympia seems laden with content. These glances are, in an odd sort of way, both disturbing and comforting to her. Several times, under his acute gaze, she is afraid she will simply break apart or disintegrate. But then she collects herself, for all around her there are the sick and the injured who require, at the very least, another's rapt attention.

Curiously, none of the patients questions her presence. Perhaps it is her gray chemise and navy skirt, or an absence of adornment that causes them to take her for a nurse-in-training or a novice; and it seem to be acceptable to them that she remain in the room during their treatment. What they cannot know, and indeed she can barely bring to consciousness herself, is that though she observes the work-ings of the clinic, she studies the physican as well. She is a novitiate, but not, as the patients believe, in the nursing arts.

For when she finally leaves the clinic that early evening, she will not be the same person she was when she entered. In the space of five hours, she will see more of human pain and suffering and relief than she has in the whole of her life. Yes, her father can tell her about the world, or she can read about it in books, or discuss it in polite con-versation at the dinner table, but always at a safe remove. During the course of the afternoon, Haskell shows her something of the real and the visceral. He opens up the seams and makes her look. And in a strange manner, he is preparing her, but not in the way either of them has imagined: It is a rapid and brutal initiation into the ways of the body, a glimpse of what is possible, a taste of future intimacy. Later, she will come to understand that it was as much his nature to initiate her in this manner as it was hers to invite this instruction.

Toward evening, the clinic begins to grow quiet, as one by one the patients are sent home or are admitted to makeshift wards. After Haskell has seen a small child with measles, he says to Malcolm, who seems to be a general handyman, though the man has evident fluency with the names of the medical instruments and tonics, "I am just going to run Miss Biddeford home, and then I shall return after I have had a meal. Nurse Paquet will be in charge until I get back."

"Yes, sir," Malcolm answers, "but before you go, Mrs. Bonneau is asking if you can attend to a young woman who is powerful overwrought with the birthing pains. She says to bring the laudanum, as it is a breech and likely to cause the mother some galling troubles."

Haskell looks at Olympia.

"There is no need to hurry to take me home," she says quickly. "My father will not miss me, as he thinks that I am with the Farraguts. And they have almost certainly given up expecting me and doubtless think me at home with my father. So I am, for the moment, in a sort of limbo of freedom as regards my whereabouts."

This is not entirely true, as she well knows; her father, having woken from his Fourth of July nap, could indeed be looking for her at this very moment. But she also knows that the day itself permits a certain latitude not normally available to her and that if she is clever, and her father has drunk enough, she will be able to excuse her absence to her father's satisfaction.

Haskell finishes washing his hands and dries them on a cloth Malcolm is holding. Olympia watches him unroll the cuffs of his shirtsleeves and fasten the links, which he has kept in his trouser pocket. He removes his apron, wads it into a ball, and tosses it into a laundry basket in the corner. There is a smear of blood near his shoulder, and his face has lost some of its color with fatigue. Later, she will understand that he is biding his time, thinking hard about the consequences of taking her with him to the room in which Mrs. Bonneau and her charge wait; for he understands, as she does not, that she is about to see something for which no preparation will be adequate and which, once witnessed, can never be erased from the memory.

He lifts his coat from the hook on the back of the door. "There is a satchel of boiled cloths in the cabinet in the next room, Olympia," he says. "It is not heavy. If you would bring that, we could go now."

The light has softened some, and there are shadows on the streets. A cool, damp breeze from the east slips through the narrow alleys and washes over them at regular intervals. The sky is a vivid azurine, unblemished by clouds. It will be a lovely evening, Olympia knows, and even now, on this ugliest of streets, the light plays wondrously upon the bricks, catching a pane of glass and making it shimmer silver, turning the tops of the leaves of the trees a trembling pink. They walk side by side, saying little, trying to ignore the filth in their path, not only the detritus of the city's daily life but also the leavings of a holiday's many revelers: broken bottles, some human waste, articles of clothing shed and not retrieved, puddles of dishwater slung from second-story windows, wrappings of half-eaten food, crockery that reeks of beer. More than once, Olympia fears for her head and wishes fervently that she had a hat. But they reach the designated row house without incident and climb the stairs to the place where the unfortunate woman lives. Haskell opens the door and walks in without knocking.

The room is no bigger than the one Olympia sleeps in at Fortune's Rocks, a cramped chamber with only one window that looks out upon a wall not ten feet away. Though it is still day, there is little light, and it takes a moment for Olympia to adjust her eyesight to the gloom. On the bed, a woman lies in apparent agony, for she writhes and clenches her teeth and then lets her breath out in sharp gusts, calling out words in a French so accented and tortured, Olympia cannot understand her. Her skirts have been rucked up to the tops of her thighs, and even from the doorway Olympia can see the blood on her skin and on the grimy pillow ticking beneath her. Her naked legs, moving and twisting on the bed, are a shock to the senses, and Olympia feels as if she had upturned a rock and come unexpectedly upon a mass of transparent worms, colorless from never having been exposed to the sun.

Olympia breathes shallowly. She fights the impulse to gag and to back out of the door.

In a moment, Haskell has shed his jacket. A quick perusal of the room indicates an absence of a water pump, and she can see him deciding to forgo washing his hands in the interests of time. As he sits upon the bed, his fingers disappear beneath the slim modesty of the thin band of cloth that hides the most private self of the woman, whose name, Olympia learns, is Marie Rivard. Haskell occupies himself thus for a moment and seems to confirm what he has been told. He speaks in French to Mrs. Bonneau, an older woman with a nervous bearing who tells him that she was summoned by one of the woman's children, who was fearful for her mother's life. And that this was largely the scene when she arrived. She adds, with much expression and many imprecations, that the young woman on the bed is a recent immigrant. There was a husband, but he abandoned his wife and children some months earlier. Marie Rivard, who must be in her late twenties, Olympia thinks — although it is impossible to give an age to the writhing apparition on the bed — has been unable to find work because she has been with child.

Olympia notices then the other occupants of the room: three children, none of whom can be more than nine years old, sitting on the floor against a wall. All are barefoot and wear soiled dresses of the most distressing cloth, dark and colorless and long wrenched out of shape. It is apparent that the children have not bathed in quite some time. The stench in the small airless cubicle is considerable.

The walls of the room are unpapered and have turned dark and greasy from years of cooking. There is no wardrobe, nor any trunk in the room, merely a shallow pantry; and when its door is opened, Olympia is surprised to discover that it is not crammed full of the occupants' belongings, but is nearly bare. Although a man's jacket hangs upon a hook, there are no other signs of a man in residence. A corner of the room, where the floor meets the joining, is burned as though there was once a fire there. Above the encrusted stove are rude kitchen implements: a colander, a knife, a pot. A few garments hang from nails hammered into moldings. She notes that there is no sign of a toy or of a plaything for any of the children. In the recesses of the sill of the window, however, is a tall stack of folded clothing partially wrapped in brown paper. Beside that package is a silver filigree frame of a man and a woman on their wedding day. The bride has on a long white satin dress with a delicate mantilla that falls forward onto her brow. The man, in a heavy woolen suit, stands as though at attention. Olympia looks from the woman in the photograph to the woman on the bed. Can it be that they are the same person? And if so, how is it that this astonishing photograph and frame have escaped being sold for food, as nearly everything else in the room appears to have been?

Haskell loses no time in spooning laudanum into the laboring woman's mouth. He uses his own utensil and takes care that no drops are spilled. The writhing on the bed lessens, and the unspeakable cries subside into low moans.

"Olympia, give me the satchel."

She hands over the bag of boiled cloths and watches with curiosity and admiration as Haskell takes a sheet from the bag, makes the bed on one side, rolls the sheet taut, and, with a trick she cannot not quite catch the mechanics of, slips the sheet under the woman and quickly fastens the bedclothes on the other side. Covering the woman's lower extremities with a white cloth, he and Mrs. Bonneau manage to remove Marie Rivard's soiled clothing.

"Olympia, would you see if you can find the pump?" he asks quietly and evenly, as though he were merely asking her for a pencil in the midst of contemplating a correction to a half-written paragraph.

"Get that pot there, and bring it back full of water. I need to wash the woman."

Olympia removes the cooking pot from its hook over the stove and walks into the hallway in search of a pump. She knows it must be out in the back of the brick house, but she cannot at first determine how to get to the rear of the building without having to go round the entire block and into the alley. She does finally discover, however, a small door in the basement that leads up and out into a parched garden. The pump in its center is rusty and jerky in its motions; but after several barren tries, Olympia finally gets the water to flow. The stench from the nearby privy is nearly overpowering, and she thinks it cannot have been emptied in some time. Breathing shallowly, she fills the pot, retraces her steps, and climbs the two flights of stairs back to the room she just left. When she arrives, she finds the door shut and the three children waiting out in the hallway. They sit on the floor, their pale legs extended before them, snipping buttons from garments of clothing they lift from the paper parcel Olympia saw on the sill, taking care not to let the cloth touch the floor. With expert motions, they flick their small knives, pop the buttons into the air, catch them easily and toss them into a can they have set in front of them. If the scene were not so haunting in its implications, the skill with which the children accomplish their task, their hands flying almost faster than the eye can see, would be astonishing and perhaps even amusing. But as their dexterity speaks only to the hundreds of hours the children must have spent honing such a skill, any astonishment or amusement Olympia might feel quickly turns to dismay.

From behind the door to the room, she hears a deep guttural cry. The children do not stir. Only the smallest child, who cannot be more than three years old, stops for a moment and sucks her thumb, which the oldest girl almost immediately bats out of her mouth with her hand.

Olympia stands helplessly with the pot in her arms, not knowing what to do for the children. She knocks once on the door, and the old woman opens it. She takes the pot from Olympia and puts it on the stove. When Olympia looks at the laboring woman on the bed, she is confronted with a most extraordinary sight. Haskell has maneuvered Marie Rivard so that she is on her elbows and knees. Haskell kneels with his arms between her thighs, his hands plunged deeply inside her. Olympia's abdomen contracts with a sympathetic sensation. But she finds that she cannot turn away.

Of the reality of childbirth, Olympia has only the haziest of notions, her knowledge of anatomy inexpert at best. Childbirth is more than just a mystery to her; it is a subject about which no polite person has ever spoken — not even Lisette, who has educated her as to some of the facts of life but who has confined herself to those bits of information absolutely necessary for Olympia to enter the first stages of womanhood. Thus she is both fearful and exhilarated by the sight of a woman's open legs, her most private place stretched sore and purple, violated not only by her physician's hands but also by the rude life that pushes relentlessly against her and makes her moan in drugged stupor. If Olympia has any conscious thoughts at all those few astonishing moments, it is to wonder at the cruelty of a God who can only with violence and pain and suffering bestow his great gift of children upon mankind.

As she watches, transfixed, Haskell appears to tussle with the infant, as if pulling a stubborn turnip from hard-packed ground. The woman screams, even with the laudanum. Copious amounts of blood spill onto the white bed sheet. But Haskell seems satisfied with the event, even as he withdraws one hand and pushes hard against the woman's belly, massaging and kneading the living mass that lies beneath. In no time at all, it seems, Haskell abruptly shifts position and gently turns the woman onto her back. He cups his palms like a priest expecting holy water. The slippery purple and blue creature slides out entirely into its new world.

Haskell takes a cloth from the satchel and wipes fluids from the baby's eyes and nose and mouth. He holds the infant at an odd angle. Olympia sees that it is a girl. Immediately they hear the first cry; and within several breaths, the skin sheds its bluish cast and pinkens. Olympia begins to weep — from relief or from exhilaration or from the shock of the birth, she cannot tell.

Haskell examines the infant's extremities and orifices and uses the warmed water to wash the child clean. He attends to the mother and extracts further matter from her womb. Exhausted by her labors, the mother falls into a deep sleep that feigns death. He gives instructions to Mrs. Bonneau, who places the clean infant at the breast of the inert mother. Haskell listens to Marie Rivard's breathing and gives further instructions. It is the first time this day Olympia hears irritation in his voice, and she thinks it must be a result of his own exhaustion or perhaps his dismay and frustration at the appalling circumstances of the impoverished family.

He washes his hands and wrists in what little water remains, using a charcoal-gray soap and producing a lather of blood and gray suds that makes Olympia have to turn away. Haskell tells the old woman to massage the uterus and that he will send Malcolm around with fresh linen and gauze to stanch the bleeding. He reaches into the pocket of his jacket and withdraws some paper dollars and hands them to Mrs. Bonneau. He tells her to buy oranges and milk and wheat bread for the children, not to give the money to any relative who is a man and not to spend it on drink. Undoubtedly grateful to Dr. Haskell for saving the life of the infant and possibly that of the newly arrived French Canadian mother as well, Mrs. Bonneau promises she will do exactly as he has asked. But when Olympia looks up at Haskell's face, she notices that he has a wry, not to say sardonic, expression on his features; and she thinks that he perhaps has little faith that his instructions will be followed to the letter.

After Haskell has cleaned himself and dressed, he gestures to Olympia, and they leave the room. Arrayed along the floor, still expertly popping buttons, are the three children of the woman who has just given birth. If they know they now have another sister, they give no sign. Haskell crouches down in front of the smallest of the three, holds her head in his hands and draws back the lid of the child's right eye. He examines her thoughtfully and then says, in French, "Why are you not outside playing on this holiday?" The child shrugs. Haskell reaches into his shirt pocket and produces a handful of saltwater taffy pieces, wrapped in waxed paper, which he distributes to the three children. Then he stands and, without knocking, opens the door to the room. He gives the old woman a further set of instructions.

"*Oui, oui, oui,*" Olympia hears from beyond the door.

They walk to the horse and buggy. Haskell helps her in, and then he climbs up and takes the reins. The sun has nearly set in their absence, and the sky has the appearance of indigo dust. They retrace their route along the trolley line and head out toward Ely and Fortune's Rocks, a distance of perhaps eight miles. From time to time, Olympia begins to tremble with the memory of the extraordinary events of the afternoon and evening. She wonders how it is that Haskell does not collapse from the sheer weight of his encounters with mortal injury and illness. But then she surmises that a physician, familiar with, if not actually inured to, the physical vicissitudes of birth and death, might take the occurrences of the afternoon as merely commonplace; though she cannot imagine how seeing the human body in extremis, as they have just done, can ever be routinely absorbed. The sleeves of his shirt are spotted with blood and other matter, and he gives off a distinctly masculine odor — not unpleasant, but testament to his own labors. After some time, he speaks.

"You must not be frightened of childbirth," he says. "What you saw just now is not unnatural or uncommon. Difficult perhaps, but not desperately so. Nature sometimes makes a thunderous entrance and a whimpering exit, though I assure you it can be otherwise. I fear I have gravely injured your sensibilities."

"Not injured," she says. "Stunned them, perhaps. And my sensibilities are not as tender as you might imagine. Indeed, I am grateful to you for allowing me to witness the birth, which was an astonishing miracle. And is it not better always to know the truth of a thing?"

"I have mixed opinions on that subject," he says thoughtfully.

"But what good does a woman do herself if she hides from the physical realities of her person? So that she might be terrified in the event itself? I wonder how I should ever have learned of such matters, for I have been overly sheltered."

"And wisely so," Haskell says. "Your father's protection has allowed you to grow and develop and blossom in an entirely healthy and appropriate manner. And if the alternative to sheltering is snipping buttons in conditions of filth and degradation, then I am in favor of such protection, even if that be suffocating." He shakes the reins, and the carriage begins to move slightly faster. "The children should be given over to the orphanage," he says heatedly.

"Taken away from their mother?" she asks.

"Why not? How can a woman who is so impoverished be an adequate mother? At least in an orphanage, under the care of the sisters, the children will have baths and regular meals and clean clothing and fresh air and some schooling. As far as I am concerned, what we just witnessed wasn't a birth, but rather a kind of infanticide."

"But, surely, we cannot blame the mother for her poverty,"

Olympia argues. "Surely, there is a man involved, who now seems to be absent."

"I would be more inclined to agree with you had I not seen some of these young immigrant women — Irish and Franco alike — drunk on more occasions than I care to think about. And there are other unfortunate women, desperate women, who at least have the good sense to ask for help, who beg to give over their children to orphanages if only spaces can be found for them."

"I cannot imagine giving over a child," Olympia says with some confusion. She has seen for herself that the Rivard children are woefully neglected, though she finds it harder than Haskell does to blame the mother. Surely a woman of her mother's station would not be expected to give up her child even if she found herself in difficult straits following abandonment by her husband, even if she drank to excess on occasion. Was a woman, mired in poverty and grieving for her lost husband, to be denied, by decree of society, all possible pleasures, all possible relief? And yet Olympia can also understand the particular treachery of taking money meant for children's food to spend on drink. And altogether, the issue seems to present a more complicated problem than can be sorted out in casual discussion.

The evening suddenly darkens, bringing with it an awareness that Olympia is on the verge of being unpardonably late. She can possibly excuse a daylight absence, but at night her father will almost certainly become worried.

"Regarding your earlier point," Haskell says, "in truth, I do not believe in shielding a young woman on the threshold of marriage and childbirth from the physical particulars of what surely awaits her. In some situations — and childbirth is one of them — ignorance can be lethal. I have come upon not a few young women in my practice who have begun birthing without ever having known they were with child."

Olympia wonders how that might be possible, since it seems to her that such naïveté would require almost willful ignorance. They pass through Ely, noting signs of life in the small village: lanterns lit in windows and shadowy figures moving along the streets, having recently been disgorged, she knows, from the trolley. They hear singing and a few drunken shouts, but for the most part the revelers have grown weary and quiet. She thinks suddenly, in the way of perfectly obvious realizations, that all of the people on the street at that moment have entered the world in a manner similar to the one she witnessed that afternoon. And she further thinks that the wonder isn't that she was present for the birth, but rather that she has reached the age of fifteen without having observed it sooner and more often.

"Did you attend the births of your own children?" she asks Haskell.

Her query seems to surprise him. As they enter the marshes, the half-moon rises and, with its pearly ripples of light on the surface of the water, illuminates all of the twisting and turning paths of the brackish labyrinth, so that the landscape becomes one of near magical beauty, the underground lair of a god, perhaps, or a passageway to the realm of a cool queen.

"I was absent for the births of my first two children," Haskell says, "and present for the last three."

"I was under the impression you had four children," Olympia says without thinking.

"The last of them was stillborn," he says. "This past March."

"Oh, I am sorry —"

"This, too, is Nature's way," he says, interrupting her. "The child would have been grotesquely deformed."

Olympia is assaulted then with disturbing images. That of Haskell kneeling between the legs of his wife, an intimate picture in stark contrast to the couple's chaste demeanor together at the dining table; and that of an infant, not at all like the one she saw that afternoon, but rather one misshapen in its limbs, pushing ferociously to get out into the world, only to perish at the moment of birth. Olympia wraps her arms around herself.

And then, in the way of random thoughts, she remembers the photograph on the sill of the Rivard room, the small picture within the silver filigree frame, the beauty and youth of the two persons who posed on their wedding day, the fine satin of the dress and the mantilla with its crown of pearls. And she wonders at the disparity between that pose of civility on the wedding day and the animal-like posture of birth within the hideous surroundings of that boarding-house room. And she further imagines that if the bride and groom in the picture had been able to foresee the circumstances in which that framed portrait would one day find itself, each of the innocents would have fled the altar in terrified disbelief.

Haskell stops the carriage.

"This has been too much," he says, turning to her.

"No," she says, "I . . ."

She inhales the salt air, as if it were her own laudanum. She tilts her head back. She can sense, but not quite see, the bats that fly near to them and then away.

"Olympia, I wish to say something to you, but not without your permission."

She rights her head and looks at him. "You do not need to ask, nor do I need to grant, permission," she says quietly.

"Our circumstances are not normal, though they feel as natural to me as it is to breathe." He says this last with quiet assurance.

"If we speak of the unnaturalness of our circumstances," she says evenly, "it will seem to us that is all we have."

With his fingers, he turns her head so that she faces him. She gives herself freely to his direction.

"Olympia, I have thought of nothing but you since the day I left your house," he says.

She briefly closes her eyes.

"I do you the greatest injury a man in my position can a young woman," he says, "which is to speak of unspeakable feelings."

In the moonlight, she can see pinpoints of moving lights in his pupils.

"This week has been unendurably long," he adds so close to her that she can feel his breath. She wants to lean into him, to rest her head on his chest.

"Mr. Haskell," she says. "I . . ."

"Have I not, in your thoughts at least, become John?" he asks quietly.

"In my thoughts of you, which are constant, you are always Haskell," she answers without any hesitation.

And there is, in the confessing of this truth, a moment of the greatest joy and release of spirit Olympia has ever felt.

"This cannot be," he says. "I cannot have created this."

"You did not."

"We can say no more about this."

"No."

"This is all," he says. "This is all we can ever have. You understand that?"

"Yes," she says.

"I forfeit all right to speak to you in this manner, and I have already trespassed upon your good nature beyond any hope of forgiveness. Indeed, by stopping here, I take advantage of your gentle spirit and of your youth, which is the worst sort of opportunism a man of my age and position can engage in. I can do you nothing but harm."

"I do not for one minute believe you guilty of opportunism," she says truthfully.

The scent of sea salt is pungent in the air, and there is as well the dank but not unpleasant aroma of mudflats and sea muck. The tide is low, but not out altogether.

"Then you are not afraid?" he asks.

"No," she says.

He puts his hands on her wristbones and slides his fingers slowly up her arms to the elbows under her loose cuffs. He says her name and presses his palms against her, as though he means to deliver the full force of himself through her skin. He removes his hands from her arms and tucks one finger inside the collar of her blouse, opening the top button with the gesture. He leans in close to her to fit his mouth to the shallow place at the bottom of her throat where she earlier directed his hand.

Olympia feels her body, for the first time, transform itself, become liquid, open itself up, wanting nothing more than more. An absolute stillness follows. It is a long kiss, if such a touch may be called a kiss, although Olympia experiences it as something different: The memory of the Franco woman with her legs open, the unruly living mass pushing against her, overtakes Olympia and seems now not an event to be feared, but rather a sensation to be savored; and it is as though she understands a thing about what will come to her in good time. She touches the back of Haskell's neck and feels the fine hairs that twirl in a comma there. He removes his mouth from her throat and presses his forehead to hers, sighing once as if only this particular embrace could give him ease.

They remain in that posture as the half-moon rises higher in its arc and the crickets scratch their repetitive tune. In the distance, they hear another carriage approaching.

"It is late, and I must go," she says. "Take me to the seawall near my house, and I will walk from there."

The other carriage comes into view, and they part reluctantly. The driver passes them with a greeting. Haskell takes up the reins, and he and Olympia journey on. When they arrive at the seawall, which is crowded with evening revelers, he helps her down from the carriage, takes her hand, and bids her good night in a manner so necessarily formal as to belie any intimacy they shared just minutes earlier.

Her father is sitting on the porch when she returns. He is smoking — a dark figure in a chair, with only the ember of his cigar clearly visible.

"Is that you, Olympia?" he calls.

"Yes, Father," she says, climbing the steps. She moves into his line of sight. He lights a candle and holds it out to her. He studies her face, her clothing.

"We have been worried about you," he says. "It is after ten o'clock."

"I went for a long walk on the beach and met Julia Fields, with whom I had a meal," she says, discerning at once that to tell the obvious lie, that she has been at the Farragut party, will lead to discovery.

"I am not certain I ever met Julia Fields," he says, somewhat puzzled. "When you did not appear at dusk, I went to fetch you at Victoria Farragut's," he adds, thus justifying at once her pragmatic deceit.

"I stopped there briefly on the porch," she says, "but I saw that to gain entrance I would have to engage in a lengthy discussion with Zachariah Cote, and so I fled, preferring my own company for a time."

It is a clever lie, for her father will easily be able to empathize with the unpleasantness of being trapped in conversation with a man who proved sycophantic and boring at table. Her father partially smiles; but then, as Olympia takes the candle from him, she sees him looking at her collar, which she has not thought to refasten. His incipient smile vanishes, and his expression turns to one of faint alarm.

"I am exhausted, Father," she says quickly, stepping past him. "Let me say good night."

But she does not bend to kiss him, as is her custom, for all about her is the distinct smell of John Haskell, as though the pores of her skin had absorbed the essence of the man, a foreign essence she luxuriates in even as she fears its consequences.

D AYS PASS into days, and it seems the entire coast lies under a gray pall that, for nearly a week, neither breaks nor gathers enough momentum to become an actual storm. But there is rain, a steady drizzle that renders nearly all outdoor pursuits unmanageable. Her sense of isolation, of being set apart from those around her, only intensifies with the poor weather; and it is as though she inhabits a warm and impenetrable cocoon in a damp and irrelevant world.

Though she paces alone on the porch, or soaks herself as she walks the beach, or eats at her dining table, or converses, albeit distractedly, with her father, or tries to read John Greenleaf Whittier or to play backgammon with her mother, every moment is devoted to — no, *claimed* by — John Haskell, so that she has no conscious thought or unconscious dream that does not include him.

Her distraction does not go unnoticed, even though those around her do not know its cause. As the days pass, she grows less able (or less willing) to dissemble and to hide her feelings; and several times she comes perilously close to revealing the true reason for her agitation. Once or twice she dangerously mentions Haskell in conversation with her father, referring more often than is prudent to the volume Haskell has written or to the work that he is doing in Ely Falls. And at a party at which Rufus Philbrick and Zachariah Cote are both present, she contrives to steer the conversation to a discussion of the mills and of progressive reforms; for simply to speak the word *mills* or *progressive* aloud in their company is rewarding and even thrilling in a secretive way. She imagines, after she does so, however, that Mr. Cote regards her with an odd and thoughtful gaze and then with the faintest of smiles, all of which causes her to wonder if she is so transparent that her true thoughts can be read upon her face.

All around her, she can see that others study her, their puzzlement turning to a smile or to a frown, depending upon what they deduce from her behavior. Her father is careful with her: He can hardly accuse her of something for which he has no evidence. And she believes that though there was between them on the porch that night the barest recognition of waywardness, he has chosen willfully to dismiss it from his thoughts. Olympia thinks her mother may be more watchful than before, but since she seldom ventures farther than her own room, there is not a great deal for her to observe. If her parents think about her distraction at all consciously, she is certain they attribute it to that temperamental state that claims many young women of her age. Or else they imagine for her an innocent romance with a boy she has recently met. Or they think she is participating in a harmless flirtation in which she, in her naïveté, has doubtless invested too much significance.

Curiously, during this period of time, whenever they have visitors to the house or she happens to observe Josiah going about his chores or her father reading, she begins to notice certain masculine characteristics that she has not ever observed before — or never knew she observed: the inch or two of skin that sometimes will show itself between a man's cuff and his wristbone when he reaches for a door, for example; or the graceful languor of men standing casually with their hands in their trouser pockets; or the way the power, the heart of the body, seems to reside just below the midpoint between the shoulders. And she is certain that though she has actually seen such masculine attributes before — that is to say, physically absorbed them with the eye — they have not previously produced conscious thoughts as they do in abundance during this spate of rainy days.

On the afternoon of the sixth day, Olympia is knitting in her room, an activity that is producing in her only a benumbed stupor. To rouse herself, she decides to make herself a cup of tea. As she descends the carpeted steps, she hears masculine voices from her father's study. She halts in her progress, her heel poised against the riser, listening intently to discern the speakers. One voice, of course, is that of her father, and there is no mistaking the other. They are talking about a book of photographs.

Taking deliberate breaths, Olympia continues down the stairs and walks, with deceptively casual posture, into her father's study, as if merely looking in to see who the company is. Her father glances over at her. He stops his speech mid-sentence. Haskell, whose back has been to her, turns. After a brief heartbeat of hesitation, he advances with the perfect manners of a gentleman and takes her hand.

"Miss Biddeford," he says, "what a pleasure to see you again."

"I trust you know my daughter well enough to call her Olympia," her father says cheerfully enough (and with what agonizing irony for both Haskell and Olympia he cannot know).

"Olympia, then," Haskell says pleasantly.

He has a bowler in his hand. She can see tiny droplets of water on his overcoat. His boots are stained black from the wet in a semicircle around the toes. His hair has been somewhat flattened by the hat, and his face is flushed, as though he had been running. In the crook of his arm is a book, perhaps the excuse for his visit.

How cunning, how capable of deceit, they show themselves to be in these few minutes as they speak the sentences of a ritual long practiced, drop their hands at precisely the right moment, and turn ever so slightly in the direction of Olympia's father so as to include him in their greetings. Her father, who seems particularly pleased to see Haskell, whose company he genuinely enjoys and whose work he honestly admires, immediately insists that Haskell stay to tea.

"I was just going into the kitchen to make a pot myself," Olympia says.

"Excellent," her father says. "Your timing, Haskell, is rather good. Olympia, bring it into the parlor. It is too cramped in here, and too cold for me, I am afraid, on the porch."

Olympia leaves their company and walks with strained poise through the dining room and pantry and into the kitchen. But once she has let the swinging door shut itself, she leans heavily with her hands upon the lip of the broad worktable and bends her head. She has shocked even herself with her deceit, with the ease of her deception.

After a time, she rights herself, fetches the kettle from the top of the stove, fills it, and returns it to the stovetop, which is still warm from lunch. Mrs. Lock, who is recently from Halifax and who will not return to the house until it is time to prepare the supper meal, has left a plate of blueberry scones on the counter. In the larder, Olympia finds butter and jam to go with the scones and sets everything on a marquetry tray from the pantry. Then she sits down on a kitchen chair to wait for the water to boil and the trembling in her hands to subside.

The kitchen is a large room that has been painted pale green with white trim. Along one wall is a series of windows looking out on a trellis and the back garden. Set into the wall opposite is a brick hearth so tall that Martha could stand upright inside it. The floors are wide pine boards, and Olympia notes that Mrs. Lock is such a fastidious cook that there is not a particle of pastry or flour or even dust in the cracks between the boards. Behind glass-fronted cabinets are the foodstuffs and the dishes, and in a corner is a polished oak ice chest.

She glances down at her lap and is suddenly stricken to discover that she has on her fawn calico, a dull dress not fit to be seen by anyone but family. She wore it today because she had nowhere to be and no visitors expected. She holds the dingy material in her fists and wonders frantically how she might swap the drab frock for another. But she knows at once that she cannot change her dress; for though she could easily sneak up the back stairway to her room, it will be worse to be seen to have altered her clothing than to remain as she is. Her hair, she realizes with further dismay, patting the hastily made knots at the back of her head, is so artlessly done on this day as to be not merely plain but unkempt.

She hears the brush of the swinging door. She turns in her chair.

"Olympia," Haskell says, and she stands.

His face is at first unreadable. In the better light of the kitchen, she can see dark circles around his eyes.

"I could not stay away," he says.

She puts a hand on the chair back. Haskell crosses the space between them.

"Your father is looking for a book in his study," he says with the careful pragmatism of the secret lover. "I said I would help you with the tray. We have only a minute, two minutes at best."

She touches the cloth of his coat at his chest. It is damp from the rain.

Haskell hooks his arm around her shoulders and draws her to him with a powerful grip. She has a distinct sense of vigor. Not accustomed to feeling small, she is nearly lost in his embrace. Releasing an arm, she reaches a hand up behind his head and pulls him toward her, her actions as instinctive to her as it is to bat a fly away from one's face. He opens his mouth, shocking her, for she has never had such a kiss. She tastes his tongue, the inner lining of his lips. Her head is tilted at an angle, and her neck is drawn long and exposed. Haskell slowly slides his mouth all along the skin there, and she shivers against him.

And then that is all. That is all the time they have.

He backs away, his empty hands forming a shape, his mouth seemingly wishing to speak a word. His tie has come undone, and unable to speak herself, she points to her own collar to tell him. She can feel the weight of her disheveled hair pulling itself loose. She tries to repin it as they stand there. Haskell's face has turned an unnatural red, and her mouth feels raw.

Her father comes through the swinging door.

"So you have found her," her father says amiably, looking at them but not really looking at them. "This is the volume I wanted to show you, Haskell. The photographs are astonishing."

He glances from Haskell to Olympia and seems puzzled by his daughter's immobility.

"Can I help?" he asks.

AFTER HER ENCOUNTER with Haskell in the kitchen, they sit on the porch, surrounded by the gray brocade of an unrelenting cloud cover. Haskell converses politely with her father, and how he manages to do that, Olympia cannot imagine. It seems incongruous — beyond incongruous — to be eating blueberry scones and speaking of photography and the new century, when only moments before, she and Haskell came together in the way they did in the kitchen. And as will happen often to her this summer, she is accosted by a moment of pure astonishment that such events can possibly be occurring in her life. If she but thinks about the kiss in the kitchen, she feels a fluttering sensation in her abdomen, and her face becomes suffused with color. She experiences the reality again and again and again, a series of brief shocks upon both her soul and her body. How can Haskell and she have done that? she wonders. They who have no right to have transgressed in that manner? And yet, in the way one may hold within the mind two separate and contradictory thoughts or theories, she believes in the next moment that they have no choice but to respond as they do, that what draws her to Haskell and him to her is as natural as it is to breathe.

She awakens the next morning to an oily green sea, the surface flat
and reflecting no light at all, a pond covered with scum. She has
spent a restless night and is not certain she slept at all; and she wonders if her perception of the color of the ocean isn't a result at least as
much of her sleep-deprived state as of Nature's inclinations.

Since it is a Sunday, and her father does not consider it proper to
interrupt one's service to God with summer pleasures, Olympia
knows they will all be going to church. She dresses in a benumbed
state, so preoccupied that it takes her nearly twice as long as usual to
complete a perfectly ordinary toilet. She descends the stairs in a distracted flurry and takes her cloak and bonnet from Josiah. He tells
her that perhaps the sun will break through the cloud cover before
the day is over. He is dressed for church himself and adds that he will
be accompanying them.

"Your mother and father are in the carriage already," he says, looking at her oddly. "You are not unwell, I hope?"

"No, Josiah, I am well enough," she says, burying her hair within
her bonnet and grateful that the hat's wide brim will hide the confusion on her face. At the doorway, he extends his arm, and she is relieved to have someone at this moment to lean upon.

It is a modest brown-shingled church with its trim painted in yellow ochre. It has a tall, wooden spire above its single gable, and atop
that is an unadorned cross that is visible from all of Fortune's Rocks.
At fifteen, Olympia has not yet suffered any crises of faith, but neither is she devout. God and his commandments, as interpreted by
man, are for her primarily social and familial obligations. When at
church, she does sometimes enjoy the sense of calm that will occasionally spread across the congregation, and the music is appealing
to her. But more often than not, she finds herself restless in that
darkened sanctuary, wishing she were out-of-doors.

The roads are muddy, and the journey is slow going. The cold
seeps in at the sides, and the four of them sit huddled, heads bent,

against the unseasonable elements. They enter the church and move to their customary pew. All about them is the smell of wet wool, the sound of cloaks being snapped to shake off the damp. The windows are arched and leaded and stained a dark red and a brownish gold. The gloom they create is dispelled only by the candles in the sconces on the walls. It is as if it were already night in the church, the faces and forms of the parishioners at first hard to discern. The pulpit, of carved cherry, is suspended from a chain in the vaulted ceiling. More than once, as a child, Olympia imagined the links of the chain giving way and crashing the pulpit and its minister to the floor, these unkind fantasies more a result of childish restlessness than a comment upon the quality of the sermons.

They sit quietly, none of them speaking, each engaged in separate reveries. Olympia thinks neither of her parents particularly devout as well, but who can ever truly know the extent of faith in another, she thinks, faith being among the most intimate and well guarded of possessions? Thus, it is not until the choir begins the processional that Olympia happens to glance to her right, past the straight-backed and uncurious form of her father, and sees who is sitting in the pew opposite theirs. Perhaps a small sound escapes her then and penetrates her father's composure, for he glances quickly at her. But she is saved from a question by the need to rise for the hymn.

It has been only a glance: a hat with a brim that all but hides a mass of silvery blond hair; a kid glove with a pearl button; a child's small boot swinging back and forth; the strain in the fabric of a blue cotton smock as a shoulder is turned to the side; the cuff of a trouser leg, wet at its hem; and above that a perfect masculine profile with no beard or mustache. He must have seen her, she thinks at once. He must know that she is there. It must have been Catherine, then, who quite innocently allowed herself to be led by the usher to the seat opposite Olympia's father, whom she doubtless plans to greet when the service is over.

Olympia sits as still as wood, determined to give nothing away. The excessive stiffness of her posture must in some small measure betray her, however, for her father glances at her again and again. But he does not speak, church etiquette requiring his silence.

If ever Olympia is conscious of another person in a room, aware only of another's physical presence — though there are at least a hundred other people in the congregation — it is that morning, during that hour and a half when she might pray, might ask for guidance, might vow to banish Haskell from her thoughts. But though she makes an attempt to speak to God, she cannot, not for the white noise inside her head, nor for the unwillingness of her soul to relinquish what it has so recently gained. And though she yearns for a glimpse of the man, it is enough just to see, from the corner of her eye, the cloth that drapes his leg, the movement of his foot.

Later, Olympia will believe that it was during that hour and a half, in that brown and ochre church, with all their families around them, with a congregation of witnesses, that she came to understand that she and Haskell would one day have a future. And that she would not put up any impediment to its unfolding.

Catherine invites them to lunch at the Highland, an invitation so genially proffered that even Olympia's mother cannot hide her pleasure at the prospect of a diversion from the claustrophobic imprisonment of the weather. In fact, Mrs. Haskell exclaims, having almost certainly planned the wording of the invitation during the pastoral prayers, they needn't return home at all; they can simply follow the Haskells to the hotel. This is all said and done in the center aisle of the church, while Olympia stands gazing fixedly at an uncharacteristically lurid depiction of the Last Supper. It would not be proper of Haskell to speak to her then; and he does not, nor she to him. But once, as they are moving to the nave, she catches his eye in the turn, and the gaze is so intimate, so knowing, that she colors immediately, a fact he cannot fail to notice.

Olympia takes it as an omen that the sky has brightened during the hour and a half they have been inside, that the west wind, now palpable, has blown out nearly all of the clouds, which form a line one can watch as they make their way out to sea. The week of constant rain has left the world shimmering with droplets on every leaf, every blade of sea grass, every beach rose. On the way to the hotel, the sheen on the rocks is so ferocious, Olympia can hardly bear to look.

At the Highland, they pass through the glass-paned front doors to a cavernous lobby with a thirty-foot-long mahogany desk; and from there to the dining room that is so large, it might accommodate a thousand diners. Set as it is for Sunday lunch, with its starched linen, polished silver plate, and clean white crockery, the dining room seems, upon entering it, an ocean itself of welcome, so far removed from the gloomy interior of the church they left just minutes earlier. And she wonders why it is that the men who design places of worship do not consider more often the appeal of light and beauty in their architecture.

Catherine, in her role as hostess, seats Olympia with her mother to one side and Martha to the other, as though Olympia were neither woman nor girl, but rather inhabited some world in between. Their posture and gestures are formal, as befits a Sunday dinner, but the meal is infused with warmth and even gaiety; and it may be that the current which Olympia knows passes between her and Haskell, who sits at the head of the table, is drawn off in part by the others. Catherine invites Josiah to dine with them, but he excuses himself immediately on the grounds that he deeply desires a walk along the beach and with it the rare opportunity to take the fine air after so long a confinement. Were it not for Haskell's presence, Olympia would have ached to join him.

Olympia listens to the light banter that accompanies the settling
in to a meal.

Catherine, you are looking well.
I am well now that the sun is out.
Has Josiah gone?
Mother, must I sit next to Randall?
And so you say you have not received your supplies yet?
Those are lovely pearls.
I thought it was rather a brilliant sermon.
And who was the soloist?
I understand they do a marvelous lamb here.
Do they?

Glancing at her from his end of the table, Haskell seems more an
attractive stranger than someone with whom she has been intimate.
And it strikes Olympia then as astonishing how willing we are to give
our hearts — and indeed our souls — to someone we hardly know.

Olympia notes that more than one person entering the dining
room turns to look at Catherine and Haskell together, the dark and
the fair, Catherine no longer hiding with her hat the loveliness of her
face or the silvery gossamer of her hair. Idly, as Olympia watches
them, Catherine reaches over to her husband and smooths a tendril
of hair behind his ear, a wifely gesture that causes Olympia to have
to look away. And she thinks that Haskell himself cannot be unaware of the irony of suffering such a caress in her presence.

Around them is an agreeable clinking of silver against china, of ice
rattling in goblets, of the low murmur of gentle and even animated
discourse. Through the windows, which are sparkling with a vinegar
wash, is the ever present surf — a steady rumble occasionally punc-
tuated with the calling and cawing of seagulls.

Her father monopolizes Haskell's attention, which is, Olympia thinks, a relief to both Haskell and her. Catherine, buoyed by her own good spirits or perhaps simply the joy of the sunshine after so many days of gloom, keeps her mother in continuous conversation — no easy task, although even she seems infected with conviviality.

Beside Olympia, there is Martha, and it is an effort to pull away from the adult debate and banter to pay attention to the girl's odd and disjointed comments, each designed, it would appear, to elicit Olympia's undivided attention. But from time to time, Martha does penetrate Olympia's reveries, reminding her of how rudely she is ignoring her. So that after the pudding, when Martha asks her if she would like to go up with her to see her room, Olympia cannot refuse without drawing undue attention to herself. As they stand and excuse themselves, Martha pulls at her sleeve, eager to be gone from the table.

"The pudding was wretched," Martha says as they move through the dining room and into the lobby. "I hate raspberries, don't you? They stick to your teeth and hurt when you bite down."

"Yes, they do," Olympia says distractedly.

"I went out this morning early, before Mother was awake, and collected all manner of pearlish seashells, which seem to have washed up on the beach with the bad weather. You must tell me what they are."

"I may not know," Olympia says.

They climb the stairs to the fourth floor, where the Haskells have rooms facing the ocean. Along the way, Olympia is struck by the pale blue walls of the hallways and their high white ceilings. Through open doors, she can see other rooms, and beyond them the ocean, which seems to lie suspended just outside the panes of glass. The effect of the blue and white is of the sky and fair-weather clouds, and she thinks the interior an inspired design. Martha takes her through a door and into a room that leads to others at either side — bedrooms, Olympia imagines, for the room they have entered is clearly a sitting room. Wisely, the beautiful windows here have not been shrouded in heavy drapes, but rather are framed with muslin. The room is suffused with a delicate light through the gauze that might have a sedating influence upon the spirit, but Olympia's senses are preternaturally alert; she is both curious and fearful of what she might find, in the way of a lover confronted with his beloved's private mail. Even as Martha chats away and lays her prized seashells upon a table for inspection, Olympia's eye travels to every surface of table and chair for some sign of Haskell and how he has lived in this space.

On a desk in a corner are several volumes and what appears to be an opened ledger filled with slanted cursive in indigo ink. A pair of spectacles lies next to the ledger, and these surprise her, since she has never seen Haskell with eyeglasses. On the pale mauve settee is a white crocheted throw curled into a soft mound, as though it recently sheltered someone's feet. On the floor beside the settee is a book, *Gleanings from the Sea* by Joseph W. Smith, a silk ribbon defining its pages.

Martha queries her incessantly. Olympia does her best to identify the girl's treasures, though there are several oddities she does not recognize — one shell a delicate opalescent, so fine it seems it might shatter to the touch.

"My best one is not here," Martha complains. "Randall must have taken it. I know he did. Wait here. I know just where he will have hidden it."

Martha strides out of the sitting room in the direction of one of the bedrooms. Olympia stands for a few moments, looking at the water. Many people are strolling along the beach and flirting with the surf, doubtless because of the good weather after such a dreary week.

Waiting for Martha, Olympia finds herself drifting slowly to the opposite doorway. She does not know precisely what she is doing or why; it is only that she wants somehow to be closer to Haskell, to understand how he lives. Silently, she steps over the threshold into the second bedroom.

It is a masculine room — there is no mistaking that — and though Catherine Haskell has obviously set her trunk upon a stand, it seems she is more a visitor than an occupant. Olympia notes a tortoiseshell brush and comb upon the bureau, above which is a spotted mirror. The bed, though made, is slightly rumpled, as though a man recently sat on it to pull on his socks. On a marble-topped table by the windows is a porcelain chamber set and a man's shaving things, a brush and mug and razor. Beside the table is a valet with a frock coat hung upon its wooden shoulders.

Emboldened by Martha's continued absence, Olympia moves farther into the room until she can see the whole of it — specifically, a wide oak bureau, the surface of which is covered with photographs. From a distance, she can make out images only: a profile, a portion of a hat, a railing such as might be on a porch. Gliding closer still, she sees that these are the photographs that were taken on the front steps of her house on the day that Haskell had his camera.

The pictures make a fan shape. At one of the edges, tucked behind the others, she notes a trouser leg. She slips the photograph away and recognizes the picture she took of Haskell on the day they had a picnic on the beach: a face, in repose; clothing loosened upon the limbs; rolled cuffs revealing legs covered with darkened hair and sand; a Franco family in the background. She closes her eyes. When she opens them, she sees the white border of a further photograph, tucked in behind that of Haskell. With her index finger, she slides it free. It is, she discovers, her own photograph. But it is not the picture itself that is so arresting; rather, it is the blurry impression of fingerprints that have stripped away the emulsion that compels her attention.

Martha steps into the room, her hand outstretched with her treasure. On her face is a look of confusion. Olympia drops the photo-

graph on top of the bureau. She assumes an attitude of slight boredom and indifference. "I was looking for a lavatory so that I might
wash my hands," she says.

"It is not in here," Martha says, frowning.

"You have found your shell," Olympia adds, moving toward her.

"It is not a shell," the girl replies. She retracts her palm and studies Olympia intently. "It is sea glass."

"May I look at it?" Olympia asks, returning Martha's gaze as
steadily as she bestows it.

"We should not be in here."

"No, of course not. Let me take this to the windows in the sitting
room so that I can see its color better."

As they leave John Haskell's bedroom and walk to the windows,
and Martha reluctantly offers Olympia her small treasure — a shard
of pale blue, the surface of the glass brushed cloudy by months or
years of battering on the rocks and sand — Olympia realizes, too
late, that the fact that she has disturbed the order of the photographs
on the bureau will be immediately apparent to their owner.

Olympia's parents are standing with the Haskells in the lobby when
they return. She does not look at Haskell, nor does she meet Catherine's gaze. She is apprehensive lest Martha, for whatever private reasons of her own, blurt out her knowledge of Olympia's having
wandered into the Haskells' bedroom. But Martha hangs back, still
puzzled, Olympia thinks, by something she can sense but not quite
understand.

Olympia's father, who has drunk more wine with his meal than is
perhaps prudent, invites Catherine and John Haskell to dine with
them on Tuesday. Catherine thanks him warmly but says that she is
returning with the children to York later that afternoon. She makes
a remark about abandoning her husband, after which she takes her

husband's hand. Olympia happens to glance up at the moment of that touch; and then, because she cannot not help herself, looks further at Haskell's face. And perhaps only Olympia can read the complex mix of anguish and remorse that resides there: anguish for his wife and for themselves, and remorse for deeds not yet committed but for which she already understands that they will one day have to answer.

Olympia waits through the long afternoon and through the night until daybreak — that time of day when there is light but the sun has not yet risen, when all the world is still for a moment, seemingly gathering itself in silence. She washes and dresses quietly in her room and listens for any restless stirring from either her mother or her father, or from Josiah or Lisette, who might be up earlier than usual. Hoping to disturb no one, she slips from her room, moves through the house, and steps outside.

The tide is dead low, the shoreline a vast flat of sand and sea muck. Long strands of sea moss droop from the exposed rocks like walrus mustaches. There are clam diggers already on the beach, and farther out, a lone boat with sails of dirty ivory moves parallel to the shoreline. At first, Olympia merely walks purposefully, holding her boots in one hand, her skirt in the other. But then caution abandons her altogether, and she breaks into a run. All the hard decisions have been made the day before. The debate, what little there has been of it, is already quashed and settled.

In the most brazen act of her short life, she sits upon the hotel steps, puts her boots and stockings back on, and enters the lobby, where she is immediately confronted with the stark reality of the night clerk. He is reading the racing form and smoking a pipe. He looks up and is clearly startled to see a young woman in the lobby at this hour.

"I have been sent to fetch Dr. Haskell," Olympia says at once, inventing an emergency as she speaks. "He is needed at the clinic. Mrs. Rivard is having a difficult birth. . . ."

The clerk snaps to attention. "Oh, yes, miss," he says at once, not eager for her to explain further. "I will go up myself. Just you wait right here."

Olympia nods. Somewhat nervous now, she moves about the lobby, inspecting the horsehair sofas, the oil portraits on the walls, the carved pillars around which velvet banquettes have been placed for the guests. It seems she waits a long time for the clerk to return with Haskell. And as she does so, she begins to doubt the wisdom of her actions. What if Catherine and the children did not go yesterday afternoon as she said they would? What if Haskell is angry with Olympia for this ruse? In fact, he will be angry, will he not? Olympia hardly knows the man. He will undoubtedly think her foolish, if not altogether mad.

Suddenly panicked, she glances all about her. She did not give her name to the desk clerk. Haskell will guess who it is, but she does not actually have to be standing there, does she? She walks quickly to the front door. But as she nears its threshold, she hears the breathless announcement of the desk clerk.

"There she is, sir. Very good."

Haskell, with his coat in one hand and his satchel in the other, sees her across the long expanse of the lobby. Olympia can move neither forward nor backward. With slow steps Haskell approaches her.

"It is Mrs. Rivard, then," Haskell says quietly.

It is all Olympia can do to nod.

"Very well, let us speak further about this on the porch."

Obediently, she passes through the door, onto the porch, and, following his lead, down the steps. Silently, they walk together to the back of the hotel. As they turn the corner, she stumbles on an exposed pipe, and in the sudden motion, he reaches for her arm.

"Olympia, look at me, please."

She turns and raises her eyes to his.

"I wish with all my heart," he says, "that it was I who could come to you. You understand that?"

She nods, for she believes him.

He will go up first, he says, to unlock the room. After a suitable interval, she is to follow.

The sun has risen, and through the windows in the hallways, the light is overbright, causing a continual blindness as Olympia passes from shadow to light to shadow. Not many are stirring in the hotel, although she does hear water running and, once, footsteps behind her briefly. Through the windows to the side, she can see wash on a line and a group of chambermaids sitting with mugs of tea on the back steps.

When she enters the room, Haskell is standing by the windows, his arms folded across his chest, his body a dark silhouette against the luminous gauze. She removes her hat and places it on a side table.

He tilts his head and considers her for a long moment, as though he might be going to paint her portrait, as though he were seeing planes and lines and curves rather than a face.

But there is expectation in his features, too. Definitely expectation.

"Olympia," he says.

He unfolds his arms and walks toward her. He puts his hands to the back of her neck. He bends her head toward his chest, where she rests it gratefully, flooded with an enormous sense of relief.

"If I truly loved you," he says, "I would not let you do this."

"You do truly love me," she says.

He trails his fingers up and down her spine. Tentatively, she circles him with her arms. She has never held a man before, never felt a man's broad back or made her way along its muscles. She no longer has fear, but neither does she have the intense hunger she will know later. The sensation is, rather, a sort of sliding against and sinking into another, so that she seems more liquid than corporeal. She brings her hands to the front of his shirt and lays her palms against him.

He seems to shudder slightly. His body is thicker than she has imagined it, or perhaps it is only that his tangible physical presence, under her palms, is more substantial than she has remembered. And it seems to her then that everything around her is heightened, emboldened, made larger than in her dreams.

"Olympia, we cannot do this."

She is taken aback, unprepared for discussion.

"It is already done," she says.

"No, it is not. We can stop this. I can stop this."

"You do not want this to stop," she says, and she believes this is true. She hopes this is true.

"I am a married man. You are only fifteen."

"And do these facts matter?" she asks.

"They must," he says.

He takes a step back from her. Her hands drop from his body. She shakes her head. She feels a sudden panic that she will lose him to his doubts.

"It is not what we are doing," she says. "It is what we are."

He briefly closes his eyes.

"I thought you understood that," she says quietly.

"We will not be forgiven."

"By whom?" she asks sharply. "By God?"

"By your father," he says. "By Catherine."

"No," she says. "We will not be forgiven."

An expression of surrender — or is it actually joy? — seems to wash over his features. She sees the strain of resistance leave his body.

"This will be very strange for you," he says, trying to warn her.

"Then let it be strange," she says. "I want it to be strange."

He tries to unbutton the collar of her blouse but fumbles with the mother-of-pearl disks, which are difficult to undo. She stands away from him for a moment and unfastens the collar herself, impatient to reenter that liquid world that is only itself, not a prelude, nor an aftermath, nor a distraction, but rather an all-absorbing and enveloping universe.

There is a change in tempo then, a quickening of his breath and perhaps of hers, too. They embrace awkwardly. She hits a corner of the settee with the small of her back and stiffens. Her clothing seems clumsy and excessively detailed. He sheds his jacket in one sinuous motion. Her blouse is undone, open to the collarbone.

"Let me lie down," she says.

If nothing is ever taught, how is it that the body knows how to move and where to place itself? It must be a kind of instinct — of course it is — a sense of physical practicality. Olympia has never had the act of love described, nor seen drawings, nor read any descriptions. Even the most ignorant of farmers' children would have more knowledge than she.

She goes into the bedroom alone, into the room where Haskell and his wife have so recently lain together. The bed is unmade and rumpled, its occupant having left it in haste. There are no traces of Catherine now, nor of the photographs that were on the bureau. Olympia takes off her dress and her hose, her corset and petticoat. Wearing only her steps-ins and her vest, she lies down and covers herself.

Haskell comes into the room and stands at the foot of the bed. "If you only knew how you looked to me," he says.

She watches as he takes off his collar and unbuttons his shirt. For the first time in her life, Olympia sees a man undress. She is struck by the way Haskell tussles with his cuff links, the way he removes the collar of his shirt as if freeing himself from a yoke. She feels odd and cold beneath the sateen puff and frightened at the thought of a man's nudity, which, in fact, she does not entirely see this day. Haskell stops short of removing his undergarments before he slides into the bed with her.

She rolls into the crook of his arm and rests her head there. She puts the palm of one hand against his vest. Uneasy and expectant, they are silent for a time. There is nothing impetuous in their actions, nothing at all. Though impetuosity will come soon enough, it is as though each movement toward the other must be taken with some forethought, some understanding of what it is they do.

He shifts his position and dislodges her from his arm, so that she is now lying beneath him. "I saw you at the beach that day. You do not remember me."

"I am not sure."

"I think I loved you then. Yes, I am certain of this."

"How is that possible?"

"I do not know," he says. "But I am sure of it. And then when I saw you on the porch the night of the solstice, I experienced . . ." He searches for the words. "As though I had known you. Will know you."

"Yes," she says, for she has felt it, too.

"You cannot know how precious this is," he says. "You will think that this is how it always is. But it is not."

He supports his weight on his forearms. He kisses her slowly on her neck. As if they had all the time in the world, which, in fact, they do not.

"I envy you," he says. "I envy your not having known anything else."

She can feel him pressing into her, a weight lowering itself, even as his hands draw up her vest and push away the rest of her underclothing. For a moment, he fumbles with something he must have had in his hand when he entered the bed, something she cannot now identify, though later he will explain his caution to her.

Does she feel pain? Not exactly. Not terrible pain. It is more a sense of greater weight, of a thrusting against her, though she does not resist. She wants to take him in.

"Am I hurting you?" he asks once.

"No," she says, struggling for breath. "No."

She is thrilled, tremulous with the event. The sun moves and makes a hot oblong of light on the topaz sateen puff, so oddly unmasculine, a spread similar to her mother's. All around them is the soft cotton of overwashed sheets — almost silky, almost white — and beyond these the austere mahogany of the carved furnishings: the wardrobe, the bed, the side tables. There are a man's garments strewn upon a chair and on the floorcloth, which has been painted to resemble a rug. She looks up at the pattern on the sage tin ceiling.

Only near the end, just at the end, does she feel a quickening within herself, the barest suggestion of pleasure, a foretaste of what she will one day have. Oddly, she understands this prophecy, even as she hears for the first time the low hush, the quick exhalation of breath, and knows that the event is over.

His weight, which has been great upon her, becomes even heavier. She thinks he does not understand that he will crush her. She shifts slightly beneath him, and he slides away. But as he does so, he pulls her with him, nestling her within the comma that his body makes, as one might cradle a child, as, indeed, he may have nestled his own children. She arranges herself to fit within his larger embrace.

For a time, Olympia listens to his breathing as Haskell dozes in and out of consciousness, a particular form of sleeping that she will come to treasure over time, to feel privileged to witness.

He wakes with a start.

"Olympia."

"I am here."

"My God. How extraordinary."

"Yes," she says.

"I will not say that I am sorry."

"No, we must not say that."

She moves so that she can see his face.

"I feel different now," she says.

"Do you? It is not just . . . ?"

"No." As though she can never return to the girl she used to be. "I did not even know enough to wonder about this," she says. "I did not have any idea. Not the slightest."

"Are you disturbed . . . ?"

"No. I am not. It seems a wondrous thing. To become one. In this way."

"It is a wonder with you," he says. "It is with you."

"I should go," she says. "Before the maids come."

And he seems sad that she has so quickly learned the art of deception. "Not yet," he says.

They lie together until they hear footsteps in the corridor. Reluctantly, Haskell stands up from the bed, trailing his hand along the length of her arm, as though he cannot physically bear to remove himself from her. He dresses more slowly than he might, all the while watching her on the bed. Only when they hear voices in the hallway — native accents, chambermaids — does he collect himself and finish dressing more quickly. He leaves the room for a time and returns with a cloth, which he gives to Olympia. She feels the sudden incongruity of Haskell with his clothes on while she lies naked.

"You will need this," he says, bending to kiss her.

Discreetly, he walks into the sitting room and closes the door so that she can dress. When she climbs out of the bed, she sees, on her legs and on the sheets, what the cloth is for. It shocks her, all the blood. She did not know. But he did. Of course he did. He knows everything there is to know about these matters, does he not?

He reenters the room as she is fastening her boots. She stands and turns to him across the bed, and as she does so, she realizes that she has not covered the stain. He opens his mouth to speak, but she waves her hand to silence him. There is a decorum to the moment, an action called for, though she is not certain what it should be. She is not embarrassed, exactly, but she does not want to discuss it. No, surely, she does not want to discuss it. Reaching down, and without haste, she brings the topaz puff up to the pillows and covers the discoloration. And she is certain that they are both at that moment remembering the childbirth they once witnessed together.

They walk together to the door. There is shame, she thinks, in his having to remain behind while she goes out. It is difficult to speak. She is glad that he does not feel it necessary to make plans to see each other again. She understands that it will happen of its own accord because now they cannot be apart.

He kisses her at the door. She leaves the room and steps into the corridor. All around her are the sounds of conversations, as though the rest of the world has come awake: the high-pitched voice of a woman, insistent, making points; the low snide chuckle of a man. The air has changed and has brought with it the smell of oranges. Behind her, she hears Haskell shut the door.

Her legs feel weak as she descends the stairs. She wonders what Haskell will do with the bloody flannel and the sheet. She catches sight of herself in a mirror in the hallway and is startled to see that her mouth is blurred and indistinct. Unwilling to go out the back door like a thief, she decides to brave the lobby, but when she walks across it, she knows that a dozen pair of eyes inspect her. She guesses that the desk clerk wonders what she is doing there, when she was to have taken Dr. Haskell to see the Rivard woman. Hotel guests, who have come down for breakfast and are waiting for their companions by the door of the dining room, glance at her as she walks by. Servants eye her as they cross the lobby to and fro with folded linens in their arms. She makes her way out to the porch, where she stands for a moment by a wicker chair, recovering her strength, unwilling yet to test her legs on the steep set of stairs. The sun is well up, but the light is muted. In the distance, she can see fishermen in their lobster boats checking their buoys.

"Miss Biddeford?"

Startled, Olympia turns. There must be an expression of fright on her face, for Zachariah Cote puts out a hand to steady her.

"I did not mean to scare you," he says.

The sight of the poet, in a gray silk waistcoat, the furtiveness of the man emphasized in the way his sudden smile appears to have nothing to do with his eyes, is like an apparition from a universe she has left behind and does not want to reenter.

"I see you in the strangest of places," he says amiably.

"Whatever do you mean?" she asks, moving a step backward.

He takes a step closer to her. "I am sure it was you, on the night of the Fourth, in a carriage by the side of the road? In the marshes?"

He cups an elbow in the palm of his hand and rests his chin on his knuckles. He studies her in an altogether impertinent manner, and she suddenly feels more naked than she did in the bedroom moments earlier. Indeed, his gaze is so frank and his smile so calculating that she wants to slap his face.

"No, it cannot possibly have been," she says.

"Then I am mistaken," he says, though he does not seem repentant. "But whyever are you here?" He makes a show of looking at his pocket watch. "It is so awfully early still. I am just about to go in to breakfast. I have had a walk. Will you join me?"

"No, I cannot," she says.

He raises an eyebrow. She leaves him standing there. She discovers the stairs and heads in the direction of the sea, which is turning a dove gray as a result of a thickening cloud cover.

*O*LYMPIA'S FATHER normally takes his breakfast in solitude or, if there are others present, immersed in a book he holds beside his plate. But on the morning after Olympia's visit to Haskell, her father looks up at her as she enters the breakfast room, and he continues to observe her as she takes her place and spreads her napkin over her lap. Though she wants to, Olympia cannot ask him to discontinue his stare, for that would be not only to acknowledge the unusual but also to speak to him in a manner that is not acceptable. Instead, she says good morning and pours herself a cup of tea. When she dares to glance up at him, she understands that his is not an angry stare, but rather one of some bewilderment, as though he needed to reassure himself that the girl before him is not, as it would appear, an imposter.

"Olympia, you look peaked," her father says, halting a forkful of shirred egg in its progress to his mouth. "You are well? You worry me sometimes. I was particularly concerned when you did not come down for supper last night."

"I am fine," she says, eyeing the food before her. She is now ravenous, and the raspberry cake looks particularly appetizing. "You distress yourself too much. Really, Father, I am fine. If I were ill, I would say so."

He takes a sip of tea.

"Well, you always have been a sensible girl," he says. "That is a pretty dress."

"Thank you," she says.

"By the way, I am thinking of having a gala partially in honor of your sixteenth birthday."

"A gala? Here?"

"Your mother and I are very proud of you, Olympia, and I have high hopes for your future."

Though the word *future* strikes an uneasy and discordant note within her, she nods in her father's direction. "Thank you," she says.

"And also I have had a letter from the Reverend Edward Everett Hale. He says he may come to visit at that time. We shall have a dinner and dancing. I have in mind the tenth of August. About a hundred and twenty? Many of the summer people from Boston, of course, and Philbrick and Legny. Yes, that would be a treat. Which means I shall require you to finish Hale's sermons before the event. You have, of course, read 'Man Without a Country.'"

"Yes, Father."

"And I shall invite the Haskells as well, since I know that John is most eager to meet Hale. Haskell's cottage is to be finished by that date, or so I am to understand. John cannot much appreciate hotel food each meal, regardless of how well prepared it is."

"The tenth is less than four weeks away," Olympia says.

"Yes, not much time at all. Invitations will have to go out the day after tomorrow at the latest. You and I will have to put together a guest list later this afternoon. Your mother will help us with writing out the invitations, I am sure."

"Yes, of course," Olympia says.

Silently, she regards her father's plans for a gala with both dread and excitement. Dread, because it will be painful and awkward to be in public with Haskell and not be able to be with him. Excitement, because any opportunity to be with each other, even if in public, seems desirable.

"If there is someone of your own you would like to invite . . . ," her father offers. Once again, he examines her face, which she hopes gives nothing away.

"No, there is no one," she says.

He nods. "I must write a note and send it. Yes, Josiah must take a note to Haskell, for I need to know whether the date is suitable for him and Catherine. I doubt John would ever forgive me if I had Hale here on an evening when he could not make it. John and the reverend share, I believe, an abnormally keen interest in motorcars."

"Let me take it," Olympia says impulsively. "I should welcome the walk."

They both simultaneously turn to look through the windows at the weather, which is not particularly fine. But she knows her father will assent to her suggestion, since he is nearly as keen a believer in her physical education as he is in her intellectual one.

"Yes," he says. "A walk is just the thing after a hearty breakfast. But leave the note at the desk. I should not like Haskell to think I am reduced to relying upon my daughter for my errands."

"Of course," she says, overbuttering her second piece of raspberry cake. Her appetite will not be appeased.

"A remarkable man, do you not think?" her father asks.

"I like him very much," she answers.

"I meant Hale," he says.

A shallow cloud cover prevents shadows and causes the landscape to take on a flat aspect that is unrelieved by color. Perhaps no palette in nature, Olympia thinks as she walks along the beach, is as capable of transformation as the seashore. Just two days earlier, the water was a vivid navy, the beach roses lovely blots of pink. But today, that very same geography is bleached of color, the sea now gray and the roses dulled.

She walks with her father's note in her pocket and her boots in her hand. She is imagining how pleased Haskell will be if she takes the note to his room. But then she has another thought: Might he not be offended, or engaged elsewhere? She does not know his schedule, nor yet know his routine.

There are few people on the hotel porch, one a woman knitting, who smiles at Olympia when she climbs the steps, and another a governess with a small child. Olympia pushes through the door to the lobby, takes the note out of her pocket, and hands it to the clerk behind the desk, who is, fortunately, a different clerk than was there the day before.

"Oh, Dr. Haskell is it then?" the clerk asks, reading the envelope. "He is just breakfasting in the dining room, miss. . . . I will have it sent in straightaway." He signals for the porter and gives the man the note.

"Thank you," she says.

She walks out onto the porch and lingers by the railing. She fastens her eyes on the ocean, though she sees nothing. She hears Haskell's footsteps behind her before he speaks.

"This is more than I could have hoped for," he says quietly. He is dressed in a blue shirt with a gray linen waistcoat. His hair is wet and still bears its brush marks.

Olympia turns. Haskell takes an involuntary step toward her and puts a hand out, as if he would touch her, but then stops himself just in time. Although he does, Olympia thinks, give himself away in the very next moment by glancing over at the woman who is knitting.

"Olympia," he says.

She cannot call him by the name that she has heard his wife use so endearingly.

"You were about to leave," she says, noting his coat and satchel.

"I have to be at the clinic." He walks closer to her. "I have thought of nothing but you," he says in a low voice only she can hear. "It is an agony to be so distracted. Yet it is an agony I wished for. That I cannot deny."

There is much she wants to say to him, but she cannot think how to form the words.

He misunderstands her long silence.

"You are sick at heart," he says. "It is why you have come."

"No," she says, feeling a flush of confusion upon her face. She finds it difficult to meet his eye, and suddenly she is acutely aware of her youth, her naïveté. But she also knows that if she allows herself to think of the damage done, she and he will both be lost, that what they have so recently begun will be tainted. "No," she repeats. "I am not sick at heart. I have joy in my heart, and there is no room for anything more."

He glances again in the direction of the knitting woman, who is now unraveling her progress. He takes Olympia's elbow and guides her down the steps. She willingly follows his lead. They walk around to the back of the hotel and stop at a small enclosure. There is a bench, a bicycle leaning against it. They are alone, though still visible from the hotel. They sit on the bench.

He trails his fingers along her skirt from her knee to her hip and lets them linger at the top of her thigh. She puts her hand over his. A chambermaid walks by the opening of the enclosure.

"This is madness," he says, reluctantly removing his fingers. For a time they sit in silence. After a few moments, he remembers the note from her father.

"What is this about a gala?" he asks, taking the note from his pocket. "It is your birthday?"

"Not that day," she says.

He reads the note through again, and then puts it away. She thinks he does not want to be reminded just then of her age.

"Of course, you cannot . . . ," Olympia says.

"But I will have to tell Catherine of this, for she will hear of it anyway," he says. "She will want to come. There will be many instances perhaps . . ."

"It is too far away," Olympia says. "I cannot think about it now. Your cottage will be completed, my father says."

He nods.

"I should like one day to see its progress."

He looks at her in a strange manner. "I cannot speak of normal things with you, Olympia, not in the normal way. It is as though I have lost the habit of normality overnight. The only subject I wish to think about and speak about is you. And why should we remind ourselves of a house in which I will have to live without you?"

"Because it is real," she says. "Because it will happen."

And he seems surprised that already she has thought of the end. "If I had any honor, I would send you away. If I cared for your honor."

His statement rattles her. "What does honor matter in the face of this?" she asks.

He shakes his head. "Nothing, nothing," he says. "Nothing at all. You amaze me, Olympia."

She looks away. A fog is rolling in along the back lawn.

"I have written a letter," Haskell says. "I did this for myself yesterday afternoon. It was not written for you to see. And it is not finished yet, it is merely scribblings. I never thought to give it to you, but now I want to, however imperfect it is."

He reaches into his satchel and removes an envelope. He holds it a minute and then hands it to her. He looks at his watch. "I have to leave you now. I am due at the clinic."

A boy comes into the enclosure and shyly deposits his bicycle. He must be a busboy, Olympia thinks, or a stable hand. Perhaps this is the employees' garden.

Haskell stands abruptly. "I wish it were not this way, Olympia," he says heatedly. "I wish it were I who could come to you."

Olympia stands with him.

"It is not worth wishing for what we cannot have," she says.

Olympia walks with deliberately slow steps along the waterline and through the fog, which is thickening, to her house. She slips as quietly as she can up to her room. But once inside the door, she tears the envelope open. In years to come, she will remember this moment as a somewhat comical scene: her sitting on the bed in a heap, her hat not yet removed, tearing the envelope to bits.

She reads:

14 July 1899

My dearest Olympia,

If ever a man felt his spirit dissolve and meld into another's, it was with you this morning. Why that should be so, I cannot say. This affair we have begun is disastrous for more reasons than I can even begin to enumerate. You are so young, and I am not. You have your entire life ahead of you, which I know that I have damaged irreparably. Forgive me, Olympia. No, do not. One cannot ask for forgiveness for that which one does not regret; and I cannot, as a man and as a lover, regret the precious moments I have been allowed to spend in your presence.

I thought that I was not of the sort to experience a great passion, that such states were fictions written by persons who wished to make more of a natural physical event than was necessary or even advisable. Indeed, my equanimity in such matters was a quality I often congratulated myself in possessing, and having in Catherine as well, who has not ever shown herself to be demonstrably passionate. I am sorry if I offend you by writing to you in such a forthright manner. God knows that if I could, I would apologize to Catherine, too, for exposing her in this way, although I know that she would not permit any apology, just as surely as I know that she would be heartsick by my betrayal of her.

Dearest Olympia, my life has been upended ever since the moment I first saw you at the beach. You do not remember me, but I remember you: a young woman in a dusty pink silk dress that seemed barely to contain the life within its folds. You walked barefooted along the sand, and every man on that beach watched you and desired you. Later, on the porch, when we met for the first time, I felt a profound shock upon seeing you, as if we two had already met.

Heretofore, my life has been one of self-satisfaction, of pride in my work, service to the community, and gratification in my family; but all that must now be something less than it was. Not enough. No, never again enough. How can I explain this to myself, let alone to you? You who are so young and have hardly begun on your journey?

I have prided myself as well in having an instinctive understanding of physical matters, when in fact I did not have the faintest comprehension, not the faintest. I thought I knew myself well — my habits have always been regular — but I find today that I am a stranger to myself, foreign. How placid I used to be, how smug. . . .

How uncommon everything about you is to me. You know much already about how to give pleasure to another, and I think to yourself, which is a quality that is not true of Catherine. Despite her love for me and her desire to please others, she does not know how to please herself. This is not a situation which distresses Catherine much, I think. When such a thing is a given, one knows not what one misses. . . . But I do not think I realized until today how very important a woman's pleasure is to a man's (and how the obverse, of course, must also be true).

You must not regret what you have done, Olympia. You must not feel shame. And I sense — indeed, this is one of the things that so astound me about you — that you do not, that you will not. Not in this. Perhaps in other things, but not in this. Is this self-deception on my part, wishful thinking? I sincerely believe not. I think you understand that which you do. Or am I so deluded as to see only what I wish to see? To wish, and therefore to believe, you to be more mature than your years, to possess a physical under-standing that eludes so many women their entire lives?

(I do not mean to suggest here that you were thinking of your own pleasure today or even that our coming together gave you pleasure, though you will one day feel such physical joy; of this I am certain.)

Forgive me, Olympia. Forgive me for taking from you what is not mine to have.

How rash this all is. How dangerous.

I met Catherine in the second year of my practice. I was much taken with her inner repose and her tenderness. Her father is a minister of the Methodist faith, a man of modest means, though learned and likable, a man whose approval meant something to me. (And, God, how this man would despise me now, if he knew! There is between men, between father and suitor, an understanding of certain aspects of a man's life that cannot be acknowledged outright, and certainly not in the presence of the woman; and so there must be, between the men, a sense of trust, of belief that the daughter who will one day become the wife will not be harmed in any way.

*And though unspoken, it is a kind of sacred trust. I had this with
Catherine's father and felt it necessary to honor. And now I experience the greatest anguish at having betrayed that trust.)*

I cannot write about this.

*I meant to describe to you, you to whom I wish to tell
everything, how it was I came to love Catherine, to want her to be
my wife. I had occasion to observe her often in the role of caretaker
to her nieces, whose mother, Gertrude, had died at an early age
from tuberculosis. I admired the way Catherine was with the children, and I saw she would be an excellent mother to her own. You
will think this opportunistic, and I fancy it was; but she, too, must
have thought me a good prospect as well, for I do not think she
loved me in any grand way when we married — rather in a cheerful and pleasant way, which makes for a good wife and a good
marriage. And I hope I have not been a disappointment to her.*

*(Although I shall be now. I shall wish her you. Every minute.
And for this reason, as well as for the secret in my heart, I dread her
return on Friday evening. I am not of a nature to enjoy deceit.)*

*Why, I ask myself, is passion, when it occurs in circumstances
outside of marriage, so absolutely wrong? This is a question that
vexes me. How can something that feels so true and honest and
pure, which is how I must describe my feelings for you, and I do
declare them love, which I had not thought possible after so short a
time (and how deluded I was again), be so ugly as to cause such
pain? And more vexing still, have no happy conclusion? None . . .
None . . .*

*I cannot deny that I have known Catherine in all the ways pos-
sible to a man and that she has been generous. So why — why? —
has this not been enough? Why? I seek a rational answer when reason is not wanted. I seek a scientific answer where science is not
invited.*

Or is it possible that such a union as I have begun now with you has for its origins a science of its own? Its own physical laws and formulae? Might we one day be able to detect this blinding thing called passion and quantify it and thus save ourselves from this helpless agony?

And yet, could I wish for that? Could I, in truth, wish this elation, this mystery, quantified and thus tamed?

I must stop now, for these are all delusions, dangerous delusions which exhaust me.

I am not a writer, but a man of medicine, infected with an illness so subversive, the patient wishes not for his own cure.

Olympia drops the pages of the letter onto the floor. She covers her face with the skirt of her dress. She sits in that posture for some time.

Never has she read such a letter. Never. Nor understood so well its meaning, nor felt that she might, apart from its specific history, have written it herself.

She releases her skirt. With an impatient tug, she unties the sashes of her bonnet.

My God, she thinks. *What have we done?*

There can be no doubt now that she has set in motion a series of events that cannot be recalled, that she has trespassed unforgivably upon a man and his family, upon a father's trust and a woman's kindness. The only remedy is to cause Haskell to forget her, so as to blunt the edges of this madness. A derangement she herself feels and for which she must now hold herself accountable.

She will never see the man again, she vows, nor permit him to see her. And if he comes to her house, she will absent herself.

How reckless she has been, how selfish, caring only for her own happiness when the greatest possible consequences were at stake. She knows that she would lose her father forever were he to discover her clandestine actions, that never again would he trust her.

She lies back upon the bed and digs the heels of her hands into her eyes. She lies looking at the ceiling for some time, and perhaps because she is exhausted, she sleeps.

She wakes with a start and sits up. She walks over to a table where there are a basin and a pitcher of water kept at the ready. She pours water over her head and face, soaking her hair. She dries her face and scrutinizes herself in the mirror.

And as quickly as tinder igniting, she forgets her earlier resolve. Her desire to see Haskell is so keen that she consciously has to fend off the urge to bend over, as though she had received a blow to the center of her being.

At the very least, she thinks, she and Haskell should discuss the questions and sentiments contained within his letter. Do they not owe it to themselves at least to do that? And if it is too dangerous to speak in person, then should she not write the man a letter? Yes, yes, she should. She will do that now.

And later she will think, How cleverly the mind deceives itself. For the need to respond is never-ending, is it not? He to her, and she to him, and so on?

She does not know what time it is. She has no clock in her room, and she does not want to show herself at this moment downstairs. She peers out at the sea, to discern in the color of the water and the sky the hour of the day, but she is greeted with the same flat light as earlier. Is it afternoon? Has she missed lunch? And if so, why has she not been summoned? She tries to dry her hair as best she can, brushing it and repinning it. She finds paper and pen in the drawer and sits down to write.

My dear sir,
*   And already I am tongue-tied, speechless (what is the equivalent of speechlessness when it be pen and paper and not the tongue?) for I cannot call you sir, nor John, which is the name that others (and*

I am thinking here of Catherine) give you, and in my thoughts, as I have said to you, you are always Haskell, so let me amend my greeting, and though the name may sound too formal, it is, I assure you, not at all, not in my thoughts of you, which are constant.

My dearest Haskell,

How far we have traveled in just a few short hours, hours spent not even in each other's company, but alone with our own thoughts and words, however inadequate they may prove. I meant, upon reading your letter, which I appreciated all the more for its spontaneity and its unfinished circumstances, to insist that we not see each other again, nor communicate, nor allow ourselves to be in each other's company, regardless of the formality of the event. And I meant to do this by not responding to your letter and by severing all that is between us with one fierce blow. But I find that I cannot. There is no part of me that can possibly hold to that resolve. Indeed, I find that I want nothing more than to be with you.

I was at first, I must confess, horrified by your letter, deeply stricken that we had gone so far, and I mean not only in the physical manner that overtook us yesterday but also in the even more consuming realm of the spiritual, which appears to have seized us and will not let us go. I wish to say to you that I am at least as responsible for what happened yesterday as you, and that no matter what happens between us, or what dreadful pass we many come to — for what good outcome can there be? None, I fear, as you do, none — I will never feel myself seduced. I do not have age, but I have will and some understanding, and though the event was new to me, I comprehended it and embraced it and could have stopped it at any point. Even now I can write truthfully that I luxuriate in the memory of yesterday, and though these memories are but faint echoes of the actual, they are treasures I would not willingly part with. The image of you is imprinted upon me as is the light upon photographic paper. I know already that no other human form shall ever be so dear.

(And yes, it was I who disturbed the photographs upon your bureau. But you knew that at once, did you not?)

Yours is the greater anguish, for you are married to a good woman. And though I share that anguish whenever my mind's eye lights upon her face, I know that you must bear the heavier burden, for I cannot know what you know, what you have had with her all these years. (And the sin is knowing that we harm her, is it not? Not simply that we lay together for those moments, but that in writing even these words, we do her conscious, incalculable harm?)

I so very much admire your work. I could not be a physician, for though I have interest in the body, I do not have the courage to face daily the threat of ugliness and death. Nor, curiously, do I have much respect for physicians of the mind, as I feel the soul to be so private a place as to resist invasion. I do sometimes think I should like to be a writer of stories or of verse, though my skills are wanting, and I am not sure what good such an endeavor would serve. I am not yet persuaded of the glorification of art over other endeavors requiring skill and craft. Is there not more good, and therefore more value, in a simply constructed chair? Or a well-made coat? Surely, your poor Rivard woman might think so. I admire you as a writer, but I admire you more as a physician, the skill and kindness of which I have had ample demonstration.

Yes, come to my father's ill-conceived gala. Come. Write my father that you will come. (And do I not now seal my fate with my greatest sin, encouraging the continuation of what we have begun, and worse, in the presence of Catherine and my father, whom we would so willingly betray?) But I cannot, in truth, write that I wish you not here. I will not speak to you beyond the expected, nor cause your wife any distress. I will be content merely to gaze upon you from a distance and know that once we were together in the most intimate of ways. I take pleasure already in imagining the silent words we shall exchange.

Know that in all things I am yours.

She reads and rereads her letter and disciplines her untrammeled thoughts with punctuation and legible cursive. She seals the note, wondering next how best to deliver it. And then she quickly conceives a plan to send it with Josiah. If Josiah should happen to mention his mission to her father, Olympia can explain by suggesting that she felt too unwell to deliver the earlier note herself and finally had to send Josiah to the Highland.

That decided, she leaves her room in search of the man. Checking her appearance for visible signs of the storm that earlier overtook her, she descends the front stairs and listens for clues as to the hour. Her father must be either asleep or in his study, she concludes, moving along the passageway to the kitchen, where she hopes to find Josiah engaged in not so great a task that he cannot be persuaded to deliver her letter. Thus it is that she moves silently through the swinging door and comes upon an extraordinary sight.

She is, for a critical second — the second during which she might have backed unseen through the door — unable to read precisely what she has inadvertently stumbled upon. She sees an indecipherable creature, half standing, half sitting, with limbs wrapped round the body in an improbable position, a flurry of clothing in disarray, a double-image of white globes of flesh, a head thrown back, the smile a rictus on the face. And then, in the next instant, propelled already inside the room, she parses the image and sees that the standing figure with his back to her — but now the face is turning toward her, the body unable to cease its thrusting — is Josiah, and that the limbs around him in a swath of stockings and petticoats are the legs of Lisette. The twinned (and then twinned again) globes of flesh are the buttocks of the man and the breasts of the woman, respectively; the rictus smile the strain of pleasure upon Lisette's face.

The act of love, as Olympia experienced it with Haskell just the day before, was fluid, seemingly a sinuous movement of the flesh. But now, seen with the shocked eye of the unwary observer, the act appears at best comic and at worst brutal, so that nothing of love or tenderness is necessarily conveyed, only the animal-like coupling of two fleshly creatures. She thinks at once of the animality of birth, which also belies its sacred context and its beauty.

Olympia leaves the room, knowing that they have seen her. She leans against the pantry wall and feels the shame that attends the inadvertent voyeur, the shock of interrupting such a private act. Though, curiously, she does not feel horror. And she is grateful that her own knowledge of the event has come as a result of having been with Haskell and not from the sight of the ungainly creature in the kitchen. For she might have been — and who can say for how long? — put off by the notion of physical love altogether.

She holds her letter still, which she tucks into her sleeve. She walks out onto the porch for air. She guesses then that her father must be away, for Josiah would not risk such an incident were he in the house. And then, suddenly, it is all around her: the realities of the body. As she surveys the sea, she comprehends, with the shock of associative leaps, that her mother and her father, too, have shared such a physical life, and that they do still. That her mother's rooms are so overtly feminine and sensual because *her father likes them that way*. She can see her mother's silk nightgown laid out upon the bed each evening, the wisteria satin sheets, the candles at the bedside table, the pots of incense and the many vases of flowers, the elaborate coiffures and toilets of her mother's evenings, and the lengthy absences of her father when he takes her mother up to her room after the evening meal. If Haskell and Josiah are sexual beings, then so, of course, are her father and mother.

Unwilling to imagine further that which should not be contemplated by a daughter, Olympia steps away from these thoughts, simultaneously catching sight of a group of boys playing with a ball on the beach. Seized by an idea, she goes up to her room, fetches some coins from her purse, and walks down to the seawall. She calls to the tallest of the boys, who runs in his short pants, his hair dried stiff into comical sculptures by the salt water and sea breezes, to where she stands.

"I want you to take a letter for me," she says. "To Dr. Haskell, who is at the Highland Hotel. Do you know it?"

"Yes, miss."

"And here are some pennies for your trouble. I wish it to be delivered now."

"Yes, miss. Thank you."

She hands the boy the letter and the coins and watches as he sprints along the hard sand near the water, his form and posture very like those of Mercury himself.

D READFUL FIRE last night in Rye. Have you heard?"

"A fire?" Olympia asks. She crouches on the floor of the porch, trying to unfasten the clasp of the mahogany case that holds the telescope her father ordered from New York for her sixteenth birthday. He intends for the instrument to be set up so that she might have excellent views of the sea and bird life, although privately Olympia suspects that her father and his visitors will use it more often than she, and that when they do, they will turn the instrument in the direction of the summer houses that curve in a shallow half-moon along Fortune's Rocks.

But she is having trouble with the latch.

"Here, allow me," her father says, bending and trailing the tails of his coat along the painted floorboards.

"You said a fire?" Her mind is only half on her task and hardly at all on her father's words.

"Terrible fire. The Centennial Hotel. An ark of a building, long past its heyday. I am told one could not open a window for fear the glass would fall out. The bellhops had to bang on the pipes with a hammer to make the guests believe that the steam heat was coming up. There, you have got it now."

She lifts from its case a brass and wood telescope, complete with collapsible tripod and several extensions. Her father, who seldom revels in material possessions, seems like a child with a new toy at Christmas. Immediately, he stands up and begins to try to assemble the instrument. But, like his daughter, he is impatient with instructions and therefore doesn't read them; and in the end it takes him twice as long to set up the new device as it might have had he studied the enclosed sheet.

"It burned within an hour," her father says. "A tinderbox. They all are. The guests smoke and fall asleep, or the fires start in the ovens. It is the fourth hotel this year to burn."

"Not one of Mr. Philbrick's, I hope," she says.

"No, Rufus has been lucky. Olympia, help me with this. Why are you just sitting there staring out to sea?"

Perhaps she sighs or makes a sound of exasperation.

"Honestly, Olympia," her father says. "I do not understand what is wrong with you. You have become so . . . so . . . I don't know. Addled. Tell me this is not permanent."

"You will need a wrench," she says.

She leaves her father briefly and walks through the house to the kitchen in search of tools, which are in a chest in the back hall. It is true she is distracted. Not only has she had no reply to the letter she sent Haskell the day before but she also has no way at all of ascertaining if he has even received it. She supposes it is possible that the boy to whom she gave the letter simply threw it into the sea and made off with the coins.

"Father, I think we should install a telephone," she says when she returns with the wrench.

"Whatever for?" he asks. "One comes away on holiday precisely to be free of such inventions."

"We might have an emergency. We did have an emergency. We might have telephoned people to come and help us."

"As I recall, we had quite a lot of help, and apart from the loss of life about which you and I could do nothing, we managed rather well under the circumstances."

Olympia reclines on the hammock and watches her father, who is not particularly mechanically minded, assemble the telescope. She thinks it better not to interfere, since two mechanically inept people will inevitably be worse than one. When he finally has the optical device put together, he peers intently into it and adjusts some knobs. He exclaims at the view.

"Olympia, here, you must see this."

She walks over to the telescope and puts her eye to the glass. At first she cannot read what she is looking at. She steps back for a moment and sees that she has the telescope focused on the post of the porch railing. Bending again, she swings the instrument up and out, and then, adjusting a knob, watches as a moving blue mass becomes the sea, a white blur a seagull, and a blot of red a fishing boat bobbing in the water. The view from the telescope is strange to her eye: She can see only highly detailed and disorienting circles within the larger reality, and it is sometimes hard to keep the whole in mind. She thinks there must be some adjustment necessary, since the picture keeps wavering in and out of focus and making her feel woozy. But when she turns the telescope in the direction of the beach, she is rewarded with the sight of the Farragut summer house with its weathered shingles, its misshapen wicker rockers, and its soft expanse of screens at its windows. She sees Victoria's mother sitting in a corner of the porch, an open window through which two white tails of curtains whip in the shore breeze, and a clothesline to one side, where pale blue sheets and pillow slips billow out and then collapse. Leaving the Farragut cottage, Olympia maneuvers the telescope slowly along the waterfront, scanning each summer house, noting certain features she has not been able to perceive from ground level — the shapes of the roofs or the number of gables —

until eventually the instrument rests upon the facade of the Highland Hotel. For a time, she studies the hotel's porch, its long front lawn, and even the windows of certain rooms she has an interest in. There are many persons about, but since she cannot see the figure she is looking for, she deduces that Haskell must be at the clinic or still in his rooms. Thus it is that she is doubly startled to hear her father say, right behind her, and with some surprise and pleasure, "Well, hello, John."

Haskell, in a wheat-colored suit, stands in the doorway, holding his boater in his hand. For one terrible moment, Olympia thinks he has come to tell her father of their affair and that he has brought her letter as evidence. But as soon as she sees Haskell's eyes, and their particular mix of anguish and anticipation, her fear gives way to reason. He walks forward and takes her hand in greeting.

"Olympia," he says, "it is a pleasure to see you again."

"And to see you," she says.

He lets her hand go reluctantly.

"Your father has been keeping you busy."

"I was just commenting to Olympia that she seems abnormally distracted this summer," her father says.

Haskell searches her face. "On such a lovely perch," he says, "I should be more than mildly distracted myself."

As good manners require, Haskell turns his attention to the telescope. "But what do you have here, Biddeford?"

"It arrived today," her father says with some pride.

"Handsome instrument," Haskell says. "May I take a look?"

He bends and peers out at the view, adjusting the focus to his own eyesight.

"This has excellent resolution, Biddeford," he says. He swings the telescope farther down the beach and adjusts a knob. "May I show you something? Come and see, Olympia."

She walks to where Haskell stands, and peers into the glass. She is aware of him hovering over and behind her and feels his leg press slightly against her own. It is some moments before she can focus properly, but when she does, she can make out the wooden skeleton of a beach cottage. It is perched atop a hillock of dunes and is surrounded with sand and cut grass. It will be, she sees, a large house with its own deep porches. A wide gable has been framed and already holds in its center a massive round window with many small panes. She wonders whose room that window will one day belong to. To Martha's? To Haskell and his wife's?

Olympia looks up and moves to one side. Her father takes her place and studies the house. "Beautifully designed, Haskell," he exclaims. "Truly. And the builders are making quite a progress. They still anticipate finishing by the first of August?"

"I am told they will be a week late," Haskell says. He twirls the boater in his hands. "Why do you not come with me now to see the house, Biddeford? If you can spare the time, I have several questions I could use some advice on."

Clearly flattered and pleased, Olympia's father, in the next instant, looks crestfallen. "Damn," he says with evident disappointment. "I should have loved to have visited the site with you, John, but I have promised myself to my dentist. Damn. If only I could reach him . . ."

"If we had a telephone, Father . . . ," Olympia says, unable to resist a smile.

Her father clears his throat. "My daughter is of the opinion that we should install a telephone at Fortune's Rocks, but I have tried to explain to her that one comes away on holiday precisely to ignore such instruments." He shakes his head. "No, I cannot go with you," he adds.

"Another time then," Haskell says politely.

"But Olympia would love to go," her father says suddenly to Haskell, as if she were not even present on the porch. "In fact, it would be an excellent diversion for her," he adds. "She has not been herself of late and could do with an outing."

Haskell catches Olympia's eye. "I would be honored to show her the site," he says. "If you think she would not become too bored."

"I doubt I should become bored," Olympia says quietly.

"Then that is settled," her father says wistfully. "And I hope you have also come to tell me, John, that you and Catherine will attend the gala we are having. Did I write you that it is in honor of Olympia's sixteenth birthday?"

The reminder of Olympia's age in both Haskell's and her father's presence sends, for a moment, a slight tremor into the air that Olympia thinks even her father must notice, for he looks first at Haskell and then at her.

"An important milestone, surely," Haskell says. "Of course, I must ask Catherine first before I can commit us to the event."

"Hale will be here," her father announces proudly.

"Hale," Haskell says, looking at Olympia as if he cannot remember why he knows the name. "Hale," he repeats. "Yes, of course." There is a pause. "Olympia, shall we go?"

He helps her up into the bottle green carriage.

"I could not stay away," he says. He climbs up beside her. "I inhaled your letter. If I could, I would have you write me every day."

"I *shall* write to you every day then," Olympia says. "But you must promise to destroy the letters."

"I am not sure I will be able to do that."

"Then I will not write them, because I will not take the chance that they might be discovered by Catherine."

"Well, then, I will tell you I will destroy them, but actually I will not," he says.

And she cannot help but smile.

Haskell does not take them along the coast road, as he suggested to Olympia's father he would, but rather veers immediately onto the Ely road. The tide is low, and the marshes are gullied out for as far as Olympia can see. The mud makes miniature cliffs and canyons within the larger labyrinth. When the two of them are out of sight of the house, Haskell draws abruptly to the side of the road.

"I have something for you," he says.

He takes a tiny velvet box out of his pocket and opens it. She is not prepared for the locket, an exquisite gold oval with her initials delicately engraved on its surface.

"I cannot," she says.

"Yes, Olympia, you can. I want you to."

The gold shines warmly in the sunlight.

"There is so little I can give you," he says. "Please accept this. Let me have the pleasure of knowing that you wear it."

He turns her shoulders so that he can fasten the clasp behind her neck.

"I shall never take it off," she says, turning back.

"I know that you cannot allow others to see it," he says. "But you can wear it like this." He slips the pendant beneath the collar of her dress. She can feel the gold falling between her breasts. He rubs the back of his finger against the cloth where the locket has fallen. And perhaps it is that intimate gesture, that one gesture out of a hundred gestures, that makes the tears come into her eyes.

"I meant to make you happy," he says, pulling her toward him. "Oh, Olympia, this is all wrong for you."

She draws away from him and dries her eyes. She sniffs once. "The question of whether or not what we do is wrong for me is irrelevant," she says, unwilling to repudiate what they have so recently won. "Of course it is wrong for me. More so for you. It is wrong altogether. But I thought we had agreed not to squander our joy by chastising ourselves."

Her hat falls backward and tumbles into the grass. He laces his fingers through the bun of her hair and draws her head back so that her throat is exposed. She is twisted, contorted on the wooden seat, and her skirt is already rucked up to her knees. Their embrace is awkward, and he cannot reach her from the side. He jumps down from the wooden seat, takes her hand, and leads her into the marshes.

Together, they sink to their knees, the tall grass bending beneath them, and he pulls her farther down so that they are lying together on their sides, facing each other. He struggles out of his jacket and slips out of his braces. He unfastens the front of her dress while she pulls his shirt from his trousers. The cloth billows out like a parachute. She slips her hand up the length of his chest, and it seems the boldest touch of her life.

Nearby, she can hear the low whomp and flutter of a bird's wing beating against the water. Something sharp digs into her side. The sun is so blinding, she has to shift his face over hers to shield her eyes. She wants to say the word *beloved* aloud. She hesitates, then does so — once, then twice, then three times — the word emerging in gasps, as if she were being pummeled. *Olympia,* Haskell whispers into the side of her hair.

He takes her earlobe into his mouth and presses the heel of his hand against her through the cloth of her dress. There is a quickening through her body. With an instinct she has not known she possesses, her hips rise to meet his hand. *How is it that the body knows?* She stretches her legs and pushes herself urgently against him. The new sensations within her are keen and knife-edged. Her shoulders slide down against the grass, and she arches her back. Haskell holds her tightly, his face buried in her neck.

They lie together in the marshes. The wet seeps through the grass. "I could not have imagined this," she says.

She wants to speak further of this thing that has shaken her body as if it were a rag doll, this thing that has left her with a curious thread of lingering desire. She wants Haskell to be inside of her, as he was in his room. She cannot think of how to tell him this except to raise her skirts.

How astonishingly bold she is becoming, she thinks.

"Is this how it is?" she asks him. "Is this the secret all men and women share?"

"Some have this," he says. "Not all. Most men do. There are women who do not ever have this, who cannot allow themselves to have it."

And Catherine, Olympia instantly wonders. *How is it with Catherine?*

"We cannot lie here," he says.

They help each other up, and he kisses her. "I will take you to the cottage now," he says. "We will sit in the sun, and our clothes will dry there."

Her legs are wobbly, and she has to pull herself up into the carriage with her hands. Her dress is damp all along one side.

Haskell takes up the reins, turns the horses around, and heads in the direction of the new cottage. He reaches for her hand, which he holds in the folds of her skirt.

"You flirt with risk," she says.

"It is not normally my nature." He presses his hand against her leg. "Sometimes I say to myself that we must never see each other again, and I am resolved in this —"

Her heart seizes up at this pronouncement.

"— and then, within seconds, I understand that such discipline will not ever be possible."

They travel the length of the coast road, Olympia praying that they will not encounter anyone known to her. After a time, he draws the buggy up to the skeleton of the new cottage. Olympia can see that it will have a stunning view, with only the Atlantic for a front yard. He helps her down from the carriage and takes her arm. She wonders if her father is even now trying to see them through the telescope, if she now exists in its circular universe. Most of the cottage has been framed, and there are many places through which one can see the ocean. Olympia begins to imagine fancifully what it would be like to enclose such a house entirely in windows — to have light always, to feel surrounded by sand and ocean.

"I am not sure I have ever seen a house being built," she says.

Together they enter the cottage and move through rooms that for now exist only in the imagination, rectangular and oblong chambers framed in pine and oak, forming a house that will one day shelter a family. She wonders how such a structure might be built, how one knows precisely where to put a post or a beam, how exactly to make a window. From time to time, Haskell murmurs beside her, "This will be the kitchen," or "This will be the sun parlor," but she does not attend him closely. She prefers, for the moment, to think of the house as ephemeral and insubstantial.

"This is the dining room," he says when they have come to a stopping place that has been partially enclosed.

And she cannot help but think of the dozens of dinners he and Catherine will one day have in this room. Perhaps even Olympia might be invited to such a dinner and will sit where she is standing now. She shakes her head quickly and turns away.

"What is it?" he asks.

"This . . . ," she says. "It is not important."

"I should not have brought you here."

"How old is Catherine?" Olympia asks.

"Thirty-four," Haskell says tentatively.

"And how old are you?"

"Forty-one."

"Do you have family? I mean, do you have brothers and sisters? Are your parents still living?"

"My mother is still living. My father is not. My mother lives with my sister in Cambridge. I have a brother who is a minister in Milton."

A sensation, as though her chest were being squeezed, overtakes her. Why, she asks herself, the first of many times she will ask this question, must love be so punishing? Why, so quickly upon the heels of the moments of her greatest joy, must she be haunted with images that produce only pain: images of Haskell with another, speaking words that might have been saved for her, sharing intimacies that she can hardly bear to think about? Why, she asks herself, as she stands in this room that is not yet a room, does she have to imagine, in the greatest of detail, a meal Haskell will share not with her but with his wife? In his letter to her, he wrote that he has known Catherine in "all the ways possible to a man." The phrase is haunting in its implications. Even as Haskell takes Olympia's hand, she is visited by an image of Haskell holding Catherine's hand; and though the persistent touch of him slowly brings Olympia to her senses and momentarily overwhelms all thoughts of the past, she feels an ache that will, if she lets it, blunt her joy and abrade the edges of her pleasure.

This time they are quick, as though at any minute her father might come looking for them or a stray craftsman might wander in. They are forced to stand, to lean against a wall. She did not think the body could so quickly want again. She feels a double guilt, the guilt of their betrayal and the additional guilt of embracing in the house that will one day belong to Haskell and his wife. But mingled with the guilt is a strange and quiet rapture, a resting in the moment, not thinking of the next thing or the next. And with it as well a distinct sense of possession. The house is not hers, but the moment is, and it cannot be taken from her.

Just before they leave, she slips a finger under the gold chain and brings the locket out from under her dress. "Thank you for this," she says, kissing him.

"It is only a locket," he says.

"No," she says. "It is not."

FOR A WHILE, she will be able to remember each of the days she and Haskell had together: what he wore on the first day, what she wore on the second, the day they lunched together in the hotel and what they had to eat, the formal way they greeted each other and spoke in public, and all the words they said in between. She will recall vividly the late afternoon they went boating in the marshes, losing themselves amidst the watery maze. And the night she left her bedroom in a frenzy, not caring if she was discovered, running barefoot along the beach, luxuriating in the darkness, and then seeing the lighted windows of the hotel as a refuge, a sanctuary, and weeping for the joy of it. She will remember every endearment and sentence of love, as well as all the words of a tearful argument she and Haskell had when he chastised himself severely for having seduced her, and she could not, with all her skill, convince him that she was at least, *at least,* as responsible as he for what had happened between them.

But in years to come, she will have only images, blurred images, a sense of how it was, but not its precise content: a face, not clean-shaven, turned slightly to the side; the smell of damp skin that sometimes followed her when she left him; an ivory crepe blouse she wore often that he liked; her kneeling on the sand, laughing at the sight of him in a bathing costume; his hand slipping from the sole of her foot, up along her calf and thigh; a plate of oysters that he had sent to his room and that they devoured beneath the sheets; the wistful tilt of his head as he stood at the threshold of his room when he waved good-bye to her . . .

Sometimes it feels to Olympia as though she and Haskell are always saying good-bye. While he works at the clinic, she conjures up reasons to be away from her house during the odd hours of his leisure, and occasionally it requires all of her wits to create suitable excuses for her absences. To this end, she has invented an entire cast of friends and acquaintances and occupations, and as far as her father is concerned, she has taken up golf in a rather passionate way. Olympia has selected the sport because her father himself does not play, and thus there seems little danger he will one day challenge her to a game — which is fortunate, since she herself has not the faintest idea of how to hit the ball or make it go into the little cups below the flags. Olympia has also created "friendships" with a number of young women, Julia Fields amongst them, to appease her parents' curiosity about her suddenly hectic social life. Once or twice, she is nearly caught at these fictions, and several times she feels acutely ashamed at how unconscionably skilled she has become at lying.

Her father, she knows, is puzzled by her new behavior and appears to reevaluate his daughter at every turn. He no longer regards her as the girl he loved and cherished in June, but rather looks at her as at a foreign creature, one who is perpetually distracted. Suddenly she has become a poor scholar who has difficulty attending to his informal lectures. She tries his patience and confuses him and makes him sad, she knows, more often than she makes him happy. As for her mother, Olympia is quite sure she thinks her daughter has a beau. Several times she has asked Olympia questions designed to cajole her into sharing a confidence, to elicit a boy's name. Occasionally, when her mother is looking at her, Olympia can see her running through the names of sons of families who are summering in the area.

Despite these awkward moments, Olympia knows she is fortunate in that both of her parents are, by nature, often preoccupied with other matters: her father with his intellectual life, her mother with a world that requires nearly all of her wits to absent herself from. For certain, there are challenging interruptions in this routine, such as when Haskell's schedule changes and suddenly permits them to be together, and he is able to get word to her; but these hiatuses Olympia disguises as best she can. Altogether, their affair is a reckless endeavor, although they have agreed never to be together when Catherine and the children come for the weekends. Nor has Haskell visited Olympia's house again.

They have been several times now to the site of the new cottage, the construction sheltering them more each day. They go in the early mornings or in the evenings when the workmen have not arrived at the site or have left already. As the frame is filled in, it becomes easier to be together behind and under the thick wooden beams and cedar shingles. They make love in the room that will be a sun parlor, under an eave that might one day grace a servant's bedroom, on the hard floor of the room at the back that will be a kitchen. On this occasion, Haskell brings rashers of bacon that he filched from the hotel kitchen and that they cook over the hearth along with slices of bread, and later Olympia will not be able to remember eating anything as delicious as those bacon sandwiches. Curiously, being together makes her ravenous, and so there is often food, and sometimes a good deal of it, and even occasionally champagne. As a result, she is filling out some and developing, in her bosom and thighs and stomach, the body of a woman — as though her outer form sought to catch up to the experiences of her inner life.

With interest, Olympia has watched as the windows of the cottage have taken shape and been glazed, as the entrance to the cottage has been fashioned and then enclosed with massive wooden double doors, as the floors have been sanded and polished and covered with painted floorcloths, as the bedrooms have been adorned with moldings and the roof overhead enclosed against the stars. It is, as the days progress, as though Haskell and she are being further separated from the universe — set off, set apart — and are allowed ever more daringly to explore each other.

It is a beautiful cottage, she thinks, with many gables and wide porches and a delicately carved tracery under and along the eaves. The upper panes of the windows have diamond panels of lavender glass, and a rich cherry wainscoting has been installed in all the public rooms. Situated as it is directly on the beach, it has an unencumbered and unparalleled view of sand and sea. It is a house in which memories will be made, a house that will be handed down from father to daughter to son, a house in which Haskell will live with his wife.

They lie on the floor, entangled in rugs and cloths stained with peach juice that has dribbled off their chins and onto the bunched material they hold to their chests as napkins. Olympia is wearing the locket and nothing else. A plate with cheese and mango chutney and the crusts of brown bread is listing precariously on her thigh, leaving a smear of amber-colored chutney on the makeshift sheet.

"Ollie is a boy's name," she protests. "From Oliver."

"No. It could be a derivative of Olivia," he says.

"But it might be from Olaf," she says, again giving a boy's name.

"Olive," he answers, taking up the challenge.

"Olney," she says, not to be outdone.

"Olinda," he answers quickly.

She thinks a minute. "Olin."

"No," he says. "I cannot accept that."

"Then . . ." She concentrates. "Ole."

"Fair enough," he says. But he will not be bested at this game. "Olwen," he trumpets.

"But that is a man's name," Olympia protests.

"No, actually it is not."

She narrows her eyes. "Oleksandr!" she cries.

He thinks awhile and tilts his head. Then he kisses her. "I believe you have won," he says graciously.

"Thank you, Dr. Haskell," she says, fitting herself against him. And then, rather abruptly, she asks: "Do you think our love for each other is the same?"

"How do you mean?"

"Well, your images and your memories surely are not so much of yourself as they are of me, while I see only you and feel only you and speak only to you. And do you not, because you are a man, with a man's sensibilities and a man's body, have different sensations than I and therefore different recollections?"

"All lovers seek the illusion of oneness," he answers. "But you are right. Most of a love affair is in the mind."

"Is it?" she asks.

"Of course, there are the times when we are together," he says. "When we express our love for each other. But do not these episodes but feed the true and ravenous lovers, which are the minds, creatures unto themselves? So that love is not simply the sum of sweet greetings and wrenching partings and kisses and embraces, but is made up more of the *memory* of what has happened and the *imagining* of what is to come."

"But if that were true," she says, "then it would not be necessary to be physically together at all. We could just simply imagine it, and be done with it. And not worry about being caught out or about hurting anyone else."

"Yes. Well . . . ," he says. "The imagination must have fuel. It must have something to base its memories on. In the beginning, when we would meet, I used to marvel how it was that we never began exactly where we had left off, but seemed to have progressed to yet another level, and then another. The mind is intolerably impatient. It can imagine the whole of a love affair in an instant."

There is a sudden and strained silence between them.

"Have you done that?" she asks quietly. "Have you imagined the whole of us?"

"Yes," he answers, "and you have done so as well."

She stands and walks to a window, having long since lost her modesty in his presence. "The house will be ready by the weekend?" she asks.

"Yes."

"Then Catherine and the children will be returning for good," she adds, stating an obvious truth that has been gnawing at her for some time.

"Yes," he answers simply. He climbs out of the bed and stands beside her at the window.

"What is it?" he asks, although he already knows.

The future lies like a thickening gas all around them. They both dread Catherine's return, for not only will it mean that the house, *their house,* the one Olympia and Haskell have christened and have loved in, will be occupied; but also it will mean that Haskell will have to move out of the Highland Hotel. Thus, they will have nowhere to meet. For Olympia, the tenth of August looms in the future not as a date of celebration, but rather as a day on which a particularly painful sentence is to begin.

"We have run out of time," she says.

"If we wallow in the pain," he says, "we shall have spent all our pleasure already. It was you who taught me this."

"My father's gala will be a grotesque charade. I shall feign illness."

Though they both know that she cannot.

Beyond the salt-encrusted windows, they can see the noontime bathers on the beach. They watch as a man in a bowler hat constructs an elaborate canopy of wooden stilts and canvas around and above the stiff figure of a woman. She sits rigidly on a collapsible wooden chair and stares at the water. The day is hot, with a sort of lemon haze all along the shore, and she is overdressed in a heavy black taffeta suit. And though she wears a hat, and her husband is frantically trying to construct the canopy, she holds a black ruffled parasol at a precisely vertical angle. The haughty and cold demeanor of the woman is a painful contrast to the too-eager-to-please mien of the husband and seems to suggest an imbalance in the marriage, if indeed it is a marriage, or a desire on the part of the man to make amends for an unknown transgression. Olympia wishes suddenly, looking at the water, that she could bathe in the sea right now and that Haskell could join her.

She rests her head on his shoulder. She knows much about him now: the tufts of hair between his knuckles, the cords at the back of his thighs, the hushed pause, as though all the world held its breath, and then the low, quick exhalation of pleasure. But sometimes doubts creep into her thoughts, and she cannot help herself from wondering: Might Catherine know things about Haskell that Olympia has not had time to learn?

"What a silly woman," Haskell says, watching the sad comedy of the chastened husband and his overdressed wife.

He moves behind her and wraps his arms just under her breasts. He looks out the window over her shoulder. "Now, *they* look to be having a better time," he says, pointing through the window at a couple with a young child sitting on a rug near the water.

The wife is dressed in a loose white shift and has her skirts pulled up to her knees. She seems relaxed, though Olympia notes that she does not take her eyes off the child playing in front of her in the water. The woman's husband has been bathing, for his costume droops with the wet. He sits beside his wife and runs his fingers up and down the thin cloth of the back of her dress. Olympia feels a keen, not to say ferocious, pang of jealousy and regret. For Haskell and she will never have what that couple have and, perhaps because it is so easy for them, cannot value as much as they might: a child, a marriage, the ability to sit outside in public and touch each other.

She turns quickly toward Haskell. There is again the lightning within her body, that endlessly repeatable lightning. The need for the relief and release only he can offer. She puts her face against the pad of his shoulder.

"We have only one more day," she says.

As if echoing the man and wife outside, Haskell strokes her back with his fingers.

"In our imaginations," he says, "we have a lifetime."

She is later than she has said she would be, and as she walks, she composes excuses: *Victoria's mother asked me to stay for tea. They were getting up a croquet match at the hotel. Julia and I were playing duets on her piano, and I lost track of the time.* The sand is hard, and her dress is wrinkled. She looks up toward her house, dreading having to enter it, and when she does, she is startled to see that her mother and Catherine Haskell and Zachariah Cote are sitting on the porch.

But surely Catherine is in York, Olympia thinks.

Olympia instinctively turns and bends to the sand as if she had dropped a handkerchief or purse.

My God, she thinks. *We might have been caught.*

Slowly, she stands and tries to smooth her skirts. Her fingers feel for the buttons at her collar to see that they are fastened. She checks to see that the locket is inside her dress. When she turns, her mother is already waving to her, beckoning her to join them. Olympia walks toward the house and makes her way up the porch steps.

"Olympia," Catherine says when she has reached them. "I am so glad to see you. How are you surviving this ghastly weather?"

"Olympia seems to have a secret life these days," her mother answers for her.

"Indeed," says Cote, flashing her a smile.

"Tell me about it," Catherine pleads. "You have a young man."

"No," Olympia says in a confused manner.

"Olympia, do sit down," her mother says.

"It is just that I have made a number of friends here this summer, and I have been much occupied with them," Olympia says in a voice tight with strain, a strain she thinks neither Catherine nor Cote can fail to notice.

"Olympia has learned to play tennis," her mother says. Beside her, Olympia can feel Cote's scrutiny.

"How delightful," Catherine says.

"Catherine has returned a day early," Olympia's mother explains to Olympia. "She means to surprise John."

"But I was seized with a sudden desire to visit your mother," Catherine says, leaning toward Olympia and placing a hand on her knee. "To discuss this exciting gala in your honor on Saturday night. Your mother has been telling me all about your dress."

"And I have come early as well," Cote says. "I did not want to have to travel north on that dreadful Friday train, and so I have slipped out of the city early. Indeed, I think I shall stay on in Fortune's Rocks for a while now." He pauses for effect. "I am sure the muse will find me here," he adds, smiling again in Olympia's direction. He accepts another cup of lemonade from Olympia's mother and settles back into his chair.

"I used to play tennis as well," Olympia's mother says in a surprising non sequitur.

Olympia hardly dares look at either her mother or Catherine.

"I was rather good," her mother adds shyly. "Actually, I had a beau once who was a tennis player. Before Phillip, that is."

Olympia struggles to attend to what her mother is saying. She wonders if she should alert Haskell somehow, tell him of Catherine's arrival. She tries to remember if they left anything at the cottage.

"He was the son of a carriage-maker in Rowley," her mother says, warming to her subject.

"Oh, Rosamund, do tell us . . . ," says Cote.

"There is so little to tell."

"Rosamund, you must," Catherine insists.

Her mother looks away and then back at her hands, which are folded in her lap.

"I met him on a day that I was asked to accompany Papa on an errand to his carriage-maker," she says. "I was young, maybe seventeen, and we had been coming north for only a half a dozen summers. Papa went into the shop, but I was left to wait in the buggy. I remember that I was very cross at this, because it was hot and I was thirsty and he seemed to be taking an inordinately long time. But while I was sitting there, a young man came over to the carriage." She raises a hand to smooth her hair and only then seems to realize that she has committed herself to her tale.

"What did he look like?" asks Catherine.

"He had pale blond eyebrows and thick blond eyelashes," Olympia's mother says.

"What was his name?" asks Cote.

"Gerald," her mother says. "He used to say that he was Welsh, but

178

my father insisted that he was Irish. I liked him very much. We talked for quite a while that day. So that by the time Papa returned, Gerald and I had somehow already arranged a meeting at a tennis club the following morning." She pauses. "Over the next several weeks, he and I contrived to meet often. I would leave the house and walk a ways, and we would meet at an arranged place. I do not know why, but on the last morning we were to be together, I had decided that I was going to tell him that I liked him, for I sensed that he liked me greatly in return."

She is thoughtful for a moment, as though if she waits long enough, she might be given a reprieve and be allowed another ending to her story. "We had planned that day to drive to the beach in Hampton for a picnic. And as we were walking onto the sand, he leaned over toward me and said something to me that in all these years I have tried to reconstruct, to hear. But before he could repeat the phrase to me, a man my father had paid to follow us came up behind him and took him away."

"Rosamund, no," Catherine says.

"I spent the rest of the summer more or less locked in my room."

"How dreadful," Cote says.

"I never heard from Gerald again," Olympia's mother says. "You see, I had no way to reach him, nor any access to anyone who would have known him. I did not even have an address to write to. But later that summer, I was allowed out of the house to attend a tennis match in Exeter. Since I was going with my father and mother, I suppose they thought little harm could come to me.

"During the interval, however, when I went in search of a glass of water, I came across a trophy case in the lobby. Inside it were medals and plaques and photographs of winning teams. Gerald's picture was in one of those photographs. I slid the glass open and reached in and removed the photograph. I hid it in my dress. When I got home, I took a pair of scissors from my sewing box and cut out his picture. I have it still."

"You must show us this photograph," says Cote.

"Perhaps I will," she says, bringing her glass to her lips. And as she does so, she suddenly looks different to Olympia, physically different, as though a portrait had been altered. And Olympia thinks that possibly such adjustments might have to be made for everyone she knows. Upon meeting a person, a sketch is formed, and for the life of the relationship, however intimate or not, a portrait is painted, with oils or with pastels or with black ink or with watercolor, and only at the person's death can the portrait be considered finished. Perhaps not even at the person's death.

"It is a lovely story," says Catherine, though Olympia is hard-pressed to see the value of having one's destiny arbitrarily denied.

"I never knew what he said," Olympia's mother adds. "How often I have wished that I could just go back and *hear* him."

Catherine reaches over and briefly holds Olympia's mother's hand.

"Doubtless you have been missing that handsome husband of *yours*," says Cote to Catherine, changing the subject rather too soon, Olympia thinks.

"I do miss him terribly," Catherine says. "Yes, of course I do. I cannot wait for the cottage to be finished. I am just on my way there now."

Olympia can feel the perspiration trickling down her spine.

"And where *is* the good doctor this afternoon?" Cote asks.

"I believe he is working at the clinic," Catherine answers. "In fact, he does not even know I am here. I mean to surprise him."

"And he will, I am sure, be very much surprised," Cote says. He turns to look over the porch railing. "My God, what a beautiful view. And, if I am not mistaken, I actually feel a breeze. What a relief to be on this lovely porch and not in Ely Falls."

"You were in Ely Falls just now?" Olympia's mother asks.

"I had need of a tailor. Some last-minute alterations. For the gala."

"Yes, of course."

"I must say, I cannot abide these Francos," Cote says.

"Really?" asks Olympia's mother, glancing quickly at Olympia.

"My tailor, such an impertinent little man with his oiled mustaches, pretending to be grander than he is. As do all the Francos, I might add."

"Olympia, dear, do you know the time?" Olympia's mother asks.

"It is common knowledge that they are all libertines and profoundly corrupt. Not to mention drunkards and dullards both."

"Zachariah," Olympia's mother says finally in mild reproof, reminding him of Olympia's presence.

"Forgive me, Rosamund. One does get carried away. But I will say they are a blight upon our Yankee cities. I fear their encroachment upon Ely and Fortune's Rocks. Indeed, some days the beach is positively teeming with them."

An odd comment, Olympia thinks, from someone who himself is not even a summer resident of Fortune's Rocks. And then, as she studies his face — its handsome planes, the aquiline nose, the lavender eyes (possibly too close together?) — she has a sudden image of a sign she once passed on the way to Ely Falls: Coté and Reny. And then she has a thought that leads wickedly to another thought and a temptation she cannot resist.

"I am surprised at your distaste for the Franco-Americans, Mr. Cote," Olympia says. "Indeed, I was just wondering: Is not Coté French?" she asks, giving the name its foreign pronunciation.

Her astute, though inexcusably rude, guess causes him to look rebuffed and to hold himself upright. He compresses his lips into a thin smile. "No, actually, it is an old English name," he says, and Olympia is suddenly certain that he is lying.

There is an awkward silence, during which Olympia can feel her mother's cold stare.

"Pity John is not here, Catherine," says Cote, "for I know he bears Olympia, and of course Rosamund as well, a special affection, does he not?"

The comment sends a small jolt of alarm through Olympia.

Catherine seems not to notice the reference to her husband and Olympia in the same sentence, even though the suggestive way in which Cote has put Olympia's name before her mother's is unsettling, not to say rude.

"He . . . well, of course . . . I think he regards Rosamund . . . and Olympia . . . Yes, surely," Catherine finishes, uncharacteristically flustered.

"Has Hale arrived yet?" Cote asks Olympia's mother, giving away, Olympia thinks, the reason for his visit.

"No. Phillip says he will not arrive until Saturday."

A quick flash of disappointment crosses the poet's face. "He will come up from Exeter or Boston?" he asks.

"Boston. Do you know the family?"

"Well, yes, I do rather," Cote says. "The New York branch. Hale's cousin married a Plaisted, did he not?"

"Lavinia. Yes."

"She is a second cousin to my aunt," Cote says, perhaps wishing to emphasize his Yankee connections. "Of course, my cousins regard Hale as something of a black sheep. Not done to have a writer in the family, is it?" he asks in what is meant to be self-deprecating wit but which somehow fails to elicit the proper response in his audience. He takes a long sip of lemonade and turns toward Olympia. "We were sorry to miss you on the Fourth. I rather think the Farraguts were expecting you at their party."

The mention of Haskell and the holiday within seconds of each other cannot be unintentional on Cote's part, Olympia thinks. She breathes shallowly so as not to betray her concern. For Cote, she realizes, is cannily feral in his instincts and will smell out any note of fear.

"I was engaged elsewhere," Olympia says.

"I daresay you were," says Cote. "But I have had the great joy of running into Olympia this summer in all manner of places," he adds to the two older women.

"Oh?" asks Olympia's mother, looking at her daughter. "And where might that have been? I should most sincerely like to know. Olympia has been rather a puzzle to me for weeks."

"Has she indeed?" he says. He gestures toward the sandwiches. "May I?"

"Of course," her mother says. "Olympia, a sandwich?"

"I am not hungry," she says quickly. "And, actually, I must go. I told Julia I would ride with her."

"In this heat?" Cote asks. "Surely not. It would be a crime upon the horses."

Olympia thinks, The gall of the man.

"Of course, we now have the pleasurable anticipation of the gala in Olympia's honor," Cote says, ignoring Olympia's discomfort and fastidiously wiping a dab of mayonnaise from the corner of his mouth. "You will be how old?"

"Sixteen," she says.

"Such a lovely age, do you not think, Catherine?"

"Indeed," says Catherine. "A lovely age. I was just saying so to Rosamund before you arrived."

Cote gazes at Olympia with open impertinence. "Why so glum, child?" he asks, taking another bite of sandwich. "Smile. Life cannot possibly be all that bad."

And Olympia, never having liked being told to smile by anyone, much less Zachariah Cote, and suddenly weary of innuendo, syco-phantic banter, and a nearly intolerable moral unease, stands up from her chair and excuses herself. She walks through the house, out the back door, and down to the seawall, where she takes off her boots and her stockings, abandons them where they lie, and runs as fast as ever she has along the hard-packed surface of the beach.

ON THE MORNING of the tenth, Olympia sits in her room, gazing out the window, unable to move or speak or read or think, enclosed within a catatonic state, as if deaf and dumb. Try as she might to banish such thoughts, she can think of nothing other than the fact that Catherine and the children are moving into the new cottage right at this very hour; and she cannot help but be pierced with the irony of Mrs. Haskell's gliding about the house, unaware of its previous tenants, thinking it is her own, all her own, which of course it now is. Olympia tries to imagine, her imagination sharpened by intimate knowledge of both Haskell and the cottage, how he will manage in such an awkward and painful situation. Surely he will not be able to share in his wife's joy. But can he feign interest? Or is he, like her, enveloped in a similar catatonic state? And if so, does Catherine notice and then comment?

Haskell and Olympia parted only yesterday, by tacit agreement not speaking of their plight, for to give it more words was to give it more life. And to give it life was to find no words, no satisfactory answers. She could not release him from his marriage, nor could she properly bid him farewell, and so they stood, mute, at the entrance to his rooms, looking at each other and then apart, Olympia having the greater burden, for it was her lot to have to walk away.

Her footsteps echoed in the stairwell. She was surprised that her legs worked at all. At the bottom of the stairs, she had to lean against the newel post before walking through the etched glass doors. It was, for her, a tearing away, not only from Haskell himself, the person of Haskell, but also from the idyll that had been the summer. For she knew that even if Haskell and she were to devise a way to be together, it would not ever be the same.

Occasionally, over the past few weeks, in the privacy of her own thoughts, she has envisioned for Haskell and herself a life together, the two of them living in rooms in Ely Falls or in Cambridge. Perhaps Olympia would help him with the clinic, or she could become a teacher. They would have children together and would make a home. But after a few moments, she cannot much enjoy these thoughts, for simultaneous with these fantasies is the realization that such a life can be had only with the unhappiness of a spurned wife and of real children; and Olympia knows that no man could sustain any happiness of his own at such an exorbitant cost. Even assuming Haskell could bear Catherine's pain, he would not be able to forfeit Martha and Clementine and Randall and May without irreparable damage. Worse than all the other horrors is the image of her and Haskell one day sitting across a table, unable to look each other in the eye. Surely it is better to long for each other than to despise each other, she thinks.

Below her on the ground floor, she can hear much activity, as deliverymen and servants call to one another across the rooms, or furniture is moved, or flowers are brought into the house. Her father has sent to Boston for the family's best china and silver and crystal, and as a result, wooden packing crates and straw litter the porch. Her parents expect a hundred and forty guests for dinner and dancing, and have set up a long white tent upon the lawn. There the visitors will dine at midnight on lobster and champagne and oysters and blueberries. Masses of lavender-blue hydrangea blossoms crowd the railing of the porch. The lawn has been groomed so fine that it resembles a putting green. Normally, Olympia would have enjoyed the preparations, and would particularly have welcomed that hour before the guests arrived, when all the house was entirely dressed, but still and silent, and she could wander through the rooms and out onto the lawn, admiring a brief moment of perfection.

She gets up from the bed and walks to the shallow closet, on the door of which hangs her dress for the evening. It is white, as indeed all of the dresses this night will be. She fingers the satin underdress with its rows of seed pearls at the bodice, and then the overgown of white chiffon that seems more like a cloud than a garment, so light and ephemeral is the material. It is an exquisite dress, a confection her mother has sent to Paris for, a dress one might wear to a summer cotillion or even to one's own engagement dinner. Since her mother has suggested pearls, Olympia is engaged in searching through her jewelry case for suitable earrings when she hears a knock at her door.

When she opens it, she sees that it is Josiah with a tray. Although Olympia is not hungry, she is immediately moved by his kindness.

They have encountered each other throughout the house many times since the day she found him with Lisette in the kitchen. Though Olympia had not known that Josiah and Lisette cared for each other before that day, she has since seen many small gestures and looks passing between the couple that, had she been more observant, might have helped her to guess earlier. At first, Josiah appeared to be alarmed each time he saw Olympia after the kitchen incident, but then, when it was evident that she would not reveal what she had seen, he seemed grateful for her silence. She wanted to tell him that it was all right and even that she was, in a way she could not explain very well, glad for him; but of course it would have embarrassed them both greatly to speak of this. Olympia has not been able to help, however, regarding Josiah somewhat differently than she always has, and she senses that he must be at least partially aware of that difference. Sometimes she wants to tell him that she, too, has a love of her own. That she, too, understands what it is to have to steal moments to be together.

But, of course, that is unthinkable.

"Thank you, Josiah," she says, taking the tray from him.

He hesitates and does not leave the doorway. She puts the tray on the dresser. She has the window raised as far as it will go. With the door open, a gust of wind blows all the papers off her desk and causes the curtains to fly up toward the ceiling.

"There is quite a stir in the household," she says, hastily bending with Josiah to retrieve the papers from the floor. "You must be insanely busy," she adds.

"We have been up since four, miss. And doubtless, we shall be up at least until four tomorrow morning. But it is a grand occasion, and your father is quite cheerful with all the preparations."

Wordlessly, she looks at Josiah, and she thinks it is the first time — the first time ever? — their eyes have truly met.

"You are not well," he says.

"No," she answers honestly.

"I am sorry to hear that."

He hands her the papers he has collected and stands with his hands clasped behind his back, his feet apart, anchored.

"Thank you," she says.

His waistcoat is stained with dark smudges, possibly tarnish from the silver. "Lisette and I . . . ," he says. "We are to be married. We plan to discuss the matter with your father tomorrow when the event is over."

"And he will be glad," she says quickly.

"I did not want you to think . . ."

"I did not think," she says.

"Shall I call your mother? Or Lisette?"

"No," Olympia says. "No, I am fine. And I shall be fine this evening. It is only the grippe."

It is an obvious untruth, but she senses he does not know what to ask or to say further.

"Just leave the tray outside the door, miss, if you do not want to be disturbed."

"I will do that. Thank you."

"And I hope you will have some enjoyment in the evening."

"I will try, Josiah."

Her limbs are heavy with a lethargy that makes it difficult to raise them to her head to fix her hair. She wonders how she will survive the evening if her energy does not return to her. Lisette has offered to come and make a chignon after she has finished with her mother, but Olympia does not think she can bear to engage in polite chitchat about the night to come with a young woman who has every expectation of imminent happiness whilst she does not.

With some effort, Olympia finishes dressing herself. She stands before the mirror to assess the outcome. She sees a young woman who looks considerably older than she did in June, who is somewhat fuller in her face and limbs, whose bosom is more prominent than it was two months earlier. Her hair has taken on some golden highlights from her reckless exposure to the sun, and there is a spray of freckles on her chest that she has not entirely been able to hide with powder. She has done her hair in a double bun and has secured it with pearl combs. The silk of the dress clings to her figure and is more revealing than anything she has ever worn before.

Altogether, Olympia thinks the sight of herself in the mirror satisfactory, but not beautiful: A smile is missing, a certain light about the eyes. For how very different a woman will look when she has happiness, Olympia knows, when her beauty emanates from a sense of well-being or from knowing herself to be greatly loved. Even a plain woman will attract the eye if she is happy, while the most elaborately coiffed and bejeweled woman in a room, if she cannot summon contentment, will seem to be merely decorative.

She sits on the bed, fighting tears and losing. If only she could speak with Haskell, she thinks. If only she could lean upon him just a moment, she would be all right. He would know what to say to her. He would take care of her. But then, in the next moment, Olympia knows this is not true. He cannot take care of her. He is obliged to take care of someone else. She wrenches the combs from her hair and lets it fall in a tangle, undoing with one stroke the patient fashioning of just an hour before. She does not care. She will not go down to the gala. She will remain in her room, and no one will be able to make her leave it. She has at least that much control over her own life, does she not? No one can force her to the party, no one can compel her to have to enter into polite conversation with John Haskell and his wife.

But then, as she sits there, the disarray of her hair all about her shoulders, her sobbing begins to subside and she lifts her head. She will have to go down to the gala, she tells herself. Of course she will. For if she were to remain in her room, the hurt to her father would be irreparable. And how selfish of her even to contemplate such a thing. Is she so weak, so hopelessly childish, that she cannot be at the same gathering as John Haskell and his wife? She thinks of the suffering that others endure on a daily basis — the Rivard woman and her children, for example — and feels shame for her overimagined torment. So little is asked of her. Can she not at least give that? Haskell has said there might be many such gatherings. Will she absent herself from those as well?

Repairing the damage she has done to her appearance takes so
long that by the time she is finished, the guests have already begun
arriving. As soon as she opens the door to her room, she can hear
those first ripples of greetings of an early evening that presage a sea
of voices, the surf rising continuously as the night progresses. When
she stands at the top of the stairs, looking down, she can see that
there are perhaps twenty or thirty persons, to whom navy-bordered
vellum invitations have gone out, already gathered in the hallway,
the women in swaths of white silk and challis and chiffon and crino-
line and moiré and satin and voile, the men all in the elegant uni-
form of white tie. At the bottom of the stairs, in a reception line of
two, stand her parents, who make a handsome pair. Her mother,
whose hair has been fashioned into an intricate series of loose knots
caught with fine ropes of pearls, stands with brilliant posture and bestows a smile only Olympia and her father know as foreign, a smile
that suggests complete well-being and welcome. It is a marvelous
performance, nevertheless, and Olympia is, for a moment, unable to
leave her perch on the upper landing for watching them.

It is said of her mother that she will be able to remember each
guest's name and make a personal greeting. That she will know the
names of her visitors' children and closest friends as well. And how
she is able to do this when she is so seldom in society, Olympia does
not know. She sometimes imagines her mother in her rooms, studying long lists of names like a schoolgirl prepping for exams. Her
father, who also has singular posture, has achieved that rare but
necessary combination in a host: poise and affability. Unlike her
mother, her father does actually know all of the guests, since he has
drawn up the lists himself. And unlike her mother, her father is genuinely fond of most of the people whom he has invited. He has
spent considerable time thinking about the introductions he will
make and how best to place a particular guest at a table or with a

group of people so as to enhance the liveliness of the evening. Many of the visitors this night will be from the worlds her father inhabits: literature, journalism, art, music, and architecture. But he will include as well a fair mixture of men of business, such as Rufus Philbrick, to ensure that his gatherings are never dull. For a time, Olympia observes her parents, noting with interest that her mother has contrived to wear the faintest shades of aqua in certain panels of her dress and that her pendant earrings are opals with a blue fire; and in this way her mother remains loyal to her nearly obsessive habits. Despite whatever longings or disappointments may trouble them, her parents radiate an air of ease and wealth and considerable respect, which in turn lends the guests a sense of security and comfort. And all of this contributes to form the desirable and necessary notion (if a party is to succeed) that this particular house on this particular evening is the only place in the world to be.

Olympia takes a breath and slowly releases it. She makes her way down the stairs. Her father looks up, and then her mother, and after that, one by one, the other guests in the immediate hallway as well, so that she descends with an audience she might have done without. But she cannot entirely mind, since it is her father's gala, and he is proud of her; and she knows enough to have the generosity to allow him this paternal pride. She can see the face of Philbrick, who smiles so broadly, one might think Olympia was his daughter, and the faces of several young men she has not met before, young men from Newburyport and Exeter and Boston who have been coming north to Fortune's Rocks with their families for years, if not for generations. Men who might, in a year or two, be considered appropriate suitors for Olympia. And she is assaulted then, as she approaches the bottom landing, with a sudden ache that nearly stops her: *How will I be able to do that?*

She has a detailed image of a succession of young men coming to call and pursuing her and perhaps asking for her hand, and her all the while having to ward them off for the secret that is in her. And it is then that she understands that she will not ever marry and will not ever have children, that she has forfeited her future. She puts her hand out to steady herself. She can see that her father is momentarily disconcerted. And then she thinks, in the next instant: *I must not think of such things now. I cannot. I cannot.* She regains her composure and continues her progress.

When she reaches the bottom of the stairs, her father comes forward and takes her hand. Both of her parents greet her with kisses on her cheek. Her father says so that many can hear, "Olympia, you are a vision." And her mother, who is less effusive but seemingly no less pleased by the effect of Olympia's gown and coiffure, smiles at her and smooths a strand of hair behind her ear.

"You make me proud tonight, Olympia dear," her father says more privately to her. And Olympia can see what might be the imminent swell of tears in her father's eyes. But in an instant, he draws himself up once again to say hello to Zachariah Cote.

Cote greets her father and then hastily — too hastily, even rudely, Olympia thinks — turns in her direction.

"Miss Biddeford," the poet says, taking her gloved hand and bowing. Though he lifts his head up, he holds her fingers tightly. She feels herself to be caught in a trap meant for a small animal. She fancies that she can actually smell the oil of Cote's hair — a cloying, sickening smell that makes her want to gag.

"You look ravishing," he says, once again forming a smile that does not include his eyes. "Like a young woman on the night of her engagement party, I should think. Or even on her wedding day."

Appalled that the man's impertinent thoughts should so closely echo her own of just an hour ago, she snaps her hand away from his fingers, like a fisherman roughly shaking off a slimy creature he has brought up with his catch.

"Oh, surely not," her mother says beside her, taking up Cote's hand. "Whatever made you say such a thing, Zachariah? I think the evening's gaiety has gone to your head. Olympia is only sixteen, as you well know. There can be no thought of her marrying yet."

Her mother says this with a lighthearted tone appropriate to the evening, but before he leaves Olympia, Cote casts a look in her direction, and there is no mistaking the coldness, the knowingness of his gaze. As if saying to her: "If you persist in this charade . . ."

Though Olympia is shaken by the encounter, it is understood that she will remain with her parents and greet the other guests, who begin arriving then in great numbers. She does this until she can bear it no longer. She excuses herself to walk out onto the porch.

A diffuse sunlit mist has rolled in with the sea and has filtered the light so that all objects are lent a salmon tinge, particularly the white dresses of the women and the long scallops of the tent. With a trick of light she does not quite comprehend, the pinkened mist has also produced an aquamarine sea with much white froth at the shoreline. It is a sight to fill the soul with the nearly unbearable sweetness of the best that Nature has to offer, an awareness that is made all the more keen and poignant with the realization that such beauty is transient, that it will soon be gone and might not, because of the unique physics of light, which she does not understand well at all, ever come again. She thinks her father must be chuffed to have Nature as well dressed on this most important evening as his family and his guests.

The beauty of the night begins to erase the memory of the unpleasant episode with Cote. Olympia makes her way down to the tent and strolls through it, looking at the tables with their elaborate settings of Limoges and heavy sterling, which bear her mother's initials in gold on the stems. Opaline flutes are ready for the champagne, and white candles flicker on every table. Already there are some guests moving along the edges, peering in. Waiters stand ready to serve them oysters and spirits.

"Olympia," a voice calls to her.

She turns just as Victoria Farragut reaches out one white-gloved hand and seizes Olympia's arm. "This is all so grand," she says. "You look ever so nice. I could not get my hair to lie smooth no matter what I did. It is this wretched humidity."

Olympia looks at Victoria's hair, which has frizzed all about her face in a way she thinks is rather becoming, and she tells her so.

"Oh, no," Victoria exclaims. "I am a fright. But you look lovely. I know that dress is from Paris because my mother told me."

Both Victoria and Olympia, somewhat to Olympia's surprise, are offered champagne. Olympia has tasted swallows of champagne at other formal parties, but until she met Haskell, she had not ever drunk an entire glass. Now, however, the dry bubbles seem achingly familiar, and for a moment she is seized with the kind of physical memories that are triggered not by thoughts but by sensations.

"This is tickling my throat," Victoria says, coughing slightly. "I do not know half of the people here. Are they all from Fortune's Rocks? No, surely, they cannot be."

"There are some guests up from Boston and Newburyport. But I hardly know most of them myself."

"My mother fussed so with her dress," Victoria confesses. "She means to find a husband. No, I should not tell you that."

Olympia smiles. "I hope she finds one," she says. "There seem to be enough eligible men here," she adds, scanning the crowd, in which men of all ages appear to outnumber the women.

"But no one wants a woman with nearly grown children," Victoria says with a small sigh. "Particularly not a woman who has little money of her own."

"I do not think a man chooses a woman solely on the basis of her fortune or lack of it," Olympia says. "Or will refuse to be interested in the woman because of a grown daughter. Is there not the matter of love?"

"Oh, I doubt very much my mother has much hope of love," Victoria says. "It is a husband she wants. With an income. Will you dance if someone asks you?"

"I suppose I shall have to," Olympia says.

"Olympia, you sound like an old woman who is tired of life already."

"I am sorry," she says. "Perhaps I am simply tired." She takes another sip of champagne and watches as Rufus Philbrick, in white beard and white tie, his studs near to bursting from his shirt, approaches them.

"Here comes someone now to ask you," Victoria says conspiratorially.

"For heaven's sake, Victoria, the man is older than my father," Olympia says, thinking immediately of, and then dismissing, the irony inherent in the statement.

Rufus Philbrick takes Olympia's hand. She introduces him to Victoria. Philbrick bows slightly in her direction. "I knew your father," Philbrick says. "We did some business together. I liked him very much. I hope you and your mother are enjoying your summer?"

"Oh, we are," Victoria says. "Thank you. And I am reminded that I should go to her. If you will excuse me . . ."

Together, Philbrick and Olympia watch Victoria thread her way through the guests who have come out onto the lawn.

"Have you made any other friends this summer?" Philbrick asks her, and Olympia has a sudden image of the night Philbrick and Haskell sat at the dinner table together.

"Actually, I have been much occupied with other matters," she says.

"I hope nothing serious?" he asks.

"No," she says. "Nothing too serious."

Olympia has an unbidden and powerful urge to tell the gruff and well-intentioned man the story of her and Haskell. To tell someone, however inappropriate. To say the words aloud, to give them life. It is a reckless urge, not unlike that of standing at the edge of a precipice and having an overwhelming desire to jump.

"To your very good health, my dear," Philbrick says, summoning a waiter to refill his champagne glass. "I think the chap who will one day snatch you away will be very lucky indeed."

Olympia looks up at the man who owns hotels and thinks how different in tone his words are from those of Cote, for Philbrick's contain nothing of the suggestiveness of the poet's.

"Oh, I hope I shall not be snatched too far away from my father and mother," she says lightly to forestall the rest of the sentence.

"You seem adventurous to me, Olympia Biddeford." He thinks for a moment. "Yes, I can see it. You will meet a cattle rancher and will go west and will own hotels and will have eight children."

She laughs. "I hope you are not as good at prophecy as you are at business."

He smiles and regards her over the lip of his glass. Around them, there seems to be a change in the pitch of the general conversation, a ratcheting up of the volume, which causes them both to turn in the direction of the porch, nearly filled now with guests.

"I had a look through your telescope," Philbrick says. "I am told it is your father's present to you on your birthday."

She nods.

"Marvelous instrument. Quite keen. I could see all the way out to Appledore with it earlier this week."

"One could not tonight," she says.

"No, but the mist is always intriguing, do you not think?"

Olympia wonders suddenly why she never sees Philbrick with a wife or children. Does he live alone? In one of his hotels? She studies the porch, where the guests seem to be converging in a cluster. She reflects once again, there in the presence of Philbrick, that each of the glittering and perfectly groomed persons at the party has come into the world in the manner of the Rivard child; and further, that most on the porch have at one time or another, if not actually often, opened their mouths and their legs and been naked in the presence of a lover and have strained for pleasure and have cried out, and perhaps have even made indecent or terrible sounds; and further, that there are couples at her house who have known each other in these intimate ways this very day. And all of this causes her to wonder at the disparity between the silk dresses and the natural postures of the body, and to think: How far, *how far*, we are willing to go to pretend we are not of the body at all.

"Ah," says Philbrick. "Hale has arrived. Our guest of honor."

"No more honored than you," Olympia replies.

He looks at her and smiles broadly. "I knew you for a democrat," he says.

They watch together as the personage makes his way out onto the porch, a woman on his arm. Olympia has a glimpse of a pale face, thinning hair. Because the man is surrounded by guests who either want to make his acquaintance or want to watch those who do, it is hard to keep sight of him; but Olympia knows that she will be introduced to Hale soon enough. It is an event she is not much looking forward to, since she has not read the man's sermons as she was instructed to do by her father. She doubts very much that Hale himself will care, but she knows that her father will mind. She hopes her father will be so distracted by the evening, however, that he will not think to question her on the matter in front of Hale himself.

But as it happens, she never does meet Hale, either that night or later.

"There is John Haskell and his wife," Rufus Philbrick says beside her.

Her heart stammers a beat inside her chest. She scans the crowd quickly and sees the couple emerging from the front door onto the porch. She notices immediately that something is amiss. It is in the solicitous way Catherine hovers near to her husband, or perhaps it is in the strain on Haskell's face. They move not toward Hale, but away, as if by tacit agreement they had decided to drift to the fringe of the gathering. Slowly, they make progress toward the railing nearest to where Philbrick and Olympia are standing.

Philbrick walks forward a few steps to greet them, but Olympia cannot move.

Haskell's hair is slightly disheveled, as if he had combed it and then, unthinkingly, run his fingers through it. His tie is poorly knotted. Catherine, in long white silk gloves, touches her husband's arm briefly. He seems not to see Olympia, who stands in his direct line of sight, but rather he appears to be gazing into that middle distance that reflects only the viewer's own thoughts. Philbrick walks up onto the porch and greets Catherine, kissing her hand. Haskell turns briefly in Philbrick's direction but seems not to be able to say much beyond the absolutely necessary.

He is not himself, Olympia thinks. He is ill.

She does not know whether to leave the area altogether or to go to them on the porch. Philbrick, doubtless made uncomfortable by Haskell's silence, begins to involve himself in a conversation with a man from Rye whom Olympia vaguely recognizes. Haskell puts his hands onto the railing and leans forward and looks down at his feet in the posture of a man who might need to be sick. From time to time, Catherine makes half turns of her head, trying to monitor her

husband's behavior. She seems more puzzled than anything else —
concerned certainly, but also disconcerted by Haskell's uncharacteristic rudeness.

But it is not rudeness that accounts for his unnatural behavior.
Not rudeness at all. And it is Catherine, in making another half
turn, who sees Olympia first.

"Olympia," she calls, her face brightening. "Oh, Olympia, look at
you. John, do you see? Does she not look marvelous?"

Haskell moves his eyes in Olympia's direction. Though there is
some distance between them, she can see him clearly. His face gives
nothing away. She waits for a sign, an indication of how she should
behave. But he only nods briefly and does not say anything.

Catherine speaks up brightly in the manner of someone who
wishes to disguise an awkwardness.

"Oh, do come up here, Olympia," she calls. "We must look at
you. I had heard your dress was a dream, but I had no idea. Of
course, it is the young woman inside that makes it shimmer, do you
not agree, John? And how is it that you are standing there alone,
Olympia, and that every young man in your father's house is not
clamoring to speak to you?"

Haskell presses his lips together.

Does Catherine know? Olympia wonders with alarm. Has Haskell told her? And is Catherine somehow, incredibly, determined
to rise above the crisis? To put it all behind her? Is that what this is
all about? What happened between husband and wife this afternoon
in their new cottage? Olympia searches Haskell's face, her eyes dart-
ing all about his eyes and mouth, but she can see nothing that answers her questions.

And then he straightens and seems to draw himself together.

"Olympia, good evening," he says. "Forgive me."

For what? Olympia wants to cry out. *For what should I forgive you?*

The fact that Haskell has spoken at all produces some small measure of relief in Catherine's features. She manages a smile.

"Come up here, Olympia, or I shall come down myself and fetch you," she says.

Olympia does as she is asked. She lifts her skirts and climbs the side stairs, the very stairs Haskell once stood at the top of as he watched her come back from the water's edge. But it is Catherine who is there to greet her this time, extending her gloved hand. Olympia is enveloped in an embrace of gardenias and castile and, underneath this, just the faintest whiff of stale breath.

Catherine's dress is gathered under her bosom in the empire style and drapes appealingly over her waist and hips. She is wearing moonstones. Her hair has been allowed to float about her face, and Olympia has the distinct impression that it is weightless, that it might suddenly dissolve altogether like spun sugar. Catherine holds her arm rather like a maiden aunt who has taken a niece under her wing. Haskell turns and bends and kisses Olympia's gloved hand. Closer to him now, she can see the tight strain of the muscles of his face.

"How do you like your new cottage?" she is compelled by politeness to ask Catherine.

Haskell turns his head away and gazes out to sea.

"Oh," Catherine says with evident delight. She brings her hands together as though she might clap them. "It is so wonderful. I have never seen such a house. One can see the water from every window, and the sea air . . . Really, Olympia, you must come to call on us as soon as possible, for I want to show you and your mother all of the rooms. The attention to detail . . . And the girls . . . Each has her own sitting room, and they are, as you can imagine, absolutely enthralled."

Catherine pauses. Olympia is meant to reply, but she can find no words. The silence extends for seconds. All around them are animated voices, which serve only to underscore that hers is not. Olympia feels a tightness in her chest.

Catherine looks from Haskell to her and back again.

"John is not himself tonight," Catherine says, apologizing for her husband's ill manners. "He has been working too hard, I fear."

"I am sorry to hear that," Olympia says.

Even Catherine, with all her social skills, can make no further headway into conversation. Haskell's strained silence is suffocating, and Olympia wants to flee. She cannot stand with this couple any longer. So great is the tension that she fears either she or Haskell will blurt out the true reason for the silence.

"If you will excuse me, I must find my father," Olympia says hastily. "He will be cross with me if I do not make an effort to introduce myself to Mr. Hale early in the evening."

Before either Catherine or Haskell can answer, Olympia leaves them and begins to make her way along the porch and into the house. Does the crowd part for her, or does she push them away? No, no, it is not so dramatic as that. She merely moves, nodding politely, slipping through breaks in the throng, feinting away from engagement. She walks into the house and through the sitting room, which is awash with persons and gaiety. She continues gliding, having no destination, wanting only to put a distance between herself and Catherine Haskell, to whom she can no longer in good conscience allow herself to speak.

As she walks, she silently chastises herself: She must never, under any circumstances, visit the woman again. She must discourage Catherine from ever coming to the house. She must avoid, at all costs, any possible chance encounters, all social engagements at which they might meet. She must leave Fortune's Rocks and go back to Boston. An excuse will have to be invented, but she can do that. Her father can be persuaded to send her back. She will go immediately. In the morning. She is in a hallway, moving away from people. She hears an orchestra tuning its instruments. The music will soon begin. *Oh God,* she thinks, *how will I be able to do this?*

She reaches the empty corridor that connects the main house to the chapel and slows for breath. She leans against a wall and puts her head back and closes her eyes. She stands in that posture, trying to calm herself, for some minutes. She can hear a viola, a waltz beginning. Will Haskell dance with Catherine? Olympia puts her hands to her eyes. She pulls the pearl combs roughly from her hair and studies them in her hands. She holds them tightly, digging the teeth into her palms.

She hears footsteps on the polished floor and turns her head. She realizes she has known that he would follow her. She watches him walk toward her, and she does not move. On his face is an expression she knows well: an expression of both anguish and expectation. He comes close to her, and she can feel his breath on her eyes. She hears a shudder, an exhalation. He bends and presses his mouth hard into her shoulder, and for a moment, Olympia is frightened. She can feel his teeth. He has not done this before. There is a wetness on her skin, and she knows suddenly that he is crying. He cries the way a man does, both silently and noisily, gulping for air. It is a loss of control so complete that the weeping triggers the lust, or perhaps it is the other way around. She wants to hold his face, to bring it up to hers, to calm him, but his mouth is on her breast, and he presses his hands so hard against her back, she can hardly breathe. They move, or lurch, along the passageway, looking for darkness, for shelter, anything to hide them. She bangs against the wall, and a picture falls. It is a wonder they do not rouse a servant or a guest. She holds his head, and they turn so that his back is against the wall. She steps on the hem of her dress and hears it tear slightly at the waist. They enter the chapel and stand looking at its deconsecrated altar, its wooden pews. Behind her, she hears the door shut. Haskell fastens the latch. Olympia glides toward the marble slab and sits on it. Haskell hovers over her. She cannot see his face.

"What happened?" she asks.

"I did not tell her," he says.

She wraps her arms around his legs and bends her head to them.

"I cannot live in that house," he says. "I cannot. I cannot."

"No," she says, rolling her forehead back and forth. And like Haskell, she is crying.

"I will go away from here," he says. "I will find a reason. I cannot be in this town."

"Let me," she says, looking up at him. "Let me be the one to go. You are needed; I am not. I have already resolved to speak to my father tomorrow."

He crouches down to put his face opposite hers. He digs his hands deep into her hair. "No, I cannot stay," he says. "There is no vista that does not remind me of you, that does not make me want you."

He puts his mouth on hers. It is a kiss, but more than a kiss. Something akin to drowning perhaps.

But the body cannot content itself with kisses, no matter how encompassing or generous. The body will go forward on its urgent course. Thus she lies down, her head against the cool marble, her legs straddling the stone. The marble is hard and uncomfortable, and she feels ungainly, her legs spread, her slippers touching the floor on either side. Haskell kneels. His cheek is wet on her thigh. He unfastens one stocking and puts his hands on her leg. She tries to raise herself up to look at his face. She calls his name. But he is lost to the most powerful sort of lust there is: that which stems from hopelessness. She is frightened — at least as much for him as for herself. And yet she knows that she cannot stop this, that it will have its own momentum, its own beginning and its own end.

And it is then that she turns her head to the side and looks through the open window of the chapel and sees Zachariah Cote move graciously away from his place upon the porch, allowing Catherine Haskell to step up to the telescope, lower her face to the eyepiece, and briefly adjust the knobs until finally the scene onto which Cote has precisely trained the instrument comes incomprehensibly into clear focus.

S HE IMAGINES it to have been like this: Catherine would have stood up, her mouth slightly parted, one silk-gloved hand pressed flat against her bosom. Cote, feigning curiosity, would have bent to the telescope and then would have righted himself, seemingly shocked by what he had just seen. *My dear,* he might have said. *I am so sorry. How dreadful for you.* Which might have penetrated the shock, might have made Catherine look up at Cote's face and see the concerned frown about the brow that could not entirely hide the sly smile at the lips. And perhaps she flinched and then drew away and had the wherewithal to slap the man. Olympia hopes that she did.

By the time Olympia reaches the center hallway, holding her dress closed at the waist where it has torn, it seems that all about her is a screeching, the sound of all the clocks of the world out of sync. Have she and Haskell caused this, this chaos, this pandemonium? Around her, people and objects are swirling, moving very fast. Haskell has gone before her, and she looks for him, for Catherine.

Her mother's face is white and frozen, and she cannot speak. Her father comes to her, a question in his eyes. *Is this true, Olympia?* he asks. She answers him, but it is as though she speaks a foreign tongue; he seems not to be able to comprehend her words. And then she sees the moment of recognition in his face, that slight shiver, and watches as the knowledge finally sets in: the ruin, the loss of everything he values — his daughter, her reputation, the possibility of ever coming to Fortune's Rocks again, the house that he loves so, the life that he loves so. And she thinks the saddest moment of the entire night is the brave manner in which her father then draws himself up and tries to maintain his poise even as the awful knowledge is seeping into his pores, the way he tries to speak to his guests, to reassure them, to remain ever the able and affable captain, even as the hull is cracking and the sea is pouring through the bulkheads.

Her father tries to take her hand, but she pulls away. She runs from room to room. Guests are leaving, calling for their carriages. She has to see Haskell. She has to find Catherine. She has to say something to Catherine.

Olympia comes upon them finally in the passageway that leads to the kitchen. Catherine has been crying and will not let her husband touch her, even though he is trying to. He looks at Olympia and does not speak. His face is ravaged.

We cannot have done this, she wants to cry out to him. *We cannot have done this.*

They go out the back entrance together. Husband and wife. He has to go with his wife. He has to see her to their new home, does he not? But what horrors will await them there? Olympia wonders. What cries will sound in the night as Catherine sleeps and then wakes and then sleeps and then wakes again, a cruel and relentless pattern?

Olympia watches Haskell leave her house, leave her standing in the passageway. The orchestra has long since stopped playing. She goes down onto her knees. She sees the back of Haskell's coat as he moves through an open door. And it is only then that she truly understands what she was meant to have known from the very beginning. He is not hers. He was never hers.

· II ·

In Exile

*O*LYMPIA AND her parents depart Fortune's Rocks on the morning of August 11 by train, leaving Josiah and Lisette, who have not, after all, been given time to make their personal announcement to her father, in charge of an army of temporary servants whose mission it is to rid the house of any trace of the disastrous gala. Her mother is tight-lipped during the journey and needs to be revived with salts from time to time by the nurse who accompanies her. Her father does not speak to Olympia until they reach the privacy of the sitting room in their house in Boston, which is not yet overly peopled with help. With barely controlled fury, he announces that Olympia has ruined the family and destroyed any chance of happiness for any of its members. Furthermore, her foolish disregard of consequences has thoroughly shredded her own future. Though he considers her seduced by a scoundrel, she will be held responsible for her actions for the rest of her life. And does she understand, he adds, spitting and spraying his question across the room with all the fury of a father whose worst nightmare has come to pass almost before he has had time to imagine it, that such an accounting not only includes the ruin of Catherine Haskell, an entirely blameless and thoroughly wronged woman, but also must encompass the lives of her innocent children as well? As for John Haskell himself, her father cannot speak, being unable even to utter the name and wanting, in these early days, to do the man, whom he has trusted as a friend, grievous bodily harm.

She sits in silence and listens to the specifics of her sentence: She will not be permitted to leave the house for the foreseeable future, and for at least a month, while he and her mother consider what to do with her and how to salvage the few remaining bits of her future, she will not be allowed to leave her room. Indeed, she is to be confined to that room with no companionship, with no access to letters or the outside world, and without any books to distract her. Her meals will be brought to her on a tray, and she will not be permitted even a walk in the park. The purpose of this deprivation, her father explains carefully, is to allow her suitable time to contemplate the gravity of her position. And then, to Olympia's dismay, her father suddenly begins to sob, right there in the sitting room, which is far worse than his ferocious scolding. He sits down hard in a chair, as if he has collapsed. She leaves her own chair and crouches down before him and implores him to stop, for she cannot bear his sadness. He draws himself up then and insists that she get off her knees. He asks if she would be so kind in future weeks and months as to omit any theatrics from their discourse, which he gives her to understand will be limited to only those sentences absolutely necessary to utter to another human being with whom one shares living space. And thus with chilly dismissal, he bids her leave the room and begin her confinement.

A worse punishment her father could not, with all the forethought in the world, have devised for her. To sit in a chair, hour after hour, and contemplate her own demise is bad enough: She will not have a husband or a family; she will not be able to continue her education, either with her father or in any institution; she will be relegated to the worst of circumstances for a woman, that of spinster-hood and utter uselessness; for the rest of her years, the scandal, which might alternately titillate or alarm others, will follow her; she will be held up as an example to young women of the ravages of sin; and, in short, she will be the recipient of that most remorseless and despicable of sentiments, which is pity. But to know that one is responsible for the ruin of innocents is nearly unendurable. Occasionally, her father knocks on the door and enters her room and feeds her bits of information he considers instructive or likely to whet the knife edges of her punishment. Catherine Haskell and her children returned to York on the eleventh of August, her father briefly announces one day, permitting her no questions in reply. Later she is told that *that man* has been stripped of his position at the college and at the clinics in both Cambridge and Ely Falls. She is not informed as to his whereabouts or how he might now make his living. She is not told how Catherine and her children will survive, only that the new cottage, in which the doomed couple spent just the one dreadful night, has been put up for sale.

Olympia is left to her own thoughts and speculations, which renew themselves each morning upon awakening and only very slowly begin to seem familiar. But after a month has passed, she learns a curious fact about herself: Her capacity for remorse is finite. The spirit does not easily submit to annihilation, she finds, and thus it will devise a way, though the path may run through the most complicated of mazes with hazards all about, to ease itself and to salve its wounds. And this she does, in the confines of her bedroom, with memory. She has recollections, both visceral and ephemeral, that no one can take away from her; and even though the events that have occasioned these memories have led only to catastrophe, they contain within them nuggets of sweetness that subsequent consequences cannot entirely sour. Thus the past becomes her companion.

*   *   *

Toward the end of October, Olympia begins to feel physically unwell. For days, she tastes something metallic at the back of her
throat, and she is plagued with biliousness. On the twenty-ninth of
October, she finally summons her courage and tells Lisette of her
malady, for she wishes her to fetch Dr. Branch. Lisette regards
Olympia silently for some minutes and then sighs gravely. Olympia
knows then, with a kind of clarity that has previously eluded her, the
exact nature of her condition. She feels light-headed for a moment,
but then, as she puts her hand to her forehead and passes through
the sensations of disbelief and shame, she cannot entirely keep a
smile from her mind, if not actually from her lips. For though she
understands fully the calamity of her situation, she also feels a seed
of joy for the seed that has lingered from her days and weeks with
John Haskell. It is something. It is *something*. . . .

Lisette volunteers to break the news to her father, but Olympia
tells her that she has courage enough for that. The next morning before breakfast, Olympia dresses carefully in a staid blue frock that
does not entirely hide her condition but does not flaunt it either.
Her father is reading Hawthorne's *Scarlet Letter* when she enters the
dining room, a coincidence she finds so disconcerting that she
nearly turns and walks out right then. There is a sharp, pinging rain
against the glass, and the smell of the coffee makes the bile rise at the
back of her throat. She wills herself not to be sick, to betray no weakness to her father.

He does not at first acknowledge her, although she senses he is
discomfited by her presence. She does not ordinarily breakfast with
him, so her arrival is somewhat suspect. As calmly as she can, she
takes her eggs and biscuits from the buffet and pours herself a cup of
hot milk. But as soon as she puts the plate and cup in front of her,
she sees that she will not be able to remain long in the presence of

this food without embarrassing herself. She therefore launches immediately into her overly rehearsed speech.

"Father, there is something important that I must tell you, for there is no hiding this, and I do not wish you to have this knowledge from —"

He turns his head and looks at her.

"I am so sorry . . . ," she says.

"Olympia, what is this?" he asks.

"I am . . . ," she begins. "There is . . ."

She touches her dress at the waist.

"No."

He says the single word quietly, too quietly, and she hears his shocked disbelief. He is rigid in his posture, and his face has gone white. He will not look at her, but rather stares straight ahead, his fingers still on his book. She has never seen a man struggle so for control. He wets his lips with his tongue. He takes a glass of water.

"Tell me this is not true," he says.

She is silent.

He takes another sip of water. She sees that his fingers are trembling. There is a long silence.

"Arrangements will have to be made," he says in a voice that is slightly hoarse with his shock.

She bends her head and nods. Arrangements for her lying-in.

"Good God!" her father explodes. "Did the man not think?"

"None of this was done to hurt you," she says.

"I shall have no reason ever again to believe anything you say," her father says calmly.

She shuts her eyes.

"This will kill your mother," he says.

And perhaps it is the exaggeration in this statement that piques her ire.

"This is not about Mother!" Olympia cries, abandoning her resolve to remain steady. "I am the one who is with child. I am the one who has lost her lover. I am the one who has suffered."

"Enough," he says sharply. He wipes his lips with his napkin and sets it on the table. "Make no mistake about this, Olympia," he says, his mouth tight with strain, his head shaking as if with palsy. "I worry about you every second of my life. But this *is* about your mother. This is about your mother and myself and our life together. This is about the unborn and innocent child you tell me now you are carrying within you. This is about Catherine Haskell and her children. This is about Josiah and Lisette, who have had to live through all of this horror with us. And though I can barely utter his name, this is about John Haskell as well, a man whose life is nevertheless ruined for all he is to blame. This is not, and I repeat *not*, only about Olympia Biddeford."

And with that her father stands. Carefully he pushes his chair in and picks up *The Scarlet Letter,* only then, it would seem, realizing the coincidence of the book, for he drops it on the table. He leaves the room without further word.

After that day, her father communicates with her by means of notes left at the dining table in the morning or brought to her by Lisette, who shakes her head at her task. One note reads: "Your mother and I will be away for a fortnight." Another: "The electrician is making repairs on Friday, so please have your room prepared." Olympia is now allowed to read, however, and because all has been lost already, she is allowed a fair variety of reading matter: Walt Whitman and Jack London and some verse by Christina Rossetti. There is also a medical text, *The Family Library of Health,* the purpose of which she assumes is to educate her further about the coming labor and birth. She reads the volume as though inhaling it, and years later she will be able to recite word for word certain key passages: *The dress of the patient should be the usual chemise and night-dress rolled up around her waist, so as to keep them from being soiled. . . . The cries emitted are generally more like prolonged grunts, and can be readily recognized at a considerable distance by one who is familiar with their peculiarities. . . . Puerperal Mania is a form of insanity liable to come on a week or ten days after confinement, in which there is frequently a singular aversion to the child, and perhaps to the husband also. A tendency to suicide is also prominent, and patients thus affected should be watched with the most unremitting care.* But she is, despite these alarming pronouncements, not as afraid of the birth as she might be; for it is difficult for the uninitiated to imagine pain.

Through all of this, her thoughts are constantly of John Haskell. To be told not to love is useless, she discovers, for the spirit will rebel. Though she thinks it unlikely she will ever see Haskell again, she cannot stop herself from remembering him, from wondering what has happened to him, from wondering if he thinks of her as she does him. She knows only (her father entering her room and making another announcement) that the Haskell home in Cambridge has been sold. She understands that Catherine and the children will remain in York with Catherine's mother for the foreseeable future, although one day she happens to notice their names in the newspaper as prospective passengers aboard the SS *Lundgren,* bound for Le Havre. Olympia tries to imagine, in the confines of her room, exactly what happened during the early morning hours of August 11 at the Haskell cottage. What did Haskell say to Catherine, and she to him? Did he leave his wife and children that evening? Or was it the other way around, Catherine rousing the children and dressing them in the dark and making a chauffeur drive them to York?

On the thirty-first of December 1899, Olympia sits at the bow window of her father's town house, which overlooks the Public Garden.

Through the lavender glass, she watches as both the reverent and the revelers pass up and down the street. A light snow is beginning to fall, thickening the dusk. Already there are people all about, most in their best cloaks and hats, hurrying in the snow to their destinations. Cabs and horses clutter the street, and as she watches, a traffic jam tightens its ring around the Garden. She has not yet lit the electric lights in the parlor, so as to better see outside the windows; and as a result, the dusk inside the room is becoming nearly impenetrable. Her father and mother and Josiah and Lisette are somewhere in the house, but Olympia can hear no sounds of human activity. Josiah and Lisette, who now live together on the top floor of the house, having been quietly married over the Thanksgiving holiday, later will go out on this new century's eve. Her mother and father will not.

Olympia and her parents have recently passed a grim Christmas, the pall of the immediate and unknowable future smothering even her father's forced attempts at cheer. There were few gifts. Olympia had crocheted her mother a lace shawl and had knitted her father a muffler, since she could not leave the house to go to the shops to buy anything else for them. Their gifts to her were ludicrously inappropriate — a pair of ice skates and a blue velvet cape — as though they wished to deny her present reality altogether. Only Lisette's gift to her, which she brought to Olympia's room on Christmas Eve (after all the others had gone to services), acknowledged her condition: a quilted yellow box filled with infant's linens, all hand embroidered with tiny yellow flowers. The woman's kindness brought fresh tears.

The fire in the grate takes the edge off the chill, but it is damp in the parlor nevertheless. Olympia wraps her shawl about her and lets the fringe fall into her lap. How she would like to be out on the last evening of the century, if only to be physically a part of the centenary milestone. Though she thinks the date an arbitrary one — for who could say on what day the counting of the millennia began? —

and not possessing mystical powers, she is much intrigued by the near hysteria and spate of prophecies that have infected the country as the last minutes of the century have drawn to a close. Already she can sense that the revelers are carousing with a license not equaled in previous New Year's celebrations. Some persons, she knows from reading the Boston newspapers, have actually built underground bunkers in order that they might survive the unfolding of the specific prophecies of Revelation, which they attach to the first day of the year 1900. Other will attend church services well into the evening. Still others have planned elaborate parties that will last until morning. Under normal circumstances, her parents would be dressing now to attend one of these celebrations. Or perhaps they might have planned, before August tenth, to hold a New Year's gala themselves; invitations for this evening went out, in some circumstances, a year ago. But, of course, all that has changed now. Her parents have not been in society once since leaving Fortune's Rocks.

As Olympia listens to the ticking of the walnut clock in the corner of the parlor, it is impossible not to imagine that her life is ticking away as well in that oppressive room of heavy damask and ornate mahogany and Persian rugs of competing patterns. How she longs for a room with large windows curtained only with diffuse sunlight. She feels the now familiar movement within her, which she has likened to bubbles of champagne rising, an image Lisette is particularly fond of. Together they have let out all of her dresses, but it is clear that even that strategy will no longer provide Olympia with a wardrobe. With little exercise, Olympia is growing bigger by the week and has long since lost any desire to hide her condition. She smooths the wool flannel over her belly and thinks, as she often does, of the impending birth, about which, curiously, she has little fear, and of the father of the child, whose whereabouts she still does not know. When it grows entirely dark, Olympia will be allowed a walk along the periphery of the park. It will be her only outing of the day, as indeed has been true all fall and winter. Josiah and Lisette will be her companions.

A light is turned on in the room, immediately creating a reflection on the window that obliterates the revelers outside.

"Lisette," Olympia asks, "do you suppose we could go now for our walk? My legs are nearly bursting for want of exercise."

"It is not Lisette," her father says quietly.

Olympia turns in her chair.

"Do not get up," he says. He walks to where she is sitting and draws a chair near to her. Her chest is tight, for he has not voluntarily entered into conversation with her alone since the day she told him of her pregnancy. Her father has lost considerable weight and has passed in his appearance, over the past few months, from a middle-aged man to an almost elderly one, and this is but one more thing for which Olympia blames herself. He has on an ordinary wool frock coat, and he has shaved his mustaches. Since he has lost some hair as well, he seems altogether smaller than he was in the summer.

"There are some matters which we must discuss," her father says, and although his pronouncement is formal, his tone is not. It contains a softness she has not heard in some time. Perhaps, she thinks, even her father cannot sustain the intensity of his anger.

"You have borne your punishment with grace, Olympia," he says to her, and her heart begins to ease at the words. "I have been too harsh."

"Father — ," she begins.

He holds up his hand. "There is no more to be said about that."

Although he draws himself up and strains for his former nearly military bearing, she notices that the center, the heart of his body, has slipped, so that he is now somewhat hunched in his posture, even as he sits.

"I have made arrangements," he says, unable to help himself from glancing at her swollen body.

"And what are they?" she asks.

He averts his eyes, turning his gaze toward the window.

"It is better if we do not talk of specific arrangements," he says.

She starts to speak, but he shakes his head.

"There can be no thought of your keeping the child," he says quickly. "It will be well taken care of, I assure you."

Though Olympia has known that such an outcome might be possible, she has prevented herself from fully imagining an absolute separation. "But, Father," she says, leaning forward, "I wish to keep the child."

"There can be no thought of your keeping the child," he repeats. "Your mother will not permit this, nor will I, and you must see that you cannot possibly survive without our support."

"But, Father — ," Olympia protests.

"Olympia, listen to me. You must trust me. In time, this entire dreadful episode will be behind you. By the fall of next year, I predict you will have recovered from this disaster entirely. And while some damage has been done that can never be repaired, I have been thinking that you can have a life for yourself. It is, after all, the modern era. Young women do go off on their own and make their own way. It is not entirely unthinkable. But you will need some schooling, some training for future occupation."

"The child is mine!" Olympia cries out. "He is mine and John Haskell's! It is we who should decide what happens to him."

Red blotches appear on her father's cheeks, and it is some moments before he can compose himself.

"How dare you mention that man's name in my presence," he says coldly.

She opens her mouth to speak further, but he holds up a hand.

"In the fall, I will send you out to the western part of the state, to the Hastings Seminary for Females," he says, and it is clear from his tone that he will not listen to opposition to this plan. "The best course for you — the only course for you — is to become a teacher. There is a severe need for good teachers, particularly in the rural parts of New England, and in this way your life will have some value to others."

"Father, do not do this to me."

He looks long and hard at his daughter's face. Olympia can imagine what he sees: an overplump sixteen-year-old girl whose judgment can no longer be trusted.

"There is nothing more to be said on this subject," he says.

She bites her lip hard to keep from crying out further. She holds the arms of her chair so tightly that she later will have cramps in her fingers.

She will refuse to obey him, she thinks. She will accept his implied challenge and set off on her own. But in the next moment, she asks herself: How will she be able to do that? Without her father's support, she cannot hope to survive. And if she herself does not survive, then a child cannot live.

Her father pretends to be examining the revelers, but Olympia knows that all he can see is himself and her, framed by the cream molding of the window's deep sill. He seems not to like what he sees, and turns back to her.

"After your training, I should like you to find a position somewhere away from Boston, where your story will not immediately be known," he says, and it is clear that he has been thinking this through for days. "Even so, you must be prepared for a life in which people will eventually know your circumstances, for I doubt there is anywhere you could go where there will not at least be a possibility of the story reaching those around you. Unless you change your name . . ."

He considers this idea for a moment.

"No," he says. "No, you will not do that. There is no need for cowardice in this family. Of course, you will be provided for. I do not think you could live very well on a teacher's salary. I shall not be lavish, merely adequate. Olympia, despite all" — she looks sharply up at him, for she detects a tiny crack in his composure — "your mother and I do love you."

Her eyes sting at this pronouncement, for she does not believe that her father has ever spoken of love to her.

Her father sighs, as though this confession has taken more out of him than he anticipated. He raises his chin and takes a quick breath.

"So, now," her father says, having ventured too far into sentiment for comfort. "Fetch your cloak and hat. I shall take you for your walk this evening in the park. And then we will come back and make ourselves some cocoa, and in this modest way we shall celebrate the new century, in which I hope you will have a life of contentment, if not actually of happiness."

Olympia tries to stand. Her father reaches for her arm, and she sees that he is disconcerted to realize just how large she has become, for it has been some time since he has stood this close to her.

She disentangles her arm from his. "You are wrong in one thing, Father," she says as calmly as she can. "Quite wrong."

"And what is that?" he asks almost absently, having discharged his duty in a timely fashion and now somewhat more relaxed than he was when he entered the room.

She looks at his face and waits until his eyes meet hers.

"You predict that by the fall of next year, I will be entirely recovered from this 'episode,' as you call it. But you are wrong. I will never recover, Father. Never. If you take the child from me, I will never get over it."

He studies her for some seconds.

"Olympia," he says. "You are so very young."

*   *   *

Shortly after midnight, in the early morning of April 14, Olympia wakes to a sensation of wetness. On further inspection, she discovers that her gown and her bed are soaked with warm fluid. Heavily, she climbs out of the bed and changes into a dry nightdress. She knows from the medical book what this means. She walks to the bottom of the stairs leading to the third floor and knocks as hard as she dares against the wall. She does not want to rouse either of her parents.

Josiah, his hair matted into a comical shape, comes to the landing in his dressing gown.

"Fetch Lisette," Olympia says.

Lisette enters the room in plaits and nightdress. She embraces Olympia and seems as excited as if it were she who is about to give birth. Since Lisette's lack of fear and good spirits are somewhat infectious, Olympia is less apprehensive than she might be. She sits on a chair in her room and watches while Lisette changes the bedclothes. When she is finished, Olympia climbs back into bed, draws up the coverlet, and waits. It is a warm night. She asks Lisette if she has ever witnessed a birth. Lisette says yes, several times. She is the eldest of seven children, and her mother "popped them out like biscuits."

"I have seen a birth as well," Olympia says.

"You have? When was that?"

"When I was with John Haskell," Olympia says, startling herself with the name spoken out loud. She has never talked of her time with Haskell with anyone, not even Lisette. "I went with him when he attended a birth. It was in a boardinghouse in Ely Falls."

"You went into the room?"

"I saw it all. The birth was breech and the woman, a poor Franco with three other children, was nearly deranged with the pain. Dr. Haskell gave her laudanum, I think, and she quieted some. But I remember him struggling to turn the baby. He had his hands —"

Olympia cannot go on, however, for she experiences then the first pain of her own. Rigid with surprise, she holds her breath until it is finished. When it has subsided, she lets out a long sigh.

Lisette stands above her. "You must not hold your breath," she says. "You must breathe each time you get the pain."

Olympia nods, shaken by the ferocity of the contraction. "Is this how it will be?" she asks.

"Listen to me," Lisette says, drawing up a chair close to her bed. She takes Olympia's hand in her own. "You are used to behaving in a certain way. You are very proper. You hardly ever get upset, and when you do, you keep it to yourself. But now is not the time to be proper. It is bad for the baby and for you. Do not worry about screaming with the pain. Do not worry about all the embarrassing things your body is going to do, because it is going to do plenty. Do you want me to fetch your mother?"

"No," Olympia says. "There is no need."

The pains come on hard then and are dreadful. Olympia is appalled, even during the first hour, which she thinks surely must be the last, since any increase of pain seems unendurable.

After daybreak, Olympia's mother, summoned by Lisette, enters the room. She has on a blue silk dressing gown tied at the waist. Her hair is rolled back from her head with rags. "Fetch Dr. Branch," she says at once to Lisette. Olympia's mother wets a cloth in a basin, walks to the bed, and lays the wrung and folded towel upon her daughter's forehead. Her face is heavily creamed and glistens in the electric-lamp light. "And I shall need hard sweets for Olympia to suck on," her mother adds. "There are some in my room in a silver jar on the dresser."

Olympia is mildly surprised at how easily her mother assumes the mantle of command. She holds the cloth against Olympia's brow, even as Olympia clenches her teeth and pulls the bedclothes into knots. Lisette returns with word that the doctor is out on his rounds and will be by as soon as he can be found. When Olympia has the pains, her mother leans over the bed and pins her arms back against the bedclothes, and oddly, this seems to help. In between the pains, her mother unwinds the rags from her hair and drinks a cup of tea that Lisette has brought, and once even gets up and inspects the quilted yellow box with its tiny treasures. Thus her mother abandons her normal air of elegance and diffidence and is as involved with the mechanics of the birth as Lisette is. She shows herself to have courage and kindness and common sense, qualities that Olympia has not noticed in her in abundance before. Once Olympia emerges from a short sleep and hears her mother chatting pleasantly, even laughing, with Lisette. Despite the pain, Olympia finds their ease together reassuring. If they are not terrified, then she should not be.

The doctor comes shortly after noon, and Olympia can smell liquor on his breath. She wonders where he has been, if he has been sharing a drink with her father in his study before he came to her, though that seems unlikely so early in the day. Olympia is barely coherent, saving all her strength to withstand the hideous and constantly recurring pain. She thinks it is knowing that the pain will come again and again that exhausts her, knowing that she cannot stop it. She begs for laudanum, and Dr. Branch gives her three spoonfuls of a brownish liquid that causes her to drift in and out of sleep, only to be shocked each time she wakes to another pain and sees her mother and Lisette looming over her.

At two o'clock on the afternoon of April 14, Olympia begins to cry out. She has been in labor for thirteen hours. Dr. Branch comes into the room and is suddenly more alert than he has been before. He tells Olympia's mother and Lisette to prop up Olympia. He then ties Olympia's feet to the bedposts. Olympia's mother speaks constantly to her in a soothing voice.

"I cannot do this," Olympia cries. "I cannot do this!"

And with that pronouncement, her child, a boy, is born into the world.

And how many times will Olympia regret begging for that drug from Dr. Branch? For if she had been alert and awake after the birth, she could perhaps have stopped them from taking the child from her. In years to come, she will remember only the briefest of moments with her son: waking to the surprise of the swaddled bundle tucked beside her in the bed, turning her head to peer at a wrinkled face, unwrapping the cloths just enough to free a delicate hand. But drugged and exhausted, she cannot keep herself from sleep. Indeed, her body, if not her heart, welcomes it.

Later, she will sift these brief moments a thousand — no, ten thousand — times for one stray glint or shard of memory she may have overlooked before. She will remember wet black spiky hair, blue eyes that were purely guileless, a tiny mouth, bowed, exquisite. She never puts her son to her breast. She never sees his tiny feet. She never hears him cry. And when she wakes finally to consciousness, the drug having leached itself from her bones, he is gone.

*O*N SEPTEMBER 27, 1900, Olympia arrives at the Hastings Seminary for Females in the western part of Massachusetts. The village in which the seminary is located is a factory town, the factory dominating the landscape, spilling down into the streets, overtaking churches and shops and the seminary itself, so that it is not possible to say where the factory begins or ends, the buildings all dark brick, even the houses of the owners. The factory produces shoes and boots, and there are many tanneries in the town, so that even the trees smell of offal. It is immediately apparent to Olympia that her father has never visited the seminary, for if he had, the near perfection of the location as a place of punishment would have strained even his sense of justice. Surely there is no crime his daughter could have committed that warrants such an exile.

Olympia will have images of this year, months that are a dull headache at the back of her neck, but no accurate sense of its passage. Cold beef on a blue willow plate. A tapestry hung over a bed. Fastidious girls who professed to be afraid of love. Darkened brick buildings in the rain. Dreams that came and went upon a fawn-colored wall. A stuck window, swollen from the wet. A girl in challis who scoured knives. A hundred eggs for custard pies. India rubbers in the washroom and a cherry desk with a green lid. A tin of matches with a slate. A wooden porch that was overhung with elms. A girl crying in the widow closet. Stiff white sheets in the drying yard. Brown-gold carpets with peacock blue chairs. An hour of recitation followed by an hour of prayer. Pale Methodist ministers who watched girls with hoops at calisthenics. *Worcester's Elements* and *Goldsmith's England*. Young women sent out to foreign lands. *Trunks must be packed by Sunday night.*

The seminary, Olympia learns, was started by Methodist philanthropists in 1873 as a place to educate the factory girls in their off-hours and therefore had the distinction of being the first evening school in the country. When it became clear to the founding fathers, however, that mill girls had precious few off-hours (and those they did have they did not want to spend in further confinement), the seminary began to direct its recruitment to the middle classes: daughters of ministers and salesmen and schoolteachers. The theory and indeed the practice of the seminary are to educate young women so that they can be sent out to teach: to Smyrna or to Turkey or to Indiana or to Worcester or to work among the Zulus in South Africa. In addition to their teaching duties, it is hoped that the graduates might also function as enlightened and Christian models for girls all over the world. It is a measure of Olympia's disassociation from life then that she regards such a prospect with equanimity: She is neither fearful of nor enthusiastic about further exile, all locations other than the Fortune's Rocks of her memories being a matter of similar indifference.

At the seminary, Olympia studies Latin and geography, mathematics and biology, and other subjects with extra courses in composition, calisthenics, vocal music, dressmaking, and household husbandry. The bent is practical; true scholars are the exception. Because neither the curriculum nor its purveyors are particularly intimidating, the establishment, much to the surprise of everyone, flourishes wildly and has many more applications for admission than there are places. Olympia finds it astonishing to contemplate how many young women are willing to leave their homes, that is to say, their villages in New England, to be sent to alien territories where one might perish from loneliness or become ill from infection. And she wonders if this collective passivity is a consequence of individual personal disasters that have rendered them unfit for marriage, or of a general lack of confidence in the future.

From its central building, the school has spread like a subdued stain, taking over vacated boardinghouses adjacent to the school's property, vying with the factory itself for turf. At the time Olympia is enrolled, from 1900 to 1903, the school owns seventeen buildings, including a gymnasium and an observatory, which has been donated by a graduate who married a Mellon. Most of the women, Olympia learns, will marry men of considerably less wealth or of no wealth at all, if indeed they marry, and not a few will remain unmarried. One woman with whom Olympia will take classes will go on to own hotels in the West, and Olympia will think of Rufus Philbrick and his predictions.

During her time at the seminary, Olympia does not have to share a room with anyone else, a circumstance for which she is grateful. (Has her father paid extra to forestall the trading of confidences with a roommate?) Her room, which is composed of a single bed with a pair of rough woolen blankets, a fireplace, a single desk, a chair, and a large window that overlooks the oval of grass at the center of the main campus, is, despite its spartan accommodations, a refuge of sorts. And since Olympia has no desire to leave or to flee this room, she begins, over time, to regard it as more of a retreat than a place of imprisonment. When she is away from it, at classes or at meals or during compulsory exercises, she thinks only of returning to its unadorned solace, where she can sit upon its narrow bed and gaze at the fawn wall opposite and see faces or imagine scenes or recall certain incidents from the past. She has left the home of nuns only to take up the habit, the habits, of the Catholic sisters. Contemplation. Meditation. Reflection. Rumination.

But not prayer. To pray is to hope, and to hope is to admit into one's spirit the pain of hopelessness. And this Olympia is unwilling to do.

Not surprisingly, Olympia develops a reputation for reticence. For to speak of even a small part of one's story might inadvertently lead to the revelation of another part one wishes to keep secret. And so she tells little of herself, a characteristic others regard with some suspicion. She is not popular, though she thinks she is not ill liked either. Rather, she is a neighbor one never knows well, regardless of well-intentioned overtures.

There is, however, one teacher Olympia particularly admires, a biologist, Mr. Benton from Syracuse, who keeps a study in Belcher Hall, a room filled with objets and books and a photograph of a woman (a wife?) he once suggests to Olympia he has lost. They take tea together quite often in her second year, when she has determined upon a course of study in biology; and perhaps it is that Mr. Benton, who is fair in his coloring and who is probably, when she knows him, in his late thirties, reminds her of her father as he was before the catastrophe, and this causes her to be fond of him. Mr. Benton and Olympia speak evenly, in measured tones, of anatomy and platelets and the circuitry of the brain, and if he senses a reserve in her that hides a wound, so does she suspect a story behind his pale facade: Perhaps the woman in the photograph is not his wife after all. They talk of life in the metaphors of cells and species, a language that permits no discursions into matters of the heart, though the physical heart itself is dissected often enough. And in this way, she thinks, they are kindred spirits. In later years, she will often think of writing to the man; but then she should have to tell him of her life and employ a vocabulary that would be as foreign to those twilit afternoons as Chinese or Urdu, and so she does not.

As for her actual father, whom Olympia sees only at Christmastime and summer vacations, the journey being too long for the brief holidays of Thanksgiving and Easter, he has resumed some of his former life, though the glitter has gone out of it, rather like a ring that has lost its diamond: Though the setting remains sturdy, it is incomplete, with its gaping hole. He does occasionally write to her. *I have reservations about your choice of biology as a course of study. It will limit your prospects in a way that the study of history will not. . . . I am sending with this letter twenty dollars so that you might buy yourself some warm clothing for the coming months. I am told that Mrs. Monckton on Hadley Street is a decent dressmaker. . . . Your mother is insisting that we go to Paris. I hope she is strong enough.*

Her father never writes about the past, nor asks her how she is, nor alludes to anything that might prompt an emotional reply. He does not ask Olympia if she is enjoying herself, if she has found any friends, or if she has been able to forget.

And if he did, Olympia would tell him this: *I am not able to forget. Not for one day. Not for one hour.*

Her father predicted she would be fine in the fall. She is not.

On no day does Olympia not wonder what has happened to her son. She feels this absence as a hole cut into the center of her body, a hole she cannot fill up with reading or with study or with imaginings, or even by bending over physically to close up the empty space. One day, when she is crossing Holyoke Street on her way to Belcher Hall, she sees a mother with a boy of about three years. His hair has a stubborn cowlick that gives him charm, and his cotton socks droop about his ankles in a manner that is nearly heartbreaking in its innocence. All about the pair is a golden light, that of the sun filtered through the translucent yellow leaves of the maples overhead.

Olympia watches the boy cross the muddy street with his mother, the child certain that if he holds his mother's hand tightly enough, no harm will ever come to him. And as they walk, a crimson leaf falls. The boy stretches out his small hand. He catches his leaf and holds his treasure aloft for his mother to see.

Olympia turns abruptly and walks back to her room, barely making it behind the closed door before she whirls in confusion and falls onto the bed. She sobs heavily, so much so that she rouses Mrs. Cowper, the housemother, who comes to Olympia's door and insists upon entry. And Olympia has to tell her that she has just learned that her mother is dying (she can still lie brilliantly when pressed) so that Mrs. Cowper will leave her alone.

And if Olympia thinks about her unknown son every day, she thinks of Haskell even more, for she has more of him to remember and thus to imagine. It is as though he, too, becomes a habit ingrained upon the bones: Her reveries of him are constant, though often vague and unformed. Sometimes she will lose his face. Early on, she loses the timbre of his voice. Most of her thoughts are of a speculative nature: She imagines a chance meeting and what they will say. He will have his back to her at a train station. She will recognize — what? — a turned shoulder, the way he stands with his hands on his hips. She will see him check his watch. He will have on a dark suit coat, a leather satchel at his feet. He will take off a narrow-brimmed fedora and brush his hair off his forehead. Silently, she will walk to his side, and sensing her, he will turn. *Olympia,* he will say, as if she had returned from the dead.

Will he dare to touch her then? There in the station, for all to see? She imagines restraint giving way to breathless revelations, hasty absolutions. She imagines remorse and also exhilaration. And she imagines Haskell's shock. For he will not have known he has a son. And then she will give herself over to him, and he will take care of her. These reveries are, without question, the happiest moments of her stay at Hastings.

A special feature of the seminary, Olympia discovers, is its innovative summer work program, a concept unique, she is given to understand, in American education. Since the majority of the students are girls from families of moderate means, many of whom can barely meet the tuition payments, it is the practice of the school to send the girls out in the summer to positions as governesses or near governesses or as apprentices to women who do good works, so that they might earn money to help with their bills. A typical summer post, for example, might be that of an assistant to an administrator of a settlement house or of tutor to a household of children who have not had benefit of schooling.

Toward the end of her third year of study, Olympia begins to think about where she might be assigned. If one is enterprising, she has already learned, one can request a certain post; and indeed most upperclassmen often return to positions held the previous summer, the most desirable of which are in Boston. Olympia, however, does not want to stay in Boston again, even though it means she could live there with her family (or particularly because she could live there with her family), for she has already spent the past three summers in those stifling rooms on Beacon Hill. These seasons were nearly intolerable for Olympia: She was able only to think about where she was not, which was at Fortune's Rocks. Each of the separate days was a small torture as she ticked off the milestones: On this day a year ago, Haskell and I met on the porch. On this day two years ago, we watched a balloon ascend into the sky. On this day three years ago, we were lovers in a half-built cottage.

To avoid a recurrence of such painful anniversaries, as well as the intense boredom and heat of the city in the summer months,

Olympia seizes upon a post that is at the opposite side of the state: "Spend the summer on a farm in the Berkshires," the advertisement outside of the dean's office reads. "A governess is needed for three children. Duties light; payment considerable."

She applies for the post in writing and is accepted. The reply comes from a woman who announces herself the sister of a widowed father who seeks a governess for his three sons. This sister (who gives the impression of sharing the household with the brother, which turns out not to be the case) hastens to assure Olympia that she is likely to be very happy on her brother's farm and to find it a pleasant refuge from the seminary. Though Olympia does not agree that she has high prospects of happiness, she does think the farm might be a refuge from both Hastings and Boston.

Olympia writes to her father to tell him of her assignment, neglecting to mention that she has actively applied for the post. It is determined, however, that Olympia will go home immediately after final examinations to visit for a brief holiday, and that after two weeks she will travel by train to western Massachusetts.

Olympia spends her time in Boston reading Emily Brontë to her mother, who sits upon her chaise, warmed by peacock tapestries and azure chenille, nursing a cup of tea, while Olympia reads of moors and grand passions. Her father, when not secreted in his study, paces the upper rooms of the town house with his hands in his pockets.

Brief though her visit is, Olympia finds she is profoundly impatient, after only two weeks, to leave that household where a faint odor of shame and failure still follows her and seems to linger in the walls and in the carpets and in the furnishings of the many rooms, like smoke after a fire. She is nineteen, an age at which most young women of her station leave the cities in the summer for the watering places along the coast of New England. They go to cotillions and parties and tennis matches and then undertake engagements to handsome or silly young men. Since such an engagement can never come Olympia's way, it is understood that it will be better if she is occupied elsewhere.

The journey back to western Massachusetts is long and arduous, although Olympia is much taken with the gentle blue roll of the landscape west of the mill towns. After they have traveled some distance into the Berkshire Mountains, she gets off the train at what appears to be a crossroads with one general store and a small stone building. When she questions the conductor as to the accuracy of this final destination, he assures her that she is at the correct place. She waits at the crossroads until her employer, Averill Hardy, arrives to take her to his house.

Mr. Hardy is a robust man of about thirty-five years. He has an abundance of hair, which seems to have gone silver at an early age, and a beard that reaches nearly to the middle of his chest. He has two wooden teeth in the front of his mouth, and he is nearly always sunburnt. With his wife, Mary Catherine, he had four sons, three of whom still live with him on the farm. The fourth has gone to Springfield. Since there are no women in the household, Averill Hardy explains to Olympia before they have even reached the farm, it is hoped she will take over the preparation of the meals, see to the laundry, and mend the clothes when she is not actually engaged in teaching his sons how to read and write. Olympia bristles at this suggestion, and questions Mr. Hardy rather strenuously at first, telling him that she has not been given to understand these circumstances. But later, when it becomes apparent to her that the poor man and his home are in desperate condition, she decides she will help; otherwise, she should have to live in near squalor, too. And since her only alternative is to give up the position and return to Boston, which she most profoundly does not want to do, she begins to give in to Mr. Hardy's expectations.

And, in fact, Olympia does not mind this work. She has learned domestic skills at Hastings, and she finds the repetition of household chores to be a calming influence upon her spirit. The farmhouse itself is similar to others in the area in that it is two stories high with white clapboards, black shutters, and an ell in the back. The building is not unpleasant, though the house is close to the barn, which houses dairy cattle and smells poorly on hot days. She has a room at the back of the house, a small room that looks out at a wall of oak and maple trees.

The boys are shy and muscular and range in age from twelve to seventeen, and Olympia thinks it rather astonishing that they cannot read. When she wakes in the mornings, they and Mr. Hardy are already up and tending to the animals and the land, which consists of a hundred acres of feed corn. The kitchen is commodious and easy to work in, and Olympia has learned enough of the culinary arts at the seminary to be able to put together some meals. Before the evening hours, Olympia will have prepared four dinners for Mr. Hardy and his sons, including a breakfast of sausages, porridge, and eggs that she will have ready within a half hour of awakening. She never eats with the men, but rather takes her meals alone at the table when they have finished theirs and have gone out again. After the noon meal, if Mr. Hardy can spare his boys that day, they will come to the parlor, where she teaches them the most rudimentary of skills. The boys are polite, and even somewhat grateful, though the eldest child, who is called Seth, is a painfully slow learner and suffers some by comparison with his younger brothers. When Olympia sees how desperately the children need even her basic tutoring, she decides she does not mind her post.

Sometimes Mr. Hardy will come back into the house before the afternoon and evening meals and will speak some pleasantry to her; but the true purpose of these visits, Olympia soon discovers, is to go into the parlor, and when he is certain she is not looking, to unlock a cabinet there and partake of spirits in a glass. She does not know when he washes this glass, for she never sees it in the kitchen. But she does, over time, come to understand that Mr. Hardy's high color is not entirely due to weathering.

One day, after Olympia has been at the farm for three weeks and has mastered the routines of housekeeping as well as the rudiments of teaching, Mr. Hardy lingers at the table after the noon meal. This distresses Olympia mildly, since she is hungry and normally doesn't sit down to her own meal until after he has left the kitchen. Generally, when she has put the noon meal on the table, she retreats to the second story of the house, where she does some mending in a chair in Mr. Hardy's room, the room he once shared with his wife and which still holds her sewing table and case. It is a pleasant room in which to linger, quite the most pleasant room in the house, Olympia thinks, and in fact the only room with any light to speak of. Mrs. Hardy was clearly skilled in the domestic arts and decorated her bedroom with much of her handiwork. Olympia is impressed by the multihued and complex-patterned hooked rugs, of which there are many, as well as the hand-pieced and intricately sewn quilts that are folded upon a chest, waiting for the winter months.

When Olympia hears footsteps on the stairs, she is startled and lays down her work. It occurs to her that Mr. Hardy might be ill and that he is returning to his room to lie down on the bed. She gets up from her chair, holding the cloth and needle at her waist.

He comes to the doorway and stands in its span. She sees that his eyes glisten or are watery, and she has a new thought: He is grieving for his lost wife. It is hot in the bedroom, with a rectangle of sun on the varnished floorboards.

"You are a good girl," Mr. Hardy says from the doorway. She thinks he may be trying to smile at her, although she is not sure of this, since he has never smiled before, and his mouth takes on a curiously crooked aspect, due to his wooden teeth, which are not pleasant to look at. It seems to her as well that Mr. Hardy is, in his demeanor, more nervous than she has seen previously.

Olympia is embarrassed to be standing there and have him speaking to her in this way when she has no hope of forming a suitable reply, and moreover not a clear understanding of why he has come up to his room. She steps toward him, thinking he will move out of the way and allow her to pass. But he takes her movement toward him as something else. There is a confused moment when she does not know where to place her foot.

Mr. Hardy, who is doubtless under the spell of too large an amount of spirits, put his arms clumsily around her and pulls her to him so that she is squashed up against his chest. She tries to resist, but cannot, and she is not certain he understands that she is resisting. Mr. Hardy, who is a foot taller, bends his head and finds her face and kisses her. It is a wet, unpleasant kiss. She feels the blunt edges of his wooden teeth. His beard is abrasive and prickly on her face and throat. She smells his bad breath, which is, she knows better than anyone else, a mixture of drink and sausage and aged cheese. Then, before she has any chance to recover, he places a large palm at the bodice of her apron and pushes against her as if he means to flatten her bosom. In this moment, she struggles and manages to turn away.

"No!" she cries.

He releases her, and she stumbles backward.

"Did you not like that?" Mr. Hardy asks in a hoarse voice. And Olympia is astonished to see that he is genuinely dismayed and possibly even surprised by her reaction.

But Olympia is speechless from the shock of the smell and feel of his person. She stands, unable to move or to answer him, still holding the needle and the cloth, praying for the incident to be over, when suddenly it is, and she realizes he has left the room.

Her hands begin to shake. She drops the needle and cloth to the floor.

"My God," she says. She sits down hard in Mrs. Hardy's chair. "This is not me," she says.

She looks down at her hands and then up at the folded quilts upon the chest. How has she arrived at this point?

Because she has been allowed to believe that she is unworthy and inferior? And why is this? Because she once was loved? Because that love produced a child? Because her father, and the world in which he has put his faith, has declared this to be so?

She shakes her head, as if to throw off her passivity.

She turns her face to the blue haze of hills beyond the meticulously mended screen of the window. She walks to the window and throws it open and leans her head out. She inhales the air, her thoughts sharpening themselves with each breath as though she had been drugged for years and were only now, with a jolt, emerging from her torpor. The air holds a promise where before there has been none. It is air that might feed a life where before there has been only starvation.

She will leave this farm and not return, she tells herself. She will end her exile. She will go back to the one place where she has been happy.

·III·
Fortune's Rocks Revisited

ALL THE WAY to New Hampshire from western Massachusetts — from the Berkshires to Springfield by carriage, from
Springfield to Rye by train, to Ely by electric trolley, and
then to Fortune's Rocks again by hired carriage — Olympia has
pondered the problem of gaining entry to a house that has been
locked for years. Will it be boarded up and impenetrable, as she suspects it will be? Or have vagabonds disturbed the quiet sleep of a
house in shame? Is it conceivable that Josiah and Lisette, in their
rush to clean up after the disastrous gala, left the door unlocked,
thus allowing the curious to enter the scene of Fortune's Rocks' most
recent, and perhaps its greatest, scandal?

The landscape is familiar and yet not, exhilarating after so many
landlocked years away but frightening in its alterations. Where once
there were long stretches of sea and rocks, now there are cottages of
varying sizes and styles, so many in Rye alone that if it were not for
the recognizable boardwalk, she might not know where she was.
They pass a bowling alley she does not recall and a new arcade that
seems like a strumpet set between two dowager hotels. Already, in
this second week in July, the boardinghouses are crowded with
holidaymakers, the beach thick with bathers in costumes that seem

more daring than she remembers. But as the carriage leaves Rye altogether and draws nearer to Fortune's Rocks, a kind of calm begins to settle over the seascape and over her agitated spirit as well. Fewer changes have been made here, with only the odd unweathered cedar shingles signaling new construction.

She unbuttons her cloak (its wool so suitable for the cool of the Berkshires, but too hot for the coast of New England in July), and it occurs to her that little of the clothing she has brought with her in her flight from western Massachusetts will be comfortable or appropriate at the beach. Beside her, the driver, a lean and angular native with a good growth of beard on his chin, spurs on the horses, and her heart kicks a beat inside her chest. They turn into the narrow winding lane that will take them to Fortune's Rocks, and she thinks: What if the house is no longer there at all? What if, in these intervening years, the cottage burned to the ground, and her father simply did not tell her? Or has he, unbeknownst to her, sold the house, and will she find, on its porches, small children who are unfamiliar to her?

But before she can wonder further, the driver rounds a bend, and she sees with a sudden ache the familiar crescent of summer houses, the rocks at low tide poking their black noses above the sea like seals, the beach at Fortune's Rocks. She strains forward in the carriage. They round yet a farther bend, and then she sees the house itself: her father's cottage, once a convent, now abandoned.

A sound escapes her, and the driver looks over at her.

The windows and doors of the cottage are shuttered, so that the house seems a face with its eyes and mouth tightly closed, betraying no secrets.

"You can't mean here, miss," the driver says with alarm in his accent of broad vowels.

She cannot, for the moment, answer the man. Does she mean here? Is this the place where women in white linen once dined in mirrored lights with glissandi of Chopin in the background? Is this the cottage that John Haskell and his wife and children fatefully visited, none of them capable of even imagining the calamity that awaited? Paint is peeling from the clapboards and the grass is two feet tall, but in the cottage of her memories, light flooded through windows and slippered feet glided silently upon polished floors.

"Yes, this is the place," she says to the driver beside her.

No houses have sprung up near to her father's cottage, and she wonders why that is. Does her father own all the land adjacent? Was this land perhaps deeded to the convent years ago? The nearest neighbor, she sees, is still the lifesaving station, its fresh white paint and red trim gleaming in the sun and causing her father's cottage to appear particularly shabby. At the shoreline, she can see many figures in varying states of undress. She remembers — the memory now bolstered by the sight of the actual landscape and thus more vivid than it has been in years — her slow walk from the bathhouse to the shoreline four summers ago, while Haskell, a man unknown to her then, watched her tentative steps.

Olympia pays the reluctant driver the fare and waits as he fetches her trunk down from the carriage. He bends with its weight. Though he offers to carry it into the house, she asks him to leave the luggage at the back door, for she does not want to reveal the fact that she has no key and cannot open that door or any other. She stands on the doorstep and watches as the driver pulls away. She waves once, hoping that she appears merely to be waiting for an unseen, if lazy, caretaker to throw open the door and invite her in.

But no such caretaker can or does emerge. When Olympia is certain that the driver has gone on, she begins to circle the house, looking for some means of entry. In her urgency to leave the Berkshires and travel to Fortune's Rocks, she has missed several meals and has hardly slept. She tries the shutters (faded now and peeling) and is not surprised to discover that they are locked from the inside. A bulkhead leading to the cellar is similarly fastened, as are all of the four doors of the cottage. She would gladly break a window if only she could gain access to one, but she cannot at first see any opening in the house's formidable armor. She does not want to summon help, for to seek aid is to announce her presence; and though she knows she will not be able to keep her residency a secret for long, she would at least like to be inside the cottage before she is assaulted by the curious.

Out by the chapel, she stands back from the house and surveys it from the lawn. Wild grasses poke beneath her skirts and tickle her legs. Shingles have come loose from the roof, she sees, and the clapboards are badly in need of paint. The porch railing has been battered by a storm, perhaps the same tempest that has denuded the dormers of their trim. There are, in fact, many repairs that should be attended to, repairs she herself cannot make, and she surprises herself with the sudden realization that she is looking at these failings of the house — a crack in a newel post, a doorframe that has warped from the damp, bricks from the chimney that have come loose — in a way she has not before, which is to say, in a proprietary manner. And it is then, during this inspection, that she sees the broken hinge.

She searches for something to stand on, for the shuttered window is just beyond her reach, and finds, to one side of the house, a table such as might be used for gardening. With considerable effort (but, oh, how her arms and legs have been toughened by her work at Hastings, work she cannot bear now even to think about), she drags the worktable beneath the window. She climbs onto its rough surface and, with a series of abrupt wrenching pulls, loosens the wayward shutter, finally tearing it free of its remaining hinge and flinging it to the ground. She brushes the rust off her fingers. She bangs on the frame of the window with the heel of her hand to dislodge it from its damp-swollen lock, and when the window gives, she cannot suppress a cry of triumph. She hitches herself over the ledge of the window, balancing for a moment on its sill and then falling to the stone flooring below.

She stands and looks at the interior of the chapel and is flooded almost at once by grief, a torrent of seawater filling a tide pool. She sees the altar and her last desperate moments with Haskell; she observes a young girl sketching by a window without a single troubling thought in her head; she sees a boy, a small child she has never known, who might have come here to play. Alone finally, with no witnesses, she sits upon the marble bench and gives in to this grief, fatigue fueling her intermittent sobs. Tears make rivulets upon her road-dusted cheek, and she wipes her nose with the hem of her skirt. After a while, she sits up, certain she is through the worst of it, and unfastens the first two buttons of her blouse. But this gesture, this innocent fumbling, triggers a memory so sharp and so sweet, she is once again shaken by small aftershocks of longing, ripples that force their way through her body.

After a time, she removes her hands from her face and glances around her. Vandals have been in this chapel and have written with charcoal or with black ink on the marble and on the walls. Waxed papers, such as fried fish might be wrapped in, are balled in a corner. A cloth hangs from a wooden bench, and when she gets up to investigate, she discovers it is a woman's undervest, its cheap muslin stained with something blue. She drops the garment onto the floor. She feels oddly violated. Though was it not she and Haskell who first desecrated this chamber? Or was that not a desecration, but rather the holiest of human sacraments? She does not know, though she has pondered this question for years. Even so, she thinks this new violation worse. The waxed papers, the scrawls, and the undervest are for her a desecration of memory, now the most dear of all her possessions.

She leaves the chapel and moves into the narrow passageway that connects the house itself, unlocking shutters and opening windows and doors as she goes, so that though there is only darkness ahead, there is light behind. The heels of her boots clicking satisfyingly on the slate floor, she passes through the kitchen with its bare cupboards and empty tables. Mice have skittered upon their surfaces, and rust has formed in the sink. She moves through the swinging door that once brought her unbidden to Josiah and Lisette. She makes her way through the paneled passageway where she last saw Haskell's face, through the dining room where they dined together, and finally into the parlor, ghostly with white shapes, undisturbed, untouched. It is, she thinks, a spectral chamber, its memories waiting to be uncovered with the sheets. A salt spray on the windows seems like a frost, and though she can hear the sea in its relentless draw and spill, she cannot see it clearly. She stands in the center of the room, which smells heavily of mildew, unties her bonnet, and lets it float to the floor. She sheds her cloak and the tie at her neck, and then bends and unfastens the cracked boots she has been wearing for weeks. She unbuttons the cuffs of the shirt she has on and rolls the sleeves to the elbow.

With a theatrical sweep, she draws off a sheet that covers a red and cream silk chair. Mice have been at the upholstery, or was it always frayed just so? She tugs off another sheet and exposes a round mahogany side table with claw feet. How heavy and dark and masculine the table looks in the whitened room. She walks to a door, unlatches its safety catch, and opens it. The sudden rush of air immediately clears her head, and it seems she can see more vividly than she ever has before. She makes her way to the railing, shading her eyes with her hand from an immense expanse of glinting and silvery light. She slowly surveys the rocks, the old orchards, the seawall, the beach. She will live in this house, she tells herself, and she will be free.

"Miss?"

She startles at the voice, which is that of the carriage driver who left her just a while before. He is standing at the foot of the porch steps, gazing up at her, cap in hand, his body long and slightly stooped.

"I come back to see you were all right," he says in his slow, unemotional drawl. "Didn't like leaving you on that doorstep there, with the house all boarded up and looking fearful as it does."

"Thank you," she says.

"I see you got in."

"Yes," she says.

"You got the water running?"

"I do not know," she says.

"Then likely you don't. Your pump is going to need a good priming."

"Yes."

She notices that his coat, a rough navy wool, is torn at the shoulder. His arms are exceptionally long and hang like unnatural appendages at his sides. His eyes, an icy blue, shine through the stubble and grime on his face.

"You won't have the electric or the gas on either then," he says. "You got somewhere to go for the night?"

"I shall stay here," she says.

He scratches his beard and looks skeptical. "It is my feeling, miss, that this is not a fit place for a young woman such as yourself," he says plainly. She tries to guess his age. Thirty-five? Forty? His face, coarsened by constant exposure to the weather, gives nothing away. "And as it is growing late in the day, I suggest you find yourself somewhere to sleep before it gets dark. Most places is full up this time of year, but my sister, Alice, she takes in boarders what are desperate."

Olympia has not thought of herself as desperate. But, reluctantly, she considers the man's proposal. He is right: If she has no water, she cannot stay here, however much she wants to.

"Yes," she says finally. "Thank you."

"You ready to go now?"

She hesitates. She cannot bear to leave this house so soon. "I . . ."

"You be ready in one hour then," he says.

"Thank you," she says. "You are very kind. What is your name?"

"Ezra Stebbins. I used to come by and deliver lobster to the house when your father and mother lived here."

"I see," she says. "You are a fisherman."

"That I am."

"You live nearby?"

"In Ely, ma'am."

She turns away for a moment and gazes out over the railing. She wonders if he knows as well why the house has been empty all these years. She draws herself up. This is but one encounter out of many she will have to endure in the coming weeks if she is to take up residence in Fortune's Rocks. She glances over to speak to the fisherman, but when she looks down at the foot of the porch steps, she sees that he is gone.

There are no chairs on the porch, only an old stool wedged into a corner of the railing. She dislodges the stool, puts it at the center of the porch, and sits on it, her skirts rumpling all about her knees. Four years ago, she and Haskell met at this porch railing. She can remember only too well the way they greeted each other, with Martha and Clementine and Randall and May in attendance, and the way she, Olympia, seemed already to understand that her meeting with John Warren Haskell was not precisely as it should be, not in any observable manner but only in that she felt, through the body, in addition to a sensation that was a combination of both shame and confusion, the distinct impression that there were layers within layers inside of which their simple, seemingly innocent gestures might one day come to be interpreted. And she wonders now if in every life there are not moments in time, perhaps four or five or even seven such moments, in which the life is transformed utterly or careens off in a direction unthought of, a direction that has seemed to be too fantastical or too harrowing to have been previously contemplated. These moments may come unbidden, when one least expects them, and often under awkward or disastrously wrong or even banal circumstances; and they may alight so softly or so fleetingly that they seem only like small birds swooping down upon the outermost branch of a tree. Except that these particular birds do not then fly away. Such a moment may be had within an evasive glance on a lover's face, or the first unwary sighting of a single word in a telegram (and *there,* one can almost see it, the life begins to veer away from its initial advance). And, most extraordinary of all, in the finite continuum of time along which each person travels, the terrible moment is fixed, immovable, incapable of being blotted out, however fervently or passionately one may later wish for this erasure.

The moment she met Haskell on the porch was one such moment, Olympia knows; and surely another was the precise instant in time when Catherine bent to the telescope, a moment Olympia shudders even to bring to consciousness (and if only one could erase such a moment as *that,* she thinks now). But was there not as well, she asks herself, a point in time when a life was made? And when was that moment exactly? That first afternoon in Haskell's room? When they lay together in the half-built cottage? In the sand, in the dark of night, when she had slipped out of the house unseen? Haskell once explained to her the manner in which he tried to prevent conception, and she sometimes saw and felt the small, wet balloons; but he also told her that such a method might not always be effective. And thus, lying on the floor of the unfinished cottage, he asked her about her monthlies, and it moves her now to think that they once had such a conversation, that she once spoke to a man of such intimate considerations; and yet how easy that was to do then. A new sadness takes hold of her, a sadness she has to shake roughly from her body as she stands up and abandons the porch for the beach.

For ten days, Olympia lives at the boardinghouse of Alice Stebbins, sister to Ezra, the fisherman who has befriended her. Olympia has a small room at the top of the house, and three meals are provided for her daily. Since the boardinghouse is in Ely, she cannot easily visit her father's cottage during this time, but she arranges nevertheless to hire a new caretaker. Water is drawn from the well and is seen to flow freely through the pumps. The electrical wires leading into the house are discovered to be in poor condition and in need of extensive repairs, a fact that does not deter Olympia from deciding to take up residence at Fortune's Rocks, as there are many kerosene lamps in the cottage. When she finally moves in, Olympia has cause to be grateful for her years at Hastings, since they have taught her enough of the rudiments of housekeeping and cooking to allow her to make the house habitable, a source of great satisfaction to her. She sweeps floors and shakes out rugs. With the water from the hand pump in the kitchen, she launders linens and bedclothes and washes windows. She rids cupboards of generations of moths; she captures cobwebs, prunes bushes, dusts furniture, and irons blouses. She airs clothing that has been abandoned, and where there are holes, she mends. She puts paper liners in all of the drawers and drags the mattresses out into the sun and beats them with a stick. She scours pots, mops floors, polishes woodwork, and takes the tarnish off the brass andirons. Gradually, the cottage begins to emerge from its neglect and even to gleam in the sunlight. The bedclothes smell of sun and sea air, and it is a joy to slip, exhausted, between the sweet, clean sheets at night.

With the small amount of money she has left from the travel expenses her father gave her before the summer began, she is able to buy food and some supplies in the village. It is a considerable walk to the store, but she goes early in the mornings, when she will be less likely to come upon someone who might recognize her. For though there are many who know the story of the catastrophe, there are fewer who might recognize her face, which, in any event, has changed in the four years she has been away. Her brow has grown more defined, her chin perhaps is sharper. When the sun is out, she wears darkened spectacles she once purchased when she was at Hastings. She knows, however, that she cannot remain unnoticed for long, nor keep the fact that she is in residence from her nearest neighbors. Already there has been some curiosity — passersby looking in at the wash on the line in the backyard, small boys peering at her as she rakes dried leaves from the underbrush — and if her neighbors know about her presence, it will be only a matter of time before her father does. Thus one afternoon not long after she takes up residence, she sits down at her old writing desk and composes a letter.

She writes her father that she is at Fortune's Rocks and that she has decided to remain there for some time. She writes that she cannot be dissuaded from her intent and that she will not return to Hastings Seminary in the fall. She adds that if he insists upon ousting her from the cottage, she will sever her ties with her family forever. She does not wish to hurt him, she says; she merely wishes to be left alone. Finally, she tells him that she is in need of funds, since the house requires many repairs, which she enumerates. In addition, she has little money of her own left.

For days after Olympia writes the letter, she expects a reply. When a letter does not immediately come, she anticipates, and then dreads, her father's arrival in person. Every time she hears a carriage on the road, she starts. On the twelfth day, however, the postman brings an envelope with familiar handwriting.

3 August 1903

My dear Olympia,

I was shocked to hear that you are at Fortune's Rocks. I do not think it a suitable place for you to be. And I am sorrier than I can say to learn that you wish to abandon your studies at Hastings. I confess I had harbored hopes that you would find some satisfaction in teaching and that you would take solace in being independent. But I cannot find it in my heart to chastise you further. Perhaps satisfaction and solace are not what you wish for yourself. I confess that I would not have cared greatly for such virtues at your age, though I value them most highly now.

You should have written to me at once, Olympia. I had a letter from Dean Bardwell within days of your abandoning your post. She was necessarily quite alarmed that you had vanished, and she managed to pass that considerable alarm on to me. I was given to understand that you had left voluntarily, but even so, I was greatly worried for you. For a time, I thought that somehow that man had made contact with you, and you had run away with him. I assume you are telling me the truth, and that you are not, in fact, with him now.

I worry about you, Olympia. I do not know how you will manage in that draughty cottage. But if you are determined to take up residence there, I shall not stand in your way. I have no desire ever to return to that house or to the coast of New Hampshire again. I will, of course, be forced to sell the cottage one day, but I have no plans for that at the moment, since I doubt I should get any great price for it in today's financial climate.

Your mother and I are sorry not to be with you on your twentieth birthday. Please know that we think of you daily. And please write to me from time to time. I need to know that you are well.

Your loving father

*P.S. Please find enclosed a check for one hundred and fifty dollars.
All bills for major repairs to the house should be sent directly to me.*

When Olympia has finished reading the letter, she bends her forehead to the kitchen table. She cannot bear to think of her father sad. For a few moments, all she wants is to pack a valise and make her way to the train station so that she might return to Boston and be embraced by her parents. She thinks of all the days her father spent with her at her lessons, how much of himself he once invested in her future.

After a time, she puts the letter on the table. Under the sink, she finds a stiff-bristled brush. She fills a pail with soap and water and, squatting to the hearth, begins to scrub away the charcoal smudges of an earlier season's fires. The stone has turned nearly black, and she has almost at once to fill her pail with clean water. She scrubs hard at the stains, for more and more it seems that only physical work can assuage the ache of irresolution.

But the pleasure she takes in those simple chores! Often, when Olympia is finished for the day, she will walk through the rooms of the house, admiring her work. She loves the way the banister gleams, the way the wavy glass in the vinegar-washed windows bends the horizon line, the manner in which the paint on the sills shines. Sometimes, when she has thoroughly cleaned a room, she will move its furniture. At first she merely shifts a table or a chair from one position to another within a room, but later, when she finds she minds the clutter, she begins to take those pieces that she can lift to the chapel for storage. The front room becomes, as a result, emptier and emptier, and she feels oddly better for this emptiness. She cannot move the piano, of course, nor the sofa, nor the English writing desk, but she takes away a crystal-fringed lamp, a chenille footstool, the furry skin of an animal that has functioned as a rug, a marbleized iron clock, an elaborate candelabra, side tables with their many skirts, a bamboo settee, tapestries that have hung upon the walls for years, heavy gold drapes that have shrouded the windows, a mahogany plant stand, a painted screen, an ornate gilt mirror, and various potted plants that have long since perished. She has a chair, a Windsor with a desk hidden beneath its seat, that she puts in the center of the room, so that when she sits on it, she can see straight out the windows to the ocean. And this she does often, occasionally getting up to make a pot of tea, or sometimes knitting, and only very seldom, reading. About books, she is cautious, for she does not want inadvertently to trigger an unwelcome emotion. For weeks now, she has been engaged in shoring up a foundation, in building scaffolds, and she does not wish the sturdy walls she has made to tumble down as a result of words on a page.

Most of the time, she wears simple dresses, since she is usually engaged in chores. But occasionally she will put on a pique or a taffeta that has been left behind in a wardrobe. Dressing and sitting in her Windsor chair and gazing out to sea is often occupation enough, and she now understands what is meant by a rest cure. She is certain that had her instincts not led her to this juncture in her life, she would never have recovered herself and might, over time, have developed various incapacitating nervous ailments that many women in their adult years, most noticeably her mother, seem to suffer.

At the end of each day, Olympia is usually deliciously fatigued, and it seems that she is always hungry. She eats sweet corn and blueberries and baking-powder biscuits and white cheese. She has milk from the milkman and bread from the bread wagon, and she strikes a bargain with Ezra so that once weekly he brings her lobster or other fresh fish. And it is, in fact, just on the heels of one of Ezra's deliveries, just as she is packing fresh cod into the ice chest, that a polished black automobile rolls up to the back gate. Through the window, Olympia watches in astonishment as Rufus Philbrick emerges from the car.

She looks down at her dress — a dull calico — and fingers her hair, unwashed now for over a week. There is no time to dress properly. For the first time since she has arrived at Fortune's Rocks, she laments the dearth of a servant to open the door.

"I hope this is not an inopportune moment to pay you a visit," Philbrick says, removing his hat and taking her hand when she has opened the door to him.

"No, of course not," she says, somewhat dazed by this entirely unexpected event.

She is surprised as well to see that Philbrick is considerably stouter than he was when she knew him, and she is at once reminded that he is, in addition to being a dandy, an epicure. Indeed, she sees that he needs to walk with the help of a cane and that he has on two different shoes, one quite a bit larger than the other. Perhaps he has the gout. He has shaved his whiskers, revealing pink cheeks and heavy jowls. His eyes are slightly pinkened at the rims. As she bids him enter the cottage, she looks once again at the faded calico she has on and thinks: *He must see me differently as well.*

He follows her into the kitchen, which, though spartan, is not unwelcoming. A vase of beach roses sits at the center of the worktable, and a pot of hydrangeas is on the sill. Still slightly rattled, she cannot at first think what to do with Philbrick. Apart from Ezra and the deliverymen, she has not had a single visitor to the cottage (and they can scarcely be called visitors). But then she recovers herself and tells Philbrick that she has lemonade and scones if he would join her for an impromptu tea. And though he begs her not to go to any trouble, she can see that he regards the prospect of fresh-baked pastries as a pleasant one.

"You are looking well," he says when they are seated in the front parlor. Philbrick has taken the Windsor chair, Olympia a lady's rocker that she brought down from her mother's room. The windows are open to the fine day, and there is the steady sound of the surf, only occasionally interrupted by the far-off screeches of small children on the beach.

"Thank you," she says, offering him a glass of lemonade.

"How long have you been here?" he asks, looking around at the room. She can tell that he is mildly nonplussed by the lack of furniture.

"I was at school at the Hastings Seminary for Females in western Massachusetts last year," she says, "but I have decided not to return. I have been here since mid-July."

"Your mother and father are well?"

"Yes, they are. Thank you for asking. Will you have some herring-paste sandwiches?"

"Yes, I think I might."

She sets down the plate before him. "Mr. Philbrick, how did you know that I was here?"

"Oh, my dear," he says not unkindly. "I am afraid I have had this news from any number of people. Did you mean to keep it a secret? If so, I fear you have greatly misjudged the nature of a small community."

She notes for the first time the remarkable costume he is wearing — a yellow and black silk vest over a pale yellow shirt, and over that a rather splendid suit of fine linen. Where does he find such clothes in New Hampshire? she wonders idly.

"No, I did not mean to keep my presence here a secret," she says, "but neither did I intend ever to announce my residency. But I am very glad of your visit, Mr. Philbrick. I have not yet had anyone come to call."

"Good Lord, Olympia. You have turned into a recluse. I merely wished to see if there was anything you needed. There was a time when I regarded your father as my greatest friend."

"Thank you," she says warmly, "but there is nothing that I need at the moment." She looks around. "Apart from a steam-heating system."

He seems taken aback. "You intend to remain here for the winter?"

"I may," she says, offering him another sandwich. Philbrick, she knows, is a man of appetite.

"Whatever for?" he asks. "Winters here are wretched."

"I am having the house prepared for winter months. And I shall shut down some rooms, of course."

"Even so."

Olympia nods. "I feel the need to live by myself for a time," she says quietly.

He studies her.

"And I was once very happy here," she adds honestly.

Philbrick sets down his glass. He folds his hands over his considerable stomach. There is a long silence between them.

"Olympia, I have great sympathy for your plight," Philbrick says finally. "In general, I am not a judgmental person. I daresay I have some understanding of difficult love and its consequences." He pauses for a moment, and in the pause, Olympia wonders fleetingly exactly what his understanding of difficult love is. "I have some understanding as well of what you have suffered as a result of having known love. For I have no doubt your relations with John Haskell were born of love. In retrospect, I fancy I saw it between you."

Olympia cannot at first reply.

"A certain current in the air when you and he were in a room together," he adds, gesturing in a descriptive manner.

Olympia longs to be able to discuss Haskell with another person. But she knows that to do so with Rufus Philbrick will be to trespass on the grounds of familiarity, to risk his perhaps already compromised opinion of her.

"Actually," Philbrick says, reaching for another scone now that he has successfully traversed the slightly treacherous landscape of love, "I rather thought you had come here for the child." He picks a crumb from his silk waistcoat.

And it seems to Olympia then that all the world holds its breath, that the floor itself gives way and falls a thousand feet. Later she will wonder how possibly she could have managed — apart from a momentary and perhaps too abrupt glance at Philbrick — to pretend that she had more knowledge of what he spoke than she did.

"Remarkably good institution," Philbrick adds.

Olympia runs her tongue against the roof of her mouth, which is suddenly paper-dry. Yet she dares not raise the glass of lemonade to drink, for she is certain that Philbrick will see the tremor in her hand.

"Some of these orphanages are appalling," Philbrick says, "but Mother Marguerite runs a tight ship, I will say that for her. The good fathers of Saint Andre are always pestering me for donations, and I suppose they finally felt it necessary to make me a member of the board." He shrugs. "Of course, I do not mind. It is a sound organization continually in need of aid."

Olympia nods politely. She realizes she has been holding her breath. She lets air out slowly so as not to betray herself.

She opens her mouth, but cannot speak.

Philbrick leans forward. "My dear," he says. "You have gone pale. I should not have spoken. I should know better than to bring up painful matters. Well, I have never been one for tact. . . ." He regards her carefully. "Please forgive an old man for having no manners."

Olympia shakes her head. "I have always admired your boldness," she says truthfully.

Philbrick wipes his mouth with his napkin. "I shall not keep you any longer, dear Olympia. I should go before I blunder further. Please feel free to call upon me if ever you should have the need. It would give me the utmost pleasure to be of assistance to you in any way."

He stands and Olympia stands with him.

"I fear I have greatly upset you," Philbrick says.

"Your visit has been a delightful respite from my daily tasks," she says quickly to deflect his suspicions. "I hope you shall come again."

Philbrick takes a card from a leather pocket case and hands it to Olympia. "You may write to this address at any time. Please give my regards to your father and mother."

She turns and walks to the door, knowing he is examining her as he follows.

"Thank you for the lemonade," he says at the door, offering his hand, "and please give my compliments to the cook."

"There is no cook," she answers.

"My God, Olympia, you really are alone," he says.

"Yes, and I prefer it that way."

He steps down onto the lawn and examines her anew.

"I always thought you would have an extraordinary future," he says.

She shuts the door behind Philbrick and waits until she hears the motor of his automobile start up. Her vision is blurry in her right eye, and a severe pain is starting in her left temple. She puts her fingers to her head, but the pain concentrates itself into a small nugget just beyond her reach. *I fancy I saw it between you*, Philbrick said. She feels nauseated and presses her forehead to the cool glass of the door. She has to clear her head and find her way to her bedroom. *A current in the air* . . . She turns to walk back into the house and has to put her hand out to the wall to steady herself. At the corner, she bends suddenly, fearing that she will be sick. *That you had come here for the child* . . . She wipes her face with the skirt of her dress and tries to concentrate. She has to find her bed. The pain grows hot and pushes against her skull. *Some of these orphanages are appalling.* . . .

Around her the hallway is spinning, and her son is in Ely Falls.

OLYMPIA LIES on her bed in her exceptionally clean house for days. It rains so much that the milk and the bread and the lobsters make a tidy and then a foul package outside her kitchen door. From time to time, she hears knocking, and she knows it must be Ezra. She does not want the man to have to worry about her in addition to all of his other responsibilities, but she cannot rouse herself to greet him.

On the third or fourth day, she climbs out of bed, weak from lack of food. Her room is stale and unpleasant. She washes herself, puts on clean clothing, and brushes her hair. She opens the kitchen door, finds the foodstuffs that have been left there, and throws them out, with the exception of a loaf of stale bread, which she toasts and eats with tea. She marvels at how her father could have given her baby to the orphanage at Ely Falls and not have told her anything about it. She thinks about how he must have blanched to have seen the Fortune's Rocks postmark on an envelope that bore her handwriting. She wonders if he is even now worrying that she might inadvertently discover the whereabouts of the boy. She imagines him pacing in the upstairs hallway.

She has known from the moment Philbrick left her house that she will go in search of the child. The days she has lain on her bed have been spent not in indecision but rather in gathering strength for the task ahead. She has had to ask herself many times if she is prepared for such an undertaking: Suppose she finds the child, what then? Can she just simply ask for him back? And if so, will they give him to her? And if she gets him back, will she be able to care for him properly once she does? The boy will be just over three years old by now. She wonders if the child has been well tended, and she prays that he has. She does not know his name.

How, then, will she be able to find him at all? What Christian name was given to him at birth? And what of his surname? Did Olympia's father allow the name Biddeford, or was he permitted to change the name to something else altogether? How are such things accomplished? Olympia has no idea and certainly cannot ask her father about these matters, since she would risk alerting him to the fact that she has discovered the child's whereabouts. And risking that, she will further risk his moving the child or journeying up to Fortune's Rocks to confront her, which she most sincerely does not want him to do.

On the morning of the seventh day, she dresses in a lavender-blue silk moiré suit left behind in her mother's mahogany wardrobe, and wears with it a broad-brimmed rucked silk hat. Experimenting in a mirror, she discovers that if she angles the hat just so, most of her face is hidden. It is not so much that she fears discovery as that she does not want yet to admit any other persons who might know her into the fragile universe she has created.

The trolley to Ely Falls can be boarded at Ely, which is three and a half miles from the beach at Fortune's Rocks. She has thought about walking but has reasoned that she might sully her skirts and boots were she to try it, and such a disheveled appearance might not serve her well in her mission. Thus Ezra, with whom she has spoken the day before, comes to fetch her and takes her to the trolley.

The lobsterman, whom she now knows is in his late thirties, is amiable company for her on the short ride into Ely.

"Was your father a fisherman as well?" she asks along the way.

"He was. And his father before him," Ezra answers plainly.

"And you like the life?" she asks.

"I have two hundred pots in the water, and that keeps me busy," he says. "I check them at daybreak before the sun is over the horizon. I have three sons, and I expect one or more of them will follow in my footsteps, though I have tried to discourage them from such a future. And I guess there's your answer. It's a hard life." He says this without self-pity, the broad vowels of his accent soothing to Olympia's ears. And indeed, when she looks down, she can see the text of many harsh incidents written upon the back of his hands. Without thinking, she reaches over and touches one of the scars, the touch startling both him and her.

She apologizes for her boldness, an apology he waves off as he explains that the deep cuts were made by lobster claws in the few seconds before he was able to peg them. She wants to ask about his wife, about what her life is like; and more, she wants to know, but will not ask — no, never would she ask this — if he loves his wife, if he thinks his wife loves him; if, in their way, they are happy together. For though her experience is limited, she knows that love is often inscrutable, indecipherable to observers, and yet it is that intimacy she most craves some understanding of. When they reach the trolley, he bids her a good journey and says that he will return for her at four o'clock.

The trolley is crowded with both natives and summerfolk, many of whom have come up from Rye, doubtless thinking to have a day of shopping in Ely Falls. There are no seats when she boards the dusty vehicle, and all the heat of the day seems to have concentrated itself within the wooden walls of the conveyance. The passengers are jostled and knocked about because of the unevenness of the track bed, and the smell of all those overheated persons is quite unpleasant. If it were not necessary to hold on to the grip with both hands to keep from falling over, she would cover her nose with a scented handkerchief.

Occasionally, through the crowd, she catches a glimpse of scenery. New houses have been built, and it seems the outer limits of the city of Ely Falls begin sooner than they did four summers earlier. They pass business signs that read PATENT MEDICINES and LIBRAIRIE FRANÇAISE and H. P. POISSON, PHOTOGRAPHER. Then FANCY GOODS, PARADAY'S SMOKE HOUSE, and BOYNOINS PHARMACY next to a sign that reads only LEWIS POLAKEWICH. There are striped awnings of many colors and tall department stores that either she did not notice on previous trips to the city or were not there before. The streets and sidewalks are thick with people and with carriages, and an air of business seems to have infected the crowd on the trolley. She gets off the trolley when most of the others do, though she has no idea where she is.

She stops a policeman in the street and is given directions to the orphanage. As she walks, the sky overhead takes on a blue-black appearance. In the distance, she can hear thunder. She begins to run but is caught in the sudden downpour and has to shelter in the doorway of a bank. After a few minutes, restless with her mission, she sets out again, only to receive another soaking a block from her destination. Running hard now, she at first mistakes the tall granite structure with its evenly spaced windows on the corner of Merton and Washington for a department store. And then, in passing, she sees above the door the words *The Orphanage of Saint Andre*.

The floor of the central hallway is made of stone. As she walks to a door marked OFFICE, Olympia's boots leave small puddles in her wake. After a moment's hesitation, she knocks on the door.

It is opened by a tiny woman in habit and wimple. The woman has small black eyes with many folds at the lids, and her mouth is deeply lined and pursed. She seems at first startled to see Olympia standing there, and then begins to regard her more closely. The sister takes in Olympia's rucked silk hat, her wet boots, and the lavender-blue skirts that cling to her legs. Her scrutiny is intense, and Olympia thinks the sister will shut the door in her face.

"Forgive me for interrupting you," Olympia says, "but I wish to speak with someone in charge of the orphanage."

"For what purpose?" the sister asks. The question is quick, in the manner of a schoolmaster who demands an equally rapid reply. The sister speaks with a French Canadian accent.

Olympia has rehearsed her speech so many times that she has thought nothing could possibly cause her to misspeak it. But so stern is the sister's countenance that Olympia finds herself stammering, even as she realizes that the stammering will undermine her position.

"I . . . I wish to find a child," Olympia says. "That is . . . I wish to ascertain the well-being of a certain child. Who will have been brought here three years ago. In the spring."

"But why?" the sister asks, neglecting still to invite Olympia into the room.

"Because . . ." Olympia draws a breath. "Because he is mine," she says quickly.

The sister sighs heavily and then steps aside. "Come in," she says.

The sister walks to a chair behind her desk and sits down. "You young girls are all alike," she says. "You think that you can just abandon your babies, leave them on our doorstep, and then come back in two or three years and walk away with them. It will not happen that way."

"No," Olympia says, moving toward the desk.

With a quick wave of her hand, the sister bids her sit down.

The back of Olympia's skirts is soaked, and she is certain it will leave a wet mark on the chair. Her hat is so heavy with the rain, she is forced to remove it. The knots she has made in her hair hang low on the back of her neck. She pushes the loosened bits behind her ears.

"What is your name?" the sister asks.

"Olympia Biddeford."

If the sister knows the name, she gives no indication. She folds her hands and presses them under her nose. "And what is the name of the child?"

"I do not know," Olympia says.

The sister's fingers are red and shiny. She wears a wedding band on her left hand.

"You wish only to know the health of this child?" the sister asks.

"I . . ." Olympia looks down into her lap. She has brought her purse, and in it a considerable sum of money. She does not like to think about having to buy her child back, but if it comes to that, she is prepared to do so.

"I am not sure," Olympia says, not quite truthfully.

"You have a husband?"

Olympia shakes her head.

The sister thrusts her chin out in a quick gesture of disapproval. "And how do you propose to support such a child?"

"I have means," she says. "I have a house."

"Where is this house?"

"At Fortune's Rocks."

The sister studies Olympia with the faint disdain of the righteous judging the privileged.

"You have a family? A housekeeper?"

"No, not at the moment. My family, that is, my father and mother, live in Boston."

"I see. Did you have money at the time the child was abandoned?"

"*Abandoned* is not the proper word," Olympia says. "The child was taken from me. I was very young."

"I can see that." The sister regards her carefully. "How old are you now?"

"Twenty," she says.

"There are procedures," the sister explains. "We do not give away children. You understand that."

"Yes."

"What name was the child left under?"

"I do not know."

"This will be difficult then," the sister says. "Who brought the child?"

"I am not sure. He was taken from me at birth by my father. He himself would not have brought the baby, but I do not know if he would have used his name for the" — she struggles for the right word — "transaction."

"Exactly," the sister says.

The nun opens her desk and withdraws a ledger that is stuffed with many papers. She peruses the journal for some time. The pages snap smartly as she turns them.

"I do not see a Biddeford here," the sister says. "Not for the time you say. Might there be another name?"

Olympia hesitates. She lowers her eyes to the middle distance on the desk. "Haskell," she answers quietly.

The sister, whose name Olympia still does not know, looks up at her.

"I see," she says, not consulting her ledger at all now. "First name?"

"John."

"And why might that name have been used?"

"He was . . . is . . . the father," she says.

"Yes, I see." The sister seems to scrutinize her anew. "And might he have brought the child here himself?"

"No, no," Olympia says. "I do not think so. My father would not speak to Dr. Haskell, nor allow his name to be spoken inside our house. I sincerely doubt he would have had dealings with him."

"And where might John Haskell be now?"

"I do not know," Olympia says.

The sister clucks and shakes her head. "You understand that this cannot be done quickly."

Olympia's heart leaps. Does that mean that securing the child might be possible? "Yes," Olympia says, and perhaps she smiles.

"And that the child may not be here at all."

The sister scowls at Olympia, causing Olympia to recompose her features. "I have prayed that this will not be the case," Olympia says, realizing at once that the sister will not much credit her Protestant prayers.

"You will almost certainly need legal advice," the sister says.

"I wish to know if the child is well," Olympia says. "And I wish to know . . . his name."

The sister nods her head slowly. What might such a woman's life be like? Olympia wonders suddenly. A life of celibacy and prayer, of service to others. Would the natural longings for love be so great that one would always feel the loss, or did longings evaporate with religious devotion?

"Many of the children are placed out before the mother can come back for them," the sister says. "Occasionally they are adopted by legal means. Why have you waited all this time?"

"It is only recently that I could even consider such an action," she says.

"The gift of a child is a very great treasure," the sister says. "Do you think that a girl who has sinned should be rewarded for her foolishness with such a gift?"

Olympia opens her mouth to speak, but she cannot answer her.

The sister rises from her chair. "I wish you to remain here," she says, and leaves the room.

Olympia sits in her wet skirts and waits for the Catholic nun to return. The room grows chillier, and Olympia shivers, from fear or from the cold or from the aftermath of fright, she cannot tell. She has nothing dry to wrap around her. Rain beats against the tall windows, the sills of which are at the level of her chin. The walls are painted brown, and the paint shines with all its nicks and dents in the electric lights. Behind the sister's desk is a large ornate cross with a suffering Jesus.

The journal with its papers — papers of differing sizes and colors — sits on the sister's desk. If she looks in that journal, Olympia wonders, will she find the name she is looking for?

She gets up from the chair to walk around the room to warm her limbs. Her skirts still stick to her thighs, and she has to peel them away from her. She is shivering badly now, and she wonders what is keeping the sister so long. Where exactly has she gone?

The sister knew the name of John Haskell. Of this Olympia is certain.

She walks to the window and looks out at the steady rain that has followed in the wake of the thunderstorm. Then she turns and studies the office, the tall oak filing cabinets partially lining one wall, the many books in a floor-to-ceiling bookcase. The only chair for guests, the one she has sat in, is severe and spartan, and Olympia thinks that the nun must not encourage many visitors.

Her teeth begin chattering, and she clenches them. She searches for a heat source, sees a radiator behind the sister's desk, but when she goes near to it and feels it, she discovers it is only lukewarm. Still, she thinks, lukewarm is better than nothing, and she leans against it. She is so cold that she no longer cares if the sister catches her behind her desk.

She listens for the sounds of children, but can hear nothing. Once, however, she does hear the clicking of heels along the stone and returns to her chair, but it is a false alarm, and within moments Olympia finds herself leaning on the radiator again. Where *are* the children? she wonders. Are they housed in this cold, granite building? Surely not. However can this be a children's home? She does not want to think about it. She has an unpleasant image of children's cots lined up against a wall, like those of soldiers in a field hospital.

The sister is gone for so long that Olympia begins to imagine she has abandoned her altogether. She wonders if she should go in search of her. She stares at her desk, mesmerized by the sight of the journal with its broken spine and its stuffing of colored papers of differing sizes. From her vantage point, leaning against the radiator, she can make out a few words in pen: *the baby which is left,* she reads. And *awful it is to separate.* Olympia takes a step closer. She reaches out and, with the tip of her index finger, opens the journal.

There is a letter lying between two pages.

24 May 1897

To the Sisters of the Orphanage,
    I scarcely know what to write but that I am the mother of the darling baby girl who was left on your doorstep with the three dollars in the basket on the night before last. I cannot speak of the terrible pain of separating from my dear one, but not being able to keep her for the reason that no one will employ me with an infant (and I have neither husband nor father to help me) I must give her up to you. Please comfort her and be kind to her and tell her

that her mother is named Francine. I cannot now tell you my other name, but I will one day when I come to fetch her, which I pray I will be able to do soon, if I am earnest and hard-working and can save up some money. She is but four weeks old, and I have not been able to pay for her baptism, so please, if you would be so kind, perform this for her. Her name is Marie Christine, and I hope you will keep this name so that I will one day be able to find her again. And if God does not permit this, I hope that we will be reunited in Heaven.

A mother

Olympia shuts her eyes. 1897. How old would Marie Christine be now? Seven years, eight years? Did the mother come back for her as hoped?

Olympia turns to another page.

15 December 1899

Sister M. Marguerite, Mother Superior,
    This child is the product of an assault upon the person of a young woman who has had occasion to come under my care. She is a decent girl but is too poor to support this child, having one other by an unknown person. I was present at the delivery of this infant, whom I pronounced to be in good health, although the girl tells me now that the boy has been weak in his breathing for several days. This child is not yet baptized. You will be well advised to place this child out if you have opportunity, since I doubt sincerely the young girl in question will ever return for him. The event that produced the child is a source of great mental suffering for the girl, and as a result of this, she has had to move away from her mother and step-father, and I hope you will take my meaning in this.

Respectfully yours,
Dr. R. Martin

Olympia's face grows hot, and there is perspiration at her hairline. She turns another page and comes upon a piece of stationery that is blank but for its letterhead. She notices the name of Mère Marguerite and decides this must be the tiny woman with the black eyes she is still waiting for. And then Olympia notices, on the letterhead, along with a dozen other names printed in the left-hand margin under the heading *Board of Directors,* the name of Rufus Philbrick. Of course. Olympia turns another page and draws a note, which appears to have been written on a scrap of brown parcel paper, toward her.

4 February 1901

Dear Sisters,

You are so kind and I know that you will love my little Charles. In your kindness, please forgive an unwed mother whose heart is broken. Please also, if I may request this, place him out to a Catholic family, as I do not like to think of him denied Heaven for want of knowing about the Church. You will forgive me if I do not leave my name.

Olympia returns to her chair and stares at the journal. Do all of the other pieces of paper in the book contain similarly wretched letters? She puts her head in her hands. She gave up her child without so much as a note or a dollar, and what excuse did she have? None. She was not poor. She was not the victim of brutality. And the child, whatever else his circumstances, had been conceived in love. That much was true. How could she have so easily given the child away?

Olympia starts when she hears the door behind her open. The sister walks by her and sits at her desk and appears to notice nothing amiss. She does not tell Olympia why she has been so long away, but neither does she look as stern as she did earlier. Indeed, she seems to have softened considerably.

"You are cold," the sister says.

Olympia is silent.

"Do you want me to fetch you a wrap? Or some tea?"

Olympia shakes her head.

"I have received permission to tell you the child's name."

Olympia presses her hands together as if praying and rests her chin on the tips of her fingers.

"It is Pierre," the sister says.

And Olympia thinks, holding her breath from the shock of the name, *His name is Pierre!*

"But I am afraid I also have some rather disappointing news to tell you," the sister says. She looks concerned, and Olympia freezes.

"The boy has been placed out," the sister says.

"What does that mean?" Olympia asks.

"The boy has foster parents," the sister explains.

"No," Olympia says. "This cannot be."

"I am afraid, my child, that it is."

"No," Olympia says with more emphasis. She places her hands upon the sister's desk. "Surely there is some way to get him back," she says. "Surely I can have him back? After all, he is mine. He is my flesh and blood. Surely no law can prevent me from having him." She is unable to keep a note of desperation out of her voice.

"I am afraid that all of this happened some time ago," the sister says softly, but with an unmistakable note of finality.

Olympia feels the blood leave her head. The sister must see this, for she asks Olympia quickly: "Will you faint?"

"Where is he?" Olympia asks, her mouth having gone dry.

The sister purses her lips and shakes her head. "I cannot tell you that," she says. "Our policy —"

"You *must* tell me," Olympia interrupts. "Please, I have to know where he is."

"I cannot," she says. "I can, however, tell you that he is with a loving mother and father. I know of the persons in question, and I know that he is being well cared for."

"Do they live here, in Ely Falls?"

"I cannot answer that," she says. "I am sorry, but this is not really such an unusual circumstance. And if you think about this from the boy's point of view, is it not better for him to have been all this time with a loving guardian in a warm home, with good food and a good bed, than to have lived with an unwed mother who is shamed and is perhaps too young to care for a young child?"

"I do not have shame," Olympia says.

The sister sits back in her chair. "How impertinent you are," she says coldly. "You come here asking for my help and I give it to you, and you dare to tell me, a mother superior of the Catholic Church, that you have not sinned? Have you no conscience, girl?"

"I have a conscience," Olympia says evenly. "I am sorry for the harm that I have done another woman and her children. But I am not sorry that I loved or was loved. And I do not think I am too young to care for a child. I would have cared for him well even when he was born."

"Ah, yes, but you did not, did you?" The nun smiles unkindly. "You will find that the law, as well as the church, will vigorously disagree that you are a fit person to care for an infant. An unwed mother, immoral in the eyes of society and a sinner in the eyes of God, is understood to be the least fit of all possible parents."

"But this is not true," Olympia says heatedly. "Would you deem a father who has raped his daughter a more fit parent than a strong, young woman who has happened to conceive a child out of wedlock?"

"No one just *happens* to conceive a child," the nun says. "There is will involved and intent. Since it is obvious you were not misled and did not suffer a brutality, it would appear that you quite willfully sinned against Nature and against God and against another woman and her family, may God have mercy on your soul."

Olympia straightens her back. "To love is not a sin against Nature, and I will never believe it so."

The nun stands. "You cannot hope to be restored to society and to the community of the righteous if you do not confess your sins and beg forgiveness."

Olympia stands as well. "I will beg," she says. "You may be sure that I will beg." She collects her purse, the purse that contains the money with which she was willing to purchase her child. Perhaps she ought to have done that immediately, she thinks, offered the money first. But it is too late now.

"You may be certain that I will beg and plead and fight and use all of the resources available to me," Olympia says carefully. "But I will one day find out my son's full name, and I will one day have him with me."

In a statement of dismissal, the mother superior crosses herself, a gesture Olympia finds distasteful as well as mildly frightening.

*   *   *

16 August 1903

Dear Mr. Philbrick,

You said to me recently that I might write you if I had need of your assistance. I would not bother you if the situation were not of the utmost importance, and I hope you will find it in your heart to permit me to call upon you and hear what I have to say.

I should like to visit Tuesday next at eleven o'clock in the morning if that is convenient for you. Please do not write my father about this letter or our previous visit. I am now twenty years of age and may speak to you, if you would permit this, as an adult.

I shall await your reply.

Most respectfully,
Olympia Biddeford

17 August 1903

Dear Miss Biddeford,

Of course, I shall help you in any way I can. I shall look forward to your visit on Tuesday, the 21st, at eleven o'clock. I trust you still have my card with my address.

I hope you are well.

Yours sincerely,
R. Philbrick

*   *   *

Tuesday dawns a brilliant day, which Olympia takes as an omen of a happy outcome. She is nervous at the thought of presenting her case to Rufus Philbrick, but whenever she feels her resolution falter, she thinks of the incomparable reward should her quest be successful. She imagines a boy named Peter sitting on her lap upon the porch while she talks to him of the ocean and the tides and the sun that always rises in the east. Of the summer solstice, of a game called tennis, and of strange-looking crusty creatures called lobsters. She will introduce him to Ezra and will take him with her to the grocer's. Together they will walk the beach and look for shells that he will put into a bucket.

Olympia dresses this day in a pale peach shirtwaist, which she irons and starches to within an inch of its life so that she will appear to be domestically capable and skilled. In her nervousness, she miscalculates how long her toilet will take, and she is ready nearly an hour before she is scheduled to be picked up. She rehearses her prepared speech, trying for a delicate balance between reason and passion. Rufus Philbrick's help is essential to her cause.

Ezra comes for her at the appointed time, and so anxious is she about her proposal that she finds it difficult in the extreme to make conversation with the fisherman. And as Ezra is by nature taciturn, the two pass the journey in near silence. When they enter the township of Rye, Olympia takes Philbrick's card from her purse and gives Ezra the address. He seems at first puzzled, even though he appears to know where it is. After a series of turns onto roads that become narrower and narrower, finally reaching a lane that is barely wide enough for the carriage, Ezra stops before a small cottage.

"This is it?" Olympia asks incredulously.

"Yes, ma'am."

"I do not think this can possibly be correct," she says.

She surveys the cottage, nestled into a landscape of thick honeysuckle with the sea not far in the distance. The cottage is weathered-shingled with two multipaned windows in the front and a large glassed-in sun parlor to the side. In the second story, if it is indeed a second story and not an attic, there are long, narrow windows that span the length of the house. It is a charming building, one that reminds her more of a gardener's cottage than of the home of a man of finance. Surely, there has been some mistake.

But then she sees Rufus Philbrick himself, in a light-blue linen suit, emerging from the sun parlor to greet her; and she can do nothing but climb down from the carriage and walk forward to take his hand.

"Mr. Philbrick."

"Miss Biddeford."

By prior arrangement, Ezra has agreed to wait for her. She waves to the fisherman and then allows Philbrick to take her arm and lead her into the cottage.

"You are very polite and so will not say anything, but you are shocked that this should be my home," Philbrick says disarmingly.

"Well, yes, rather," she answers, smiling slightly. "I had imagined . . ."

"Indeed. I am a man of few needs, apart from my vanities, and I discovered that I much prefer living in a small house to rattling around in a manse that is clearly too large for a single man. Also, I do not care for the constant invasion of privacy that servants must necessarily cause. Therefore, I decided, some years ago, to swap grandeur for freedom, and I must say I have never regretted the trade. My housekeeping skills are minimal, not to say nonexistent, however, and so I have a housekeeper who comes in twice a week and cooks for me. But I am rambling on and on when you are standing here in need of food and drink."

"No, no," she protests as she gives him her parasol. "Please do not go to any trouble."

"Nonsense. I seldom have visitors, and Mrs. Marsh has made marionberry pie. We shall go into the parlor and take a small lunch of sandwiches and so forth and then the pie. Or would you rather sit out here?"

Olympia gazes around her at the sunporch, the white beaded boards rising to the chair railing, the large windows in a bank above it. Some of the windows have been latched to the ceiling, so that breezes move through the screens. Around the sun parlor, someone has planted beach roses and flox, and to one side she can see the ocean. Through the open doorway of the cottage, she catches a glimpse of part of a kitchen. Unadorned. Yellow wood.

"Here would be lovely," she says.

He asks her to sit in one of two wicker rockers he has drawn up to a small round table. With no discernible limp, he disappears into the kitchen. His foot must be better, she decides. She gets up and follows Philbrick into the kitchen. She asks if there is somewhere she might wash up.

"My dear. Of course. Walk straight through there, and at the end of the hallway, you will find the lavatory."

Olympia does as she is instructed, admiring a small parlor that looks more like a man's study than a sitting room. On an intricate walnut desk with many compartments are half a dozen silver frames of varying sizes with photographs of what must be family members, including several of handsome young men who might be Philbrick's younger brothers. In another corner is a grand piano, too large for this modest room, and on it a sweet-scented bouquet of flox in a pink glass vase. Beside the piano, there is a small silk settee as well as an ornate captain's chair, not unlike her father's. A Persian rug covers the floor and even licks at the walls. It is a room filled with furniture that clearly used to belong to a larger house — pieces too cherished to abandon.

Along the hallway, papered in tasteful green-and-black stripes, are several good oil paintings. She recognizes one by Childe Hassam, another by Claude Legny. At the end of the hallway are two rooms, and she guesses that the lavatory will be on the right. She realizes her mistake at once, however; she appears to have entered Philbrick's bedroom. Its accoutrements are obviously masculine: the double bed, ill made; a cherry dresser, bare but for a man's hairbrushes and humidor; another bureau of bleached pine on which a bowl and pitcher sit. She turns to leave, but something odd about the room causes her to linger a second longer than she might, and it is then that she notes the second set of boar-bristle brushes, the two identical paisley silk dressing gowns on hooks beside the bureau, the two sets of striped pajamas folded, one under each of the pillows of the double bed. Two matching stained-glass lamps sit on bedside tables, and next to each are large gold glass ashtrays with the remains of cigars in each. She moves closer to one of the tables, picks up a photograph in a marquetry frame. The young man has a beautiful face, seen in profile, a cloud of pale hair lit from behind. The face is smooth, unlined, the planes of the cheeks high and dramatic.

Olympia is unnerved but not stunned, not stunned as she might once have been. And neither is she disturbed. But though she cannot know for certain, and though she cannot truly understand this knowledge, she cannot help but regard Philbrick as a somewhat different man than he was just moments ago. And as she thinks about the pictures of the other young men in silver frames on the walnut desk (perhaps not brothers after all), she remembers Philbrick's statement about love, words she thought slightly odd at the time but now make perfect sense. *I daresay I have some understanding of difficult love and its consequences,* he said to her.

Portraits, she thinks as she replaces the marquetry frame. We are all unfinished portraits.

When she returns to the sun parlor, Philbrick comes through with plates of sandwiches and a pitcher of iced tea, condensation dripping from the glass. The sight of Philbrick in blue linen amidst these humble surroundings — and further, the image of Philbrick in his paisley silk dressing gown conversing with a young man standing at a bureau and knotting his tie — moves her, and for a moment she forgets her manners and cannot help but stare at the man. But then she is herself, the smell of the food awakening her, the vision of the gruff Philbrick bearing plates of sandwiches so astonishing that she wants to smile despite the gravity of her mission.

She opens her mouth to speak, but he holds up a hand.

"I know you have come on important business," he says, "but it is my belief that one should never discuss serious matters on an empty stomach, as such a condition will lead only to light-headedness and a faint heart."

This is logic Olympia cannot argue with; and besides, she is unexpectedly ravenous. Later she will remember this small lunch as one of the half dozen best meals of her life, the simplicity of the food and its circumstances fueling a hunger that had lain dormant for weeks.

For a time, they speak of fish paste, blue willow plates, the lamentable license in bathing attire, and the garish arcade in town. "You are a woman of appetite," Philbrick says appreciatively when between them they have devoured nearly all of the sandwiches. "Now, you must have some of Mrs. Marsh's incomparable marionberry pie."

He brings from the kitchen two white plates stained with dark juices. "It is a local berry," Philbrick explains, handing her a dessert plate and fork. "A cross between a raspberry, a blueberry, and a cranberry."

Olympia tastes the pie, a claret droplet falling from her fork and onto her peach shirtwaist. Philbrick reaches forward to dab the spot with his napkin. For a time, they eat in companionable silence, the only sounds the industrious buzzing of bees outside the sunporch window. "This is delicious," Olympia says after a time. "Both sweet and tart. I did not know such a thing existed."

"A well-kept secret," Philbrick says.

Olympia sets down her glass. "Mr. Philbrick," she begins. "I know you are a busy man, and I will not take too much of your time. Let me tell you why I have come."

"Please do. What is this grave matter?"

"In April of 1900, as you know, I gave birth to a baby boy," she says boldly, the blood pounding in her ears at her audacity. She has never spoken that sentence aloud to any person before. Philbrick, who has been leaning forward to put his glass on the table, slowly sits back in his chair.

"The child was immediately taken from me," she continues. "My father had made arrangements. I do not know to whom he gave the child. I know that he himself did not leave the house that day or the next day."

"I see," he says.

"When you came to my house, I did not know that the child had been brought to Ely Falls," she says.

Earlier, she made the decision to be forthcoming and honest with Philbrick, for she knows him to be a man who can detect falseness in a person. And if he detects this in her, she will fail in her campaign. "It was a shock for me to comprehend that the child had been placed with the Orphanage of Saint Andre. Shortly after your visit, I went to the orphanage to inquire about the boy."

"Did you indeed?" Philbrick asks, appraising her closely.

"I spoke with a sister there."

"Mother Marguerite Pelletier, I suspect," he says. "Small but formidable?"

"Very."

"And you survived."

"Barely."

"Go on."

Olympia takes a breath. "The sister would tell me only that my son's name is Pierre. And that he has been placed out."

"You did not know the name of the child before?"

"No, I was never told. It was not a subject my father would discuss with me."

"No, perhaps not." Rufus Philbrick dabs at the corners of his mouth with his napkin. "You want to know where your son is?" he asks.

"Yes, yes, I do. I want to know his whole name. I want to know where he is, with whom he is living. I want to know if he is well."

"And?"

She folds her hands in her lap. "I could lie to you," she says, "and tell you that I wish merely to ascertain if the boy is well, but I do not want to be false with you if I am asking for your help. My hope is that one day I may have him to live with me."

Philbrick seems to take in the whole of her now, as if gauging her moral weight. He folds his fingers under his chin. "This is a very grave undertaking."

"Yes, I know that," she says. "But I cannot say truthfully to you that I will not try to win him back. He was taken from me, *stolen* from me one might say, and I am heartsick at the loss. I have already lived with this for some time now. I believe I have paid a heavy price."

Philbrick is silent. He adjusts his tie and looks down at his large stomach, as if assessing its comfort. Then he leans forward, emphasizing the seriousness of what he is about to say.

"I have always regarded you, Olympia Biddeford, as a responsible and gifted young woman. I confess I was shocked and saddened at the events which occurred four summers ago. It seemed so unlike you, I hardly knew what to think. I was distressed for your father, of course, who was my friend, and I was very concerned about Mrs. Haskell and the children. I am sorry to bring this up again, but these things must be said."

"Yes."

"Actually, I was not as shocked to hear of a child as I might have been. It is, sad to say, a not uncommon occurrence. Hence, the existence of the orphanage."

"Yes."

"But let me ask you this, Olympia. Are you prepared to take a young child, barely more than a baby, from his home? From the only mother he has ever known?"

She has thought about this question and has rehearsed her response. "She is not the mother," Olympia says quickly.

Philbrick shakes his head. "You have wronged one family already. I am sorry to say this harshly to you, but there it is. Are you quite certain that you wish to do this again? Surely you do not expect a foster mother to give up her child so easily?"

"He is not her child," Olympia repeats.

"I doubt very much the woman in question will see it that way."

"But what if the woman is not caring for the boy properly?" she asks. "What if she has many other children and thus little to go around? What if she is Franco? Indeed, she almost certainly is Franco to judge from the name of the boy. Do I want a child of mine to be raised in a culture he was not born to?"

"But what if the mother is a loving, caring woman?" Philbrick asks. "Does station or income or culture matter in such a case? Do you not think of what is best for the child?"

"I do," Olympia cries. "I do. And I think I shall be best for the child. I have some means. I have no other responsibilities. I know that I can take good care of the boy. That I will be a good mother. I sincerely believe this."

Olympia hears the note of near hysteria in her voice and tries to compose herself. "Mr. Philbrick, I cannot argue my case, for it is an argument written in the blood of my body. It is a debate more heartfelt than reasoned."

Philbrick stands up then and walks to a window.

"Am I to be eternally punished by not even being allowed to know the whereabouts of my own child?" Olympia asks. "Shall you not at the very least tell me whether he is well cared for and what his situation is? Am I to be denied that simple knowledge for the rest of my life?"

Philbrick turns. "Let me think about these matters, Olympia. They are difficult."

"I know."

"I believe I can answer at least one question for you," Philbrick says. "I cannot say for sure what name the child has now, but I do know he once had the name of Haskell."

"My father gave the name Haskell to the boy?" Olympia asks.

"It was John who brought the child," he says quietly.

Olympia turns her head away and stares through the screen at an old lilac bush, now divested of its blooms. Philbrick leans toward her, but she waves him off.

"No, I did not know," she says. "I thought only that my father, having heard about the orphanage and reasoning that it was far from Boston, had made arrangements."

"And doubtless he did," Philbrick says. "But he made them with Haskell."

She shakes her head. It is inconceivable to her that her father communicated with John Haskell during that terrible time before the birth. Inconceivable that Haskell would have given over his own child. But then, as she removes a handkerchief from her purse beside her, she remembers an argument she and Haskell once had in a carriage on the way back from the Rivard birth, and how he advocated life in an orphanage for a child over life with an unwed mother who was ill prepared for her lot.

"You never heard from John himself then?" Philbrick asks, again quietly.

"No."

Philbrick clears his throat. "I daresay the child is thriving," he says. "Although it has been some time since I inquired. Actually, I am ashamed to say that it has been years. This is news to me that the child was placed out."

"How dare my father and Haskell conspire to take the child from me!" Olympia blurts out suddenly. In an instant, anger has replaced shock.

"Oh, my dear," Philbrick says. "Of course, you know they did it for you. I am certain they thought it best for you."

"They could not possibly know what was best for me," Olympia says heatedly. She stands. "I must leave you now," she says, only then remembering her manners and the lovely lunch. "Mr. Philbrick, thank you for a truly wonderful luncheon. And I do mean that sincerely. I envy you your house."

"Do you indeed?"

She studies him for some sign of how he lives in this modest cottage, some clue to his secret life; but he remains, in his blue linen, only a kindly, if blunt, man of finance. "You will not write my father?" she asks.

"No," he says, walking her to the door. "I can promise you that. This matter is between you and me."

They move out onto the front lawn. In the lane, Ezra is waiting.

"I will try to discover the whereabouts of the child," Philbrick says, "and then determine for myself if he is being well cared for before we will discuss this again. I do not like to be the arbiter of your future, but you have placed me in this position."

"I can think of nothing else to do."

"I shall write to you," he says. And with that he bends and kisses Olympia at the side of her mouth, which is nearly as astonishing to her as the news she has so recently had to digest.

A S SHE HAS been doing each of the eleven afternoons since she visited Rufus Philbrick's cottage, Olympia sits looking out to sea, an occupation that consumes nearly all of her time. Sometimes she brings a book with her onto the porch, even occasionally her mending, but these, she has come to understand, are mere accessories to the true task at hand, which is no task at all, but rather the necessity merely to be patient, to sit and look out over the water and to wait for a letter.

She watches a fisherman working from his boat not fifty feet off the rocks at the end of the lawn. A not unfamiliar sight, the boat bobs in the slight chop while the man hauls in wooden pots from the bottom of the ocean. The craft is a sloop, no, perhaps a schooner, laden with barrels of bait and catch — a charming sight, but testament only to a life more harsh than any Olympia has ever had to endure, even during those wretched weeks at the Hardy farm. Prior to meeting Ezra, Olympia had hardly ever given any thought to such men or to their families. She has passed by the rude fish shanties from which the lobstermen work dozens of times, seeing the shacks and the boats themselves and even the men aboard them as mere backdrop to the true theater of Fortune's Rocks, the life of the privileged summer colony at its leisure; when of course it was much the other way around, these farmers of the sea being the time-honored inheritors of the native beach and its environs. And it strikes her again, as it has so often lately, how easy it is not to see what is actually there.

With a sudden and impatient gesture, Olympia puts down the book she has been pretending to read, a dull treatise on Italian landscape painting. All her thoughts circle in upon themselves, and no progress is ever made. It is this wretched idleness, this hideous state of suspension to which she has sentenced herself. Seven, eight, sometimes ten times a day, she walks to the back door with its letter chute and stares at the barren floor, willing an envelope to the painted surface. Although the post is often irregular, she has come to know well the postman's habits, and she frequently finds herself at the place where the back walkway meets the street, engaging the slightly bewildered man in conversation, ever hopeful of an envelope with her name on it.

She stands up and begins to pace along the length of the porch. Why is it taking Rufus Philbrick so long to reply? Is it possible he has simply decided not to pursue the inquiry after all? But would he not then write to her of this decision? He has seemed always to be a man of his word, and if he said he would try to help her, then surely he must be doing so.

Patience, she counsels herself. But she is tired of being patient, weary of remaining passive.

She picks up her book and then immediately puts it down. Surely there must be something more lively to read than the nearly impenetrable prose of an uninspired Italian art critic. She makes her way through the house and into her father's study, where some few volumes remain, damp and swollen and sadly misshapen though they are. She has scarcely ventured into this room since her return to Fortune's Rocks, the presence of her father having permeated the very walls and flooring of this small chamber, so that it seems that he is always here, sitting in the captain's chair, eyeing her judgmentally.

So with a sidelong movement (and avoiding for the moment the sight of the captain's chair), she enters the study and searches the nearly barren shelves for a book that can at least physically be read and that might hold the promise of engagement. As she scans the titles, however, *Clapp's Marine Biology, A Short History of the Zulu Nation,* and *Nepos De Vita Excellentium Imperatorum,* hope of success begins to dwindle. Disappointed, she turns to leave the study, meaning to go back to the porch, but her eye then lights upon a dark volume with gilt lettering, a book held together with string and lying facedown on the floor beside her father's chair, almost as though he had dropped it. And when Olympia realizes its title, she marvels that the book has survived at all, that it was not flung across a room or burned in the grate, for it is the very same volume that once introduced her to the breadth and scope of John Haskell's mind.

She picks up the book and sits in the only chair in the room, forgetting for the moment its spectral occupant. She unknots the string that binds the book, and immediately a number of letters slip from the pages onto her lap. She knows well the pen, that masculine hand, not her father's, and the sight of Haskell's writing makes her sit back in the chair. It is some time before she can open the letters themselves. Of course, she thinks, when she unfolds the first one; of course, Haskell would have corresponded with her father that summer.

10 June 1899

My dear Biddeford,
Thank you for your most welcome invitation to join you and your family at Fortune's Rocks the weekend of June 21st. You are

quite right in discerning that Catherine and the children will not much care for hotel life on their weekend visits, but neither do we wish to . . .

26 June 1899

Dear Biddeford,

How can I possibly describe to you how very delightful our visit with your family was during this past weekend? Such an excellent stay it was, apart from the tragedy of the shipwreck, and what a considerable wrench it was for us to have to leave you all! Catherine is in high spirits, feeling as she does that she has found a true companion and future confidante in Rosamund. I, of course, enjoyed my discussions with you and Philbrick immensely as always. And the children are in thrall to your astonishing daughter, Olympia. . . .

2 July 1899

My estimable Biddeford,

No, I confess I do not see the point of your argument regarding the merits of Zachariah Cote as a poet and should be indifferent to the publication of his shorter works in your much-admired Quarterly. *I find he lacks the muscle to temper his verse, which is shot through with baroque description and feminine whimpers. But of course, this is why you are the editor of this excellent journal and I am only a man of science. . . .*

11 July 1899

Dear Biddeford,

Thank you for your kind invitation to join you for dinner at the Rye Club on the 14th, but I am expecting that day a visit from the eminent physician Dwight Williston of Baltimore, and thus will be engaged. . . .

18 July 1899

Dearest Rosamund and Phillip,

John and I accept with pleasure your kind invitation to a Gala evening on the Tenth of August, 1899, in honor of the Sixteenth birthday of your daughter, Olympia.

With Anticipation and Fond Regards,
Catherine Haskell

Olympia crumples the letters in her fists, and then, regretting this impulse, lays them flat against her lap. How extraordinary that all that summer there was this other bond between her father and John Haskell, a man her father much admired, an admiration that was much reciprocated. And how twice (no, thrice) betrayed her father must have felt — by his daughter, by his friend, and by this fraudulent correspondence with its attendant ironies. Had her father reread these letters in light of the discoveries the night of the gala? No, she thinks, he could not have, for certainly he would have destroyed them in a fury.

The book falls open at its flyleaf, and she reads the inscription there. *For Phillip Biddeford and his engaging intellect, this humble offering. Yours sincerely, John Haskell.*

She tucks the letters back into the book and closes its covers. Is Haskell once again working in a mill town? she wonders. Or can he have forfeited his training as a physician? Has he abandoned the writing as well? Or might she one day wander into a library and open a literary or political journal there and come across his name as the author of an essay published therein? She looks through the open door that gives onto the dining room, that elegant room with its double mirrors and buffets, its graceful proportions and its view leading down to the sea. She glances up at the chandelier, a crystal confection that resembles nothing so much as a necklace strung upon a woman's throat. She fingers, at her own neck, the locket Haskell once gave her, a locket she has never been without, not during her time at the seminary, not during her exile in Boston, and not even during the difficult moments of her son's (their son's) birth.

She closes her eyes and lets the memories wash over her, as they are wont to do, an incoming tide she has learned to let overtake her and then ebb away. And when it is over, she sets the book down upon the marble table beside her father's chair, and stands. She will go mad if she stays in this house a moment longer.

The sand has a crust upon it that crumbles as she walks. Men and women, in heavy cotton bathing dresses, stand at the water's edge, looking forlornly out to sea. Almost every summer Olympia can remember, there is a week in August when the water seems stagnant with dark clots of seaweed, slimy with jellyfish on its surface. No one bathes in the sea during this week for fear of the stings from these gelatinous creatures. Most know well the story of the hapless Tommy Yeaton, once the lone constable of Fortune's Rocks, who went bathing for pleasure on a Saturday afternoon in August and had the misfortune to be assaulted by a school of jellyfish. The man perished on the following morning as a result of fever caused by the stings, and Olympia remembers her father telling her this story from time to time as they walked along the beach, doubtless wishing to deliver a cautionary tale.

But soon, she knows, the beach will be deserted. There is only a week remaining until the end of the season, when most of the summerfolk will leave Fortune's Rocks. She finds that she is looking forward intensely to the fall, when the beach will be silent but for the gulls and the sea, and the cottages will be boarded up. The days will grow colder, and inland the leaves on the trees will change their color. She will get in a good supply of tinned fruit and vegetables and dried cod, and coal as well for the stoves. It might be necessary to move downstairs for the winter, she thinks; indeed, she almost certainly will have to do that. She imagines herself alone in the front room, looking through the long floor-to-ceiling windows on a cold November day, gazing down the expanse of beach, thinking of each of the other cottages shuttered and waiting for its owner once again to return to bring it back to life; and that image causes such a sudden and unexpected pang of something like grief that she stops in her progress. It is, surprisingly, she recognizes at once, grief for her father; for she sees, more clearly than she ever has (and perhaps she has not, until now, been able to allow herself to see this before), how crushed her father must have been to have his daughter, his only child, fall so far from grace, to have all his hopes dashed beyond reclamation. Was Olympia not his experiment, his pride? She remembers the night of the dinner party with Haskell and Philbrick in attendance, and the manner in which her father spoke of his daughter's superior learning. And it was true then, she thinks; she did have a singular education. But for what purpose?

Olympia crouches on the sand and wraps her arms around her legs, resting her forehead on her knees. Her hat slips backward off her head. She thinks of all the hours her father spent instructing her, all the days of lessons and debate. What will he be doing with those hours now?

"You all right, miss?" she hears a voice beside her ask.

She looks up quickly into the face of a boy. He is frowning and seems slightly puzzled by her odd posture. She sits back on the sand and props herself up with her hands.

"Yes," she says, reassuring him. "I am fine now."

He stands politely, in his dry navy bathing costume, his hands folded neatly behind his back, a position that incongruously suggests the military. The boy has yellow curls and a splash of freckles below his eyes, which are a blue so pale as to resemble water in a glass.

"You are sad," he says.

"A bit."

"Because of the jellyfish?"

She smiles. "No, not exactly."

"What is your name?"

"Olympia."

"Oh."

"What is yours?"

"Edward. I am nine."

She offers her hand, which he takes, as a boy trying to be a man will do.

"Are you on holiday?" the boy asks.

"No, I live here."

"Oh, you are lucky."

Olympia sits up and wraps her arms around her knees. "But I have not lived through a winter yet. They say the winters are difficult."

"I live in Boston," the boy volunteers, sitting down beside her. "May I?"

"Yes, of course," she says, smiling at his attention to manners. "You are here with your brothers and sisters?"

"One sister, but she is only a baby," he says, implying that a baby is of not much use.

Olympia glances around her and sees no concerned adult. "Will your mother and father not worry where you are?"

"I shouldn't think so, miss. They are in France now. I am here with my governess."

"And will she not worry about where you have got to?"

"When I left her, she was sleeping on the porch." He gestures toward a large, weathered-shingled cottage with white trim beyond the seawall.

Olympia nods. "But you do know all about how you should not go into the water without an adult with you?"

"Oh, yes. But I should not go in today anyway."

"No."

She watches the boy stretch out his legs, which are long and spindly and dry. He digs his heels into the sand.

"Are they terrible?" the boy asks suddenly. "The stings?"

"I have never been stung myself. But I have heard that they are."

"And you die?"

"You *can* die from them. But not always. Sometimes you just have the fever. There once was a policeman who got stung. His name was Tommy Yeaton. He swam into a school of jellyfish and got stung dozens of times. He died the next day."

The boy seems to consider this new fact.

"Would you like to have a footrace?" he asks her suddenly.

"A footrace?" she asks, laughing.

"Yes," he says. "We could start here and . . ." He scans the length of the beach. "Do you see there? That striped umbrella in the distance?"

"Yes."

"Shall we say the first one to the umbrella wins?"

"Well . . . ," she says, hesitating. She cannot remember the last time she participated in a footrace. Surely not since she was a child herself. But the boy's request is so earnest, she finds it hard to resist.

"Why not?" she says, beginning to unlace her boots.

The boy jumps up. He draws a long line in the sand. "This will be our start," he announces excitedly.

"All right," she says. She discreetly pulls off her stockings and stuffs them into her boots.

The boy steps up to the start, leans forward, and puts a foot behind him in the traditional racing stance. Olympia leaves her boots and stockings with her hat, stands on the line beside the boy, and lifts the skirts of her yellow gingham just enough so that she will not trip.

"Are you ready, miss?"

"Yes, I think I am."

"When I count three then?"

The boy races flat out, his chin up, his hair flying behind him, as if he had been taught to run this way at school. Olympia, feeling slightly awkward at first, bends into the run and tries to keep pace with him. Almost immediately her hair comes loose from its pins and flaps heavily against her neck. The boy, both wiry and strong, looks over his shoulder, and, seeing her so close to him, picks up his pace. The balls of Olympia's feet dig into the sand. Her muscles feel pleasantly strong after so many weeks of domestic work. She lifts her skirts higher so that she can stretch her legs. She feels at first mildly embarrassed to be cavorting so, but then this embarrassment turns to a distinct sense of exuberance until she is nearly giddy with the event. She raises her face to the sun. *My goodness,* she thinks, *it has been so long since I have felt like this.*

As they draw closer to the striped umbrella, Olympia glances over at the boy and can see that she might inadvertently win the race. The boy runs with grace and determination, but his young legs are tiring. Olympia pretends then to be winded and slows her pace slightly. With the prize in sight, the boy, finding new energy, sprints forward to the umbrella, startling its owners, who are sitting on canvas chairs beneath it, and gathering so much momentum that he pitches into the sand. When Olympia reaches him, he is sprawled with his legs splayed open, trying to get his breath. She bends, taking in air. The boy has sand on his forehead and on his upper lip.

"You won!" she says breathlessly with her hands on her knees.

He is so winded that he cannot even smile. In a moment, however, a look of concern crosses his face. "You did not let me win, did you?" he asks.

She rights herself. "Of course not," she says. "I would never do that."

He brushes the sand from his face and limbs.

"I would race you again tomorrow if you like," he offers.

"That would be fine," she says.

"And perhaps tomorrow you will win," he adds shyly.

She tries not to smile. "Then I shall look for you," she says, "and tomorrow I *will* win."

"Well," the boys says. He stands up, but he seems reluctant to leave. "Do you have a boy?" he asks suddenly.

"Yes," she says simply.

"What is his name?"

"Peter."

"Would he like to race with us, do you think?"

"I think that perhaps he would, but actually I think we would beat him rather badly. He is only three years old."

"Oh," says the boy with evident disappointment.

"But I know he would like to meet you one day," Olympia adds quickly. "He is very fond of nine-year-old boys just like yourself."

"Is he?"

"Oh, yes."

The statement produces an unexpected smile. He glances in the direction of the shingled cottage.

"You had better go back now," Olympia says. "I shall look for you tomorrow," she says.

He nods. He begins to walk slowly away, then turns and waves once quickly. She waves back to him. He breaks into a run then, and Olympia watches him sprint to the place where they met on the beach, as if he were already practicing for tomorrow's event.

She watches him until he is only a speck.

Yes, she thinks. *I have a boy who is three.*

She glances at her feet, encrusted with sand. She touches her hair, which lies tangled in knots along her back. Inside her dress, she is perspiring from her exertion. She makes a feeble attempt to tie up her hair without pins, but its weight almost immediately pulls it loose.

She does not want to go back to the cottage just yet, for to return to the house is to wait for a letter, and she does not want to reenter that numbing state of suspension. She sets off once again toward the far end of the beach. She will collect her shoes and socks and hat later.

She walks briskly, still buoyant with her earlier exercise, and it is only when she sees the Highland Hotel in the distance that she slows her steps. She has not ventured this far along the beach since she returned to Fortune's Rocks. She takes in the porch, the guests sitting in the rockers, the windows in the upper stories, a certain window through which a gaily colored cloth snaps repeatedly, as if a woman inside were shaking out a bedspread. The hotel looks remarkably unchanged, although it seems there are more people about than she remembers from before. She recalls a sea of white linen, an opened ledger with slanted cursive. She can see muslin curtains at the windows, the way a shirt was flung upon an ochre floorcloth. She can hear a voice: *If only you knew* . . . She can almost feel the silky cotton of the overwashed sheets, can nearly make out the sage tin ceiling with its raised pattern. She can hear the echo of her own footsteps in the stairwell.

She notices then a gathering of people at the southern end of the porch. A late-season party, she deduces, and thinks: *How fashionable the women look in their bishop's sleeves.* And then as she casually scans the guests, her eyes fall upon a familiar figure. She stiffens as she recognizes a certain self-conscious tilt of the head, a distinctive profile, a flash of white teeth. He has on a yellow-and-black checkered waistcoat, and he sports a new monocle. He has grown his whiskers in the muttonchops mode, a style Olympia has never found attractive. While she watches, Zachariah Cote throws his head back and laughs, and Olympia, even at a distance, can see that the gesture is exaggerated for his audience. She has heard that Cote is successful now, that his verse has become popular; he publishes in ladies' magazines and is admired by married women in particular. Olympia has several times seen his poems in print, and she has remained steadfast in her opinion that they are dreadful: dripping with sentiment and overlaced with a penchant for the morbid. And she is seized with a sudden bitterness that it should be Cote, of all of them, who has fared so well. That it is Cote — and not her father or her mother or John Haskell or Catherine Haskell or even she (no, especially not she) — who is welcome upon that porch on a late summer day in 1903.

And yet, was not Cote, of all of them, the only one who acted with true malice? Did not Cote actually *invite* Catherine Haskell to inspect the view in the telescope, knowing what she would find there? And were not Olympia's parents and Catherine Haskell utterly blameless but for an innocent, if intimate, association with scandal? Though Olympia would not absolve herself of any of the guilt associated with the catastrophe, her anger grows as she stands in the sand. *What an ass,* Catherine once said of the man. Olympia thought the observation fitting then, and does now. She wonders if Catherine Haskell herself ever had occasion to come inadvertently upon the poet's verse, and if she did, how she managed the experience.

And it is as she is having this thought that Cote, still dissembling for his audience, turns slightly and spots Olympia on the sand — in her yellow gingham, her feet bare, her hair in knots along her back. She resists the impulse to walk away and instead returns his gaze as steadily as he bestows it. She can see the man's surprise, his momentary bewilderment, the quick questions as his mouth relaxes from its smile.

The woman beside Cote speaks, and he briefly acknowledges her; but he does not remove his eyes from Olympia. The woman glances in her direction, doubtless wondering who it is that has captured Zachariah Cote's attention so thoroughly. But if the woman recognizes Olympia, she gives no sign.

Olympia holds her ground as Cote extricates himself from the cluster of admirers and makes his way down the porch steps toward her.

What extraordinary nerve, she thinks as she watches him walk closer.

He stops when he is three feet away. For a moment, neither of them speaks.

"Miss Biddeford," he says finally. He stares at her a long time, as if assessing how this encounter might unfold. A small smile begins at one corner of his mouth, the smile of a chess player who has possibly seen his way to a checkmate. "What a delightful surprise," he says.

"I should think there is nothing delightful about it," Olympia responds evenly.

"Of course, I knew you were in residence," Cote says, ignoring her rude reply. "It is hardly a secret."

She is silent.

"But are you truly living alone?" he asks. "Astonishing to think of it." His posture is eerily familiar to her: One arm is folded across his chest, his chin resting on the knuckles of his other hand.

"How I am living, I believe, is none of your business, Mr. Cote."

He puts his hands to his heart. "Oh, I am wounded," he says, mocking her.

She continues, "But I am glad for this opportunity to tell you that I consider you to be the most despicable of all men."

She watches as he takes in her bare feet, her disheveled hair, the unfashionable yellow gingham.

"This is rather rich coming from you, do you not think? But then I must make allowances for your impertinence, as you are certainly the most unfortunate of all women."

"No," she says. "I think the most unfortunate of all women is the woman who will one day be your wife. Or have you been refused already?"

"My, my, but you have changed, Olympia Biddeford. You used to be so sweet. And so accomplished. I did not know you for such a sharp tongue."

"I would, on this occasion, wish my tongue as sharp as a razor," she says.

"You little witch." Cote's lips are suddenly bloodless. "How dare you address me in this manner? You who have committed the foulest of sins? You who have displayed your wanton nature for all to see? Did you think I was blind to you and John Haskell? I knew from the moment I saw you by the side of the road in his embrace what you two were plotting. And I held my tongue. I held my tongue for weeks, Miss Biddeford. But you, you who were so much grander than I, could barely bring yourself to speak to me. Did you think that I would not notice your condescension? And did you think I would then stand idly by forever and watch you and Haskell carry on, with no thought of consequences? Did you think I could just let you ruin not only Catherine Haskell's life but also those of your mother and father — whom I must say I can no longer admire? My God, Olympia Biddeford, you used to come to this hotel to fornicate with that man!"

He sputters this last and actually points at the hotel, causing several of the women on the porch to turn to see what the commotion is about. Olympia glances down at her hands and notices, for the first time, how red they are, how raw their knuckles.

She looks up at Cote. She knows, as indeed she has known all along, that he will shortly return to the porch and will tell all of the assembled guests of this encounter; and she imagines, briefly, exactly how he will narrate the story of the scandal and her family's disgrace. She can almost feel the exquisite pleasure he will take in retelling this familiar tale.

"What I did," Olympia says to Cote, "I did for love. What you did, you did with the heart of a snake."

She turns then and walks away, slowly and with a steady gait, striving for as much dignity as a woman in bare feet and gingham can manage. Her temples are pounding, and she can barely breathe; she forces herself to move forward without looking back. When she is certain she is beyond his ken, the trembling in her body begins in earnest, so much so that she has to walk into the sea, even with its seaweed and the threat of jellyfish, so that the shock of the icy water upon her feet and shins and knees might bring her to her senses. But when she is in the water, she finds she cannot move, either one way or the other; and thus she remains in that position, the only bather on the beach, the focus of many curious stares, until her feet become so numb that she can no longer feel them beneath her skirts.

When she returns to the place where she has left her shoes and stockings and hat, the boy, Edward, is waiting for her. He jumps up when he sees her approaching.

"I was worried for you, miss. You have been such a long time in coming back."

She reaches out to touch the top of his hair, which is thick with curls and silky.

*   *   *

1 September 1903

Dear Miss Biddeford,

Forgive my tardy reply to your request, but it took me some time to discover the answers to your queries, and more time to ponder the wisdom of passing this information on to you. Mother Marguerite, as you know from experience, is quite a formidable gate-keeper, and even as a member of the Board, I found it took nearly all of my powers of persuasion to convince her to allow me, so to speak, in the door.

Now, Olympia, heed what I have to say here. I have written the facts you have requested on a separate piece of paper and have sealed it within the enclosed envelope. But I am going to urge you to have the courage to destroy the envelope before opening it. What is written here has the potential to cause both you and very many other persons considerable anguish.

If you have further need of me in this or in any other matter, please feel free to call upon me at any time.

I remain faithfully yours,
R. Philbrick

She lays the enclosed envelope on the table and studies it for some time, partially out of respect for Rufus Philbrick and his warning, and partially out of fear of what she might find. But within minutes, she knows that she has neither courage nor sound judgment in this matter and that her desire to discover her son's last name and his circumstances outweighs all other considerations. With hungry eyes, she rips open the second envelope.

The boy is called Pierre Francis Haskell. He was baptized 20 May 1900 at Saint André's Church. He was given into the care of Albertine and Telesphore Bolduc, both employees of the Ely Falls Mill, who reside at 137 Alfred Street in Ely Falls. He is healthy and has been so since birth.

Olympia shuts her eyes and brings the crumpled piece of paper to her breast. She has a son, she thinks calmly, and he is healthy. She has a son, and his name is Haskell.

*L*IGHT-HEADED FROM the press of bodies, Olympia emerges from the trolley at the corner of Alfred and Washington Streets. The sky, too brilliant, casts a dull white light upon the streets, turning elms to nickel and women's faces to porcelain. It is among the worst of days the New Hampshire seacoast has to offer: the hot, close air unrelieved by even a breath of east wind. Perhaps there will be a storm.

With Philbrick's letter in her hand, she moves along the sidewalk, checking the wrought-iron numerals beside the doors. Alfred Street, she discovers, is both commercial and residential, the ground level taken over by shops, the upper stories of the buildings left for housing. Today, nearly all of the windows of those upper stories are open, with people leaning on sills, fanning themselves, hoping for an errant breeze. Olympia finds the numbers 135 and 139 and deduces that 137 must belong to the narrow building without a number sandwiched in between, an ochre brick edifice next to a dental office. She checks her piece of paper, not quite daring to believe she has found the correct address. Wishing to remain as anonymous as possible, however, she quickly puts the paper in her purse and casts about for a suitable place to linger.

Two possibilities appear to her: a bench under an elm about twenty yards north of the house, and a bakery behind her that is advertising in its window tea cakes and jelly rolls. Deciding that the bakery might be stifling in the heat, Olympia makes her way instead to the bench.

Alfred Street is crowded with men and women trying to stand in the shade of the shop awnings, the men in collarless shirts, their braces hanging from their waists, and women in open-necked blouses with sleeves rolled. A vendor selling ice cream and tonic has attracted a considerable following of children, some of them barely dressed, who hover around the vendor, doubtless looking for a stray ice chip to suck on. Olympia, thirsty from her journey, is momentarily tempted to buy herself a cold drink, but the prospect of calling publicly to the vendor and thus drawing attention to herself seems unwise.

She wishes she had not worn her hat and that she *had* worn her white lawn, which is much the coolest dress she owns. As it is, she is awash in perspiration against the back of her thighs and inside her boots. She studies the signs in the windows across the street. TEETH. ARTIFICIAL SETS. $8.00, she reads. SILVER FILLINGS. 50 CENTS. Near the dentist's office is a drugstore promoting, in a hasty scrawl on a cardboard sign, COLD SARSAPARILLA. All of the doors to the shops along the street have been thrown open, and Olympia can see many shop owners, identifiable by their white aprons, standing in the doorways, some smoking, some wiping sweat-stained necks with handkerchiefs.

Despite the extraordinary heat and the distractions of the street, however, Olympia keeps her eyes trained upon the small blue doorway that is poised over three stone steps nestled between the buildings of the druggist and the dentist. And as she does so, she becomes aware that a man in a suit of buff-and-brown check has taken a seat beside her. In the stagnant air, the smell of an unwashed body mixed with the cloying scent of cheap cologne, and this in turn overlaid with the smell of cigar smoke, nearly makes her gag. She moves an inch or two away. To Olympia's dismay, the man leans even closer to her and asks her when the next trolley is. Without fully turning in his direction, she says that she is sorry, but she does not know.

"I, for one, am off to the beach," he announces. "I cannot tolerate the heat of this foul city a minute longer."

Olympia remains silent, unwilling to encourage the man in conversation.

"Let me make a proper introduction," the man says. "Lyman Fogg, traveling purveyor of Boston Drug, 'administered by the wife in coffee for the treatment of alcoholic excess in husbands.' Our slogan, by the way."

He extends his hand, and Olympia, who has just removed her gloves because of the heat, is forced to put her own in his. The man is absurdly overdressed in a woolen suit and top hat, which he wears at a rakish tilt and from which an oily black curl has fallen onto his forehead. With his free hand, he stabs his cigar into his mouth and takes a quick puff, the exhalation hanging as though suspended in the air in front of them. His coloring is remarkably florid, and Olympia observes that in addition to the nearly intolerable smell, the man is giving off heat as well.

"Powerful hot, is it not?" he asks. He takes off his hat, revealing a brim that is black with sweat. Olympia turns away from him to watch the doorway.

"You waiting on the trolley yourself?"

"No," she says politely. "I am just resting."

"Well, aren't I the one in luck then?" the man says jovially. "Because I was just saying to myself, 'Lyman, that is a fine-looking bench with a fine-looking woman sitting upon it, so why don't you just make yourself an introduction?'"

Even with her head turned slightly away, Olympia can smell alcohol on the man's breath. He settles himself back against the bench and in doing so contrives to inch even closer to Olympia.

She removes a perfumed handkerchief from her purse and puts it to her nose, hoping he will take the hint. But the man seems impervious to her distress.

"Now I would say," he begins speculatively, and she can sense the man's eyes upon her, "that you are not from these parts, which causes me to wonder and even to be so bold as to inquire what a fine young woman such as yourself is doing sitting on a bench on Alfred Street, which, though not without its charms, is not a fit location for a lady?"

From the corner of her eye, Olympia can see the blue door between the dentist's office and the drugstore open. A woman in a mauve cotton dress leans against the door, apparently holding it open for someone else. She has her hand extended into the building.

"No," the man beside her continues, "I can safely assume that you are from over to Fortune's Rocks, where all those fancy cottages are. Am I correct in this assumption?"

Olympia watches the woman in the doorway bend slightly to speak to someone in the interior of the building.

"Miss?"

"What?" Olympia asks distractedly. "Oh. Yes. I am."

"Well now," the man beside her says, chuffed to have made such a good guess. "And may I ask your name?" he adds, perhaps emboldened by his success.

The woman in the doorway touches her dark hair, which is arranged in a pompadour with fringe at the front. She smooths her hand over the bodice of her dress, three tucks extending from the yoke to the waist. She might be thirty, Olympia guesses. Over the skirt of her dress, the woman has on a black apron. She steps back into the building, letting the door swing almost shut. She emerges with a boy.

"Or perhaps I am being overforward," the man beside Olympia is saying.

The mother and the boy, hand in hand, stand at the top of the cement steps, as though assessing the scene before them. Olympia can see clearly the child's features.

Walnut hair. Hazel eyes. The resemblance is unmistakable.

Olympia presses her knuckles to her mouth.

The man beside her looks over sharply. "Are you ill, miss?" he asks.

The want is instinctive and overwhelming. Later, she will recognize this strange sensation within her as a double want: for the boy as well as for the father before him.

She watches the woman and child descend the stone steps. The boy has on faded blue short pants with a matching jacket. He turns and begins to walk with his mother away from Olympia. She can see only the back of the child now, the neatly cut hair, the scuffed brown leather shoes, the short plump legs. Olympia stands.

"Oh now, miss," the man beside her says, standing as well. "There is no need for this. I hope I have not offended you. Perhaps I am being too forward? If so, please forgive a weary salesman in this heat."

Olympia is losing sight of the woman and the boy in the crowd on the sidewalk. Panicky, she takes a step forward.

"May I start again by suggesting that we dip into that drugstore over there, where I am bound to tell you I am rather well known, and have ourselves two of those cold sarsaparillas they are advertising in the window, which, I may assure you, will be given to us free of charge?"

Olympia shakes her head distractedly. "Leave me," she says impatiently, although it is she who walks away.

She crosses the street and moves briskly, searching for a mauve dress in the crowd. She is jostled rudely, and perhaps she jostles rudely in return. She picks up her pace, nearly running now, until she sees, at the next corner, the figures of a woman and a boy entering a shop. The sign over the door reads CONFECTIONERY.

Olympia moves closer to the store and stands as near to the shop door as she dares. She pretends to be examining the contents of her purse, as though searching for something she has misplaced. She puts a frown of concentration on her face.

This is madness, she thinks to herself, though she does not alter her posture. *I do not even know if this is the correct woman and child.*

And then, in the next instant, she thinks, *Of course I do.*

Around her, there are men and boys, their braces loose, their shirts collarless. She can hear them call to one another, but she cannot make out their words. When the woman and the child emerge from the shop doorway, the boy has in his hand an ice-cream cone that is dripping all around its rim and onto his tiny fist. Perhaps alarmed by this food that moves, the boy seems about to cry. The woman bends and takes the cone from him and licks all around its edge, catching the drips. She returns it to the boy, who seems much relieved.

Olympia is standing so close to the pair that she could reach out and touch the boy. The resemblance is astonishingly keen. She might be looking at the face of John Haskell as a child.

The woman in mauve cotton, perhaps aware of Olympia's odd

stare, takes the boy's hand and leads him farther along the sidewalk. Olympia remains frozen with her purse still open, barely able to breathe. In a moment, the woman bends down and picks up the boy and kisses him on the cheek. Olympia can just make out the boy's small brown shoes, well worn and cracked.

A hard knuckle of jealousy sends a jolt through her body, causing Olympia to drop her purse. Coins and hair combs clatter to the surface of the sidewalk.

Overcome by a momentary paralysis, she is unable to bend to collect her things. She smells cigar smoke and is dimly aware of the man in buff-and-brown check crouching to retrieve them for her.

"Now I am convinced you are not well," the man is saying beside her. She feels a hand at her elbow.

"I followed you," the man is saying. "I hope you will not mind, because I could see that something was not right with you."

He leads her into the darkened shop. He tells her to sit on a metal chair. She does so, slipping heavily onto its hard surface. Between them there is a round glass table.

"And then I could not help but see you searching through your purse. You must have had a most terrible fright, for your face went dead white." He holds up a mug from a vacant table. "As white as this cup."

When she looks at the man, she sees unkempt eyebrows, shrewd green eyes, a plump pink mouth with a shred of tobacco on its lower lip; but, try as she might, she cannot form a coherent face. A field of bright white spots obscures the vision in her right eye.

The man leans toward her, and she can smell anew the alcohol on his stale breath. "Have you misplaced something very valuable to you?" he asks her.

The field of white spots expands, nearly blotting out the figure before her. Olympia begins to laugh, and she can see that her laugh astonishes the man.

And she thinks, as she feels herself falling — falling ever so slowly, a feather wafting lazily in the heavy air — *Yes, yes, indeed. I have misplaced something of great value.*

*   *   *

The sky is heavy and foul with a strange yellow light. The air is still, too still, worse than yesterday, sulfurous. When she reaches the bay, she takes off her boots and wades into the black muck that twice daily reveals itself at low tide. Her feet are long and white and smooth, quite the most tender part of her body, and to step inadvertently upon a clamshell or a large sea-pebble is painful. She thinks how odd it is that one should be so strong and muscular elsewhere but have the roots of the body so vulnerable.

Seaweed of many varying colors and textures has strewn itself against the tide line, along with horseshoe crabs and jellyfish that have beached themselves and lie transparent on the top of the muck. She has to watch closely where she treads to avoid their unpleasant gelatinous texture as well as their sting. The seaweed at the high-tide line resembles, in its dried state, nothing so much as shredded newsprint. She has heard of people who make soups and stews of this sea vegetation, but she is quite sure she herself would not care for it.

With the clam rake that Ezra has lent her, she harvests the small mollusks that hide in the muck. In this way she occupies herself for the better part of an hour, filling her bucket nearly to the top with littlenecks. The skirts of her yellow gingham have more than once been sucked into the mud and dragged out again, so that her feet and the hem of her dress look as though they have been coated in molasses. She walks to a large rock that enters the sea and sits on it, rinsing her feet and the bottom of her dress. When her feet are dry, she puts on her stockings and boots.

Yesterday, when she collapsed inside the confectionery at Ely

Falls, Lyman Fogg caught her just before she fell from the stool. Almost immediately, she regained consciousness with a ferocious headache. The man fed her sips of water as she forced herself to gather her strength despite the pain in her head. She allowed him to walk her to the trolley and even to accompany her to Ely, but when they reached the station she thanked him, bade him a firm farewell, and, in spite of his many protests, took a carriage alone to her house. Once inside, she went upstairs and fell upon her bed. She drifted into a deep sleep and did not wake until nearly noon today.

She will not go back to Ely Falls, she tells herself. She has seen the boy, and that is enough. She will write Rufus Philbrick and thank him for helping her, and he will be pleased to hear that she has now put the matter to rest.

It is an effort to move in the thickish air, but Olympia collects her pail of littlenecks and makes her way back to the cottage. It is as though the sea and the shoreline and the houses beyond are covered with a dull yellow film and cannot breathe. She will steam the clams for her meal, she decides. She has oyster crackers to accompany them and some milk, and she will make a stew of the broth.

She washes the clams repeatedly, as Ezra has taught her to do. She finds a large pot and puts water on the stove to boil. Immediately, the kitchen becomes stifling. She throws open all of the windows, and when that does not help much, she walks into the front room and opens the windows there.

She gazes down at the beach, nearly deserted today, a result partially of the unpleasantness of the air and partially of the fact that so many families have already left and gone back to the city. A sharp crack of thunder startles her, and for a moment she thinks that something heavy and sharp has fallen onto the floor above. And then the sky lowers itself, like night coming on too early. The wind starts, beating against the cottage. The frames of the windows shudder from the irregular gusts of wind.

The temperature drops precipitously. Chilled, Olympia finds a shawl on a chair and wraps herself in the crocheted wool. The sky, despite its menace, is oddly beautiful; and she thinks about how a disaster, though horrific in its particulars, may create a scene of great beauty. A blazing hotel, for example, may elicit fear and sometimes bravery from the witnesses of this catastrophe, but will it not also move these same observers with its very majesty?

The shipwreck was an event she remembers for its paradoxical beauty in the midst of horror and fear. She recalls the moment John Haskell passed by her with the child. What was she thinking then? That though she did not want to be noticed, she could not mind being seen by John Haskell? That she could not then have willingly removed herself from that cool white sand, into which her bare feet had burrowed, save for the most dire threat from her father? That though she sought to attend to the rescue operation only, she could not keep her eyes from the form of John Haskell, a form that she and all around her could see only too well, since the sea had already soaked through the man's dressing gown and the nightshirt he wore underneath?

And what precisely was it that passed between her and Haskell on the beach for those few seconds near daybreak? It cannot have been love — no, of course it cannot — nor even infatuation, which needs, she imagines, rather more experience with each other than they had then, so early in the summer. No, it was instead a kind of recognition, she believes, as though each of them knew the other not only from the day before but also from some future date.

The rain assaults the house from a nearly horizontal angle, sneaking in under the eaves of the porch. A gust of wind knocks over a wicker chair on the porch, and too late she remembers that there are sheets on the line.

But it *was* love, she tells herself. Of course it was. Even then. Even that night. For had not she and Haskell already entered into that dangerous state of thrall which may be called love or obsession or romance or simply delusion, depending upon one's proximity to the event and one's ability to believe in the notion that two souls which stir in the universe may be destined to meet and may be meant only for each other?

Already the sea is clawing at the sand, eroding the beach and creating great gullies. The erosion will endanger the cottages, she knows. Leaning against a windowpane, she can feel the wind vibrating the glass. Did she not understand the consequences of allowing herself to fall in love with John Haskell? Can she ever have been that heedless? Or did she imagine herself charmed, untouchable, merely skimming the surface of disastrous and lethal matters, as a gull will fly above the ocean, alighting neither here nor there, but always teasing the waves?

She glances up, draws the shawl more tightly around her. *Where will the boy be now?* she wonders. And where do he and the woman go on their walks? Why did the woman have on a black apron? Olympia recalls the boy's worn brown leather shoes, nearly heartbreaking in their shabbiness. Hand-me-downs surely, for the boy cannot have used them so himself.

Great love comes once and one time only, Olympia understands now. For by definition, there cannot be two such occurrences: The one great love remains in the memory and on the tongue and in the eyes of the once beloved and cannot ever be forgotten.

She puts her head in her hands.

Why must love be so punishing?

A monstrous wind catches the house, and she can feel the wood shudder in its embrace. With awe, she watches as the wind beats along the beach, blowing the tips off the breakers, heaving stray brush and driftwood and seaweed high into the air. A gull remains motionless over the water, unable to make headway against the wind, and then is blown backward by a gust. Farther down the shore, a large piece of tin is lifted off a fishing shack. The wicker chairs slide along the painted porch floor and hit the railing with a series of dull thuds. Upstairs, Olympia can hear glass breaking.

The hurricane pummels the coastline all the way up to Bar Harbor. Through the night, Olympia huddles in the kitchen, listening to the crack of wood, the heaving of the sea, and the high whine of the wind. Near to the side of the house, a pine tree falls, missing the cottage by inches, and, once or twice, when the wind is particularly fierce, Olympia climbs under the kitchen table for safety. She thinks of Ezra and hopes that he made it in to shore before the storm. No one out in a boat would survive the seas this night.

From time to time, Olympia walks to the window at the north side of the house and looks out to the lifesaving cottage. Its beacon is lit, and she can hear, intermittently, like Morse code being sounded from a great instrument, the foghorn from Granite Point. The wind strains the beams of her own cottage, and Olympia is sometimes startled by the creaking of the wood, as if the house were a ship foundering at sea.

By daybreak, parts of the beach have been eroded nearly to the seawall. Houses have been lifted off their foundations and porches have been sheared clean from their pilings. Olympia's own front lawn is littered with debris — leaves and branches and, ominously, a man's oiled jacket. All along the crescent of Fortune's Rocks, cottages have lost their windows and their roofs. Where the beach has not been gullied out, it is covered with metal caskets and shingles and glass and broken wood. Only the sea, as though victorious in some unnamed struggle, remains undaunted, its enormous breakers rolling in a stately manner all along the newly drafted shoreline.

Tentatively, people begin to make their way to the beach to survey the damage. Olympia throws a shawl over her shoulders and steps out onto the porch. The air is clean and sharp, as though freshly laundered. She walks to the seawall and looks back at her own cottage, where she sees that a chimney pot has fallen over. But though she studies her house, her thoughts lie elsewhere, and she wonders, as indeed she will wonder a thousand times (and it is as if she understands already that because she will never be free of this particular worry, she must claim it for her own or go mad with the distance, with the powerlessness of the distance) what has happened to the woman and the boy. Doubtless the storm will have had less impact inland, but can those boardinghouses withstand the terrifically high winds of a hurricane? And what of the electrical lines? Will there be fresh water? And is the boy, whose true name Olympia cannot yet utter, safe?

On the tenth day after the storm, Olympia boards the first trolley car out of Ely Station for what becomes an arduous journey of an hour and a half to Ely Falls, three times the length of a normal trip to the city. All along the route, Olympia and her fellow passengers are mildly dazed as they survey the wreckage of the storm: telephone and power lines still down, carriages overturned, and rooftops caved in by fallen pines whose shallow roots could not hold them upright in the high winds.

In the wake of the storm, the weather has grown cooler. For the first time since returning to Fortune's Rocks, Olympia has taken the wool suits out of her trunks, aired them out on the porch, and hung them in the shallow closets of several bedrooms. For her trip into Ely Falls, she picked out this morning her best day suit, a jacket and skirt of dove wool challis that she likes to wear with a high-necked white blouse and velvet tie. Her hat, a plum toque, sits at an angle on her chignon. Already she is aware, glancing at her fellow travelers on the trolley, that fashions have changed in the four years she has been away. Skirts are longer, sleeves are fuller, and altogether the clothing seems less fussy.

With several other travelers, Olympia alights at the corner of Alfred and Washington Streets, where men stand on scaffolds repairing a roof and reglazing windows. She has read, in the *Ely Falls Sentinel,* that seventeen millworkers perished when a spinnery collapsed during the hurricane, the owner of the mill unwilling to cancel the night shift despite repeated pleas from the workers to suspend operations. Olympia read the list of the dead like a wife examining a list of war casualties, her eyes skimming quickly over names, looking only for a single surname. Unlike the mood of the city on Olympia's previous visit — which was, though oppressive with heat, oddly playful — today the city's inhabitants seem solemn, even somber. Olympia walks along Alfred Street, noting the boarded-up windows that still remain in many of the shops.

Midway up the street, Olympia is startled by a signal whistle, much like that of an oncoming train. Within minutes, the street is thick with men and women moving quickly toward the doorways of the boardinghouses. Olympia glances up at the clock tower at the corner of Washington and Alfred: five minutes past noon. Clearly this must be a dinner break.

She finds the doorway of number 137 and once again sits on the bench across the street. Several women enter the blue doorway, but not the woman Olympia is searching for. She ponders the wisdom of accosting someone on the steps of that building and inquiring about the Bolduc family, but as there is not much common sense to be had in this proposition, she abandons the idea. She sees almost immediately that she will not be able to remain long on the bench; because the weather has grown colder, there are fewer people lingering in the streets, and thus she will be more conspicuous than she was on her last visit.

At precisely ten minutes to one, dozens of persons emerge from the boardinghouse entryway, the women pulling on gloves, checking purses, holding hats as they move briskly along the sidewalk back to work. By one o'clock, the street is silent.

Chilled beneath her dove challis, Olympia walks to the bakery and steps inside. A serving girl in a black dress with a blue apron glances up at Olympia with surprise, as though the bakery were closed.

"May I have a cup of tea?" Olympia asks.

"Dinners are gone now," the serving girl says, "but I suppose I can always make up a cup of tea."

"Thank you," Olympia says. She takes a seat near a window and arranges for herself an excellent view of number 137. She slips off her gloves and puts them in the pocket of her suit. Emboldened by the thought that she might well leave Ely Falls without a scrap of further information about the boy, she asks the waitress when she returns with the tea if she knows of a family named Bolduc.

"I should say so," the girl says in an accent that sounds Irish. "Dozens of Bolducs hereabouts. Which one would you be wanting?"

"Albertine?" Olympia asks, her breath catching in her throat. "Telesphore?"

"You're in luck then," says the waitress, wiping her hands on her apron. "They live right across the street."

Olympia smiles at her apparent fortune.

"But which are you wanting?" the girl asks. "You won't find Albertine at home today until after four o'clock when the first shift is ended. But if it's Telesphore you're wanting, he'll be home until four. There," the girl says, pointing at the blue door. "That one

319

there is where they live. You don't look a relative, so you must be a friend."

"A friend," says Olympia.

"I expect you know the boy."

"Yes," says Olympia.

"Sweet little one, isn't he?"

Olympia nods.

"I do not know when husband and wife see each other," the girl says. "What with the two shifts and all. One goes in, the other comes out. Ships passing in the night. I can probably get you a bowl of oyster stew if you're hungry."

Olympia, not wishing to reject anything the young woman has to offer, answers that stew would be most welcome.

The chowder is watery, but Olympia forces herself to eat it. She sips it slowly, stalling for time, not wanting to leave her perfect vantage point. The waitress brings her oyster crackers and scones and sweet pastries and then excuses herself, saying she'll be in the back room, having her own dinner.

For a time, Olympia sits at the table, which is now warmed by the afternoon sun. She has had so much to eat that she almost dozes. But at 3:50 by the clock tower, she comes alert when she sees Albertine, dressed today in a rather severe black cotton dress with a black apron, running up the stone steps into the blue doorway. Five minutes later, a man in a blue workshirt and black cloth cap (his head is bent, and Olympia cannot quite catch his face) comes out of the door and walks down the steps and onto the sidewalk. Confused now about what she should do, for she has no real intention of knocking on the blue door, Olympia sits a bit longer. And in a short time, she is rewarded for her patience. At twenty minutes past four, Albertine Bolduc once again opens the blue door. Olympia braces herself for the shock she knows will come, but when the boy emerges, standing on the top step and blinking in the sunshine,

Olympia understands that no preparation will ever be adequate for the blow that hits her with such force that she has to press her knuckles to her mouth.

The boy's thick walnut hair appears to have been recently cut, using a bowl for a pattern. It hangs fetchingly just over his eyebrows, enhancing the luminous hazel of his eyes. His eyes dominate his face, its tiny nose, its bow mouth, and its plump double chin. He reaches instinctively for his mother's hand, and together they descend the three stone steps. He has on longer pants today and a gray handknit sweater with a matching woolen cap. Only the shoes, the cracked brown leather shoes with the ties, are the same as before.

Olympia places a number of coins on the table and leaves the shop unobserved. She follows the pair at a discreet distance. She is aware of a particular form of madness that has overtaken her and that is making her behave in ways she would not have believed were possible. She feels uncomfortably like a spy, which, of course, she is. But even understanding the absurdity of her actions, she cannot turn her eyes away, nor can she let the woman and child disappear from sight. Remaining at least a block behind them, Olympia follows the pair down to the corner of Alfred and Washington, and then along Washington to Pembroke, which is lined with boarding-houses, identical brick buildings with small windows and unpainted picket fences bordering scruffy front lawns. Albertine and the boy enter one of these boardinghouses, the boy running up the front steps and pushing open the door as though he has done this a hundred times.

Olympia, unable to follow the woman and boy onto Pembroke for fear of being caught out, stands at the corner and watches this small tableau. She wants to sit down and wait for the boy to come out again, for to leave is to let the boy go, and it is some minutes before she can bear to turn away and head back to the trolley stop. It is nearly five, and she must, she knows, catch the last car to Ely or be stranded in Ely Falls.

For a time, she walks blindly, unable to stop thinking about the boy. Will this be all she has of him? Ever? These stolen glimpses? For there can never be any interaction with Albertine, Olympia understands now. Never. Nor can Olympia continue these clandestine sightings without risking discovery. And that she is not prepared to do.

She cannot go on like this. She cannot. She must put this obsession away, as she once vowed to do. She must forget the boy and move on with her life. She must find a position, perhaps as a governess or a teacher. Possibly she could ask Rufus Philbrick for assistance in this matter. She imagines the man would be considerably more enthusiastic about helping Olympia find employment than he was about aiding her in her search for her son.

Consumed with these thoughts, Olympia walks without noticing where she is going, so that after a time, when she looks up, she discovers that although she still remains in the business district of Ely Falls, she does not know where she is. When she glances around, she notes the Bank of New Hampshire and the office of the *Ely Falls Sentinel.* There is a funeral parlor and an insurance company that seems to occupy all of one massive stone office building. There are various other offices with signs out front or in the windows or, more discreetly, on brass plates beside doorbells. She notices, across the street, on the ground level, a black sign over a door. A black sign with names carved in gold. TUCKER & TUCKER. ATTORNEYS AT LAW. She turns away from the sign and stares through the glass window of the bank into the lobby. The bank is closed, and she wonders what time it is.

The offices will be shut, too, she tells herself. Even if she were to knock on the door, there would be no answer. And if no one is there, this will be a sign, a message, will it not? She will then be able to walk away from this matter. She will go back to Fortune's Rocks and stay there and not return to Ely Falls. Yes, this will be a sign. A sign she will not be able to ignore.

And thus armed with these fragile delusions, Olympia walks across Dover Street, Ely Falls, on September 14, 1903, and enters the law offices of Tucker & Tucker, father and son, attorneys at law, to announce that she intends to reclaim her boy, Pierre Francis Haskell, and that they must help her do it.

·IV·
The Writ

A ND YOU SAY you met him at your father's house," Payson
Tucker is saying.

On his lap, the young lawyer has a marbled notebook not
unlike the ones in which Olympia used to practice cursive when she
was younger. Tucker makes notations from time to time, dipping his
pen into a striped glass inkwell behind him on his desk. The room is
small — polished wood and brown leather and brass studs — and
reminds Olympia of her father's library in Boston. And perhaps it is
that association, or Tucker's serious and attentive manner, that lends
his questions authority.

"We met on the twenty-first of June in 1899 at my father's cottage
in Fortune's Rocks," Olympia says. "I remember particularly because it was the day of the summer solstice."

"And you were how old?"

"Fifteen." She watches Tucker carefully for a reaction, but his face
is impassive.

"And how old was Mr. Haskell?"

"He was forty-one at the time."

"And you are how old now?"

"Twenty."

Tucker adjusts his gold-rimmed spectacles and studies her for a moment. "And John Haskell was at your home visiting your father?" he adds.

"Yes," she says. "He was there with his wife and children."

"I see," Tucker says noncommittally, and Olympia wonders what exactly he does see. She hazards a guess as to his age — twenty-five, twenty-six? — but he seems a man wishing to appear older, the already receding hairline helping with this effort. He is a slender man with mustaches, pale skin, and black silky hair that occasionally falls, when he bends his head, forward onto his cheek.

"Can you give me their names?" he asks.

"Catherine," she says. "That is — *was* — his wife. Actually, I do not know if they are formally divorced. I have heard only that she is living without him, and I do not believe they have been together since August of 1899. The children's names are Martha, Clementine, Randall, and May."

Just moments earlier, when Olympia entered the offices of Tucker & Tucker, she interrupted Payson Tucker in the act of gathering together his case and his hat to leave for the day. She introduced herself, stammering a bit, and said she had need of a lawyer. Tucker seemed a bit startled and gestured for her to sit. Since then, she has been answering his questions as best she can.

"How old were they at the time?" he asks.

"Twelve, in the case of Martha. The others were younger."

"And where is John Haskell now?"

"I do not know."

Tucker puts the pen down. "Perhaps it would be better if you just told me the whole story, from the beginning," he says.

Olympia glances away for a moment toward a towering oak bookcase. There are hundreds of volumes on its shelves, leather-bound books with difficult titles. She hesitates, uneasy about sharing the details of the most private acts of her life. For words, she knows, even in their best combinations, must inevitably fall short of the reality. And not all the words that she has could describe the joy and happiness she and Haskell had together. Instead, she fears she will risk reducing these most sublime experiences to mechanical movements, pictures only. Images at which another might cringe. At which an unwary observer, who has suddenly and inadvertently drawn back a curtain upon a pair of lovers in their most intimate moments, might be shocked. And will not such an interruption, this other pair of eyes, ultimately change the event and take something precious from it?

"I can tell you what happened," Olympia says to the lawyer, "but first I must make you aware of something important."

"Yes, of course."

"Though I was very young and understood little of the magnitude of what I was doing, I was not seduced. Never seduced. I had will and some understanding. I could have stopped it at any time. Do you understand this?"

"I think so," he says.

"Do you believe me?"

He considers her thoughtfully, holding his pen between his thumb and forefinger and unconsciously flipping it back and forth. She wonders if Tucker & Tucker means father and son, or brother and brother. "Yes," he says. "Yes, I do. I do not think you would say this if it were not true."

It is warm in the office, and she removes her gloves. "John Haskell and I were in each other's company several times that first weekend," she begins. "And then we met again on the Fourth of July. We became . . . intimate . . . about two weeks after that. I knew him for only seven weeks during that summer."

"And John Haskell and his family were living where?"

"Haskell lived at the Highland Hotel. At Fortune's Rocks. Catherine and the children were staying in York, Maine, with her parents until their cottage at Fortune's Rocks was completed."

"Yes, I know the Highland. And you . . ." Tucker hesitates, removing an imagined piece of lint from the sleeve of his chalk-striped frock coat. "You went with him to this hotel? Or he came to you at your house? Or did you meet elsewhere?"

"Usually, I went to him at the hotel," she says with difficulty, thinking, *There was nothing usual about it.* "He came to my house on three other occasions, one of which was the last time I ever saw him."

"And when was that?"

"August tenth."

"What happened on that day?"

Olympia looks down at her lap. Her hands are clasped so tightly that her knuckles are white. She thinks about the last time she saw Haskell, about all the days leading up to that last time. About all of the days during which she might have stopped Haskell and Catherine from coming to her father's house for the gala. But she did not. For she had, she knows, already entered that phase in a love affair when all meetings with the beloved are to be desired, no matter how formal or awkward, for they offer not only an opportunity to gaze upon the lover but also a chance to experience that peculiarly delicious thrill of silent communication in the midst of an unknowing audience. Olympia could tell Payson Tucker that she wished her father had not invited the Haskells or that she was anxious lest she cause Catherine Haskell, whom she truly admired, even the smallest concern, but to do so would be disingenuous, not to say altogether false.

"My father had a party, and the Haskells came to it. Catherine Haskell discovered us together that night."

The lawyer dips his pen into the inkwell and makes a notation. "She discovered you, or someone else did and told her?"

Olympia averts her eyes.

"If this is too painful . . . ," he says.

"Mrs. Haskell had some help," she says. "A man by the name of Zachariah Cote."

Payson Tucker lifts his eyes from his notebook. Olympia catches a flash of light from his lenses. "The poet?"

"Yes," she says, mildly surprised that Tucker has heard of Cote. "I have not seen John Haskell since then," Olympia adds.

"Where did he go?"

"He stayed in their new cottage the night of August tenth. I do not know where he went after that. I believe he left Fortune's Rocks and Ely Falls."

"He was living in Ely Falls as well?" the lawyer asks.

"No, he was a physician with the Ely Falls Mill infirmary."

"Oh, I see. And when did you discover you were with child?"

Tucker asks the question as if it were one fact of thousands, a mere sentence in a paragraph. Olympia opens her mouth to speak, but cannot. She can feel the heat spreading into her face. Tucker, watching her closely, leans in her direction. A wing of hair falls forward, and he tucks it behind his ear.

"Miss Biddeford, I know these are terrible questions. And I think you have shown great courage in your answers. But I require this information if I am to take on your case. I also need to know if you have the stamina to face certain realities about your past. Believe me when I say to you that this is but the mildest foretaste of the questions that will be put to you if you decide to go any further with your suit."

Olympia takes a breath and nods. "My family and I left Fortune's Rocks on the morning of August eleventh," she says. "My parents live on Beacon Hill in Boston. I discovered I was with child on the twenty-ninth of October."

"You were examined by a physician?"

"Not immediately."

Tucker leans back in his chair. Behind him on the desk, fitted into a silver frame, is a photograph of a handsome woman in her thirties — his mother, surely, Olympia guesses. When she was a young woman.

"Miss Biddeford, this next question is exceedingly difficult, but I must ask it. Is there any possibility that another man, a man other than John Haskell, could be the father of the boy you speak of?"

Despite Tucker's warning, Olympia is shocked, not so much by the question itself as by the notion that she could ever have had such a relationship with anyone but Haskell. "No," she answers vehemently. "No possibility whatsoever."

"Good," he says, and he looks genuinely relieved. "That is fine. Did you then contact John Haskell to tell him of the news?"

"No."

"Tell me what happened on the day you were delivered of the child?"

"I am not sure what happened. I had been given laudanum toward the end of my confinement, and it made me sleepy, so that when I woke from the ordeal, the child had already been taken from me."

"But you saw the child."

"Yes."

"And you knew it was a boy."

"I was told it was a boy."

"You had a physician with you? Or a midwife?"

"A physician. Dr. Ulysses Branch of Newbury Street in Boston."

"Was it he who took the child from you?"

"I do not know. I assume whoever it was did so at the request of

my father, since he had once or twice referred to 'arrangements' that
had been made. Though he never spoke directly to me, either then
or later, about what had been done with the child."

"Did you ever ask him outright?"

"No," she says. "I did not." And it strikes Olympia as odd now
that she did not. How was it that she accepted her fate so willingly?

"Your father left your house that night?"

"No, he did not."

"Then he must have given the child to someone else?"

"Yes. I do not know precisely to whom he gave the child. But I
have reason to believe the baby shortly entered the care of John
Haskell himself."

"The reason that I am lingering on the details of the birth is that
the issue of how and when the child was taken from you may be important," he explains.

"Yes, I understand."

"How was it you came to know of the child's whereabouts?"

"By accident," she says. "Soon after I arrived in Fortune's
Rocks — that is, returned to Fortune's Rocks, this July — I had a
visit from an old friend of my father's, Rufus Philbrick —"

"Yes, I know the man," Tucker says, interrupting her.

"During this visit, he inadvertently let slip about the child's being
in the Saint Andre orphanage."

"And how would he have known this?"

"He is a member of the board of directors," she says. "The next
day I went to Saint Andre's and spoke to a nun who I believe is called
Mother Marguerite Pelletier. She told me the child had been at the
orphanage but had been placed out. She told me the boy's first
name. She would not tell me his last name."

"But you say the child's name is" — Tucker consults his notes —
"Pierre Francis Haskell."

"Yes," Olympia says. "I paid a call on Rufus Philbrick and asked him to find me the boy's whereabouts. He told me the child's name had once been — if not still was — Haskell. Later he was able to confirm this."

"What else did he tell you?"

"He could tell me little else on that particular day, but later he wrote me that the boy's guardians are Franco-Americans, Albertine and Telesphore Bolduc. They live at one thirty-seven Alfred Street here in Ely Falls and work at the Ely Falls Mill. The boy is three years old, and Rufus Philbrick's letter said that he was healthy. I have seen the boy, and he appears to be so. That is all I know. Oh, and he was baptized into the Catholic faith."

"You spoke to the boy."

"No, I saw him from a distance."

Tucker removes his spectacles and cleans them with a handkerchief. "Did anything about the boy's appearance suggest that he was the son of you and John Haskell?"

Olympia knows she will never forget the shock of seeing the boy's face. "Yes. Definitely. He looks very like his father. I believe anyone would remark upon this resemblance."

Tucker puts his spectacles back on. "Have you spoken to either Albertine or Telesphore Bolduc?"

"No."

"Have you told anyone of your desire to reclaim your child?"

"Only Rufus Philbrick."

"And you say you saw the boy again today?"

"Yes."

Tucker sits back in his chair and folds his hands in front of his chin. "I cannot tell you today whether or not it is possible to pursue this case," he says.

"I understand."

"I will need to investigate certain matters."

She nods.

"To do this, I will have to hire a private investigator. This is usual in these cases. . . ."

"Yes," says Olympia.

"I am sorry to have to broach the subject of fees, but I fear —"

"I have money," Olympia says quickly. "Money is not a difficulty."

"Very well then," he says, standing, and she takes this as her cue to stand as well.

"May I call your carriage?" he asks. "Or do you have a motorcar?"

"Mr. Tucker, I live alone," Olympia says. "I have neither carriage nor motorcar, and I believe I have missed the last trolley to Ely. If you would be so kind as to call me a cab. . . ."

Tucker takes the gold watch from his vest pocket and consults it. "Yes, yes, of course," he says. He turns and appears to be looking for something on his desk. "Can you be reached on the telephone?"

"No."

"I shall need your address then."

"Yes, of course."

"I may have to visit you in Fortune's Rocks from time to time to discuss this case," Tucker says casually. He turns back to her with an address book in his hand. And she is surprised to see, in his face, that Payson Tucker finds her interesting, or intriguing, or possibly even attractive. And that because of this, he will take her case. For a moment, Olympia ponders the uneasy question of whether or not to use this attraction to gain what she wants.

And then she thinks about the boy, her son, in his cracked leather shoes.

"I will look forward to your visits," she says.

When Olympia returns to Fortune's Rocks, she writes to Rufus Philbrick to tell him that she has hired a lawyer to look into the

335

matter of the boy. She also writes to her father to ask him for money, neglecting to explain the reason. While she awaits a reply from each, she contemplates possible ways in which she might earn extra funds to pay for an eventual custody suit; but she can see no immediate manner in which to secure a living, apart from hiring herself out again as a governess, which she most sincerely does not want to do. To pass the time, she reads books and newspapers, but the outside world seems to her more and more remote, particularly as the summerfolk desert Fortune's Rocks. The days grow colder still, and she wonders if she will, after all, be able to remain in her cottage.

On the twenty-eighth of September, Olympia receives a letter — but not from Rufus Philbrick or her father.

27 September 1903

Dear Miss Biddeford,

I shall be staying at the Highland Hotel on 2 October and would be pleased if you would dine with me there. I understand that this may be awkward for you, and if you prefer, I will be happy to suggest an alternative venue. In either event, may I call for you at six o'clock on the evening of the second? I have some information regarding your custody suit that I think you will want to hear.

Respectfully yours,
Payson Tucker, Esq.

Olympia sits down at her kitchen table with the letter in her hand and reads it through once more. The Highland Hotel. She can see its high ceilings, its cavernous lobby, its long mahogany desks. She has not thought she would ever again be able to enter the Highland, but it seems cowardly now to have to say to Payson Tucker that she cannot do that, particularly so if she wishes to impress him with her courage and resolve. She takes her pen and ink from the drawer in the kitchen table and begins to write.

29 September 1903

Dear Mr. Tucker,

I should be pleased to dine with you at the Highland Hotel on the evening of the second of October. I shall expect you to call for me at six o'clock. I look forward most sincerely to hearing your information.

In anticipation of your arrival, I remain,
Olympia Biddeford

She blots the letter, puts it into an envelope, and seals it with wax. She glances about her kitchen.

So it is beginning, she thinks.

*   *   *

Olympia dresses for the evening of October 2 in an emerald velvet suit with black braid piping and frog closures. The suit, though somewhat out of date, squares her shoulders and flatters her waist. With the suit, she wears a high-necked ivory silk blouse that once belonged to her mother and was left behind in her closets. Olympia chooses pearls for her jewelry: drop earrings, a rope at her neck, and a bracelet. She fusses for nearly an hour with her hair, forming wide wings at the sides and a double bun at the back. When she is dressed, she studies herself in the glass in the kitchen and is somewhat surprised to see that her face looks considerably older than she has remembered it, its planes more accentuated. Her figure is thinner as

337

well, somehow longer, or perhaps this is just an illusion created by the suit. No, she is definitely thinner. She seems foreign to herself and yet oddly familiar, familiar from a time when it was not unusual to dress in velvet and pearls or to spend an hour on one's hair.

Payson Tucker comes for Olympia at precisely six o'clock, as he said he would, in a smart lemon and black motorcar. His white shirt shines in the headlamps as he passes in front of the automobile after helping her in. He seems larger, more adroit than she has remembered him. Since it is only Olympia's second time in a motorcar (though she does not tell Tucker this), she is more than a little tremulous when they begin to move faster than seems prudent along the winding narrow lane that abuts the seawall and the summer cottages of Fortune's Rocks.

"You must be one of the few people still in residence on the beach," he says.

"I think I may be."

"You do not mind being so isolated?" he asks.

"No," she says. "In fact, I am rather afraid I am enjoying it."

At the hotel, a valet takes the car from Tucker, who touches Olympia's elbow gently as he guides her up the long set of stairs. Although she has prepared herself, she hesitates a bit when they enter the lobby, a misstep she tries to hide with conversation.

"What brings you to the Highland so late in the season?" she asks Tucker.

"I have business in Fortune's Rocks both today and tomorrow," he answers, moving her firmly through the lobby, "and it seemed pointless to make the journey back and forth to Exeter, which is where I live. And besides, it has given me an excellent opportunity to see you again."

He leads her into the dining room, which seems not to have changed at all. There are, she notes, only a few diners on this Tuesday in October. Olympia and Tucker are led to a table with white candles and late-summer roses, and as she sits, she takes in the sparkling goblets, the silver champagne buckets, the heavy cutlery, the massive crystal chandelier at the dining room's center, and then the menu (haricot mutton, turkey with oyster sauce, mock turtle soup, apple brown Betty), reflecting that it has been four years since she was last in society. And she further reflects how very much, when she was, she took for granted its luxury, its furnishings, its food, its accoutrements, as if they were her birthright, her due, with hardly a thought — barely even an imagining — of those who would never have such luxury offered to them. Perhaps obliviousness is necessary, she thinks, to enjoy, or even to bear, this excess.

"The hotel will be open only a week longer," says Tucker.

"It seems there are not many in residence. You shall be rattling around."

"If I may say so — and I hope you will not be offended by this — you look very lovely tonight," Tucker says. He takes off his spectacles and puts them on the table beside his plate. She is startled to see, without the buffer of the gold-rimmed eyeglasses, how intensely black his eyes are, how long and silky his lashes.

"If I am offended by such a pronouncement," Olympia says, "I do not know how we shall proceed with my case. As I recall, we spoke of rather more disturbing matters during our first meeting at your office."

Tucker's hair, worn straight back from his forehead tonight, is shiny with hair wax or with oil. This must be a new fashion as well, Olympia thinks, and she is certain that her emerald suit, no matter how altered, will be seen to be hopelessly out of date.

"You live with your family in Exeter?" she asks.

"I live with my mother and father and sister," he says. "I am in practice with my father, who was kind enough to take me in. Had you come a half hour earlier to our offices, it would be he who would be your advocate."

"Well, then, for once in my life, I must be glad that I was late," she says.

"And I, too, am exceedingly glad," Tucker says with perhaps rather more warmth than Olympia is comfortable with.

A waiter arrives with champagne, which, when she takes her first sip, is so dry that it seems to bubble right up through Olympia's nose.

"Do you like oysters?" he asks.

"Yes, I do."

"I feel obliged to mention, since I do not wish to deceive you, nor compromise your suit in any way, that I am only one year out of the Yale School of Law," Tucker says disarmingly when the waiter has left them. "I have discussed your case with my father, and if you would prefer that he represent you, I will not be insulted in any way. In fact, I would advise you to consider this option carefully. My father has rather more experience with the state courts than I do, although your case is unusual, and I am sorry to say my father has not brought forth a suit similar to yours. In fact, I cannot find a like case in the county files at all."

"Is it so unusual? My case?" she asks.

"It would appear so. As far as I can tell, such a suit has been put forth before only twice in New England."

He seems about to speak further, but stops himself, brushing his mustaches with the back of his fingers.

"And the outcome of these two suits?" she asks after a time.

"In neither case was the petitioner successful," he says quietly.

"I see," Olympia says.

"I was quite fascinated to read of the history of your house," Tucker says, in an obvious attempt to change the subject.

"You have had occasion to read of my house?" she asks, looking up.

"I thought I recognized the address when you were in my office. Six months ago, while I was working on a case for the Catholic Diocese in Ely Falls, I came across a few old documents relating to the convent," he says. "Did you know that the church was forced to close the convent's doors? It appears there was something of a scandal there."

"No," she says. "I was always under the impression that the church had decided to move the sisters into Ely Falls so that they could run the hospice and the orphanage. I am sure that was what my father was told."

"Yes, I do not doubt that it was. The scandal seems to have been kept rather quiet. The Catholic Church had — has — tremendous political influence in Ely Falls." He pauses while the waiter serves the oysters in a large silver tray with cracked ice and lemon and horse-radish sauce. "The house was set up in the late 1870s to house young women who were felt by their families to be wayward or to have gone astray. A convent within a convent, as it were," Tucker explains.

"Schoolgirls?"

"Some were as young as twelve. Others as old as twenty. A few of them were victims of brutalities upon their persons or were servant girls who had been taken advantage of by their masters."

Olympia lays down her oyster fork. "Mr. Tucker, you surprise me with this story."

"Miss Biddeford," he says in the manner of a man who has become aware of a terrible social gaffe, "I am so very sorry. Forgive me."

"Not with the story itself," she says. "But with its obvious parallel to my own situation. I assume we are speaking of unwed mothers."

"Of course, I did not intend . . . I cannot think why I have . . . I suppose I simply do not think of you as I do those unfortunate girls. I am most sincerely sorry if I have offended you."

"No, no," she says, waving her hand. "Do not trouble yourself. I cannot pretend that I am not surprised by this news, and I am clearly more than a little sensitive about my own situation, but I must tell you, Mr. Tucker, in the same breath, how tremendous a relief it has been for me to have someone to speak to of such matters. I have kept them in my heart for all these years and have confided in no one. And in not being able to speak of facts that are true, one watches them grow and distort themselves and take on greater significance than one ought to allow, the result being that one is crippled by the actions of one's past. Indeed, I have lived these four years with no other reality."

Tucker is silent for a moment. "I am sorry that the past has burdened you so, Miss Biddeford," he says with evident concern, "and yet I confess I am honored to be the recipient of these closely held truths."

Olympia touches her mouth with her napkin. "I am not usually this priggish," she says quickly. "Please continue with your story. You have whetted my curiosity."

"Well, it is a grim tale altogether. The infants were taken from the girls at birth and given to the orphanage. In those days, such infants made up the bulk of the population of the orphanage and were largely the reason for its existence. But not all of the girls were in such dire straits. Some were merely thought, because of excessively high spirits, to be troublesome to their families."

"And the families had them put away because of this?"

"Yes, with the idea that the girls would then be 'broken' — like horses, I suppose. The discipline was quite severe. The girls were forced to take vows of silence, as the members of the order themselves had." He pauses. "It beggars the imagination."

"I am dismayed, Mr. Tucker, to think of my father's house being used in this manner. I had envisioned something altogether different, something rather more peaceful and contemplative."

"Quite."

The waiter brings the next course, which is the turkey. "The scandal came to light when one young woman, who had been committed by her guardian for 'wanton and lascivious behavior,' accused a priest of assaulting her and took him to court," Tucker continues. "Before the case was settled, it was discovered that the priest — whose name has been stricken from the records, I might add — had been physically examining the young women to ascertain if they were . . ." Tucker pauses. Olympia can see that he is blushing. "It is impossible to put this delicately," he says. "According to the results of this examination, the girls were then segregated on the theory that those who were seen to be less than . . . intact . . . might corrupt the innocents."

"I see."

"The case was settled out of court. And as part of the settlement, the church agreed to close the house down. The nuns, most of them of course blameless, were moved into Ely Falls. The two sisters who collaborated with the priest were sent back to Canada. As you are doubtless aware, the Sisters of the Order of Saint Jean Baptiste de Bienfaisance now have a remarkable record of good works, many at considerable sacrifice. And they no longer keep vows of silence as they once used to do."

"Not very practical."

"No. Quite. Indeed, the silence was seen in retrospect to have allowed the molestation to continue."

"And what happened to the girls?"

"There is no mention of that in the records."

Olympia tries to imagine their fate. "Would their families have taken them back in?" she asks.

"I do not know."

"I see. The oysters were delicious, by the way," she says.

He smiles. "You have an appetite, Olympia Biddeford."

Somewhat abashed, she smooths the napkin in her lap. "That is the second time I have heard that said of me this fall," she says.

"It is an admirable quality, your considerable appetite," Tucker says. "I cannot bear women who feel obliged to appear delicate in their constitutions, when, in fact, they are not. Most women must eat as regularly and as heartily as men. And why should a woman not enjoy her food? Indeed, it is one of life's greater pleasures, do you not think?"

He waits until the waiter has left them. "Miss Biddeford, there are some matters which we must discuss," he says. "If I could, I would delay mentioning such unpleasant subjects forever, but clearly I cannot if we are to proceed with your suit. But I should like to say before I begin that I am thoroughly enjoying your company, and I am hopeful that we shall one day have a meal together when it will not be necessary to discuss business."

"Yes," she says. "Thank you."

"May I speak frankly now?" he asks.

"Please."

"I do not wish to discourage you," he says, "but I must warn you that your case is difficult. In most states that have decided the matter, the biological mother has fewer rights than the surrogate maternal figure. You, of course, are the biological mother, and Albertine Bolduc will be seen to be the surrogate mother."

Olympia is discomfited by the mention of another woman as the mother of her son, however much she has known this to be true.

"Furthermore, an unwed mother is the least likely person to be given custody of a child. An unwed mother who has been seen to have abandoned her child has essentially no rights to the child at all."

"I see," she says.

"I know that this is difficult," Tucker says. "Please tell me if I am already upsetting you too greatly."

Olympia struggles for composure. She must, she knows, steel herself for all manner of revelations. She cannot afford to be discouraged so soon. And she thinks now that Tucker's discussion about the provenance of her father's cottage must have been a deliberate attempt to prepare her in some small way for the even more difficult matter of her own case.

"No, I am fine," she says. "Well, I am not fine. Of course I am not. But I understand I must hear what you have to say. Indeed, I wish to know everything you know, for I cannot make any intelligent decisions otherwise."

Tucker nods. His hand hovers close to hers on the tablecloth, and she senses that under different circumstances he might touch her, but now will not.

"That is why it is so important that we establish that you did not abandon your child, but rather had the child stolen from you," he continues. "I have some further facts I should like to tell you if you think you can bear them."

"Are they so terrible?"

"They are . . . difficult."

"I am as ready as I ever shall be," she says.

"Shortly after his birth, the boy was given to Josiah Hay by your father," Tucker begins.

"Josiah!" Olympia exclaims before she can stop herself.

Tucker puts up a hand. "Only to transport the child," he says. "He and his wife, Lisette, took the child and journeyed up to Ely Falls by train the afternoon of the birth."

Olympia's head swims with the news. Lisette! How is that possible? Olympia thinks back to the day of the birth. Was Lisette at her side after she delivered? She cannot remember. No, perhaps she was not. Was it not, in fact, her mother who sat with her all that long day as Olympia drifted in and out of consciousness?

"They brought the child to John Haskell, who was staying at a hotel in Ely Falls. It is my understanding that John Haskell examined the child and dismissed Josiah and Lisette, who took the next train back to Boston. Dr. Haskell then took the child to the Saint Andre orphanage. He had already made arrangements."

"I find this so difficult to comprehend," Olympia says. "I do not know how he could have given up the boy," she adds, momentarily benumbed.

"Do you need some time?"

Olympia shakes her head.

Tucker puts his glasses back on. "Very shortly," he continues, "the boy was taken on by Albertine and Telesphore Bolduc. They have not formally adopted the child because John Haskell cannot be found, and he did not sign the appropriate waivers before he left. Such an adoption, even if the Bolducs had the money for the legal fees, which they have not, has not, therefore, been possible. It will, however, become possible simply by the fact of your bringing this suit."

"I *can* bring suit then?" Olympia asks.

"Legally, yes. In John Haskell's absence and considering that he has abandoned the child."

"But you are telling me that if I lose, the Bolducs may legally adopt the boy."

"They will be bound to by state law."

"I see," Olympia says. "And do you know where John Haskell is?" Olympia asks.

"No. If I did, I assure you I would tell you. We contacted the former Mrs. Haskell, who divorced her husband two years ago, but she has not responded to us and apparently will not. We did have a conversation with her attorney, however, and he gave us to understand that Dr. Haskell sends money regularly to Mrs. Haskell via an arrangement with the Bank of New Hampshire."

Olympia shuts her eyes, dismayed to learn that Catherine has been brought into this matter. Dismayed that Catherine has been asked to contribute information. And Olympia realizes then, in a way she has not before, that she has begun something that will be larger than herself and that she will not be able to stop.

"Albertine and Telesphore live with the child in one room," Tucker says. "Albertine works as a carder at the Ely Falls Mill from five-thirty A.M. to four P.M., six days a week, combing raw cotton so that it can be spun into thread. A hazardous job, I might add, because of the high incidence of white lung. You do know about the white lung?"

"Yes."

"For this labor, she makes $336.96 a year."

Olympia looks steadily at Payson Tucker.

"The couple seem to have made adequate arrangements for the child's care," Tucker continues, "however difficult these arrangements may be for the couple themselves. I am bound to tell you that their industriousness and their careful attention to the needs of the child, as well as the sacrifices that this has entailed, will be seen in a favorable light by any judge."

Olympia nods.

"I have more to tell you," Tucker says, "and I have to warn you that it is worse."

Olympia looks up. "How can anything be worse?"

Tucker folds his arms on the table and leans toward her. "I will tell you right now that you should not go forward with your petition," he says. "Let me explain what will happen to you if you do. The trial will be grueling. You will be seen to belong to the lowest rung of society, that of unwed mothers. Your transgressions will become public knowledge in ways you have never imagined. Very likely, the story of this trial will be considered newsworthy by the Boston papers. In the two cases I spoke of earlier, the damage to the principals was considerable. One of the young women committed suicide shortly after the trial."

Olympia feels her hands go cold. Out of sight of Tucker, she wraps them in the folds of her skirt.

"I am sorry to be so harsh," Tucker says. "But I want you to understand that if you continue with your petition, you will be left with no reputation whatsoever when it is over, no matter what the outcome. I do not think the Bolducs' lawyer will spare your sensibilities or will care for your delicacy. The irony is that even I cannot spare your delicacy. I will need to be as ruthless as the opposition."

"And what are my alternatives?"

"The alternative is simple, Miss Biddeford. Do not put forth your petition."

Olympia looks at Payson Tucker, at his gold-rimmed spectacles, his oiled hair, his well-groomed mustaches. "Then I should never see my son," she says.

"That is correct."

"I will never hold him."

Tucker is silent.

"I will never teach him," she says, her voice rising. "I will never dress him. I will never speak to him, or he to me."

"No."

"Then there is no alternative, Mr. Tucker. I must proceed."

Tucker sighs and leans back in his chair. He surveys the overdressed dining room and its few patrons. "Then let me help you," he says simply.

Clouds have covered the moon, and she can see only those portions of the road the headlamps of the automobile illuminate: a flash of stone wall, the shingled corner of a cottage, a stark silhouette of a telephone pole.

"I have ridden in a motorcar only once before," Olympia confesses. "At school. A benefactor came to visit. I was one of the students asked to accompany him in his automobile up a small mountain to visit an observatory."

"Where were you at school?"

"Not a place you have ever heard of, I can assure you. The Hastings Seminary for Females. In the town of Fairbanks in the western part of Massachusetts."

"Did you enjoy it?"

"The drive or the school?"

He smiles. "Well, both, actually."

"I was terrified during the drive. I was certain we would slide sideways off the mountain. I spent the entire time at the observatory wondering how I could get down without going back in the motorcar. As for the school, I disliked it intensely."

Olympia watches with interest as Tucker shifts the gears. And she thinks that she should like to learn to drive an automobile. She imagines the luxury of being able to drive herself back and forth to Ely Falls.

When Tucker opens the door of the motorcar, she is enveloped in a fine mist, like cobwebs, against her face and hands. "Is it raining?" she asks.

"Just," he says, once again taking her elbow.

"It is very dark tonight," she says, feeling her way along the slate path.

"Shall I wait while you light a lamp?" he asks when they have reached the stepping stone.

"No, I know my way. Thank you."

In the dark, she cannot see his face. She extends her hand, and he takes it, his grip firm and warm against her own.

"I am sorrier than I can say to have to be the bearer of such bad tidings," Tucker says. "I have admired you from the moment you entered my office."

Olympia withdraws her hand. She catches, on the air, a faint whiff of castile. It has been a long time since she stood this close to a man.

"Do you love him still?" Tucker asks suddenly.

And Olympia is not as surprised as she might be by the young lawyer's question, for she understands that Payson Tucker has perhaps waited all evening to ask it.

"I cannot imagine not loving him," she answers truthfully.

She hears the motorcar drive away, leaving only the rumble of the surf. With her hat and gloves still on, she walks through the rooms of the house, seeing it anew, imagining it filled with young girls sentenced to silence, separated from their unforgiving families. How extraordinary that this house, in which she has known both luxury and love, in which John Haskell once kissed and held her, in which Josiah once dallied with Lisette, in which orchestras have played and women have danced and men have talked and smoked, should have had all this time such an abhorrent history and yet have given away nothing of that suffering and sorrow.

She wanders upstairs, enters a seldom-used bedroom, and sits on the bed. It is a benign room, papered in blue forget-me-nots with delicate crewelwork curtains shrouding the windows. In the light of an amber-beaded lamp, long discarded from her mother's dressing table, she can see the scars of wet cups and glasses that remain on the surface of a mahogany bedside table. She tries to hold in her mind the two images of the house, its past and its present, the convent and the holiday retreat, and it is then that she understands — or has a vision of — what she will one day do with her father's summer cottage.

THE HEELS of Olympia's boots echo sharply along the slate flooring of the courthouse. To either side of the cavernous hallway are bronze busts on tall stone pedestals and between them lie low leather benches, so that sitting on one as she waits for Payson Tucker, Olympia feels dwarfed and insignificant, which she supposes was the architect's intention. The law is greater than the men who make it, the bronze men seem to be announcing. The law is greater than those who petition for its intervention.

She watches as the snow on her boots melts into wet puddles on the stone. The glass in the high windows opposite is obscured by dirt and age, and she can neither see nor hear the snowstorm that is beginning to cripple the city outside. She will need to spend another night in the Ely Falls Hotel, she knows, since it will be almost impossible to return home in this weather.

It has been a severe winter at Fortune's Rocks. All through the months of January and February snow has fallen about the cottage and on the beach and even on the rocks near to the sea. As Olympia has waited for the hearing to begin, gusts have shaken the house and drifts have risen to the windows. Some weeks, she has not been able to leave her cottage, and when she does manage to make her way to

Goldthwaite's for provisions or into Ely Falls for a meeting with Payson Tucker, the talk is always of the storms. *So unusual on the coast to have such snow. When will it end?* She understands, from these comments, that she could not possibly have chosen a worse winter to take up residence at Fortune's Rocks.

In the distance, she can see Tucker coming toward her from the opposite end of the long corridor, a spindly dark figure emerging from a kind of dusk. She catches a flash of his spectacles before she can see his face. And beyond him now, there are other persons entering the corridor as well, as if a trolley had made a stop. The fur collar of Tucker's overcoat is frosted with snow, and his spectacles fog in the sudden warmth of the building, so that when he reaches her, he seems a face without eyes. He sets down his cases in front of her.

"Miss Biddeford," he says, taking off his spectacles and wiping them with a handkerchief from his pocket.

"Mr. Tucker."

He unwinds his muffler, and a radiator hisses beside them.

"Are you ready?"

"I hope I am," she says.

"I shall call you first, as we have discussed. Although it may not happen straightaway. It will depend on what motions and so forth are put forward by Mr. Sears."

"Yes, of course."

"Dreadful storm. I hope they do not postpone this hearing yet again." Tucker looks away a moment and then back again. "There is something we need to discuss before we go in," he says, "because I do not want you to be surprised or caught off guard in any way."

"Yes?"

He sits beside her on the bench. He smells of wet wool and again castile. "I have summoned your father," he says.

Her face must register her considerable shock, because he immediately puts his hand over hers.

"I have been trying to reach him for weeks," Tucker says, "but he has been abroad with your mother."

"Italy," Olympia says. "But why have you done this?"

"I cannot prove your case without him and Josiah Hay as witnesses."

"You have called Josiah as well?" Olympia asks, suddenly hot inside her coat. She withdraws her hand and unfastens the top several buttons. "How could you do this without consulting me?"

"Miss Biddeford, you have hired me to put your petition before the court," he says, sliding his arms from his own overcoat.

"Yes, but —"

"And I must do so in the best way known to me. And that may require actions or words or maneuvers that you and I will not necessarily discuss."

"My father is coming here? Today?"

"Yes. I trust he might. If he can get through in the storm. I hope he came last night before it began."

She turns her head away. She has not even told her father that she knows of the boy's whereabouts, never mind that she has requested a custody hearing.

"If you truly thought you could put forth your petition without help from any other persons," says Tucker, "then I fear I have misled you."

"My father knows nothing of these proceedings," she says.

"Well. Yes. He does now. Now he does."

"Was he shocked by this news?"

Tuckers ponders the question. "He seemed a bit taken aback, but not as much as I had expected. You, however, may be surprised to learn that he was most eager to help in any way he could. In fact, I rather imagined he sounded relieved."

"You spoke to him?"

"I wrote to him initially — and repeatedly, I might add. I spoke to him yesterday morning by telephone."

"My father has a telephone?" she asks.

The room is small, wood-paneled, a chamber meant for hearings and not for audiences. Its intimacy is unnerving to Olympia, for within minutes Albertine and Telesphore Bolduc enter the room and sit, as instructed by the bailiff, across the aisle from Olympia and Payson Tucker. The Franco-Americans are as close to Olympia as they might be in a church. Though Olympia has twice seen Albertine, the Franco woman has never seen Olympia, and so for a long moment the two women regard each other across the aisle. Their mutual gaze is disconcerting, but Olympia forces herself not to glance away. If she would go forth with her petition, she tells herself, she must be able to look this woman in the eye.

And such deep-set eyes they are. The features of the woman's face, though not fine, are sharply delineated. It is a face one reads immediately, and thus immediately Olympia can see that Albertine Bolduc is angry. But mixed with the anger is also curiosity. Is she searching for a likeness in Olympia's face? Or a reason for this suit? Or an indication of Olympia's resolve? Albertine's thick dark hair begins low on her brow, and there is perhaps the merest hint of a mustache. Her lips and cheeks are red — by nature, Olympia is certain, and not with paint. She has on a black woolen suit, either inexpertly tailored or borrowed from another woman. Despite her ill-fitting garments, Albertine holds herself with good posture, the ruffles of her collar barely touching her chin. Her husband, who sits just beyond her, suddenly leans forward to see what it is his wife stares at so intently. He seems then to remember his cloth cap and removes it. His mustaches are damp, his cheeks coarsened by the weather. He says a word to his wife, and when she answers him, she hardly moves her mouth, shocked perhaps into rigidity.

A stout balding man with side whiskers and a monocle takes his place next to Albertine, blocking Olympia's view. He sets a leather case on the table in front of him. And then before Olympia can absorb further the presence of her adversaries, the bailiff is announcing the judge.

"All rise for presiding Judge Levi Littlefield."

The judge enters the chamber with a vigorous sweep of his robes. He is short and slight and sandy-haired, with no beard or mustaches or spectacles, and he looks considerably younger than Olympia has expected. Only his robes lend the man authority, as do those of a minister.

"He seems so young," Olympia says to Tucker when they sit.

"He is not as young as he appears," Tucker says. "And do not let his looks fool you. He is quite shrewd and tough."

"Mr. Payson Tucker," says Judge Littlefield, reviewing the documents laid out in front of him, "as counsel for the relator, you have a matter to put before the court."

Tucker stands and approaches a lectern set up between the lawyers' tables. He is so tall that he has to stoop to read what he has written. He has cut his hair, Olympia notes, and oiled it back from his forehead. Sitting as she is, behind and to the left of him, she can see only a profile. There is a slight tremor in Tucker's hand. Is it possible this is Tucker's first case? she wonders. She has never asked.

"I have here a writ of habeas corpus for the body of a male infant child, Pierre Francis Haskell, aged three years, ten months, and thirteen days, currently of Ely Falls, New Hampshire."

"Yes, Mr. Tucker. Proceed."

"That Albertine and Telesphore Bolduc of one thirty-seven Alfred Street, Ely Falls, New Hampshire, have for three years and approximately ten months restrained the said child of his liberty. That this restraint of liberty is a result of an unlawful and clandestine removal and retention of the child on fourteen April 1900 from the mother of the child, the relator, Olympia Biddeford. That this unlawful removal was carried out at the direction of the petitioner's father, Phillip Arthur Biddeford of Boston, Massachusetts, thereby depriving the infant child of his liberty and depriving the said mother of her maternal rights and solace. That on fourteen April 1900, the child was unlawfully delivered unto the care of the father of the infant male, Dr. John Warren Haskell, address unknown. That on fifteen April 1900, said father unlawfully delivered the child into the care of the Orphanage of Saint Andre of Ely Falls, New Hampshire, unlawfully charging them with placing out the child."

"Mr. Tucker, is the child here?" Littlefield asks, interrupting the lawyer.

"Your Honor," says Tucker, "the respondents have requested permission to have the child remain with Albertine Bolduc's parents, who live a block from the courthouse, during this hearing. He will stay with them until the day the judgment will be read, at which time the boy shall be brought to the courthouse."

"And this is acceptable to you?"

"Yes, sir, it is. We should not like to see a small child confined in unfamiliar surroundings."

"No, quite. Are Phillip Biddeford and the Orphanage of Saint Andre represented here today?"

"Phillip Biddeford has declined representation and agrees to provide testimony on behalf of the relator. I believe the Orphanage of Saint Andre has also declined representation and has agreed to provide testimony on behalf of the respondents, who are represented by my colleague Mr. Addison Sears."

"Is this true, Mr. Sears?"

"Yes, Your Honor, it is."

Looking up from his notes, Tucker addresses the judge less formally. "Your Honor, because this trail of unlawful events inevitably leads to the child being in the custody of Albertine and Telesphore Bolduc, and because this is not a criminal case but rather a petition for custody, the relator can only sue the Bolducs as foster parents for custody. It remains to be seen whether criminal charges will be brought at a later date."

"Am I to understand that the father of the infant male child cannot be located?" Littlefield asks.

"That is correct," says Payson Tucker.

"Very well," says Judge Littlefield. "Let us proceed."

Addison Sears, who is not even as tall as Olympia, rises and moves to the lectern and adjusts his monocle. Olympia notes that he has not one but several diamond rings on the soft fingers of his left hand. His frock coat is finely cut, in stark contrast to the clothes of his clients. He takes a long drink from a glass of water he has carried to the lectern.

"Good morning, Your Honor," Sears says in a tone that suggests he knows the judge personally.

"Good morning, Mr. Sears," the judge says amiably.

"Your Honor, this is a simple case," Sears begins, still riffling through his notes as if he were not really beginning at all. "There is no statute in the land that would prompt a court to give custody of Pierre Francis Haskell to the young person sitting to my left."

He pauses to let the implications of the words *young person* have their full effect.

"Let us consider the facts," he continues. "A wanton fifteen-year-old girl, a mere child herself, with a child's faculties and lack of mature judgment, fornicates with a man nearly three times her age, causing this man to commit adultery and to leave his wife and four children." Sears pauses to allow the impact of this moral transgression to settle upon the court. "She then gives birth to an infant male, whom she abandons," he continues. "Through the years, she shows *no interest whatsoever* in his welfare. She does not support the child, either morally or financially. She does not inquire as to his health and well-being. She never visits him. *And then she seeks custody of this child?*"

Sears shakes his head, as though bewildered.

"In truth, Your Honor, if these were not such serious proceedings, this situation would be laughable."

Judge Littlefield does not laugh. Sears tucks his fingers into his paisley vest pockets.

"Without resorting to the obfuscation of the language of our esteemed profession, I should like permission to set forth the respondents' position in a manner that the young person to my left might understand," says Sears, looking pointedly at Tucker, who did not, of course, think to reject the obfuscation of the language of the law himself.

"Very well, Mr. Sears. Proceed."

"The task of the respondents today is twofold," says Sears. "We shall prove that Olympia Biddeford is not a fit parent for this or any other child. And we shall prove as well that it is in the best interests of the child to remain in the care of Albertine and Telesphore Bolduc, who have been the boy's foster parents almost from birth."

Sears takes another drink of water and then clears his throat.

"We shall show, Your Honor, that the relator, Olympia Biddeford, when she was only fifteen years of age, an age, I might add, when one's character is being formed, participated in an improper sexual relationship with a man who was married and had four children of his own. That Olympia Biddeford not only is guilty of wanton and lascivious behavior but also has shown herself to be depraved, vulgar, and vile."

Sears slowly turns and looks directly at Olympia. Despite her desire to remain calm, her cheeks burn, as though proving Sears correct in his accusations. He then abruptly turns his back on Olympia, suggesting that he cannot even bear to look at her.

"Your Honor, the courts of this land have consistently decided that if a child is left with an immoral mother, then that child is in danger of becoming immoral himself. Unwed mothers have, in nearly all cases brought before the courts, been denied not only custody but also visitation rights.

"Olympia Biddeford has shown no interest in the child's welfare," Sears continues. "She abandoned the boy on the day of his birth, never inquired as to his whereabouts, never contributed a penny to his care, never knew where he was until last fall. Moreover, she has never even met with or spoken to the child. According to the law of the land, a mother who abandons her child, who lets this child remain too long with a surrogate family, loses her custodial rights and legal standing. As there are no other cases on point with written decisions in the state of New Hampshire, making the case before us today one of first impression, I should like to make reference to other cases stated in the respondents' memorandum. If I may refer to the 1888 decision of the Connecticut Supreme Court in *Hoxie* v. *Potter*: *'The courts do not feel called upon to sunder the ties that have been permitted to grow up, and believe that the happiness of the boy and the rights and feelings of his foster parents will be best subserved by leaving custody where it now is.'*"

Olympia glances at Tucker, who is staring at his notes in front of him.

"Olympia Biddeford may be a mother by nature, but she is not by nurture," Sears pronounces. "And even if she were a morally upright woman, *which she clearly is not,* she would have to be considered an unfit guardian on the basis of her age at the time of the child's conception, which was fifteen years, her marital status, which continues to be unwed, and her inability to provide a religious education for the boy. She herself is not a member of any church, nor does she attend services on any regular basis."

Sears turns quickly and points at Olympia, a gesture so sudden that she flinches.

"Perhaps Olympia Biddeford seeks rehabilitation by having the child restored to her," the lawyer says, as though the idea were a novel one. "This was once, in fact, a not uncommon if misguided notion of the courts. And I quote now from the 1873 decision of the Tennessee Supreme Court: *That if a woman be an unmarried mother, the surrendering of her child removes the one great influence toward a restoration of character through maternal affection. Her love for the child and fear of separation may prove her salvation.*'"

Sears looks up at the judge and holds out his hands, palms up. "But, Your Honor, the state of New Hampshire does not *care* about the rehabilitation of the mother. It must and does care first and foremost about the welfare of the child."

Olympia presses her own hands tightly together in her lap. *But I, too, care about the welfare of the child,* she wants to cry out.

"So let us, for the moment, put aside the character of Olympia Biddeford," Sears continues. "And let us consider only the best interests of the child."

Now Sears turns and gazes at Albertine and Telesphore Bolduc, who both immediately look down into their laps, as if about to be chastised themselves. The couple appear to be at least as uncomfortable with these proceedings as Olympia is.

"Citing for a moment the New York case of *Chapsky* v. *Wood* in 1881," Sears says, "*When reclamation is not sought until a lapse of years, when new ties have been formed and a certain current given to the child's life and thought, much attention should be paid to the unlikeli-*

hood of a benefit to the child from the change. It is an obvious fact that
ties of blood weaken and ties of companionship strengthen by lapse of
time; and the prosperity and welfare of the child depend on the ability
to do all which the prompting of these ties compels.'"

Sears, seeming to study his notes for a moment, creates another
pause.

"Mr. and Mrs. Bolduc have been foster parents to Pierre Francis
Haskell since ten days after his birth — in effect, all of his life. The
child knows no other parents. The Bolducs have lavished upon the
boy all the love and affection they might have lavished upon their
own blood child had Albertine not been a barren woman. Mr. and
Mrs. Bolduc are of sufficient age to care for the boy: They are both
thirty-two years old. They have a stable marriage, having cohabited
in a state of wedded solace and bliss for eleven years. They are both
longtime members of the Parish of Saint Andre, the Roman
Catholic church of Ely Falls, and attend services regularly. They have
expressed a passionate desire to extend to the boy a proper religious
education. Moreover, they are deeply woven into the fabric of the
Franco-American community here in Ely Falls and are part of a large
extended family with many cousins and aunts and uncles and grand-
parents who dote on the little boy. As Your Honor is doubtless
aware, the Franco-Americans are known for their strong family and
cultural ties, which they refer to as *la Foi*. In addition, these foster
parents are hardworking. Though both are employed by the Ely Falls
Mill, Mr. and Mrs. Bolduc have made adequate, not to say excellent,
arrangements for the boy's care at great sacrifice to themselves. You
shall hear testimony from Albertine Bolduc regarding her love and
devotion to the boy."

Sears removes his monocle and lets it fall upon his chest.

"Your Honor, it would be a crime — *a crime* — to take the boy
away from the only parents he has ever known. And as the state of
New Hampshire is not generally in the business of committing

crimes against its citizens, the respondents request that the writ of habeas corpus put before us today by the counsel for the relator be set aside forthwith."

The lawyer takes his seat next to the Bolducs and then pinches the bridge of his nose with his thumb and forefinger, as if he already knew the judge's disposition.

"Motion to set aside the writ of habeas corpus denied," says Judge Littlefield matter-of-factly, and Olympia understands that Sears's speech was never intended to persuade the judge to dismiss the suit, but rather to put forth the arguments of the respondents. And this the lawyer has done, she has to concede in spite of her agitation, in rather excellent fashion.

Beside her, Tucker is standing.

"Your Honor," he says. "I should like to call Olympia Biddeford to the stand."

She and Tucker have agreed that she should dress conservatively, neither hiding her class and wealth nor flaunting them. To this end, Olympia has purchased a suit of charcoal gray gabardine, which she has on over a high-collared white blouse. With it, she has worn a matching hat, a black velvet tie, and small pearl earrings.

Tucker, without notes, stands up slowly and approaches her in the witness box.

"Miss Biddeford," he says kindly and with a smile, which, though doubtless much rehearsed, puts her at ease, as it is meant to do. "How old are you?"

"Twenty years."

"And you live where?"

"Fortune's Rocks."

"And prior to living at Fortune's Rocks?"

"I was a student at the Hastings Seminary for Females in Fairbanks, Massachusetts," she answers, making sure, as Tucker has advised, that the word *seminary* is emphasized.

"For how long were you in residence at this seminary?"

"Three years."

"And the purpose of this female academy?"

"To train young women so that they might be sent out to foreign lands for the purposes of teaching children and setting good examples of Christian womanhood."

"And were you in agreement with the aims of this seminary?"

"I was not in disagreement," she says carefully.

"You fully intended to be such a missionary yourself?" Tucker asks, emphasizing the word *missionary*.

"I assumed that was my future. Yes."

"And how did you acquit yourself at this school?"

"I acquitted myself well, I trust."

"Is it not a fact that you consistently ranked number one or number two in a class of two hundred and seventy young women?"

"Yes."

"Is it not a fact that you could, if you so chose, accept a teaching position right now, without further schooling?"

"Yes," she says. "I imagine I could."

"Then tell the court why you have chosen not to do so at this moment."

"I wish to have my son with me."

There is a muffled gasp from Albertine Bolduc, who brings a gloved hand to her mouth. Her husband puts his arm around her shoulders.

"I think that we can safely say," says Tucker, ignoring the small outburst, but looking pointedly at Sears, "that the staff of this religiously oriented seminary considered you neither wanton or lascivious nor depraved, vulgar, and vile."

"Your Honor." Addison Sears is on his feet. "Would you be so kind as to ask counsel for the relator to desist in this line of questioning, as the answer calls for conjecture on the part of the witness?"

"Mr. Tucker," says the judge.

Tucker seems unruffled by the mild reproof. "Miss Biddeford, how do you support yourself?"

"I have money from my father."

"Would it be correct to say that as far as the foreseeable future is concerned, money is not a subject you need worry about?"

"One always wishes to be prudent with money," she says carefully, "but, yes, I think you could say that was true."

"So that, if you were to receive custody of your son, you would not have to leave the house to go to work?"

"No, I would not."

"And thus you could care for the young boy full-time?"

"Yes, I could."

Tucker turns and glances at Albertine Bolduc, as if physically to point out the difference between his client and the Franco woman. He walks back to the table, where he briefly consults his notes.

"Miss Biddeford, I know that these are painful questions. But let us now go back to the day of the child's birth."

Olympia takes in a long, slow breath. No matter how many times she and Tucker have rehearsed these questions, they always make her anxious.

"Where did you give birth to the child?" ·

"In my bedroom in my father's house in Boston."

"And what day and time was this?"

"Two o'clock on the afternoon of April fourteenth, 1900."

"Was it a normal birth?"

"Yes."

"And what happened immediately after this birth?"

"The boy was taken from me."

"By whom?"

"I do not know. But I do know that it was upon the instructions of my father. I doubt, however, that he personally handled the child himself."

"And why is it you do not know for certain who removed your child from your arms?"

"I had been given laudanum by my mother's doctor."

"This would be Dr. Ulysses Branch of Newbury Street in Boston."

"Yes."

"How much laudanum were you given?"

"I believe three spoonfuls."

"So you were asleep."

"Yes."

"Do you remember the boy at all?"

Not once during their informal rehearsals has Olympia been able to answer this question without her eyes welling up. "Yes," she says as evenly as she can. "I remember some things. I was drifting in and out of consciousness."

"Tell the court what you remember."

"I was told the child was a boy. He was swaddled and laid beside me. I remember black spiky hair, beautiful eyes. . . ." She bites her lip.

"That is fine," Tucker says quickly, having established his point. "Was it your desire that the child be taken from you at birth?"

"No."

"Had you made your feelings on this subject clear?"

"Yes, I had spoken of this to my father."

"And what did he say?"

"That he had made what he called 'arrangements.' And that if I kept the child, he would disown me."

"But, Miss Biddeford, did you not care more about the child than about being disinherited?"

"Yes, I did care more about the child," Olympia says with fervor. "But I reasoned that if I went against my father's wishes, I would have no way to support myself and that I could not survive. And that if I did not survive, the child would not survive."

"Miss Biddeford, tell the court why it is you have put forth your petition now, as opposed to, say, two years ago or one year ago."

Olympia looks at Tucker and then takes in the entire courtroom before her — Judge Littlefield, the clerk, the bailiff, the Bolducs, Mr. Sears. What she says now, Tucker has told her, may be everything.

"My child was stolen from me," Olympia says. "I have suffered greatly with this loss. I have thought about my son every single day since his birth and have wanted him with me. But until recently, I was not of an age nor was I in the proper circumstances to petition for the child's return to me. Nor did I even know where he was, as this knowledge was kept from me all these years."

Tucker nods encouragingly. And it occurs to Olympia then that something is profoundly missing from these proceedings. The boy himself. Her son. Though she would not wish him here, would not wish him to have to listen to any of this testimony, the event seems patently hollow without him.

"But I do not seek to have the child returned to me simply because I wish to have my 'property' restored," Olympia says. "No, I believe that I shall be a good and loving mother for the boy, that I can offer the boy certain advantages in terms of comfort and education that are not normally available to all children."

The intensity of Albertine Bolduc's angry stare is almost more than Olympia can bear. She tries to focus only on Tucker's face, his spectacles.

"Mr. Tucker, my heart aches for the loss of my son," Olympia says with unfeigned passion. "Our separation has been unnatural and painful. I pray that the court will redress the terrible wrong that has been done both to me and to the boy and that we will one day be reunited, as God and Nature have meant us to be."

Albertine Bolduc closes her eyes. Telesphore, who still has his arm around his wife, glares at Olympia with what can only be hatred. Tucker stands motionless, allowing Olympia's words to settle over the courtroom.

"No further questions, Your Honor," Tucker says, taking a seat.

And then Addison Sears is standing. "Your Honor, I have some questions I should like to put to the relator."

"Yes, Mr. Sears, proceed."

The portly Mr. Sears takes his time shuffling his notes as he approaches Olympia. It is so cold in the chamber that for a brief moment, Olympia can see the lawyer's breath.

"Good morning, Miss Biddeford," Sears says, not even looking at her, but rather at his notes.

"Good morning," she says in a low voice.

Sears glances sharply up at her. "I think you will need to speak up, Miss Biddeford, or the court will not be able to hear you."

And immediately, she understands that he is setting a pattern of scolding, of chastising the child. She raises her chin. "Good morning," she repeats in a louder and clearer voice.

"Miss Biddeford, are you or have you ever been married?"

"No."

"And if you were to receive custody of the boy, you would, of necessity, be forced to care for him as an unwed mother. Is this not true?"

"Yes," she says simply.

"Miss Biddeford, you have told the court that before arriving at

Fortune's Rocks you were at school. But is it not true that directly before coming to Fortune's Rocks, you were in fact in the employ of Averill Hardy of Tetbury, Massachusetts, and not, as you have said, at the Hastings School for Girls?"

The deliberate misnaming of the school is not lost on Olympia, nor, she imagines, on the judge. "Yes," she says, "that is true. But as it was a summer work-study program administered by the Hastings Seminary for Females, it was considered part of my education at the seminary. It took place under the auspices of the staff there."

"Yes, quite," says Sears. "You were employed as governess to Mr. Hardy's three sons, is that not correct?"

"Yes."

"And is it not true that on twelve July of last year you abandoned this post? That you left these three boys without a tutor and did not even tell them you were leaving?"

"The circumstances were such that . . ."

"Did you not in fact leave Mr. Hardy's employ under *suspicious* circumstances?"

"Your Honor." Tucker is standing. "Mr. Sears is not allowing the witness to finish her answer."

"Mr. Sears."

Addison Sears makes a show of bowing slightly to the judge. When he turns back to Olympia, he is smiling. "I apologize for my small interruption, Miss Biddeford. Doubtless I am too eager to discover the truth. Please, by all means, finish your answer."

But Olympia cannot finish her answer. For while Tucker and Sears have been sparring, the bailiff has responded to a knock on the courtroom door and has opened it. Phillip Biddeford, his overcoat dusted with snow, his bowler in his hand, stands at the threshold.

He seems flustered, disturbed by his surroundings, as if unable to read them immediately. And then he catches sight of his daughter in the witness box with the judge towering over her, and this sight must appear to him so unnatural, so wrong, that he pales and actually brings a hand to his chest. Olympia leans forward as if she would go to him, realizing only then how utterly confining the witness box is, a small and temporary prison. She cannot go to her father, nor can she even speak to him. And worse, she will have to continue to answer Sears's hideous questions with her father in the room.

The bailiff leads Mr. Biddeford to a bench. Tucker, who has leaned around in his seat in an unsuccessful effort to signal to Biddeford, turns back again to Olympia.

But it is Sears who has the floor.

"Please, Miss Biddeford. I believe the question was: 'Did you not abandon these three boys with no explanation and without even bidding them farewell?'"

Instinctively, Olympia reaches for the locket inside her blouse and touches it through the cloth. "Mr. Hardy made unwanted and improper advances toward me, and I thought it prudent, for my own personal safety, to leave at once. It was hardly a situation I could explain to Mr. Hardy's three sons."

"I see. So you found yourself once again involved in an improper amorous relationship."

Tucker leaps to his feet, furious this time. "Objection!"

"Miss Biddeford's moral character is a relevant issue," Sears says quietly, as though he has anticipated Tucker's consternation.

"Your Honor, in describing Miss Biddeford's interactions with Averill Hardy as a relationship, and, moreover, an amorous one, counsel is mischaracterizing the witness's testimony," says Tucker heatedly. "Miss Biddeford was molested by Mr. Hardy — not the other way around."

"Do we not agree that this is a matter Miss Biddeford might clarify for us herself?" Sears asks.

"Yes, the court agrees," says Judge Littlefield. "In future, Mr. Sears, you will put appropriate boundaries around your questions."

"Yes, Your Honor, I shall."

Sears bends a finger under his nose as if lost for a time in deep thought. Then he turns suddenly in Olympia's direction.

"Miss Biddeford, when did your sexual relations with Dr. Haskell begin?"

The bluntness of the question not only stuns Olympia but also seems to startle Tucker, who looks sharply up from his notes. Neither has prepared for such a frontal attack. Despite Olympia's best intentions, and Tucker's advice, Olympia glances down into her lap. *My God,* she thinks, *I cannot have my father listen to this. I cannot possibly answer these questions in front of him.* She looks up and silently implores Tucker to do something.

Tucker, either seeing the desperation on Olympia's face or having similar thoughts of his own, stands. "Your Honor, counsel for the relator requests that Mr. Phillip Biddeford, the relator's father, who has just arrived, be removed from the courtroom during this sensitive questioning of his daughter."

Littlefield nods. "Bailiff, please show Mr. Biddeford to another room, where he can await a summons or" — Judge Littlefield checks his pocket watch — "a recess."

Olympia watches as her father is led away, and it seems to her that he has to lean on the bailiff's arm for support. Sears returns his attention to Olympia.

"The question, once again, is, 'When did your sexual relations with Dr. Haskell begin?'"

"On July fourteenth, 1899."

"And what was the nature of these sexual relations?"

"Objection, Your Honor," says Tucker from his seat. "Does the witness have to answer this abhorrent question?"

"Objection sustained," Littlefield says. "Mr. Sears, the court will not countenance such questioning of the witness."

"Miss Biddeford," Sears says, "where did you meet Dr. Haskell for the purpose of this sexual congress?"

"At his hotel."

"This would be the Highland Hotel of Fortune's Rocks?"

"Yes."

"You went to his room?"

"Yes.

"This is a room he occasionally shared with his wife when she came to visit on weekends?"

"I believe so," Olympia says, wondering how Sears can possibly know such facts.

"Would it be accurate to say you initiated these relations?"

Olympia thinks a moment. It is a question she has long pondered herself. "Yes," she says finally.

"And you were aware Dr. Haskell had a wife and children?"

"Yes."

"You had, in fact, met this wife and children and had dealings with them?"

"Yes."

"They were, indeed, guests at your house from time to time?"

"Yes."

"On how many occasions did you engage in sexual congress with Dr. Haskell?"

"I do not know."

"More than a dozen?"

"Possibly."

"Did you always go to the hotel?"

"No."

"Where else did you go?"

"To a building site."

"To a building site?" Sears asks incredulously. He turns away from Olympia and glances at Albertine and Telesphore.

"Dr. Haskell was building a cottage," Olympia adds.

"At Fortune's Rocks?"

"Yes."

"And you engaged in sexual congress with him in this half-built cottage?" Sears asks.

"I have already said that I did."

The tension of Sears's inquisition is producing an excruciating headache at the back of Olympia's neck. For how long will these terrible questions go on?

"Miss Biddeford, at the time you were engaging in these reprehensible acts, did you consider your actions wrong?"

"I considered it wrong to harm Catherine Haskell," she says. "I did not consider it wrong to love John Haskell."

"Catherine Haskell being Dr. Haskell's wife?"

"Yes."

"Do you now consider your conduct during that time to have been sinful?"

"No, I do not."

"Truly, Miss Biddeford? Do you attend church services?"

"I have done so."

"When was the last time you attended a church service?"

"Last June," she says.

"I see. That would be eight months ago. Will you, if you are given custody of the boy, then consider your conduct sinful?"

"Your Honor," says Tucker, again on his feet. "The witness cannot know how she will feel at some future date."

"Mr. Sears."

"Let me put the question another way, Your Honor. Miss Biddeford, how will you explain the circumstances of your son's birth to him when he is of an age to understand such things — if, indeed, such unnatural acts can ever be understood?"

"I shall explain them in the way I would hope Albertine Bolduc would explain them. That is to say, I shall tell my son the truth."

Shaking her head, Albertine whispers to her husband.

"Miss Biddeford, have you ever contacted the child?"

"No."

"Have you shown any interest in his welfare?"

"I have put this petition forward."

"In any other way?"

"I have had interest in the boy ever since he was born."

"Have you indicated any such interest to any other person prior to moving to Fortune's Rocks in July of last year?"

"No."

"Have you ever met the child?"

"No."

"Miss Biddeford, do you love John Haskell still?"

The question is swift and clean, a blade slicing to the bone. But Olympia does not hesitate in her answer. "Yes," she says at once, and it is the first time during the proceedings that Addison Sears himself looks at all surprised. He takes a drink of water. "Can you possibly now foresee a day when you might repudiate, in the interests of your child, your love for John Haskell?" he asks.

Tucker is on his feet, but Olympia is answering the question. "No," she says in a clear voice. "It will never be in the interest of the child to repudiate my love for John Haskell."

"Your Honor, I have no further questions."

Olympia meets her father during the noontime recess in a small chamber to one side of the courtroom. He falters and has to use his hands on a table edge to pull himself upright. It has been only eight months since Olympia last saw her father, but he seems scarcely familiar to her. His face is chalky in color, and he appears to be frail; and she does not know if this is a result of his shock in the courtroom, at the sight of his daughter in the witness box, or of age. Perhaps her father is unwell. When she embraces him, she kisses him, even though it is not their custom.

"My dear," her father says.

They clasp each other's hands, the kiss having unleashed a torrent of feeling in Olympia. They sit in the leather chairs at a library table. Tucker stands discreetly at the door.

"Must you go through with this, Olympia?" her father asks.

"I will have my son restored to me, Father," she says. "But I am distressed at the thought of the anguish this is causing you."

"I do not have anguish if you do not," he says. "And I no longer care about scandal. You should know that your mother did not agree to my . . . disposing . . . of the boy in the manner I did. She was most upset with me. And now . . . Well, I can hardly speak of now."

"You have told her?"

"Yes, of course. I felt I must. She is bound to hear of it. Olympia, please let me help you. I wish to make amends. I shall stay here as long as I am needed. I will tell you, however, that I am bound to testify, for I have been summoned."

"Do so, Father," she says. "Tell the truth. It can only help me."

"You must need money."

Olympia sits up straighter and glances over at Tucker. "Mr. Tucker has been kind enough to defer all fees until such time as I can pay him."

"Well, that is a matter Mr. Tucker and I shall settle between us," her father says. "You must not try to be so independent, Olympia. It is not good for the heart."

And she thinks, as she gazes all about her father's face and his coat, rumpled and wet from his journey, that of course her father has wisdom about some matters.

"Father — ," she says, but she cannot finish her sentence, for the door opens. Judge Levi Littlefield enters the room.

"Oh, excuse me," he says. "I did not realize anyone was in here."

Littlefield, who appears considerably smaller without his robes, seems for the first time to see the other person in the room.

"Phillip," he says, advancing.

Olympia's father stands. "Levi," he says, putting out his hand.

"I am sorry you have had to appear in this matter. You came last night?"

"This morning."

"And missed the brunt of the storm, I hope?"

"Just."

"Well, I shall leave you to your conference."

With a small nod in Olympia's direction, and hesitating only slightly, Littlefield backs through the door.

"You and Judge Littlefield know each other," Tucker says to Phillip Biddeford.

"A matter of pigs straying into the orchards and creating a general nuisance, as I recall," Olympia's father says. "Levi settled the matter with considerable grace and wit."

Olympia remembers the invasion of the pigs from the Trainer farm. Six years ago? Seven?

Tucker smiles. "I imagine it was one of the more amusing matters to come before the court."

"I daresay it was."

"Father," Olympia says, "let us take Mr. Tucker to lunch, and ascertain as well that you have a room at the hotel. There can be no thought of your journeying back to Boston until this weather has turned fine again."

"Olympia," her father says, turning to her, his face having regained some of its color. "I have missed you so very much."

*   *   *

Counsel for the relator calls Phillip Arthur Biddeford to the stand:

"Mr. Biddeford, did you on the afternoon of fourteen April 1900 conspire to unlawfully remove the infant male child Pierre Francis Haskell from his mother, your daughter, Olympia Biddeford?"

"Yes, Mr. Tucker, I did."

"Did you take the child yourself?"

"No, I did not. I had my wife's personal maid take the child and bring him downstairs to me, whereupon I immediately bade my personal manservant, Josiah Hay, to transfer the child to its father, Dr. John Haskell."

"And you had made prior arrangements with Dr. Haskell?"

"Yes, I had."

"How so?

"By post."

"At your instigation or at his?"

"At mine. I had written to the man through his lawyer."

"And your agreement was?"

"That he would undertake to place the child with an orphanage. He was well suited to do this, since he had often worked with charitable institutions in Ely Falls and elsewhere."

"Mr. Biddeford, tell the court why you made these arrangements and contrived in a clandestine manner to steal the child from your daughter."

"I was concerned for her reputation."

"Do you regret having done this?"

"Yes, very much so. I pray my daughter will one day forgive me."

*   *   *

Counsel for the respondents wishes to put questions to Phillip Arthur Biddeford:

"Mr. Biddeford. When you discovered your daughter was with child, what were your thoughts?"

"I was horrified."

"Did you consider your daughter too young to bear a child?"

"Yes, Mr. Sears, I did."

"Did you consider her too young to raise a child?"

"Yes, I did."

"Your daughter was sixteen at the time?"

"Yes."

"Did you consider her a child herself?"

"Yes, Mr. Sears, I did."

"Did you, at the time, give any thought to the welfare of the child himself?"

"Some, yes."

"And what was that?"

"I thought, at the time, that he would be better cared for by an institution, but now I regret —"

"We will confine ourselves to answering the questions at hand, Mr. Biddeford."

"Yes."

"And if you gave, at the time, some thought to the welfare of the infant child, what other concerns did you have?"

"I was concerned for the ruination of my daughter."

Counsel for the relator calls Josiah Hay:

"Mr. Hay, we have heard testimony that on fourteen April 1900, you were given temporary custody of the infant male issue of Olympia Biddeford by her father, Phillip Biddeford, for the purposes of transporting the child to Dr. John Haskell. Is this true?"

"Yes, Mr. Tucker, it is."

"What did you then do with the child?"

"My wife, Lisette, packed a suitcase of the little boy's things and we took a carriage to North Station and there boarded the train for Rye, New Hampshire."

"Your wife went with you?"

"Yes, sir, she did, and she cried all the way, I can tell you."

"Were you aware that all of this was done without the knowledge of Olympia Biddeford, who was barely conscious as a result of drugs that had been given to her during her confinement?"

"Yes, sir, and that is why my wife was crying."

"And what happened when you got to Rye?"

"We took a carriage to Ely Falls direct. Mr. Biddeford had given us quite a sum of money for the journey."

"And there you met with Dr. John Haskell?"

"Yes."

"And where was this?"

"At the Ely Falls Hotel."

"Tell the court what happened at that meeting."

"We went up to the man's room. I had known him from before, from when he used to visit Mr. Biddeford's house. And we handed over the child."

"And then what happened?"

"And then Dr. Haskell, he lets out this great cry. Oh, it is too terrible to report."

"I am afraid you must. Tell us precisely what happened, Mr. Hay."

"Well, he lets out this great cry, and then he puts the child on the bed and undresses it and looks it over in a tender manner, and he seems to collect himself and he tells us the child is healthy, which had been worrying my wife greatly, so she was much relieved, sir."

"And then what happened?"

"Then Dr. Haskell walked over to the door, where my wife and I were standing, and he thanked us, and he shook my hand, and my wife says to him, 'You make sure that child is well placed out,' and Dr. Haskell says that he will."

"And then?"

"And then he asked after Miss Biddeford and wanted to know how she was and how the birth had gone, which my wife was able to inform him on, having been present through the whole ordeal. And then the baby started to cry and I handed over the suitcase and Dr. Haskell went to the child and held him, and my wife and I left the room. We spent the night in the hotel, since it was too late to start back for Boston."

Counsel for the relator wishes to call Mother Marguerite Pelletier:

"You are a mother superior in the Order of the Sisters of Saint Jean Baptiste de Bienfaisance, is that correct?"

"Yes, it is."

"And, as such, you are director of the Orphanage of Saint Andre?"

"That is correct."

"Prior to fifteen April 1900 had Dr. John Haskell ever contacted you?"

"Well, yes, the doctor had been in touch with the orphanage on several matters prior to the fifteenth of April of that year, since he was often in a position of needing to place out infants of mothers who had perished giving birth or of young girls who could not care for the infants."

"I see. And had he been in touch with you regarding the matter of the issue of Olympia Biddeford?"

"Yes, sir, he had. Though he did not tell us the mother's name. Only that he would be bringing to us sometime in April an infant who would be without mother or father, and would we make certain that there would be a place for the child. And, of course, there always would be, since Dr. Haskell had treated so many of our children and had not ever charged for his services."

"And did Dr. Haskell bring that infant to you on the morning of fifteen April 1900?"

"Actually, sir, it was in the afternoon of April fifteenth. He came to my office with the infant."

"And what happened?"

"He seemed most distraught by the plight of the child and deeply concerned that it be well cared for. Although he did not tell me of the circumstances of the infant's birth, and I did not feel in a position to ask, I did think that perhaps the matter concerned Dr. Haskell personally, since he was in such a distraught state and also because he gave the child his name. Though not unheard-of, this was unusual. And also he gave the orphanage a considerable sum of money for the child's care. He was insistent that we place the child out as soon as possible, and he charged us with finding the infant a household with two parents."

"And then what happened?"

"He kissed the boy on the forehead and gave the child to me."

"And did you place the boy out as you had been charged?"

"Yes, sir. We placed the boy with Mr. and Mrs. Bolduc."

Counsel for the respondents wishes to put questions to Mother Marguerite Pelletier:

"Mother Marguerite, did you have occasion last August to meet the relator in this case?"

"Yes, Mr. Sears, I did."

"Can you describe for the court that meeting?"

"She came to my door wanting to inquire about a certain child. I believe I quickly ascertained that the child in question was hers. She gave me some facts about her situation."

"And what fact led you to discover that her child was the infant child Dr. Haskell had left in your charge on fifteen April 1900?"

"She told me the name of the father."

"I see. And then what happened?"

"I left her in my office and went to have a discussion about this matter with Bishop Louis Giguere, who is also one of the directors of the orphanage."

"And what did you and Bishop Giguere determine?"

"We determined that we would tell the young woman that her child had been in our care but had been placed out to a loving couple. We also decided to tell the young woman the first name of the boy, but not his surname."

"And why was that?"

"We wanted to protect the privacy of the child as well as that of the foster parents."

"And how did Olympia Biddeford react to this news?"

"She was quite upset."

"Was there anything unusual in your discussion with Olympia Biddeford that day?"

"Yes, there was."

"Will you tell the court what that was?"

"Well, Mr. Sears, unfortunately I see many young girls in similar situations. They think they can just abandon their babies and get on with their lives, and then from remorse or guilt or whatever feelings are motivating them, they show up on our doorstep wanting the child back. And I thought at first Olympia Biddeford was like the other young women I have seen. Except that she was not."

"And how was that?"

"She was unrepentant. I asked her if she was ready to seek forgiveness for her sins, and she let me know in no uncertain terms that she did not think her actions at all sinful and that she would not ask for forgiveness for something she did not consider wrong."

"Do you recall the specific language of that exchange?"

"I told her that no one just *happens* to conceive a child, that there is will involved and intent, and that she had obviously sinned against Nature and against God. And she said, 'To love is not a sin against Nature, and I will never believe it so.' She was quite insolent, I thought, and had the gall to tell me, a mother superior of the Catholic Church, that she was not sorry she had loved or had been loved in an improper relationship."

"And then what happened?"

"I prayed for her soul."

Counsel for the respondents wishes to call Dean Bardwell of the Hastings Seminary for Females:

"Dean Bardwell, thank you for journeying from western Massachusetts to Ely Falls, which, as we all know, is a considerable distance."

"Yes, sir, it is. But when I received your offer of funds for the journey, I felt I could do with a bit of rest at the seaside."

"Yes. Well. Dean Bardwell, do you remember the relator, Olympia Biddeford, from when she was at your seminary?"

"Yes, Mr. Sears, I do indeed."

"What can you tell us about her stay there?"

"She distinguished herself academically. She was quite superior in her studies. All of her teachers gave her excellent recommendations."

"And what would you say of her personal adjustment to the school?"

"She was what I would call a recluse. She kept to herself. If she had any friends at the school, I am not aware of them. This is highly unusual, I might add. One would expect that in three years a young woman would form some attachments."

"Would you say that Olympia Biddeford was antisocial?"

"Yes, sir, I would."

"Would you say that Olympia Biddeford is academically prepared to go out into the world and accept a teaching position?"

"Yes, most definitely."

"Would you recommend her for such a position?"

"No, I would not. I cannot recommend someone who has previously abandoned an employer without cause."

"How were you informed that the relator had abandoned her post as governess to the sons of Averill Hardy in July of last year?"

"I received a letter in the mail from Mr. Hardy. That was the first I heard of it. Miss Biddeford did not see fit to inform us herself. He said that he was glad the girl was gone, because one of his sons had revealed that she had made what might be considered to be improper advances to the boy."

"Would you allow Olympia Biddeford to reenroll at Hastings?"

"On the basis of that letter, no, I could not."

Counsel for the respondents wishes to call Zachariah Cote to the stand:

"Mr. Cote, you are a published poet of no small reputation within the literary community, is that correct?"

"Yes, Mr. Sears, I have been fortunate in my career."

"Would you tell the court how it is that you came to know Olympia Biddeford?"

"I was a guest at her father's house in Fortune's Rocks on several occasions."

"And what was your opinion of Olympia Biddeford when you met her?"

"She was obviously very well educated. She seemed nice enough, although perhaps a little too sure of herself."

"Did that opinion change at any time that summer?"

"Yes, sir, it most certainly did."

"Can you tell us about this?"

"On the Fourth of July 1899, I was returning from a celebration in Rye. The Burning of the Wagons? Do you know about this? The farmers roll their hay wagons into the center of town and set them on fire? . . ."

"Yes, Mr. Cote. I am sure we have all heard of this local custom. Please go on."

"Well, my driver had decided to return to Fortune's Rocks by way of the road through the marshes, as it is the quickest route. I was staying at the Highland Hotel at the time."

"Yes, go on."

"Well, as we came around a corner, I saw a couple embracing by the side of the road."

"And can you tell us who that couple was?"

"Yes, sir, I can. It was Olympia Biddeford and Dr. John Haskell."

"Are you certain of this?"

"Yes, I am. The lantern from my carriage lit up their faces."

"What was your reaction?"

"I was deeply shocked, sir. Dr. Haskell was a married man. And Olympia Biddeford was only fifteen years old."

"And did you tell anyone of this sighting?"

"No, I did not. Although I thought there might be a future date when I would feel compelled to speak of this to Phillip Biddeford."

"And did you see Olympia Biddeford again that summer in unusual or compromising circumstances?"

"Well, yes, Mr. Sears, I did. Once while I was staying at the Highland, I happened to be returning to the hotel after an early-morning walk and I met Olympia Biddeford on the porch."

"What time was this?"

"It cannot yet have been eight o'clock."

"How did she appear to you?"

"Well, I must say I was quite shocked by her appearance. She appeared . . . how shall I say . . . disheveled?"

"Did you speak to her?"

"Yes, I did. I attempted to engage her in conversation."

"And how did she respond to this attempt?"

"I thought her impudent. She refused my invitation to breakfast and rather ran off, I am afraid."

"Mr. Cote, did you know Catherine Haskell?"

"Yes, I knew her well as a matter of fact. A lovely woman. An excellent wife and mother."

"Did you and Catherine Haskell ever have occasion to catch Olympia Biddeford in a compromising position with Dr. John Haskell?"

"Yes, I am afraid we did."

"Can you tell us about that?"

"Well, sir, it is a delicate matter. It was on the occasion of an evening dinner dance at the home of Phillip Biddeford, August tenth, 1899. While I was with Mrs. Haskell on the porch, she happened to look into a telescope that had been set up there and inadvertently pointed it through a window in the chapel, which was attached to the cottage. And there she saw a most disturbing, not to say shocking, sight."

"Did you see this sight as well?"

"Yes, sir, I did. Noticing Mrs. Haskell's considerable shock, I bent down to have a look myself."

"And what did you see?"

"I saw Olympia Biddeford and Dr. John Haskell in a state of . . . how shall I put this . . . *in flagrante delicto*?"

"In the *chapel*, Mr. Cote?"

"Yes, sir, in the chapel. And if I may offer a further detail, on the *altar,* sir."

"The altar, Mr. Cote?"

"Yes, sir.

"And what was Mrs. Haskell's reaction?"

"She went white in the face."

Counsel for the relator wishes to put some questions to Zachariah Cote:

"Mr. Cote, you are a poet, are you not?"

"Yes, Mr. Tucker, I have said that."

"Of some reputation?"

"Of no small reputation, I am bound to say."

"And were you possessed of this not entirely modest reputation during the summer of 1899?"

"I trust I was."

"Mr. Cote, in June of 1899, did you submit a half dozen poems to Mr. Phillip Biddeford, editor of *The Bay Quarterly,* in hopes that he would publish them?"

"I may have. Is this relevant?"

"Judge Littlefield will determine what is relevant, Mr. Cote. Your answer, please?"

"I am not sure."

"Think, Mr. Cote."

"As I say, I may have."

"Would it be correct to say that Mr. Biddeford rejected these poems for publication?"

"If you must put it that way."

"I am not a poet, Mr. Cote; I prefer to speak the plain truth."

"I do not recall exactly."

"Perhaps this will refresh your memory, Mr. Cote. Is this not a copy of a letter Mr. Phillip Biddeford sent to you?"

"I am not sure."

"Take your time."

"It appears to be."

"And what is the date?"

"August fourth, 1899."

"Which means you would have received it shortly before the evening of August tenth, the night of the dinner dance at Phillip Biddeford's house?"

"I may have done."

"Mr. Cote, would you be kind enough to read the letter aloud?"

"Really, Your Honor. Must I?"

"Mr. Tucker, is this necessary?"

"Your Honor, I wish to show that Mr. Cote may not be an impartial witness in this matter."

"Very well, then. Proceed."

"Mr. Cote?"

"Yes?"

"The letter?"

"Yes, very well, Mr. Tucker. I shall read the letter if I must. But I should like to lodge my considerable protest at this invasion of privacy."

"Mr. Cote, a custody hearing is nothing if not an invasion of everyone's privacy."

"*Dear Mr. Cote. I am returning your several poems to you, since I find I cannot publish them in* The Bay Quarterly *as I had hoped. Though certainly unique in their style and content, they are not suitable for this publication. In future, you may want to consider a modest reining in of your descriptive powers, the result of which might be, I believe, less sentiment in your verse. Yours sincerely, Phillip Biddeford.*'"

"Mr. Cote, did this letter make you angry?"

"It was disappointing, surely. And wrongheaded in its judgment, I might add."

"But you went to Biddeford's gala on August the tenth nevertheless."

"Yes, I did. I had written that I would go, and I am a man of my word."

"I am sure that you are. Mr. Cote, to your knowledge, was Olympia Biddeford ever wanton in public?"

"How do you mean?"

"Were she and Dr. Haskell ever demonstrative in public?"

"No, not unless you count that time in the chapel."

"Was the chapel at all visible from any of the public rooms of the dinner dance?"

"No."

"Did anyone else besides you and Mrs. Haskell see Olympia Biddeford and Dr. John Haskell together that night?"

"I do not know."

"Mr. Cote, is it not a fact that Catherine Haskell did not just happen to look into the telescope the night of the dinner dance, but rather was invited to do so by you?"

"Certainly not, sir."

"You who had been watching the couple all night and knew they had gone into the chapel?"

"No, Mr. Tucker."

"And had, in fact, adjusted the telescope so that it was pointed directly into a window of the chapel?"

"No, Mr. Tucker, most certainly not! And I resent your scurrilous suggestion!"

"Your Honor, I have no further questions for this witness."

"Very well, Mr. Cote, you may step down."

"But, Your Honor, I should like to respond to the completely unfounded insinuation of Mr. Tucker."

"I am sure you would. You may step down now."

"Very well, but I do not like what has been said here."

"No, I am sure you do not. Since it is so late in the afternoon, we will recess for the day and, if this dreadful weather permits, go to our homes. Mr. Sears, you have other witnesses?"

"Yes, Your Honor, tomorrow I shall have Mrs. Bolduc to the stand."

"Very good. Now let us retire to our dinners."

S HE FIGHTS her way through the slush, the skirt of her suit saturated with dirty snow, as she walks from the hotel to the courtroom, a distance of only three blocks. The sun is up, high and strong, and she can smell spring in the air — spring, which is only twenty-two days away now. Perhaps she will survive the winter after all. She has a sudden and intense desire to return to the cottage at Fortune's Rocks, for by today, the snow will be melting on the front lawn, and quite possibly there will be some green beneath, new growth.

Olympia and her father dined at the Ely Falls Hotel last night and again this morning, the dining room shabby but their affection for each other not; and it was a joy to both of them to once again speak of the world outside Fortune's Rocks. He said that he was most eager to know what she thought of Roosevelt and the controversy in the Philippines, and she teased him about finally installing a telephone. He confessed he had purchased a phonograph machine as well, and he rather thought that it was a French recording of the cellist Pablo Casals that had finally made Mother nearly well.

"Father, you should return home," Olympia said when they were sitting in the library of the hotel after breakfast with their coffee. "I appreciate your having come, more than I can say, but Mother needs you more."

"But do you not want support at the trial?"

"I shall manage with Payson Tucker. He is good support. And thank you for taking care of his fees. I promise I shall come to visit as soon as this is over."

And I shall bring the boy, she thought privately.

"Very well," her father said, "but only on the condition that you allow me to send Charles Knowlton over to the cottage to see what it requires by way of further repairs. If you are going to continue to live there, Olympia, certain aspects of the house must be altered. I do not know how you have survived the winter."

"Actually, I have moved into the kitchen," Olympia said, and her father laughed at this idea. And Olympia thought that if such a thing were possible, her father had grown younger in the twenty-four hours he had been in Ely Falls. Indeed, he seemed almost to be in high spirits when he left her for the train.

But the infection of high spirits begins to dissipate as Olympia nears the courthouse, for she has an increasing dread of reentering the hearing chamber. It is a dark, claustrophobic room, too small for such grand passions, for such need, for such antipathy. And she has as well a sour taste in her mouth from having had to reveal thoughts and feelings that one should never have to speak of in public. As strongly as she wants to win her suit, she is not without sympathy for Albertine Bolduc, who will have to take the stand today and will have to answer many of the same questions Olympia did yesterday.

But dread is quickly replaced with bewilderment as Olympia rounds the corner to the entrance to the courthouse. For arrayed all along the stone steps are many persons, some with hastily hand-lettered signs. LA SURVIVANCE! she sees scrawled on a board. JE ME SOUVIENS! she sees scrawled on another. A man, hanging over the stone balustrade, catches sight of her as she stands frozen at the corner. *"Ici la jeune fille!"* he yells to the crowd. Frightened, Olympia watches as the throng moves quickly toward her, carrying their placards with them. Before she can think what to do, she is surrounded by men who are shouting rude questions and remarks at her: *"Ou est le docteur?"* "Miss Biddeford, why are you suing for custody?" *"Ou est la justice?"* A sign is thrust in front of her face, and she puts her hands up to ward it off. She feels then a strong tug on her arm, which she resists frantically until she hears the familiar voice of Payson Tucker and looks up to see his spindly figure towering above the others.

"Leave her alone," he commands in a surprisingly deep voice. "Let us pass."

He takes hold of Olympia's arm and walks her through the crowd, which parts under his direction. He runs her up the steps and through the courthouse doors, which are opened for them only. He ushers her quickly into an anteroom.

"Are you hurt?" he asks at once.

"No," she says, though she is badly shaken. "I do not think so. But I do not understand."

"It is a disaster," Tucker says, looking for an electric light switch and, failing to find one, drawing back the dusty drapes at the window. "A disaster." He opens his briefcase. "Have you seen the newspapers?"

"No," she says, but already she feels a foreboding.

"Take a look at these."

There are two newspapers, the *Ely Falls Sentinel,* with which she is familiar, and *L'Avenir,* a French-language paper she has occasionally seen on newsstands but has never picked up. BEAUTIFUL DAUGHTER OF BOSTON BRAHMIN SEEKS CUSTODY OF FRANCO CHILD, reads the headline of the English paper. FORTUNE'S ROCKS SCANDAL, shouts the Franco paper, Olympia translating, with a subheading: THE BREAK-UP OF A FRANCO FAMILY. The editors of both newspapers have commissioned drawings of Olympia. The portrait in the *Ely Falls Sentinel* is in an oval, much like a cameo, and it shows the young but serious face of a pretty woman who resembles more than anything else a Gibson girl. The drawing that accompanies the story in *L'Avenir,* however, shows a woman in a low-necked dress that reveals a great deal of bosom. The woman's lips are parted, and hair wisps float around her face. Neither picture looks much like Olympia.

"Oh," Olympia says, sitting down.

"This is precisely what I did not want to have happen," Tucker says, picking up one of the papers and slapping it with the back of his fingers. "The city is polarizing. The Francos are passionate about their own community and now will rally around the Bolducs. And the Yankees, threatened by *la Survivance,* will demonstrate the worst sort of prejudice, as only they are capable of. This has been simmering for years, it is always there, and occasionally there is an event, like this suit, that brings it to the fore. This is Sears's doing, I know it is. He has nothing to lose from this, and everything to gain. Indeed, I suspect that is why he has taken the case. For the publicity. He certainly is not in it for the fees."

But Olympia has another thought, one she voices to Tucker. "To me, this gesture has the imprint of Zachariah Cote all about it," she says. "This is how he would repay you for having shredded him on the stand yesterday."

Tucker looks at Olympia and then seems to see her face for the first time.

"Miss Biddeford," he says, putting the paper down. "Here I have been ranting on about class warfare, when, of course, the hurt is to you."

"You tried to warn me about this," she says.

"Yes, but a warning is nothing compared to the shock of the reality. I know that."

Tucker removes the newspapers from the table and puts them in his case. "Are you sure you wish to continue with this case?" he asks. "It is not too late to withdraw your petition."

"I am glad my father was not here to see this," Olympia says, standing and walking to the window. "What is this *la Survivance?*" she asks, looking down at the crowd. "I know it means *survival*, but in this context?"

"It is the rallying cry of the Franco-American community. To keep their culture and their language pure and uncorrupted by the influence of the Yankees. An effort, I might add, that history has shown to be doomed to failure, which I think makes the Francos all the more determined. Of course, you and I know that this suit is not about class or culture, but they will have it differently."

"Are you sure?" she asks. "Are you so sure this is not about class or culture?"

"I have not thought so," Tucker says. "But it shall become so now."

In the small hearing chamber, the sounds of the growing crowd outside can be heard through the sole, shrouded window. Albertine looks frightened and clutches the hand of her husband. Judge Littlefield enters the chamber, and even he, Olympia notes, appears to be somewhat rattled.

"I had hoped to handle this affair privately behind closed doors," Littlefield says at once when he is seated, "which is where it should remain. But occasionally, through no fault of the court, a legal affair is made public, and that public determines it has need to be witness to the facts of the case. This private dispute has found its way into the newspapers, and I hope I shall never discover that any of the parties present in this room has been responsible for this breach of confidentiality." Littlefield glares pointedly at Sears, who, in turn, looks startled and bares his palms, as if to say: It was not I.

"When a case has been made public," Littlefield continues, "and the public decides it is being denied access to it, it is possible that one or both parties may be injured. Therefore, it is with great reluctance and after much deliberation that I have made the decision to sit in public. We shall now adjourn to a larger chamber, and as I do not wish to expose any of us to personal injury from the crowd that has gathered outside, I shall ask the bailiff to escort you through the entrance behind me. The public shall be let into the chamber through another entrance. Bailiff?"

Tucker waits for Sears to show Albertine and Telesphore Bolduc through the door behind the judge before he leads Olympia to this exit. Taking her arm, they pass through the door into what seems like a dark warren of tiny chambers, and Olympia thinks of lambs being led to the slaughter. Because the way is murky and labyrinthine, Olympia instinctively draws closer to Tucker. For part of the way, there are no lights at all, and he puts his arm around her shoulder to guide her. It is odd to feel a man's protective touch again. When they approach the entry to the assigned hearing room, Olympia can hear shouts of encouragement to Albertine and Telesphore. Tucker takes her hand.

"Mr. Tucker, I am more than a little apprehensive," she says, looking down at their clasped hands.

"Miss Biddeford," he says, "there is something I should like to say to you."

In the twilight of the chambers, all that she can see is the suggestion of a face, his eyes.

"I know that this is a dreadful moment," he says.

"Mr. Tucker," she says.

"It is only that I wish to say how much I have admired your

courage and that I have hope that one day we shall have occasion to be friends and not merely colleagues."

Olympia withdraws her hand. "You have picked an exceedingly odd time to announce your admiration," she says.

"Yes. Indeed. I have. But is there ever an opportune time and place for such pronouncements?"

"No, perhaps not."

Olympia considers Tucker. "I should not like to quash hope in any person, having much need of it myself," she says carefully. "And I should particularly not want to disappoint you, since I am already more grateful to you than I can say. But I cannot offer any person more than I can give."

"I understand."

"Please call me Olympia. It is absurd of us to stand on ceremony when we are surrounded by too much pomp and protocol already."

"Thank you, Olympia," he says.

"My God, Tucker," says Judge Littlefield, emerging from the gloom and startling them both. "If I discover that it was Sears who has caused this pandemonium, I shall have him disbarred. Tell me it was not you."

"No, sir," says Tucker, more than slightly flustered to have been overheard in his private petition. "There is no advantage to me in having the courtroom packed with members of the Franco community."

"No, quite."

"And if I may say so, sir," Tucker adds, "one cannot be certain that it was Sears either."

"No, perhaps not. But who then?"

"A disgruntled witness perhaps?" Tucker suggests, looking at Olympia as he does so.

"Let me think on that," Littlefield says. "And tell your father that he still owes me a barrel of apples."

"Sir?"

"An old bet, Mr. Tucker. An old bet."

Littlefield advances toward the door and holds it open for them.

"This could be a circus," Tucker says quietly to Olympia as he shepherds her toward the entryway. "And it almost certainly will be painful. From the sound of it, I think there are rather more Franco supporters than Yankee in there. Think only about your cause and remember, it is not the public who is making the decision."

"No, I should hope not," says Littlefield.

Inside the larger hearing room, it is as Tucker has forewarned: He and Olympia enter the chamber to a chorus of shouts of *"La Survivance!"* Olympia is aware only of scores of men in gray workshirts and cloth caps calling out and raising their fists. *Why are these men not at work?* she wonders. Judge Littlefield, by design, enters immediately after them and swiftly takes up the gavel. He pounds sharply and impatiently upon the table before him.

"Let you make no mistake about these proceedings," he begins, addressing the crowd. "Such outbursts will not be tolerated in this courtroom, and anyone who so much as utters a word will be thrown out forthwith. Mr. Sears, let us proceed with dispatch." And whether it is the tension of the proceedings or his refusal to believe that anyone but Sears could be responsible for the mayhem, Littlefield is harsher in his command to Sears than he might be.

"Counsel for the respondents calls Albertine Bolduc to the stand."

To a hum of muffled murmurs, and a severe look from Littlefield, which momentarily silences the crowd, Albertine Bolduc walks to the witness box and steps inside. It is immediately obvious to Olympia that the woman is terrified, for her hands tremble visibly. She has on the same suit and blouse as she did the day before, and she has fashioned her hair, once again, into a high pompadour with fringe at the front.

"Your Honor," says Mr. Sears, himself dressed in a pinstriped frock coat of dark navy, the diamonds on his fingers sparkling in the electric lights, "I wish to enter into the case several exhibits."

"Yes, Mr. Sears, go ahead."

The chamber is large, with many rows of benches and even a gallery, which appears to be packed. On the walls are portraits of grave men with somber expressions.

"I have here a document issued by the Orphanage of Saint Andre and another by the state of New Hampshire," says Sears. "I also have several photographs."

"Let these documents and photographs be marked as exhibits by the clerk of the court," Littlefield requests.

Sears lets the documents be recorded and then takes them back. Holding them close to his breast, as if they were near and dear to him, he approaches Albertine Bolduc in the witness box.

"Good morning, Mrs. Bolduc."

"Good morning."

"I have some documents here that I should like you to take a look at and identify for me."

Sears shows her the first one, placing it in her trembling hand. "Can you tell the court what this is?"

"Yes," she says, her voice barely audible. "Is certificate of guardian from orphanage."

"And this one?"

"Is certificate from state to being foster," she says haltingly.

Sears takes the two papers from her and hands them to Judge Littlefield.

"And, Mrs. Bolduc, can you identify these two photographs?"

"Yes," she says. "This one? Is of my little Pierre and me when he is five months. And this one here, this is Pierre in wagon with chicken. He is one year."

"Who took these photographs?"

"Is overseer in the mill who is being friend to me and Telesphore."

"Thank you," says Sears quickly, delivering the photographs to the judge, who studies them for a moment. Oddly, Sears seems abrupt with Albertine on the stand, perhaps uneasy with her obvious lack of education, a fact seemingly heightened by her broken English.

"Your Honor," says Tucker, "may we see these photographs?"

"Yes. Clerk, give these documents and photographs to counsel for the relator."

And Olympia will later think: *There are some moments in life for which there can be no preparation.*

The first photograph shows a seated woman holding aloft an infant in a long white dress. The woman's arms are hidden inside the dress. Her face is wrinkled into a broad smile, a pretty smile, over even white teeth. She has on a blouse with a wide white collar and cuffs, and a skirt of a darker shade. The baby has what looks to be a necklace around his neck and tiny kid booties upon his feet. The baby, looking toward the camera, as the mother is, is also smiling broadly, a wide toothless grin. One can almost hear the baby's laugh. The mother, though grinning, is looking at the photographer with sly delight, as if to say, *What do you think of my marvelous treasure?*

In the second photograph, a boy is reaching forward to try to touch a large rooster that has been harnessed to a tiny wooden wagon in which the boy is seated. Around them are long grasses and leaves, suggesting a rural setting.

Olympia thinks: *He was such a beautiful infant, and I have lost all of those years already. No matter what happens here, I can never get them back.*

Tucker, seeing Olympia's reaction to the photographs, quickly summons the clerk to take them away.

"Mrs. Bolduc," Sears says. "Tell us in your own words how it was you came to have the boy in your care."

"My words?" she asks, confused. She glances up at the judge for help.

"In English, please," says Littlefield, and there is some disgruntled muttering in the courtroom.

Albertine Bolduc squints into a ray of sunlight that has momentarily fallen onto the witness box. She moves her head to escape its glare. "I am married eight years and am not having any infants," she begins. "And I am asking of the sisters about the orphanage. And they are telling me of how I will get a baby. For the doctor is telling me that I am not having any children of my own, which is big sorrow to me and Telesphore."

"Yes," says Sears. "Go on."

"And in April of 1900, I am getting a visit from Mère Marguerite, who says there is a baby."

"This would be Mother Marguerite Pelletier?"

"Yes, she come on Sunday afternoon to me. And she tell me that there is baby for me if Telesphore and I want. And I am saying yes, no matter what we have to do, we do want. And then Telesphore and me, we do not go to shift in the morning and we get the baby."

"And what date was this?"

"Twenty-three April 1900."

"And you signed the documents I showed you earlier."

"Yes, I did."

"And tell me about how you felt that day."

"When I am seeing the boy, he is so tiny, I have love in my heart at once. And, Telesphore, he does, too, I can see this. And we take the boy home and we make a bed for him, and we are loving him all the hours of the day."

Tucker glances at Olympia.

"Was the boy healthy?"

"Yes, he is healthy. He grows."

"But, Mrs. Bolduc, how did you go back to work once you had the infant in your care?"

"Telesphore and I, we are going to overseer and are asking to work different shifts to take care of baby. And we are good workers, so he is saying yes to us."

"Where is the boy now?"

"He is with my mother."

"Your Honor," says Sears, "I have here an affidavit from Sister Thérèse Bracq, a visiting nurse with the Orphanage of Saint Andre, who cannot be in court due to a long-term chronic illness, attesting to the fact that repeated visitations to the Bolduc household have shown that the boy is being well cared for and that he is almost always with one of his parents. She adds that various members of Albertine Bolduc's extended family have helped as well to raise the boy."

Sears hands the document to the judge, who briefly peruses it.

"Now, Mrs. Bolduc," Sears continues, "tell me how you felt when you heard last fall that Olympia Biddeford, the natural mother of the boy, was seeking custody of the child."

There is a cry of *"Non!"* from the back of the courtroom. Little-field immediately bangs his gavel. "Bailiff," he says, "eject that gentle-man." They wait while the spectator, a man with a sign and a blue scarf, is removed from the courtroom.

Albertine glances over at Olympia, and it is the first time since they entered the courtroom yesterday that the two have looked each other in the eye.

"I am not believing this," she says, as if directly to Olympia. "I am not believing this. The boy is ours. He cannot be taken away, I am saying to Telesphore. And he is shouting and being very angry. And I am telling him to be quiet for the boy. And I am holding the boy and I am telling him I will never leave him. And then someone is telling us of you, who sometimes take the cases of the poor."

"Yes, thank you. What does the boy call you?" Sears asks quickly, seemingly wishing to change the subject. And not from any modesty, Olympia guesses, but because he does not wish the court to linger on the word *poor,* an attribute no lawyer in a custody suit wants to emphasize in his client.

"He is calling me Maman, of course."

"And your husband?"

"Papa."

"The boy knows no other parents, correct?"

"Yes."

"Tell me, Mrs. Bolduc, why have you not adopted the boy legally?"

"The father is not being found. But we are wishing to. And the sisters are telling us that after five years we can do this."

"And when will you enroll the boy in school?"

"At six years."

"Thank you, Mrs. Bolduc, that will be all."

Olympia watches as Sears returns to his table, lifts the tails of his frock coat, and takes his seat. In the witness box, Albertine removes a handkerchief from her purse and wipes her upper lip.

"Your Honor," says Tucker, rising to his feet. "I have some questions to put to Albertine Bolduc."

The judge makes notes and does not respond for a moment. In an impulsive gesture of encouragement, Olympia reaches over and touches Tucker's hand. He looks down at her hand and then at her face.

"Yes, proceed," says Littlefield.

Tucker, reluctant to withdraw his hand, slowly rises to his feet and approaches Albertine Bolduc. He studies her for a time before he speaks. Albertine, uncomfortable with the silence, begins to fidget.

"Mrs. Bolduc," says Tucker finally. "I wish to ask you some questions about your background."

"Yes?"

"You are an American citizen?"

"Yes."

"You were born here? In this country?"

"Oh yes."

"In Ely Falls?"

"Yes, my mother is working in the mill forty-seven years now."

"Forty-seven years?" Tucker says with seeming surprise. "That is quite a lot of years, Mrs. Bolduc."

"Yes," she says. "And she is having seven children."

"Did she? That strikes me as extraordinary."

"Oh no," says Albertine. "Is not. Is many Franco families who are working many years in the mill with many children. Is common."

"Can you give me another example?"

"My sister is working for twenty-four years and she is having four children and one who is dying." Albertine crosses herself.

"And she is how old now? Your sister?"

"Thirty-two years."

"That would mean she entered the mill when she was . . . eight years old?"

"Yes, this is true."

Sears struggles to his feet. "Your Honor, I do not understand the relevance of this line of questioning."

"Mr. Tucker?"

"Your Honor, I wish to establish the cultural context in which this boy will be raised. I think these questions are quite relevant."

"Very well, proceed."

"And how about you, Mrs. Bolduc? When did you enter the mill?"

"I am going in at eight years, like my sister."

"I see. And did you go to school?"

Sears, having just sat, is on his feet again. "Really, Your Honor, I do not think Mrs. Bolduc's schooling or lack of it is at all relevant to her ability to properly mother a child."

"Your Honor," says Tucker, moving slightly toward Judge Littlefield. "Once again, I wish to establish the context in which the boy will be raised. I think this is highly relevant, for no man or woman can be a parent in a vacuum. A boy is not just raised by the parents, but is raised into a community. The court cannot make an adequate judgment about the custody of the child without a full understanding of the composition of this community."

The judge ponders Tucker's point and studies the tall young lawyer. A long silence ensues and even the spectators are quiet, awaiting a judgment from Littlefield. "Very well, Mr. Tucker," he says finally. "Mr. Sears, you will, for the moment, allow Mr. Tucker to pursue this line of questioning without further interruptions."

Tucker walks back to Albertine and moves so close to her that he could rest his arm on the witness box. "Mrs. Bolduc," he asks, repeating his question. "Did you attend school?"

Albertine looks into her lap. "No," she says. "I did not. My mother is not having the money for the school."

"And this is because she would have sent you to a Catholic school, and Catholic schools cost money?"

"Yes. The school of Saint Andre."

"Is that where you will send your foster son?"

"Oh yes."

"And at this school, your foster son will speak French and have his lessons in French. Is that correct?"

Shouts of *"La langue"* and *"Je me souviens!"* erupt from the back of the courtroom. Littlefield bangs his gavel, visibly seething at this continued defiance of his orders. "Baliff, eject the persons who have just spoken out. And if I hear one more sound from any of the spectators, I will remove not only the speaker but this entire audience. Is this clear? Mrs. Bolduc, you may answer the question."

Albertine, clutching her purse, blinks at Tucker. "Yes, is important to me," she says. "We are all believing in *la langue*."

"Tell me why this is so."

"If we are giving up the *français* and speaking only the English, we are losing our life . . . our . . ." — she searches for the word — "'*La culture.*'"

"I see. So you attend Saint Andre Church?"

"Oh yes."

"How often do you go there?"

"Every Sunday."

Olympia wonders why Tucker is asking Albertine these questions, for they seem designed to emphasize her fitness as a parent. Is not the practice of religion a point Olympia's own lawyer might not want to bring up again?

"Mrs. Bolduc, what do you do in the mill?" Tucker asks.

"I am carding. I comb the cotton."

"And you work how many hours a day?"

"I am working ten and a half hours."

"And your pay is?"

"I am making more than three hundred dollars a year."

Tucker smiles at Albertine. "Would it be correct to say that you have some pride in your work, Mrs. Bolduc?"

"Oh yes, I am having the pride. I am good worker and am supervising many other women."

"In general, do you believe that a child should be taught the work ethic?"

She seems puzzled. "I am not understanding you."

"Should a child be taught that work is a good thing?"

"But yes," she says, confused. "Everyone must work."

"Exactly," says Tucker. "And what other values would you want to teach Pierre?"

"Honesty, yes? And kindness to others. Obedience, yes?"

"Of course. So let me be clear about this," says Tucker. "You would hope that your foster son would be raised as a French speaker. Correct?"

"Yes."

"You would hope that your foster son would be raised as a Roman Catholic."

"Mais oui," she says quickly.

"You would promote the moral values of honesty and obedience and kindness to others."

"Of course."

"And you would promote the work ethic which is so dear to the Franco-American community."

"Yes, I must."

"But you would not have Pierre go into the mills at age eight, as you had to do."

"No," she says, shaking her head.

"You would wait until he was ten."

She seems to think a moment. "Ten, yes," she says.

Tucker pauses.

"Ten, definitely?" Tucker asks.

"Ten, yes, I think so. Definitely."

There is a moment of silence. Then Sears, galvanized, rises to his feet and begins to speak, but even Olympia can see that it is too late. She watches as bewilderment and then comprehension pass across the features of Albertine Bolduc. At the respondents' table, Telesphore puts his head in his hands.

"Mr. Sears, sit down," says Judge Littlefield.

"But, Your Honor," Sears says.

"Sit down, Mr. Sears."

The courtroom is preternaturally quiet, as though something large and ponderous has settled upon it.

"I have no further questions, Your Honor," says Tucker into the silence.

"You have no further witnesses?"

"No, I do not. But I should like permission to address the court."

"Your Honor," says Sears, now alarmingly pink in the face. "This is highly unusual. Mr. Tucker cannot address the court at this point."

"The petitioner's suit is completed," says Tucker.

Littlefield thinks a moment. "This may be somewhat unusual, Mr. Sears, but it is not unprecedented. Mr. Tucker may perhaps jeopardize the petitioner's own suit by making his address now, before he has heard the respondents' other evidence. But if he chooses to do so, he may."

"I do choose to do so," says Tucker.

"Your Honor, this is highly irregular."

"Yes, Mr. Sears. I understand that. But, I repeat, not unprecedented. Mr. Tucker, you may proceed."

Sears, shaking his head, sits reluctantly. Albertine, clearly stunned by the abrupt ending to her interview as well as the potential damage she has done to herself, remains motionless in the witness box. Judge Littlefield, glancing in her direction, asks her politely to step down. But Albertine is deeply shaken and, in a bitter moment of irony, is forced to take Tucker's hand so that he may help her back to her seat. Sears, furious, rises at once to take her from Tucker.

Tucker returns to his desk and removes another set of notes from his briefcase. He looks at Olympia as if he would speak, though he does not. She watches as he walks slowly to the lectern. Her future, her entire future, is in the hands of this young man, barely out of law school, a man who perhaps has never argued a case before.

"Your Honor," he begins, "my address to the court, while not incendiary in intent, may be seen as being so by members of the

407

Franco-American community, and as this court is not a forum for political debate, and as I should not like to be interrupted in my summation by shouts and catcalls from the gallery, I request that the court be cleared for this part of the hearing."

Immediately, the gallery seems crowded with noisy confusion — shouts in both French and English. Albertine, alarmed, swivels in her seat to examine the spectators. Littlefield bangs his gavel hard until finally there is silence. "Mr. Tucker, I have been searching for a valid reason to clear this court for the past hour. Thank you very much. Bailiff, will you help the audience to vacate the courtroom forthwith. Anyone who resists will be arrested."

At the lectern Tucker remains motionless.

"Mr. Tucker," says Littlefield, when the audience has been removed. "I think we are finally free of potential disturbances. You may begin."

The aura of stillness surrounding Tucker begins to spread through the courtroom, as if in concentric circles.

"Your Honor," he begins, "we cannot guarantee the education of the child once we bind over custody. The Texas Supreme Court in 1894 recognized this when it likened parental authority to a trusteeship subject to public oversight:

"'The state, as protector and promoter of the peace and prosperity of organized society, is interested in the proper education and maintenance of the child, to the end that it may become a useful instead of a vicious citizen; and while as a general rule it recognizes the fact that the interest of the child and society is best promoted by leaving its education and maintenance, during minority, to the promptings of maternal and paternal affection, untrammeled by the surveillance of government, still it has the right in proper cases to deprive the parent of the custody of the child when demanded by the interests of the child and society.'

"Your Honor, we have seen here that Albertine and Telesphore Bolduc are deeply embedded in the Franco-American community of Ely Falls. They have said so, and their own counsel has said so. But the Franco-American community in this city has consistently shown itself to be in conflict with progressive views of childhood. As of this year, only three hundred and twelve of out of a potential eight hundred and seventy-one school-age Franco-American children in this city have attended any school at all. That is only one-third, Your Honor. Seventy percent of all Franco-American children in this city between the ages of eight and fourteen work in the Ely Falls Mill. Let me remind the court of the child labor laws in this state: No child under the age of twelve is to be employed in any manufacturing or mechanical establishment. Nor any child under the age of fifteen during vacations of public school unless he has attended school for sixteen weeks of each year preceding his sixteenth birthday.

"How is it then that so many children are working in the Ely Falls Mill?" Tucker asks rhetorically. "The answer is simple. The parents of the Franco-American community evade the child labor laws by lying about their children's ages. This is not opinion, but fact. They do so not because they are bad people. They do so because they do not believe it is wrong within the context of their culture and because they are desperately poor. I quote from a recent editorial in the Franco-American community's own newspaper, *L'Avenir:* 'The child labor statutes of this state are badly enforced and ineffective since so many Franco-American parents falsify their children's ages. Even the good sisters of the Order of Saint Jean Baptiste de Bienfaisance have professed shock and dismay that so many young Franco-American children are working in the mills.'"

Tucker pauses to let the opinion of the sisters settle over the chamber.

"I have here in my hand a number of photographs that I should be glad to submit to the court," Tucker says. "These sorry photographs were taken at the Ely Falls Mill this year. One shows six children, each of whom cannot be more than ten years old, looking dirty and exhausted, standing between looms that are at least two feet taller than they are. Another shows a poorly dressed boy, barefoot I might add, standing on a box to reach the controls of his machine."

Tucker walks to the dais and hands the photographs to Judge Littlefield, who studies them. Sears does not ask to see them.

"Your Honor," says Tucker, "we have long known about this situation here in Ely Falls, but we have more or less chosen to look the other way. I believe the city officials, both Yankee and Franco alike, have concluded that 'Petit Canada' should police its own. Which is not the matter precisely before the court, except insofar as it is relevant to the future of one little boy, Pierre Francis Haskell.

"This boy, if left in the custody of Albertine and Telesphore Bolduc, will enter the mills sometime before his twelfth birthday. Let me tell you what this will mean for him. Not only will he be deprived of schooling, but he will also work eleven hours a day, six days a week, with no fresh air or sunshine, and most likely in a lint-filled room. He will be subject to a wide range of diseases, including measles, diphtheria, and the treacherous white lung. He will probably be stunted in his growth and will compromise his eyesight. He will have no exercise except for the repetitious motions of his job. He will live in worker housing that is commonly infested with cockroaches, rats, and mice, and where filth and poverty encourage the breeding of diseases such as smallpox and cholera. Bishop Louis Giguere himself wrote the following this year in L'Avenir: 'The worker housing is indescribable in print. There are vile privies, stinking cellars of rubbish, and perilous stairways. Sewer pipes contain large holes that emit a noxious gas. The buildings are without adequate ventilation and water supply.'

"Your Honor, I do not mean to suggest that the specific room in which Albertine and Telesphore Bolduc reside is so indecent, but as a member of the Franco-American community, Pierre Francis Haskell will grow up in this environment. Moreover, he will emerge into adulthood, if he makes it into adulthood, with no place else to go except back to the mills. He will have no education to speak of, no other skills except the one he has learned at the looms. Is the state prepared to sentence Pierre Haskell to such a life? For make no mistake: To grant custody to Albertine and Telesphore Bolduc is to give the boy a life sentence of missed opportunities and poverty."

Olympia glances over at the respondents' table. Sears has his hand on Albertine's arm, as if to restrain her. Telesphore mutters angrily, *"Non, non, non."*

"Your Honor," says Tucker, "both women in question here today stand to either suffer terribly or have great joy as a result of your decision. But as my colleague Mr. Addison Sears himself said before the court, we cannot care about the joy or suffering of the mother. We must care first and, if necessary, only about the welfare of the child. And there can be no question but that the boy will be better served by being remanded to the custody of Olympia Biddeford, who guarantees, by her own example, the boy's education, his financial security, and very likely his higher education as well. We are speaking here today of making either a future millworker or of making a doctor or a professor or even a judge. To take these opportunities away from the boy is nothing short of a crime."

Tucker pauses.

"Your Honor, Olympia Biddeford was herself a child when she discovered she was with child. Since that day, she has conducted herself in a manner any Christian woman might envy and aspire to: She has secured a higher education, she lives a clean and sober life, and she uses wisely the advantages given to her by dint of her birth, namely, good descent and respectable fortune. I do not think any of us here today doubts for one minute that she will be a good mother to the boy."

At the lectern, Tucker gathers his notes together.

"The court is entrusted with the decision of a great question of morals as well as law: To whom belongs the custody of the child?"

Tucker looks pointedly at Judge Littlefield and then slowly turns to Olympia. He holds her gaze for what seems a long minute.

"Let us restore a child to his rightful mother," he says.

*J*udgment *to be read tomorrow three o'clock. Will collect you eleven o'clock for meal. Courage. Tucker.*

She slips the yellow telegram into the pocket of her dress. Closing the back door, she watches as the lithe telegraph boy sprints out onto the road with his tip. She walks directly into the butler's pantry and pours herself a drink to steady her nerves, which is not like her. For what occasion did she purchase this bottle of whiskey? she wonders. The decanter is old, cut-glass, her mother's mother's. Drink in hand, she moves into the front room and stands at the windows. The dying sun turns the water teal, a color nearly leached in the next instant. She sets her glass on the windowsill and unpins her hair, holding it in great handfuls in front of her.

A judgment has been rendered. Her fate is sealed, and she does not know what it is. She is surprised at how quickly the waiting is over. Tucker said it would take at least a week for Littlefield to arrive at an opinion, but it has been only four days. She is not prepared for this.

She sits in her Windsor chair and takes up again the nightshirt she has been working on. She slips the pearl-headed pins from the fabric and pokes them into the old horsehair pincushion she once

413

embroidered as a child. With her scissors, she snips the tails of thread still caught in the seams. All about her on the floor are scraps of linen and cotton. The nightshirt might have been finished earlier, but all afternoon she has been disturbed by recurring images of the hours she spent in the courthouse last week, vivid pictures that make her pause in her sewing and set her needle and thread in her lap.

She thinks of Tucker and the way he returned to their table after his final address, his face white, his hands trembling slightly, and how she understood, even then, how difficult it had been for him to put forth that particular argument, knowing as he did that he was taking on an entire culture. Where another man might have been exuberant, Tucker had seemed subdued. "A risky gambit" was all that he said to her when she later tried to thank him.

She thinks of Sears as he was delivering his own address at the end, the stout, bald man stabbing the air and hurtling accusations at Olympia, his anger at Tucker fueling every word. His summation, not unlike his opening statement — although more ferocious and perhaps more persuasive — was at least as strong as Tucker's. Numerous times Sears made the point that one could not judge the behavior of an individual by the behavior of a culture. And when he was done, it was not at all clear to Olympia which argument might have moved the judge more.

She recalls her own time in the witness box, the wretched questions she was forced to answer about the manner in which she and Haskell had once loved each other. She thinks of her father in the box as well, pale and shrunken, clearly wondering how it was his life had arrived at this terrible juncture. She thinks of Josiah's astonishing story of journeying up to Ely Falls with the infant, a journey that would have been a torment for Lisette. She remembers Mother Marguerite in her habit and starched wimple, each word she spoke having the weight of truth. She thinks of Dean Bardwell in her tweed suit, with her unexpected tale of Averill Hardy and his self-serving accusations. And she thinks of Cote squirming at the end of his testimony, and how deliciously satisfying it was to see the man left hanging, how even Judge Littlefield appeared to be certain Cote was lying.

And then, in her mind's eye, she sees Albertine Bolduc in the witness box — Albertine with her broken English, her obvious love for the boy, and her painfully eloquent photographs. Olympia shakes her head quickly. She cannot think about Albertine now.

She lifts the nightshirt, holds it away from her, and studies it for a moment. Last month, in a moment of whimsy, she purchased in Ely Falls five horn buttons of different animal shapes, which she has put on the shirt: an elephant, a monkey, a bear, a giraffe, and something that might or might not be a buffalo. She walks with the shirt into the kitchen, where she has set up the ironing board and has put the iron on the stove to heat. As she presses the seams flat, she thinks about the trunk upstairs, nearly filled now with shirts and short pants and socks and underclothes and sweaters and jackets that she has sewn or knitted for the boy. It has been a true labor of love, and something more — the only thing that has kept her calm during the long winter months of waiting for the hearing to begin.

The doorbell rings again, surprising her. She holds the iron in her hand and listens. Two summonses in twenty minutes? Perhaps it is another telegram. Has Littlefield, in his impatience, read his judgment today? No, surely not. She puts the iron on a brick and walks around the corner into the back hallway.

He is standing at the door, having already rung. She can see his face through the glass panes. She puts a hand out to the wall to steady herself. He has on a suit jacket, a gray fedora. A vest that buttons high on the chest. Beyond that, she cannot make out much because the sun is behind him, low in the sky and glinting painfully through the bare trees.

A moment of joy. Then of disbelief.

As if in a trance, she moves the six or seven steps to the door and opens it.

"Olympia," he says.

She backs away from the door, and he steps over the threshold.

He gazes steadily at her, as if he, too, cannot believe in the apparition before him. She turns and walks into the kitchen, knowing that he follows her. Her heart beats so hard inside her chest, she has to press a hand to the bodice of her dress to still it.

"Olympia," he says again.

She turns, and he removes his hat.

His face is older, but still he has high color. His hair, which has been cut short, is receding slightly at his brow. He seems leaner to her, more wiry than she has remembered. But it is his eyes that claim her most. They are old eyes, older than his body, hollow and lined, as if the weight of the past four years — no, nearly five now — had settled in those orbs, had done its damage there.

They stand on either side of the kitchen table, each taking in the other.

"I came as soon as I heard," he says finally, breaking the silence.

She cannot speak.

"I have been away. Deep in the country. I have come just now by train from Minneapolis."

She shakes her head and puts a hand on a chair back to steady herself.

"Minnesota," he says.

She lifts her chin.

"When I returned to the boardinghouse in Minneapolis where I was staying, there was a letter from Mr. Tucker. And I have read just now about the suit in the newspapers. Indeed, there is hardly any other news at all."

Turning her back to him, she stares out the window over the sink.

"No one knows I have come," Haskell continues. "I shall not tell anyone. Not even Tucker. I fear my presence, as I am still legal guardian, would complicate and perhaps jeopardize your suit."

She sets her jaw hard.

"I am at the Dover Inn," he says. "I daresay I shall not run into anyone I know there."

She pivots and leans against the lip of the sink.

"Olympia," he says, laying his hat on the table.

"Would you like some tea?" she asks in a quavering voice, and she can see that he hardly knows how to answer her. "I shall put a kettle on," she adds. "If you would leave me for a moment, I shall bring it into the front room."

He hesitates, but then he seems to understand. "All right," he says, and with reluctance, he walks through the swinging door.

When he is gone, she wraps her arms over her head and sinks to the floor, the skirts of her dress billowing up and out as she falls. She leans her head forward into her arms and weeps silently. Of all her imaginings, scarcely sane, she has not imagined this. She is gullied out, like the clay in the marshes. He has done this to her.

She pulls herself to a standing position. She finds a handkerchief in the pocket of her dress and blows her nose. Hardly knowing what she is doing, she fills the kettle with water, only then realizing that she cannot leave him waiting for her in the front room.

He is looking out at the ocean, his elbow resting on the thin window ledge, his other hand in the pocket of his trousers, and she sees that he has not lost the elegance of his gestures for all his time in the country.

He hears her skirts and turns.

"I have never been here when it was not summer," he says. "The beach is quite majestic without people."

"Nature is often seen at her best without people," she says.

417

"You know, I hardly feel the guilt now," he says. "What is left is the punishment."

"Your children," she says.

"The guilt is dulled. It is the loss I feel most keenly. The lost years one can never have back."

"Why did you go so far away?"

"Catherine requested it. I could not refuse her."

Olympia is silent, thinking of that request and of the circumstances under which it would have been made.

"To think I have not seen you since that night," he says, studying her intently.

"It was a terrible night."

"More dreadful than any I have ever experienced," he says. "I was awed by Catherine's pain, by its depth. It would not exhaust itself. She threw herself out of the carriage on the way to the cottage."

"I did not know."

"She fractured her wrist."

"I was not told of this."

"I had no idea she loved me in that way. She hardly felt the pain of the injury to her arm. It was the other injury that claimed her."

"I remember her beauty," Olympia says.

"Yes."

He keeps his eyes on Olympia's face. And it is she who turns away.

"What do you do in Minnesota?" she asks.

"I work among the Norwegian immigrants and the Arapaho. I have an office, but I am seldom in it. Most of my patients live far from town. Sometimes I am gone for days."

"It is hard work?"

"Only to watch their suffering. We scarcely know the meaning of the word by comparison."

And she can see then that the high color in his face is from the sun. His hands, too, are sunburnt. Perhaps there is, she thinks, a brute strength through the shoulders he has not had before. And in his hands, grown larger.

"You have seen the boy?"

"Yes." She hesitates. "He is very like you."

She watches him attempt to master the features of his face.

"Has all your work been . . . punishment?" she asks, thinking of the Indians.

"In its way. An exile."

She smooths her skirts. She still has on her apron. Under it, a gray shirtwaist. "I, too, was sent into exile," she says. "After the birth."

"The school."

"Yes. It was a kind of prison."

"You know I had the boy," he says. "For a day."

"Yes."

"I did not know I could feel so much love," he says. "I lay on the bed with him all night. I had hired a wet nurse, who came to the room from time to time. I had planned to bring the boy to the orphanage first thing in the morning, but I could not bear to part with him. In the end, the wet nurse had to remind me that he needed better care than I could give him."

The image of the man and the infant on the bed together seems unbearable to her now.

"I thought I would die after I left him there," Haskell says. "Literally. I wanted to die. I thought of drowning myself in the Falls."

"Did you not feel a similar love for your other children?" she asks.

"I must have," he says, "but Catherine possessed them so when they were infants." He pauses. "Martha will go to Wellesley."

She has forgotten that Martha is of an age to go to college. "We might have been there together," Olympia says.

"It was knowing I had only the one night," Haskell says, explaining. "It is time that determines the intensity of love."

"Is it?" she asks.

Restless, he begins to walk around the room. "I had started drinking," he says. "I had been wandering. I had a post office I would call at from time to time. It was there I got your father's letter. It was a brutal letter. But no less than I deserved."

"I knew nothing of any of this."

"And then after that night with the boy, I could see how banal the drinking was, how trite the ruin. So I went west."

She tries to imagine him among the Indians.

"You are even more beautiful," he says.

She looks away.

"You never used to wear your hair down."

"I do not usually wear it down," she says. "I have just taken it out."

"I used to weep for the wreckage," he says. "For the lives that must now always be something less."

She thinks how familiar he is to her and yet how foreign. He is years older, not in his body, but in the eyes, which have perhaps seen too much.

"The most unforgivable," he says, putting his hands into the pockets of his coat and shaking his head. "The most unforgivable is that I would do it again. If I believed in such a thing, I would get down on my knees and pray to have those moments with you restored to me."

She is startled by this pronouncement. It seems blasphemous, to fly so in the face of God. And yet has she not done the same? In a Catholic orphanage? In a courthouse?

"Without the cost," she says.

"Even with the cost."

"You cannot mean that," she says. "You cannot know the cost. The cumulative cost."

"No," he says. "I cannot."

He sits in the Windsor chair, the scraps of linen all about his feet. "Will you win your suit?" he asks.

"I do not know. The judgment is to be read tomorrow."

"I shall go back, of course. Though I should like to know the judgment. I like to think of you with the boy."

"I want him with me passionately," she says.

"I should like to see him."

"You could see him as I have had to," she says harshly. "Standing across the street and hoping to catch a glimpse of him."

"I am sorry you have had to do that."

"I had to answer questions about you," she says. "I had to tell them of us. When we were at the hotel together and at the cottage."

"My God."

"It was unspeakable," she says. "Not the admitting to the deed. That I have long since gotten over. It was having to tell it aloud, having to tell it to people I did not know and did not want ever again to see. When I was sitting in the witness box, I felt I was being stripped of my clothing. Worse."

"Olympia, I am so sorry."

She shrugs, as if to say, *It does not matter now.* She asks him: "Do you enjoy practicing medicine in Minnesota?"

"The need is desperate." He glances around. "Do you live here alone?"

"Yes."

"How extraordinary."

"Is it?"

"I think so."

"I came in here to say I did not make the tea."

421

"I am not sure I could hold a teacup steady," he says.

"Would you like a drink of spirits? I was having one when you came."

"Were you? How unlike you. But then how would I know what is like you now? Yes, thank you."

She walks into the pantry and pours him a glass of the whiskey. When she returns, he is staring out the windows again. He takes the drink from her. There is within him, she thinks, some great strength that she herself does not have access to.

"I am so very sorry, Olympia. To think of your giving birth so young and losing the child in the same moment. It is more than anyone should have to bear."

"I would not wish you to be sorry," she says.

"I am happy simply to be in this room," he says. "I have imagined this a thousand times."

But even this happiness, she sees as she glances up at his eyes, must necessarily be less than it was. He has sacrificed his children. He has made them sacrifice him. What happiness can there be after such a loss?

"I did not ever stop loving you," he says. "Not for one minute." He takes a drink of the whiskey. "It must be said. There is joy, even now, in saying it. I would not have thought such love could be maintained over so long a time. But there it is. There is no point in saying anything but the truth," he adds.

"I have felt relief in speaking the truth to Mr. Tucker," she says. She wraps her arms around herself. With the sun down, the room is colder. "There is something I want you to see," she says. "Upstairs. But wait here a minute."

She walks into the kitchen to fetch the nightshirt. When she returns, she asks: "Will you come with me?"

He follows her into the front hallway and up the wide staircase. They move along a darkened corridor. She pauses outside a room, not her own, and opens the door. She walks to a table and turns on a lamp, revealing a child's bed covered with a blue and white crocheted coverlet. On the floor is a navy hooked rug with a red star in its center. There is a nursery table and chairs, a wooden toy box, painted red. Blue curtains with a star pattern are at the window. From the ceiling hangs a mobile of tin stars.

"I found the furniture in the attic," she says. "It used to be mine. I made the rug and the curtains and the mobile," she adds, not without a note of pride. "My room is next door. I thought he would want to be close to me. I am sure he will be frightened. I am frightened."

She walks to a tin trunk, kneels, and opens it. Inside is the boy's wardrobe. She folds the nightshirt carefully and lays it on the top. She closes the trunk.

"I know that you will be a good mother to him," Haskell says.

She looks up at him in the doorway.

"I shall go now," he says.

She is not prepared for this so soon, and, in not being prepared, she resorts to manners. "You have a carriage?" she asks.

"I shall walk to Ely and take the trolley from there. The walk will do me good. Though I shall falter in the marshes."

She stands.

"You have not said anything about how these years have been for you," he says.

"No, I cannot."

"Your face is exquisite. More formed. As though your character has been completed."

"But we are all unfinished portraits," she says.

"Will you not at least give me your hand?" he asks. "We never said a proper good-bye."

"No, we did not. We could not."

She walks to him in the doorway and extends her hand, which he takes. His skin is coarsened with calluses.

"We made a child together," he says. "It hardly seems possible."

"I have often wondered when," she says. She glances at the room that will be her son's. "He may be here tomorrow. To think of it."

"Love him," Haskell says suddenly. "For me as well."

She squeezes Haskell's hand with all her strength, digging her nails into his skin. The want is sharp, the sorrow too keen.

"You could have come back at any time!" she cries.

"I made myself stay away. Can you not see how far I had to go?"

"You could have kept the child!"

"No, Olympia. I could not."

He draws her toward him, burying her face. He weeps like a child himself, hiccuping with the weeping, with no shame, with no thought of hiding this from her. She is speechless with the relief his body offers her.

He holds her head in his hands. He kisses her, and she remembers the softness of his mouth, his taste.

"I shall never believe that this is wrong," he says.

She looks at him, having already decided. She shuts the door and leads him along the hallway and into the room with the blue forget-me-nots on the walls and the amber-beaded lamp on the scarred mahogany table, unwilling yet to take him into her own room.

"I remember this room from the night of the shipwreck," he says, glancing around.

She walks to the narrow bed, having forgotten how to begin. "We shall have this whole night," she says. "We shall sleep beside each other this whole night, and no one will disturb us."

"No one," he says. He listens, as if astonished. "What perfect quiet." And she thinks: Where he has been has perhaps been crude and noisy.

"Have you loved another?" he asks quickly.

She shakes her head. "Have you?"

"I tried to be with other women. To lessen what we had. If I could cheapen it, I thought, then it might be bearable."

She feels a quick stab of jealousy. Other women's bodies.

"But I could not," he says. "I kept seeing your face."

He traces the outline of her mouth with his finger. "It was this that tormented me most," he says.

He kisses her, a chaste kiss, unlike the one before.

"Do you still have the locket?" he asks.

She nods.

"Then let me see it."

She unfastens the buttons of her dress. He leans over to turn on the lamp. She bares her chest, the locket lying just above her corset. He takes it in his fingers.

"It is evidence you truly loved me," he says.

He lets the locket fall and traces the curve of her breasts as he did her mouth.

"I was tormented by the memory of this as well," he says.

She does not sleep for fear of waking and finding him gone. In the middle of the night, Haskell dresses himself and walks down to the kitchen to forage for food. He comes back with bread and butter and jam and more quilts to burrow under. He undresses and climbs back into the narrow, single bed with her. Above the quilts they can see their breath. Beside them on the mahogany table, a thick wine-colored candle burns down, creating a waxen waterfall to admire.

She thinks, as he sleeps beside her: A love affair is the sum of many parts — the physical, the sense of being set apart, the jealousy, the loss. It is not a trajectory, not a straight line, but rather a deck of playing cards that has been shuffled, this thing fitting into that thing fitting into this thing.

"You cannot go away now," she says, waking him. "I could not bear to lose you again so soon."

"You are distracted," Tucker says to her from across the table. "Well, of course you are."

The walls of the restaurant are covered with red silk. On the tables are small bouquets of early daffodils. The white linens are heavy and embossed, quite the most beautiful table linens she has ever seen. The room is crowded this noontime, mostly with men, although there are some women in suits and toques. How is it that such a place exists in Ely Falls?

Olympia studies her plate. On it is an enormous piece of roasted beef that just moments earlier a waiter sliced for her on a silver cart at tableside. She cuts a small bite and dips it into the horseradish sauce. "I had no idea that such a place was here," she says.

"It is the only decent restaurant in town. I eat here often."

"Do you?"

She watches as he cuts into his beef. She guesses he has on his best coat for the judgment: a fine charcoal worsted, and with it a blue and black silk tie against a snowy shirtfront. His hair has been polished back from his head in a nearly unbroken line. Only his slight impatience with the waiter, and even perhaps with her, betrays his anxiety. Her own anxiety appears to have manifested itself as a complete lack of appetite, so that it is an effort even to chew the small piece of beef she has put into her mouth. She takes a sip of water.

"What was the bet?" she asks.

"The bet?"

"Littlefield said your father still owed him a barrel of apples."

"My father bet Littlefield I would never go into the law. Littlefield took the bet. My father sent the apples the very next day."

She thinks: Would it not be better to love Tucker? Was that not the way it was supposed to be?

"You understand what will happen today," Tucker is saying. "We will walk into the chamber and sit, and Littlefield will come out, and then he will read the judgment."

"And then it will be over."

"And then it will be over."

He lifts his glass of wine. "You wore that suit the night we had dinner at the Highland," he says.

She looks down at the green velvet, scarcely knowing what she has on.

"I will give you and the boy a ride back to Fortune's Rocks," Tucker says.

"The boy has probably never been in a motorcar," Olympia says. "He may be frightened."

"It will be better in an automobile than on the trolley so late in the evening. And there may be some unpleasantness."

He means the Francos, she thinks. "Thank you," she says. She attempts another bite. "What I find most difficult is the absolute finality of the judgment. It seems there ought to be an easing. Not so abrupt."

"Custody suits are always exceptionally difficult," says Tucker. "But the courts have found over the years that a clean break is actually better for the child, particularly at this age. Most children, when they are grown, do not remember anything of when they were three."

"Then if I win, he will not remember her."

"Probably not."

"It seems unduly harsh," she says.

This morning, Olympia made Haskell leave the cottage early. She washed her hair and then cooked a meal of roasted chicken and cornbread, her own favorite meal as a child, so that she and the boy might have a supper waiting for them when they returned to Fortune's Rocks in the evening. Lacking anyone to consult, she has read two books on maternal care and family life. She has also purchased a French grammar, which she has been reviewing daily for weeks, having had the realization that of course the boy will not speak English.

"Mr. Tucker, you have been very kind to me. I hope it shall go well today for my own sake, but also for yours."

"You cannot eat," he says, looking down at her plate.

"No, I cannot. I am sorry."

"It is perfectly understandable."

He reaches his hand across the table, and as he does so an entirely new anxiety presents itself: After the judgment is read — perhaps not today, not this afternoon, but one day soon — she will have to tell Tucker that she cannot, after all, offer him any hope.

When they reach the courthouse, it is as before, with newspaper reporters and Franco supporters standing all about the entrance. Tucker, who has left his motorcar at the restaurant and has walked Olympia to the courthouse, sees the crowd before they see him. He makes an abrupt about-face, taking Olympia with him. "I know of a side entrance," he says. "I should like to avoid the crowd both coming and going today if I can."

Tucker holds her elbow as he leads her into the chamber. And she is glad of his support, for when she sees Albertine in her black suit, holding a string of rosary beads, her lips silently moving and her eyes shut tight in prayer — and then Telesphore with his eyes closed and his arms crossed, himself in an attitude of either prayer or sleep — Olympia has a sudden and clear picture of just how terrible this hour will be. Tucker leads her to her seat, carefully placing himself between Olympia and Albertine.

"The judge will be here soon," Tucker says. "In a few minutes, it will all be over."

And indeed, as Tucker says this, the bailiff asks the court to rise and announces the judge. Levi Littlefield and Addison Sears come into the courtroom simultaneously from opposite directions, Littlefield once again entering with a great sweep of his robes, Sears running up the aisle like a boy late for class. Littlefield ignores the lawyer's tardiness. Indeed, the judge seems somber this day, almost sad. His mouth is tightly drawn, and he does not look at either Olympia or Albertine, but only at his notes.

"I shall deliver the opinion of the court in the case of *Biddeford* v. *Bolduc,*" Littlefield says. He puts on his glasses. Olympia looks around at the dark wood paneling of the chamber, the electric lights in shaded sconces on the walls. In a moment, her future will be decided.

So this is it, she thinks.

"In this case, the writ of habeas corpus was issued at the insistence of Olympia Biddeford and directed to Albertine and Telesphore Bolduc, commanding them to have before the court the body of Pierre Francis Haskell, the infant son of the relator."

Littlefield looks over his half glasses at the assembled in the chamber.

"The relator has argued that the infant boy was taken unlawfully from her, and by a series of unlawful actions then placed into the custody of Albertine and Telesphore Bolduc, who have raised the boy for more than three years now."

With a sidelong glance, Olympia can see that Albertine is leaning forward, as though trying to translate Littlefield's every word.

"Albertine and Telesphore Bolduc make return that they are possessed of the custody of the child; that, as its foster mother and father, they claim and are entitled to such custody for the proper and necessary purposes of its care and guardianship, and for no other purpose; that they have in no respect restrained said child's liberty or detained him illegally; and that the child's tender age does not admit of being separated from them due to the potential injury to his spiritual health."

Littlefield takes a drink of water.

"In this sober matter thus presented to the court, we have seen that the issues of this case are far-reaching. We would, if we could, resort to legal principle; but occasionally, a case presents itself to the court for which there are no legal precedents."

Olympia glances over at Albertine again and, as she does so, hears a slight movement at the back of the courtroom. She turns to see who has entered the chamber. Haskell sits immediately. The bailiff, noting Haskell's physician's satchel, must think he has been asked by Littlefield to be present in case of medical need, for he does not speak to Haskell or ask him to leave.

Tucker glances at Olympia, then turns to see what it is that has so captured her attention. He quickly turns back to Olympia. His eyes dart all about her face. He will not know Haskell by sight, but might he guess at the man's identity from her demeanor? She watches Tucker's expression as curiosity gives way to comprehension.

"There are two questions before the court today," Littlefield continues. "The first is: Shall the court redress a wrong and recognize that the child was unlawfully taken from its mother? And second: To what extent is the court charged with guaranteeing the continued well-being of the child?"

Littlefield licks his finger and turns a page.

"The court not only must consider the care that the boy has received from his guardians to date but also must scrutinize the community into which the child will be given up. For we are bound to recognize that the community and the environment of the home will either harm or help the child in his future life. If the court is given, no matter how briefly, the charge of ensuring the child's welfare, it must take into consideration all future likelihoods."

Olympia closes her eyes.

"However strong the allegations against the character of Olympia Biddeford, which in his pleadings have been made by the counsel for the respondents; however clearly the respondents have shown themselves to be careful caretakers of the infant boy; however injurious it may be to the boy to be separated from the only parents he has ever known, the court is bound to say that the respondents have failed to satisfy the court as to the future education and well-being of the boy."

Beside her, Tucker seizes her hand. She looks at Tucker and then over at the respondents' table. Sears sits impassively, studying the handle of his briefcase. Albertine and Telesphore appear not to understand what has been said, even though they seem to sense something amiss. Albertine looks wildly all about her.

"The court," Littlefield continues, "however much it may be loath, in this particular instance, to do so, cannot allow a boy to remain in a household in which he may, in future, by influence of his guardians or by persons influential to the guardians, or by circumstances beyond the guardians' control, such as poverty or undue influence of community, commit crimes against the state."

A cry pierces the chamber. Littlefield looks up from his brief. Albertine, her hands in the air, cries, *"Non! Non! Non!"* Littlefield does not ask for order, as if he has realized that it is the right of the woman to disrupt the court. Albertine turns and grabs her husband's arm.

"In addition," Littlefield continues, "the court is bound to acknowledge that the guardians in this case, Albertine and Telesphore Bolduc, though blameless, received the child into their care as a result of an unlawful separation of the child from the natural mother. The court is therefore presented, in this case, with a dual charge: to redress the wrong that was done both to the infant child and to its natural mother, Olympia Biddeford; and to ensure the continuing nurture of this child by guaranteeing, insofar as the court or any institution can guarantee the future, its healthful security and education."

Telesphore puts his head in his hands. Albertine flings her head back against her chair.

"I therefore issue the following decree, endorsed upon the writ of habeas corpus."

Albertine begins to sob, a deep, continuous sound.

Littlefield, obviously rattled, clears his throat. "On ten March 1904, this cause having been heard upon the returns and amended return, suggestions and further suggestions, filed by the respective parties, and remaining of record, and upon the evidence, written and oral, adduced before the court, it is considered that the within named infant, Pierre Francis Haskell, has been unlawfully restrained of his liberty and detained by the parties to whom the within writ is directed, or any or either of them, and that the said infant be remanded and restored to his mother, Olympia Biddeford, in the said writ named."

"He is yours," Tucker says beside her.

"Bailiff," says Judge Littlefield, removing his glasses and wiping his forehead with a handkerchief. "Bring in the boy."

Sears is on his feet. "Your Honor, may the mother and father say a last farewell to the boy?"

Littlefield pinches the bridge of his nose. "The foster parents may say good-bye to the boy, but I forbid them to upset him. If Mrs. Bolduc and her husband cannot control themselves, I will have them removed from the chamber. I do not wish a spectacle on my hands."

"Your Honor," says Sears, "may Mr. and Mrs. Bolduc bid farewell to the boy in private?"

"No, the court cannot permit that. What happens shall happen before all."

The door at the back of the chamber opens, and the bailiff appears with his charge. The boy is dressed in a navy coat and cap, with long gray stockings leading into the same broken leather shoes. With eyes wide, he glances around, perhaps slightly apprehensive, but excited, as if sensing an outing. Olympia watches as Albertine, with extraordinary selflessness, attempts to compose herself so as not to frighten the boy. She stands and slips the rosary into the pocket of her black suit. Telesphore, behind her, stands with his shoulders severely slumped, as though his back were broken. Sears steps out into the aisle and moves around the table behind Telesphore.

The bailiff brings the boy past Haskell, who holds himself as if at church or at some solemn occasion requiring respect. The resemblance between the boy and the father is so acute that Olympia thinks that all must now see. The boy looks quizzically at Olympia and Tucker and Littlefield and then, midway down the aisle, spots his foster mother.

"Maman," he cries, breaking loose. "Maman."

He runs on fat legs along the aisle to Albertine. With an instinctive gesture, long practiced, Albertine bends and picks up the boy and holds him tightly to her breast. He burrows into the wool of Albertine's suit. And then she holds him slightly away from her, his legs hooked around her waist, his arms around her neck. She speaks to the boy in French, and he cocks his head slightly to the side, as if pondering his mother's instructions. But when he looks at his mother's face again — red and swollen — Olympia can see that he senses something is not as it should be. Albertine turns and hands the boy to Telesphore, who buries his huge head in the boy's neck, unwilling to have the child see his devastation. With a quick kiss on

the cheek, he gives his foster son back to Albertine. The sleeves of
Albertine's misshapen suit envelop the child. Her hat slides off her
head. The entire room seems on the verge of some large and terrible
explosion.

And then, though minutes pass — and it is too soon, even Olympia can feel that it is too soon — Albertine is forced to help the boy
slide down off her body. She turns him around so that he is facing
Olympia.

Albertine fixes Olympia with a stony look. Her face is puffed and
raw. The boy, bewildered, does not move. The aisle might be a
chasm. The bailiff once again takes the boy's hand.

"Maman?" the boy calls over his shoulder, questioning.

It seems an obscenity to Olympia to hold out her own arms in Albertine's presence, but she must welcome the boy somehow. She
crouches down so that she is his height. She says his name.

"Pierre."

The boy studies this new person before him. Why has his mother
told him to go with her? Perhaps she is a friend of his mother's? But
if she is a friend, why are Maman and Papa crying?

"Maman?" he calls again over his shoulder.

Olympia reaches out a hand and touches the boy. Tentatively, he
moves in closer to her.

A terrible sob — elemental and primitive — escapes Albertine.

The boy freezes, as if suddenly comprehending the meaning of
the small tableau.

"Non!" he cries, pushing Olympia's hand away. He runs back to
his mother, who bends double over him, sheltering him in the folds
of her skirt.

A long moment passes.

"Bailiff," says Littlefield with obvious reluctance.

The bailiff, his face red, clearly hating this job, awkwardly reaches
in to try to snatch the boy.

"Mr. Sears," says Littlefield. "Please speak to your client."

Sears reaches around Telesphore and touches Albertine on the arm.

Albertine straightens, then bends to face the boy. She speaks to him and points to Olympia. The child is silent. Albertine tilts her foster son's chin upward so that she and he are gazing directly into each other's eyes.

From across the aisle, Olympia can see the look that passes between mother and child — a look that will have to last a lifetime, a lifetime of lost days, a lifetime of days that must now always be something less.

Olympia glances up at Tucker, who has gone gray in the face with this responsibility. She searches down the aisle for Haskell, who stands tight-lipped, his hands folded in front of him. And then she dares to look again at Albertine Bolduc, who in this moment will lose the child who has been her son. The anguish is more than any woman should be forced to endure, more than another woman can bear to watch.

"No," says Olympia.

The bailiff glances up at Olympia and then over at Littlefield.

Olympia stands. "Do not."

Tucker puts a hand on her arm.

"Miss Biddeford?" Littlefield asks with some bewilderment.

"I withdraw my petition," Olympia says quickly.

"But Miss Biddeford, a judgment has been entered on your behalf."

"I will not take him," she says.

"Miss Biddeford."

"I cannot."

Albertine is cradling the boy. Olympia turns and walks briskly down the aisle past Haskell, who does not speak or attempt to stop her. She moves through the massive doors of the chamber and out into the stone hallway with its bronze busts. Her heels clicking loudly, she walks the length of the hallway to the door of the court-house and opens it. She flinches, having forgotten the mob that has been waiting for her. Quickly now, so as not to lose her resolve, she makes her way blindly through the reporters and the men with signs. She emerges onto the sidewalk, turns, and moves as fast as she can to the next corner. And it is only then, with the crowd behind her and all her life before her, that she truly understands what she was meant to have known from the very beginning. He is not hers. He was never hers.

YOU MUST NOT hold your breath. You must breathe each time you get the pain."

The girl grunts with a sound hardly human. The thin blond hair is wet and matted against her forehead. Both the calico shift and the bedclothes are rough and wrinkled with perspiration. If it were not so near the end, Olympia would change them yet again.

Occasionally, the girl's father, in overalls and woolen shirt, his face unshaven, comes to the door and looks in, though he seems to do this out of duty and not from any desire to see his daughter. Olympia prays that the child to come is not the product of the father and the girl. Earlier, the girl told Olympia she was fifteen, which Olympia guesses is correct. There seems not to have been a mother for at least a decade.

The girl grunts again and pulls on the sheet that has been tied to the post at the foot of the bed for this purpose. Olympia anoints the girl's vulva with lard and gently examines the progress being made by the descent of the head. Earlier, Olympia covered the horsehair mattress with a sheet of rubber and then spread old newspapers all along that to absorb the birth matter. She has brought with her clean flannels, scissors, coarse sewing cotton, muslin, and a paper of safety pins, all of which she has laid out upon the only table in the room. She has washed the girl's nipples with a solution of strong green tea and made her a birthing skirt out of yet another clean sheet. Olympia soaks the washcloth in the ice-cold water the father has been bringing from the well, wrings it out, and places it on the girl's forehead.

"Go look out onto the road," Olympia says to the father, who seems to need occupation. "He must be coming soon."

Olympia fears that the girl's pelvis will be too narrow. Olympia could possibly manage the birth herself, but she would rather that Haskell were here with his greater experience and his forceps. Already the girl has been in labor for twenty hours, and her strength is nearly depleted.

Olympia glances around the room. Some attempt, she can see, has been made at cheer, although the girl is clearly not a skilled housekeeper. Faded red curtains, misshapen from many washings, are fastened onto the two windows of the room with small nails hammered into the frames. On the floor is an oiled cloth, the design of which has nearly been erased by wear. A knitted blanket, with several holes, is folded at the foot of the bed, away from the mess of the birth. But even these touches of human habitation cannot hide the rude truth of the room, one of only two in this small cabin so far from town. The walls are not plastered, and the beams of the peaked roof are exposed. With no wardrobe, the girl and the man hang their clothes on wooden pegs. Outside, Olympia can hear the bleating of sheep, a constant but not unpleasant sound.

And then she hears another sound, a motor, distant at first, fading away altogether and then louder as it makes its way up the rutted dirt road. The girl is lucky in giving birth this week; in another week, the roads will be so muddy that no motorcar will make it at all. Olympia sees a flash of scarlet and beige and waits for the familiar thunk of the automobile door.

Haskell enters the house without knocking, a habit he cannot break even when they go visiting.

"Olympia," he says when he comes into the bedroom. He sets down his satchel and slips off his coat. He puts his hand on her shoulder. It is his need, Olympia knows, to reassure himself that she is still there, even after all these years.

"She is wanting to bear down," Olympia says. "But her pelvis, I think, is too narrow."

"How far along is she?"

"Past half a dollar."

Haskell walks to the table where the basin is, rolls his cuffs, and washes his hands, exclaiming at how icy the water is. Olympia glances at his broad back. His hair is graying some now, even though his beard is still walnut. He walks to the other side of the bed and looks down at the girl, who is so exhausted that she falls asleep between the pains. Through the window, Haskell and Olympia can see the father standing beside the Pope-Hartford, clearly more interested in the motorcar than in the progress of his daughter.

"No mother present?" Haskell asks.

Olympia shakes her head.

Haskell narrows his eyes. "Tell me this is not what I think it is."

"I do not know. I have had the same thought. I pray not. The girl refuses to say who the father is, but that could be for any number of reasons."

In the eight years they have been working together, she and Haskell have attended incestuous births before. Once they birthed a woman who made no attempt to hide her obvious physical affection for her brother, a situation that rattled Haskell no end.

"What is the father's name?"

"Colton."

She bends to the girl. "Lydia, this is Dr. Haskell," she says as the girl is awakened by another pain.

439

In answer, the girl grits her teeth and makes again the short rhythmic grunts.

Haskell lifts her birthing skirt and examines her.

"I am not sure about the pelvis," he says. "But it is definitely near time. How did you get here?"

"Josiah."

"The Reverend Milton called you?"

"Yes, I tried to reach you at the clinic. Josiah said he would stop by to see if he could find you. Apparently the father only went to the minister after his daughter had been in labor more than ten hours. I think they thought they could manage the birth themselves."

Haskell shakes his head. In synchronous movements — which are the same, yet never exactly the same — Haskell slides the girl down along the bed, lifts her knees, and gently secures her ankles to the bedposts while Olympia props her up into a half-sitting position with pillows and sacking behind her. As she does this, she speaks constantly to the girl so that she will not be unduly afraid. Earlier, during a respite from the contractions, Olympia explained to Lydia the procedures that would happen, having surmised, rightly, that the girl had no idea whatsoever about the birth to come. Even so, the child looks frightened half out of her mind, simply from the pain if nothing else.

"She can bear down now," Haskell says.

"Lydia," Olympia instructs. "Strain as if at stool."

The girl strains. She grunts and pants for breath. And then, on Olympia's instructions, she repeats the process. And then again. And then again.

"The head is presenting," Haskell says after a time. "I shall not need the forceps after all. Lydia, bear down hard now. Push with all your might."

The girl screams as if she were being torn apart. Outside by the car, the father freezes. The head is born, and Haskell passes his finger around the infant's neck to find out whether the navel-string is wound around it. "Lydia, bear down hard now," Haskell commands, this time with some urgency in his voice. He pulls on the cord, loosens it, and slips it over the baby's head.

"Now, massage the uterus," Haskell says to Olympia.

Olympia places her hand upon the lower portion of the girl's abdomen and presses upon the uterus. The infant, slippery and purple, emerges into the world. Haskell grasps the child firmly with both hands and immediately attends to it, suctioning the mucus from the mouth. Olympia hears the infant, a boy, make his first astonished cry. On the bed, the girl weeps, a particular kind of weeping Olympia has seen often but never witnessed outside the childbed, a combination of relief from pain and joy and exhaustion and something else — fear about the days and nights to come. In the doorway, the father is white-faced.

While Haskell attends to the child, Olympia massages the girl's uterus into a hard ball to prevent flooding and tries to provoke a contraction forceful enough to expel the placenta. After Haskell has cut the cord, Olympia gently pulls on it, and the afterbirth comes away. "Lydia, stop," Olympia says, twisting the afterbirth round and round upon itself and withdrawing it. She sets it aside to be examined later. She stands.

"Let me," she says, lifting the infant out of Haskell's arms. She receives the child into the flannel, and it seems, as it always does, a most elemental gesture, to take a child from a man.

Olympia tucks the robe around her legs and ties the scarf over her hat and under her chin. The ride is jarring from the ruts as they enter the village and turn onto the main road out of town.

"I shall go back tomorrow," Olympia says.

"The girl has no one?"

"Not as far as I can tell."

"I did not like the look of the father."

"Nor I. I shall have to call Reverend Milton about the family. John, I think she may need to be taken in."

"Is there room?"

"Yes, just. Eunice will be going to Portsmouth tomorrow."

"As tutor to the Johnsons?"

"Yes."

"And the infant?"

"My dear, the 'infant' is a year and a half."

"Is she? Has it been that long since Eunice came?"

They enter the city limits of Ely Falls. Since the mills have begun to close, the city is slightly less bustling than it used to be. If Ely Falls goes the way of Lowell and Manchester, it will not be long before they will pass empty boardinghouses and collapsed mill buildings. They head east onto the Ely road.

"How was the clinic?" Olympia asks.

"Much the same. Though I did see a dreadful case of accidental poisoning by oxalic acid. The woman had mistaken it for Epsom salts and given it to her husband. The man died within twenty minutes of reaching the clinic. It was terrifying to watch his struggle, Olympia. The pain in his esophagus and stomach must have been beyond imagining. I tried magnesia and chalk, but he was too far gone for that."

"Are you sure it was an accident?" Olympia asks.

Haskell turns briefly in his wife's direction. "My dear, you do have a devious mind," he says, reaching for her leg. "Well, the police are bound to investigate any accidental death. Also, a man came by trying to sell me an X-ray machine."

"And will you buy it?"

"Yes, I think I might. I am rather convinced by the research."

He massages her thigh through her skirt. "And Tucker came round today," he adds.

"Did he?" Olympia asks.

"He needed to discuss some matters having to do with fund-raising. He said he was getting married."

"To whom?"

"A woman named Alys Keep."

"The poetess?"

"Yes, I believe so."

"How extraordinary."

"He asked after you."

"Did he?"

"You know, I think he has a special fondness for you. There is something in the way he inquires about you that is always a little less than casual."

Haskell withdraws his hand to shift the gears, and as he does so, she thinks about meeting Tucker and about her custody suit and about the terrible months afterward. The nights she roamed the house, crying for the boy. Haskell would hear her and come find her and then ease her back into bed. It was Haskell who finally, one day when she was away, dismantled the room, taking the children's furniture back to the attic.

He pulls suddenly to the side of the road and makes a turn onto a narrow lane. She glances out the window and sees that they are in the marshes. He switches off the motor.

"John?" she asks, surprised that they have stopped.

For answer, he turns toward her and unfastens the top three buttons of her blouse. He tucks his fingers into her corset.

She laughs. "John?" she asks again.

"In a moment, we shall be at the house," he says, "and will be surrounded by twenty-three girls and will not have a moment to ourselves. And then I shall have to go to the clinic, and when I come home, I shall probably be so exhausted that I will fall asleep immediately."

"No, you will not. That is just an excuse."

"Do I need an excuse?" he asks, massaging her breast.

"No, perhaps not," she says.

"We were here once, in the marshes," he says, unbuttoning her blouse further.

She can see and feel that day as vividly as she can the polished wood and leather of the interior of the car. The wet seeping along the length of her skirt. The whomp and flutter of a bird's wing. The sun stuttering through the grasses. It was the first time she understood the nature of sexual passion.

His beard brushes against the skin of her chest, and she can smell the natural oil of his hair. They do not remove their coats. They might be young lovers, she thinks, with nowhere to go.

They park in the driveway and enter, as they always do, through the back door, Haskell carrying both of their satchels. Maria is on the telephone in the hallway, reading a grocery list into the mouthpiece.

"Six dozen eggs, four pounds of that cheese you sent us on Monday, seven chickens . . . Can you wait a minute?"

Maria puts her hand over the mouthpiece and turns toward Olympia. "I am just calling in the groceries to Goldthwaite's," she says. "You have a visitor."

"I do?" Olympia asks, unwinding her muffler.

"A Mr. Philbrick."

"How extraordinary," she says.

"I shall just run up and change my shirt," Haskell says, hanging his coat upon a hook, "and then I shall come in and say hello." He checks his pocket watch. "But I am needed at the clinic. Ask Rufus to stay to dinner. I shall be back by then."

Olympia watches her husband walk through the kitchen, snatching a biscuit from under a cloth on his way. She guesses he has not eaten since breakfast.

"Maria, did you give Mr. Philbrick tea?"

Maria, who came to them only seven months ago, has proven herself the ablest of all the girls and thus has been rewarded with the job of assistant to Lisette.

"Yes."

"And where is Josiah?"

"In his office with the accounts."

Olympia tucks a stray wisp of hair behind her ear. When she opens the swinging door, the cacophony of the house greets her like a rush of warm air. She likes to think of it as organized cacophony, though often it is not. She walks past the dining room, remodeled to hold two long refectory tables, and then past a sitting room in which Lisette is reading from a medical text. Around her, in a circle, are eight young women, some merely girls still, between the ages of fifteen and nineteen, some Franco, some Irish, some Yankee, all pregnant. All have been dismissed by their families. When it is their time, the girls will give birth upstairs and then will stay on for as long as they need to. When they have recuperated, they will contribute to the household by assuming various jobs — in the nursery or with the laundry or with the meals. The only rule is that they may not abandon their infants.

As Olympia makes her way toward the study, she remembers the night she first had the idea, sitting on the bed in the room with the blue forget-me-nots on the walls. In the months following the custody suit, Haskell helped her to bring the idea to life, even as he was starting up his own clinic in Ely Falls. Haskell and she moved into her mother's old rooms, refurbished the other rooms to accommo-

445

date young mothers with newborns, and gradually, over a year's time, took in girls whom Haskell either saw at the clinic or came to his attention. By the following year, girls and their families were begging for places, and still Haskell and Olympia continued to remodel. In the summer, when the weather turned fine, they were going to have the chapel converted into a dormitory.

But they have not had their own child. And they have been told they may not ever. Not long ago, in Boston, a specialist suggested to them that Olympia's infertility was probably a result of her having had to give birth at such a tender age.

She turns the corner and finds Philbrick in the study, once her father's, now her own. Still robust at sixty, Philbrick is dressed in a dark maroon jacket with plaid trousers. Ever the dandy, she thinks, eyeing as well the empty sandwich plate on the side table.

"Olympia," he says, standing.

"Mr. Philbrick. Please sit."

The room is considerably more feminine than it was when it was her father's. Books still line one wall, but on the other, Olympia has put her pictures — the paintings and drawings by local artists she began collecting half a dozen years ago: a Childe Hassam, a Claude Legny, an Appleton Brown, an Ellen Robbins. A red and white silk settee has replaced her father's old captain's chair, but she still has his desk. And she has never replaced the objets — the malachite paperweight, the bejeweled cross, and the shells — that remind her of the days when her father would sit in his chair, reading one of the hundreds of books that were warping in the damp.

"It has been too long," she says, sitting.

"You have an extraordinary household," he says.

"It is the people within it who make it so," she says.

"I have long wanted to see it. Of course, I have heard much about it. How many do you have here?"

"We have twenty-three girls. Eight of them have not yet given birth. The others will stay on as long as they need to. We have had several girls three years now."

"A marvelous enterprise."

"Our neighbors do not think so."

He smiles. "No, perhaps not. But more and more are understanding the need for settlement houses such as yours. I always said you would have a remarkable future, Olympia."

"And I hope that future shall include me," says Haskell, crossing the small room to greet Philbrick.

"John," says Philbrick, standing once again. "I have heard nothing but good things about your clinic."

"Thank you, Philbrick. Please sit. It has been a rewarding venture. And we have been fortunate in our funding."

"So I understand. It is always difficult to maintain a private hospital. But your endowment is substantial now?"

"Yes, it is, and I am able to hire two new physicians this year. Indeed, I am afraid I must leave you now to go to interview a young man from New York about one of the positions. I shall be back for dinner, though, and I hope you will stay and dine with us?"

"Thank you," Philbrick says. "I should like that very much."

Haskell bends toward Olympia and kisses her. "Unfortunately, Rufus, with this household and my clinic, Olympia and I must often make appointments simply to see each other," Haskell says.

Philbrick considers the couple. "It does not appear to have bruised the marriage any," he says amiably.

"Nothing shall ever do that," says Haskell. Olympia glances quickly up at her husband, who smiles genially at Philbrick, and perhaps only she can see the thing that has gone out of him and can never be replaced, no matter how much pride he has in his work, no matter how much love he has for his wife. For he has had to forfeit his children — once, as a result of having chosen love; twice, as he watched Olympia walk away from the boy; and now, a third time, in marrying a woman who most likely will not have another. Olympia thinks often about desire — desire that stops the breath, that causes a preoccupied pause in the midst of uttering a sentence — and how it may upend a life and threaten to dissolve the soul.

"Tell me, how are your father and mother?" Philbrick asks when Haskell has gone.

"My father visits often," Olympia says. "Indeed, it is he who supports us. My mother is well and will come for the summer."

"I hope I shall see them."

"Then you shall. They are taking a cottage farther down the beach."

"Olympia, I have come on a serious matter."

The abrupt change in Philbrick's tone takes Olympia by surprise. "Yes?" she asks.

"Albertine Bolduc has passed away."

The handle of Olympia's teacup slips from her fingers, and the cup rattles into its saucer. She sets it down on the marble table for fear of dropping it altogether.

"She died six months ago," Philbrick says. "From the white lung. One might have anticipated it."

Olympia looks away. She seldom allows herself to think of the boy, to imagine him. She has, over the years, tried to put such thoughts away. She has tried not to think: *He is nine now. And now he is ten.*

"Telesphore Bolduc has been caring for the boy," Philbrick says, "but he is ill himself. Tuberculosis. The boy is eleven."

Olympia says nothing.

"A tender age, as you know," Philbrick says, eyeing her carefully. "It was Telesphore who asked me to come to you."

"Was it?" she asks, scarcely believing what she is hearing.

"As you know, you are, by decree of the court, still his legal guardian."

"I surrendered that responsibility," she says.

"Yes, I know. And it was an extraordinary thing you did."

"I have sent money from time to time," she says, "but I have felt it necessary to keep myself at a remove."

"Of course," Philbrick says. "But it is not only money that the boy is needing right now."

"Then I do not understand."

"I know that this is neither here nor there in terms of your responsibility to the child, considering past events, but it would be necessary for you to approve any decision to place the boy back with the orphanage."

"He must go to the orphanage?" she asks.

"I am afraid so. He is still a minor. And I would guess that he would not have much success at being placed out from there, since parents looking for children are rarely if ever interested in eleven-year-old boys."

"What about the rest of the family?"

"Most are gone now. The family has been hard hit by the closing of the mills. Many have already had to move farther south."

"Yes, I see."

"I have taken an interest in the boy from the very beginning," Philbrick says. "Well, I felt bound to, didn't I? I visit him from time to time. I would take him in myself, but it is not me whom the boy needs. He is still sad. But you will find that he is quick. He has an untutored intelligence."

"I will find . . . ?"

"He is here," Philbrick says quickly.

"He is here? In this house?"

"I have brought him with me. The boy does not know anything

449

about you," he adds. "I have merely told him I needed to pay a visit to a friend. Forgive me for this intrusion upon your privacy, Olympia, but I did think it best. I felt it important for you at least to set eyes upon the boy before you decide his future."

"Mr. Philbrick, you have given me a shock."

"No greater than you can bear, or have I gravely misjudged the woman?"

"Where is he?" she asks.

"On your porch. I rather think he has taken a fancy to your telescope."

With an unsteady gait, she walks from the study to the front room, overstuffed now with furniture to accommodate all of the girls and their infants when the entire household gathers in the parlor after the evening meal. Through the windows, she can see the boy on the porch. He is tall, his hair badly cut. He has on a sweater that perhaps once was ivory. She watches as he circles the telescope, bending to peer through it, moving it back and forth, seemingly searching the sea for something important.

She takes a shawl from the back of a chair and walks out onto the porch.

"Hello," she says.

"Oh, hello," the boy says, looking up from the telescope. He takes a step forward and holds out his hand.

Polite, she thinks. Well mannered. His fingers are cold from having been so long outside.

"You must be freezing," she says.

"Oh no," he says quickly, snatching his hand away, clearly not wanting to be told to go back into the house. "You live here?"

"Yes," she says. "I am Olympia Haskell."

450

He is spindly, at an age when the bones grow too fast for the rest of the body. And spindly, he does not resemble Haskell as much as he used to. Though the hazel eyes are the same. Strikingly the same.

"You are the woman Mr. Philbrick has come to visit," the boy says. Awkwardly, and perhaps cold after all, he stuffs his hands into the pockets of his trousers.

"Yes."

"Is this yours?" he asks, gesturing with his elbow to the telescope.

"Yes, it is."

His English, though accented, is not poor. He has had some schooling somewhere, she thinks.

"Do you go to school?" she asks.

"I used to," he says.

Olympia nods.

"Mr. Philbrick is taking me to Boston with him in June," the boy says. "We shall see the science museum and the Public Garden."

"I used to live at the edge of the Public Garden," she says.

"Did you?" he asks with keen interest. "Is it true that in the spring the children have races with miniature boats in the pond?"

"Yes. If you are there on the right day."

"Last year we went into Portsmouth."

"And what did you think of that city?"

"I liked the place where they build the ships."

"The shipyard."

"Yes. Can you see France?" he asks, gesturing again toward the telescope.

"No."

"Can you see the stars?"

"Yes."

"How is it that one can see the stars, which are so far away, and cannot see France, which is closer?"

"That is an interesting question," she says. "I think it has some-thing to do with the curvature of the Earth. And also the stars are brighter."

"Could we see Ely Falls if we pointed the telescope in the right di-rection?" he asks.

"I am not sure. Perhaps if we got onto the roof, we would be able to see the steeple of Saint Andre's."

"I should like to do that," he says.

"Then you shall come back to visit and we will do that."

"Well, surely you would not go onto the roof," he says, seemingly alarmed at the thought of a grown woman on a rooftop.

"No, probably not. But my husband would."

"Is your husband here now?"

"No, he will be back this evening."

"Oh," says the boy with evident disappointment.

"Well, you shall definitely come back to visit in the daytime when he is here," Olympia says.

"I have been to this beach," he says.

"Have you? When was this?"

"I came for the Fourth of July."

"And did you have fun?"

"Oh, yes. My mother made a picnic, and she went into the water with me."

The boy's face tightens suddenly.

"There is a man in that fishing boat out there," Olympia says quickly, pointing out to sea.

The boy stoops to the telescope. "I can see him," he says. "He must be a lobster fisherman. Here. Would you like to see?"

The boy takes a step backward to make room for Olympia. She, too, bends to look. In his excitement, the boy stands so close to her that she can feel his elbow and his upper arm.

She can see the lawn, too close, the chapel that will shortly be made over into a dormitory. The rocky ledge. The sea. She turns the knobs, focusing. There is the fishing boat, a man in oilskins pulling in a pot. In the distance, hardly visible, she sees another boat and behind that the Isles of Shoals, merely a hazy suggestion. Beyond the islands, there is France. And then there are the stars. And farther still, there are the lost years and a history written upon the bones.

But here there is a boy, and his name is Pierre.

Acknowledgments

The court opinions cited in italics in this work of fiction are, in fact, true ones, and portions of the final judgment are taken from the court transcript of the Pennsylvania case of *d'Hauteville* v. *Sears, Sears and d'Hauteville*. I am grateful to John Martland for reading and editing the trial section of my novel and to the following works for providing me with information regarding child custody law in the late nineteenth century: *A Judgment for Solomon* by Michael Grossberg; *From Father's Property to Children's Rights* by Mary Ann Mason; and *Governing the Hearth* by Michael Grossberg.

I also found inspiration or bits of history in these works: *Gleanings from the Sea* by Joseph W. Smith; *The Cities on the Saco* by Jacques Downs; *La Foi, La Langue, La Culture* by Dr. Michael Guignard; *Biddeford in Old Photographs*, compiled by Loretta M. Turner; The Images of America series for Saco, Hampton, and Rye; *From Humors to Medical Science* by John Duffy; *The Library of Health*, edited by Frank Scholl; *America 1900, The Turning Point* by Judy Crichton; *A World Within a World: Manchester, the Mills and the Immigrant Experience* by Gary Samson; *Working People of Holyoke* by William Hartford; *Women at Home in Victorian America* by Ellen Plante; and *A Memory Book: Mt. Holyoke College 1837–1987* by Anne Carey Edmonds.

I would like to thank Michael Pietsch for his continuing encouragement and brilliant editing; Stephen Lamont for his elegant copyediting; Ginger Barber for her wisdom in literary and financial matters; and John Osborn for his guidance and assistance, as well as for his confident eye and ear.